This special signed edition of

RAMSEY CAMPBELL
Master of Weird Fiction

is limited to 100 copies.

Ramsey Campbell

S. T. Joshi

This is copy

RAMSEY CAMPBELL
Master of Weird Fiction

RAMSEY CAMPBELL
Master of Weird Fiction

S. T. JOSHI

FOREWORD BY RAMSEY CAMPBELL

Published in May 2022 by PS Publishing Ltd. by arrangement with
the author. All rights reserved by the author. The right of S. T. Joshi to be
identified as Author of this Work has been asserted by him in accordance
with the Copyright, Designs and Patents Act 1988.

FIRST EDITION

ISBN
978-1-78636-723-5
978-1-78636-724-2 (signed edition)

Design and layout by Alligator Tree Graphics.
Printed in England by T. J. Books Limited.

PS Publishing Ltd
Grosvenor House
1 New Road
Hornsea, HU18 1PG
England

editor@pspublishing.co.uk
www.pspublishing.co.uk

CONTENTS

PREFACE

In the realm of modern weird fiction, there are few living writers whose work is sufficiently rich and variegated to justify a full-length critical study. It is not my place here to engage in a polemic for or against some of the more popular figures in the field; but I can say with confidence that Ramsey Campbell, although by no means the most widely known living writer of horror fiction, is worthy of study both because of the intrinsic merit of his work and because of the place he occupies in the historical progression of this literary mode. Campbell, having now surpassed his seventieth year, has been publishing for some fifty-five years and has been a professional writer for more than forty; he has thirty-five novels and hundreds of short stories, novelettes, and novellas to his credit; and he represents a bridge between the "classic" weird writers of the first half of the twentieth century and today's diverse crop of best-sellers, although he himself is in many ways still in advance of his younger colleagues in the provocative dynamism of his work.

Campbell himself has facilitated the study of his work by making available documents that ordinarily would only see the light after an author's death. He has been generous enough to allow his juvenilia, written at the age of eleven, to be published; and, more significantly, he has issued his own bibliography of his work. (It should be made clear that the impetus for the publication of this bibliography did not come from Campbell.) This bibliography—although proceeding only to the mid-1990s, and therefore not incorporating his work of the past two and a half decades—is doubly valuable in that it lists items in order of composition, not publication, and gives their dates of writing (by year only), allowing one to gain a precise idea of the growth and development of Campbell's output. Although I have decided on a thematic rather than a chronological study of Campbell's novels and tales, I will frequently have occasion to refer to the progression of a given theme or element in his work; hence, when I wish to refer to the date of composition of a given item, I place the date in brackets.

I presume my system of citations is readily understandable. I cite all major works by a series of abbreviations and page numbers in the text; the edition used, when not the first, is indicated with an asterisk in the bibliography. In those cases where I only discuss a story without citing from it, I have not identified the collection in which it appears, as the reader can ascertain that information by consulting the contents of Campbell's story collections in the bibliography.

Writing about a living author, especially one with whom one is acquainted, is not an easy task. I trust that my objectivity will not be questioned, and that I will not be deemed an uncritical partisan. Critics of unrecognised authors do have a tendency to lapse into occasional drumbeating and pompom-waving; but I would not have written a book about Campbell if I did not think that his work merited detailed attention. Ramsey Campbell has read nearly the whole of this book, but I have not written it on the assumption that he will be my only reader.

In every way this monograph should be regarded as merely a preliminary study of Campbell. Because much of his work is not widely known to the general public, I have felt the need to provide fairly detailed synopses of his major novels and tales, and this has reduced the space available for analysis. While I have chosen to study Campbell's work thematically, I am aware that many other perspectives could be employed.

Although the opinions in this book are of course my own, I have also received much useful information from Stefan Dziemianowicz, Michael A. Morrison, and Steven J. Mariconda.

S.T.J.

MY ROOTS EXHUMED

BY RAMSEY CAMPBELL

Probably the commonest question horror writers are asked is why they write what they write. In my case one answer seems to be that the aesthetic taste I developed first was for terror. My earliest memories of reading are of being frightened—which is not to say that everything I read scared me, but that I remember the reading that did. I was no older than four, and may well have been younger, when I encountered *More Adventures of Rupert*, the 1947 volume of a British children's annual. One illustrated story, "Rupert's Christmas Tree," introduced me to supernatural horror.

Consider the imagery. The title page of the story shows the silhouette of a small spruce tree prancing uphill against a lurid moonlit sky, an image that haunted me for many years. The tale itself has Rupert, a young bear in a red pullover and yellow check trousers, searching for a Christmas tree in a forest near his rural home. Having rescued a mysterious little old man from a tangle of brambles, he's rewarded by being led blindfolded to a secret plantation from which he chooses a tree that mysteriously reappears outside his home. ("The tree is coming," he tell his parents, a decidedly ominous announcement.) It is first seen by the glow of a flashlight, an image I remember giving me a premonitory chill.

After the Christmas party, Rupert hears a high-pitched laugh from the direction of the tree, and (to quote one of the couplets with which the illustrations are captioned for slower readers)

As Rupert lies awake that night,
Again that voice gives him a fright.

By now I too was distinctly apprehensive. He leans out of the window and hears "a little scratchy noise in the dark shadows." Downstairs he finds that the tub in which the tree stood is empty, and a trail of earth leads out of the house. Much to my infant dismay he follows it and sees what I dreaded—"the tree, using its roots for legs, moves rapidly away into the gloom." The panel that was altogether too much for me shows the tree clinging with clawlike roots to a rock against a moonlit sky and leaning towards Rupert the ornamental fairy that is the best it can do for a head. The moral of the tale appears to be that he shouldn't have been so inquisitive, but that was lost on me. What strikes me now is the macabreness of the imagery—the small unlocatable voice, the noise in the night, the trail of earth, the scrawny silhouette. One trusts that the reticence of the telling was intended to prevent the youthful reader from being too distressed, but it had precisely the opposite effect on me.

So, before long, did *The Princess and the Goblin*, George MacDonald's fairy tale. The descriptions of the animals that had mutated in the goblin mines—"the various parts of their bodies assuming, in an apparently arbitrary and self-willed manner, the most abnormal developments"—strike me as reminiscent of the early scenes at the farm in Lovecraft's "Colour out of Space." Lovecraft had read at least MacDonald's fantasies for adults, but I wonder if the goblin novels might have been part of the childhood reading of M. R. James, with whom they share the technique of showing just enough to suggest far worse (at least to me).

Not even the best-loved tellers of fairy tales always reassured

me: the Grimm Brothers may have, but not Hans Christian
Andersen—the fate of the brave tin soldier and his beloved seemed
cruel enough to be real, the spectre of Death and the strange
heads that peered over the edge of the emperor's bed in "The
Nightingale" were capable of invading my bedroom at night, and
the angelic spirits that bore up the little mermaid came too late
to make up for her having to feel as if she trod on sharp knives at
every step. Perhaps I was destined to believe more in knives than
angels.

Events that only might happen, or even that the audience was
assured would not, troubled me as well. In *The Princess and the
Goblin* the princess had only to fear that an old castle staircase
up which she could flee a stilt-legged creature "might lead to no
tower" for me to be obsessed with what could have befallen her
then. Sometimes I saw reasons for terror where nobody else may
have. In Disney's film, the entire scene in which the seven dwarfs
perform a song and dance to entertain Snow White was rendered
terrifying for me by the sight of an open window that framed a
space too dark, too suggestive of the possibility that something
frightful might appear. But it was another image that set me on
the course I was to make my career: the cover of an issue of *Weird
Tales*.

It was the November 1952 issue. I saw it in a sunlit window of
a newsagent's in Seabank Road in Southport, a train ride up the
coast from Liverpool, and I must have been seven years old. I had
never wanted to own anything so much. I couldn't imagine what
dread pleasures might lurk behind such a cover, but owning the
picture would have been enough—a painting of a terrified bird
or birdlike creature cowering beneath a luminous green sky while
two monstrosities with immense human skulls for heads and very
little in the way of bodies advanced towards it across a black desert.
I pleaded with my mother—the price was only a shilling—but was
judged far too young. It took me a decade to locate a copy of the
issue, only to find that the cover depicted a vulture perched on a

rib-cage near two half-buried skulls while two greenish skeletons, possibly ambulatory, hovered in the background. It seems clear that on that summer day in 1953 my imagination was dissatisfied with the image and so dreamed something stranger into existence, an approach it has taken to reality ever since.

Though I was forbidden lurid magazines when I was seven, my mother did let me use her tickets to borrow adult books from the local library, which presumably could be trusted not to allow anything too disreputable or sensational onto its shelves. Little did she, or indeed I, know that many of the anthologies multiplying on those shelves drew on the pulps for their material, and I wasn't much older than seven when the gruesomeness of "The Colour out of Space" proved almost too intense. Other tales haunted me too—Le Fanu and Bradbury seemed especially powerful, though above all it was M. R. James whose work suggested that nowhere was safe: not one's bedroom, where a sheet might take it into its head to rear up, nor the bed itself if you were ill-advised enough to reach under the pillow.

Given that my childhood was already a place of some terror, it may reasonably be asked why I scared myself with fiction too. It can hardly have been that the fiction was a medium that carried away some of my actual fears, since remembering it at night only brought me close to panic, or closer than I already was. Let me suggest that reading the fiction may have been my method, however unconscious I was of this at the time, of dealing with the experience of terror by discovering some aesthetic pleasure in it. In time, as the intensity of the effects of reading it began to lessen a little, I was able to develop a clearer notion of what I valued in the field.

Two books were especially important in shaping my view of it: *Great Tales of Terror and the Supernatural*, edited by Herbert A. Wise and Phyllis Fraser, and *Best Horror Stories*, edited by John Keir Cross. Crucially, neither book drew its material wholly from the ghetto the genre had started to create for itself. Wise and

Fraser have Poe next to Balzac, Thomas Hardy between Bierce and "The Monkey's Paw," Hemingway beside John Collier; in the Cross book Angus Wilson keeps company with M. R. James, Faulkner with Bierce, and I was given my first flavoursome taste of Graham Greene. Crucially, over forty pages are occupied by "Bartleby," Herman Melville's tale of psychological horror, in which the eponymous clerk is destroyed by his own apathy. It is the longest story in the book, and Cross apologizes in his preface to those readers who feel cheated by its inclusion. I was only eleven, but I didn't feel tricked out of any portion of the fifteen shillings I'd saved up to buy the book, which shows that my concept of the genre was already pretty large. Reading "Bartleby" satisfied some expectation, whereas I felt compelled to reread "The Skull of Barnaby Shattuck" in one of the last pulp issues of *Weird Tales* because, try as I might, I could detect no weirdness. (I assume there was none, just an editor desperate to fill an issue.)

I'd been permitted pulp magazines since I was ten. I collected them avidly, in particular the British digest reprints remaindered for sixpence, and—perhaps excited by being able to possess the previously forbidden—initially wasn't too critical. Paul Suter's "Beyond the Door," for instance, gave me quite a turn, and it was years before I realized that its payoff ("THE THING BEFORE ME WAS NOT A DOG!") was a coarsened version of the climax of M. R. James's "Diary of Mr Poynter." My critical taste wasn't long in developing, however. It was in my very early teens, perhaps even earlier, that I bought a paperback of one of Christine Campbell Thomson's *Not at Night* anthologies and found it dismally unsatisfactory, not in lacking gruesomeness—the book was a trough of that—but in the utter absence of good prose. I later encountered Thomson's boast "From the first, I set my face against literature" but believe me, I didn't need to be told. Her influence was apparent in the increasingly pornographic and decreasingly literate *Pan Books of Horror Stories* before Steve Jones and David Sutton rescued them from their downward trend, and her regrettable tradition may be seen in a more recent teeming of writers bent on outdoing each other in disgustingness. No doubt they encourage one another, but there's no reason why anybody else should.

At fourteen I read an entire collection by Lovecraft and determined to model myself on him. Having done so to the best of my ability, with a good deal of editorial advice from August Derleth, throughout my first book, I let that persuade me I knew all there was to know about Lovecraft, whereas in fact I had yet to appreciate how his career was an exploration of numerous different modes of horror fiction in search of the perfect form. By now, aged seventeen, I was turning towards the mainstream, not least in search of the kind of disquiet I'd come to crave. I found it in Beckett (the unmercifully disturbing *How It Is* and *The Unnameable*), in Thomas Hinde's first-person studies of madness (*The Investigator, The Day the Call Came*) and Paul Ableman's *I Hear Voices*, in Sartre's *Nausea* and just about everything available by Kafka . . . Films proved rewarding too. Having spent more nights in cinemas than out of them once I looked old enough to be admitted without an adult—many of those nights devoted to catching up on horror films in decaying Liverpool cinemas in the midst of blitzed streets that became my personal Gothic landscape—I began to discover in subtitled movies an unease even more to my taste: the terrifying dream that begins *Wild Strawberries*, the achingly unpeopled streets at the end of *The Eclipse*, the interpenetration of surreal nightmare and bleak social observation in *Los Olvidados*, the instant dislocations of *Last Year in Marienbad*, a film that (along with the tales of Robert Aickman) convinced me that an enigma could be more satisfying than any solution. This view, and the influence of much else cited above, is apparent in *Demons by Daylight*, my second published book.

I find it hard to see much in it now except flaws, but it was my attempt to address in horror fiction some of the concerns I'd found in the contemporary mainstream and, by finding them there, in myself. Reading Nabokov, *Lolita* and *Pale Fire* in particular, had liberated my style—the first effects can be seen in 1963, in "The Stone on the Island"—but had also made me impatient with what I saw as the narrowness of my genre, though Fritz Leiber's urban supernatural tales had shown me a way forward. Of course it was my mind that was narrow, not the genre, whose edges I've yet to find, and whose power at its best to convey awe I continue to strive to achieve. For the past few years I've tried to follow the fine example of Brian Aldiss in allowing as much of the whole of my personality into my tales as possible. I hope I can take a few people with me while I continue to explore—not that I need the company, but the trip might be rewarding for us all, and some fun as well. My good friend S. T. Joshi will indicate the route so far. Those half-buried misshapen objects that protrude here and there from the landscape are memories, and quite a few of the grotesques who pop out from behind unlikely bits of scenery will be me, wearing various masks. Think twice about snatching them off. What they conceal may be stranger or—horror of horrors!—just dull.

Wallasey, Merseyside
3 June 1998

I. BIOGRAPHY AND OVERVIEW

Ramsey Campbell emerged at a critical juncture in the history of weird fiction. The distinguishing feature of horror, fantasy, and supernatural fiction, as opposed to mainstream fiction, is the freedom it allows an author to refashion the universe in accordance with his or her philosophical, moral, and political aims. The result, as Rosemary Jackson[1] has pointed out, is a kind of "subversion" whereby the laws of Nature as we understand them are shown to be suspended, invalid, or inoperable; and this violation of natural law (embodied in such conceptions as the vampire, the haunted house, or less conventional tropes such as incursions of alien entities or forces from the depths of space) often serves as a symbol for the philosophical message the author is attempting to convey. Unlike science fiction, however, the horror story often foregoes any attempt at a scientific justification of the supernatural phenomena; and the degree to which an author can convince the sceptical reader of the momentary existence of the unreal is frequently an index to his or her skill as a practitioner of the form.

In the fifty-year heyday of the "Gothic" novel—from Horace

1. Rosemary Jackson, *Fantasy: The Literature of Subversion* (London: Methuen, 1981).

Walpole's *The Castle of Otranto* (1764) to Charles Robert Maturin's *Melmoth the Wanderer* (1820), and including the work of Ann Radcliffe, Matthew Gregory ("Monk") Lewis, Charles Brockden Brown, and an endless array of their largely mediocre imitators and disciples—many of the basic themes, tropes, and elements still used by modern horror writers found literary expression.[2] The ghost, the vampire (as in John William Polidori's "The Vampyre" [1819]), the haunted house or castle, the artificial man (Mary Shelley's *Frankenstein* [1818]), and many other devices were exhumed over and over again in the hundreds of Gothic novels of the period, to such monotonous effect as to incur Jane Austen's well-deserved parody, *Northanger Abbey* (1818). Indeed, the amount of scholarly attention devoted to the Gothic novel—from Edith Birkhead's seminal study, *The Tale of Terror* (1921), to the present day—is far out of proportion to the actual literary merits of this body of work.

It was Edgar Allan Poe (1809–1849) who definitively established the weird tale as a viable literary form. Scorning the stale Gothic stage properties except for half-parodic purposes (as in "Metzengerstein"), Poe showed how the short story is best suited to convey terror by its compactness, potency, and unity of mood and effect. Poe's chief contribution to the form was an unremitting realism—not of incident (for the horror tale, as an account of something "which *could not possibly happen*,"[3] cannot be held to realistic standards of plot or incident), but of psychological

2. For a comprehensive history of the field, see S. T. Joshi, *Unutterable Horror: A History of Supernatural Fiction* (Hornsea, UK: PS Publishing, 2012; 2 vols.). Lovecraft's "Supernatural Horror in Literature" (1927) has not been excelled as an historical outline of horror fiction from the eighteenth century to his own day.
3. H. P. Lovecraft, letter to August Derleth (20 November 1931), in *Essential Solitude: The Letters of H. P. Lovecraft and August Derleth*, ed. David E. Schultz and S. T. Joshi (New York: Hippocampus Press, 2008), 416.

motivation. Poe's direct influence on Campbell may be negli-
gible, but in his acute exploration of abnormal states of mind Poe
achieved heights of psychological terror that perhaps only Campbell has come close to equalling. There are relatively few instances
of the standard "monsters" of horror fiction in Poe's work—a fact
that has caused the otherwise penetrating scholar Noël Carroll[4]
to deem Poe's work altogether out of the realm of the weird—and
in this sense Poe is also an important precursor of Campbell. Also
like Campbell, Poe—in spite of such stories as "MS. Found in a
Bottle" and "A Descent into the Maelstrom"—is lacking in what
H. P. Lovecraft would call the "cosmic quality":[5] his horrors are
manifestly human in origin.

The half-century after Poe saw the proliferation of horror
fiction in a multitude of forms and by a wide array of authors.
Aside from the prolific J. Sheridan LeFanu (1814–1873)—whose
"Green Tea," "Carmilla," and *Uncle Silas* are landmarks—few
authors focused solely on the supernatural, and many were distinguished practitioners of mainstream fiction. What this suggests
is that the horror story was not—and, in my view, would not be
for many years—a distinct genre but merely a mode of writing to
which authors of varying persuasions could turn to convey moods,
emotions, and philosophical conceptions not otherwise possible in
the literature of conventional realism. Robert Louis Stevenson's
The Strange Case of Dr. Jekyll and Mr. Hyde (1886), Bram Stoker's
Dracula (1897), and Henry James's *The Turn of the Screw* (1898)
are only the high-water marks of a plethora of horror literature
produced on both sides of the Atlantic. Much of this work was still
in the old-time Gothic mode, little influenced by the new thinking

---

4. Noël Carroll, *The Philosophy of Horror* (London: Routledge, 1990).
5. H. P. Lovecraft, letter to Clark Ashton Smith ([17 October 1930]), in
*Dawnward Spire, Lonely Hill: The Letters of H. P. Lovecraft and Clark Ashton
Smith*, ed. David E. Schultz and S. T. Joshi (New York: Hippocampus
Press, 2017), 248.

typified by Poe; but Ambrose Bierce (1842–1914?) became a formidable posthumous disciple of Poe by his compressed short tales
of supernatural and psychological horror.

What may be termed the "Golden Age" of weird fiction—the
period from, roughly, 1880 to 1940—was distinguished by the
emergence of five or six leading writers whose single-minded focus
on horror produced a legacy that perhaps may never be excelled.
The Welshman Arthur Machen (1863–1947), the Irishman Lord
Dunsany (1878–1957), and the Englishmen Algernon Blackwood
(1869–1951) and M. R. James (1862–1936) created permanent
landmarks in all modes of the horror tale.[6]

James perfected the ghost story in his four collections of tales,
and his *Collected Ghost Stories* (1931) remains a seminal volume. Far
from the wispy, sheeted form of standard legendry, James's ghosts
are aggressively violent, animalistic, and vengeful, sometimes
pursuing hapless victims for no greater sin than undue curiosity.
James's scholarly erudition—he was a recognised authority on
church history and mediaeval manuscripts—formed the perfect
pseudo-realistic background for the incursion of the supernatural.

Lord Dunsany, in such early works as *The Gods of Pegāna* (1905)
and *Time and the Gods* (1906), abandoned mundane reality altogether for a quaintly decadent, aesthetically refined imaginary
world of gods, demigods, priests, and heroes, laying the ground-
work for the more popular "Middle-Earth" of J. R. R. Tolkien,
whom Dunsany surely influenced. Later works by Dunsany are
set nominally in the real world, but they continue to embody the
essence of fantasy—the wilful disregarding of the laws of Nature
and their replacement by an ontology derived wholly from the
author's imagination. The work of Dunsany and Tolkien (1892–
1973) definitively established fantasy as a subclass of imaginative
fiction.

---

6. For a study of these four writers, as well as of Lovecraft and Bierce,
see S. T. Joshi, *The Weird Tale* (Austin: University of Texas Press, 1990).

Blackwood and Machen, both profound religious mystics, expressed their dissatisfaction with the mundane world—its inexorable industrialisation, its growing secularism, its decreasing stores of poetry and imagination—by horror tales that are in many instances scarcely veiled philosophical and political jeremiads. Blackwood's *The Centaur* (1911)—a heavily autobiographical work in which a man, disgusted with the modern world, comes upon a herd of centaurs in the Caucasus mountains and rediscovers that closeness to Nature which contemporary civilisation has lost—is an intensely vital novel. But Blackwood's most influential works are those less openly philosophical tales which display an extraordinary skill at the manipulation of supernatural elements: "The Willows," that haunting tale of the eerie and nebulous creatures encountered by two travellers sailing down the Danube (which Lovecraft, with some justification, called the finest story in all weird fiction); "The Wendigo," about a harrowing monster in the wilds of western Canada; and the tales in *John Silence—Physician Extraordinary* (1908), in which that "psychic detective" probes all manner of hauntings, apparitions, and spectres. Although not gifted with a polished style, Blackwood possessed an intensity of vision and a skill in psychological analysis that justify his standing as perhaps the greatest weird writer in English literature. As for Machen, in the vast array of his stories, novels, essays, and journalism is found a substantial body of supernatural work—"The Great God Pan" (1890), about the offspring of Pan and a mortal woman; "The White People" (1904), a poignant and horrific account of a young girl unwittingly initiated into the witch-cult; *The Three Impostors* (1895), an episodic novel containing powerful sequences about horrors in the Welsh mountains ("Novel of the Black Seal"), the loathsome effects of tainted drugs ("Novel of the White Powder"), and other monstrosities—that perpetuates his memory among a small but devoted cadre of readers.

    The situation in America during the "Golden Age" was quite different. A number of writers produced the occasional horror novel or tale, but only one significant figure, H. P. Lovecraft (1890–1937), devoted his entire career to the supernatural; and he did so in a peculiar way—by means of the pulp magazines. Although some of the magazines in Frank A. Munsey's wide chain (notably the *Argosy* and *All-Story*) had included random tales of terror in the first two decades of the century, it was not until the foundation of the pulp magazine *Weird Tales* in 1923 that the field gained a forum focusing solely on the form. But this focus had both virtues and drawbacks: in its thirty-one-year run, *Weird Tales* certainly published a vast quantity of weird fiction, but it created a literary ghetto by publishing the work of amateurs and hacks who could never have found a haven for their stereotyped, ill-written products in any other venue. The mainstream magazines accordingly became closed to the weird except when it was written by the most eminent writers, and there slowly developed a prejudice against horror fiction of any kind. In truth, the fault may not fall solely on *Weird Tales* and its equally juvenile congeners among the science fiction pulps; in the United States, with its Puritan moral tradition, the horror story had always been looked upon with suspicion as somehow unwholesome, morbid, and depressing. Poe did not enter the canon of American literature until at least half a century after his death, and he still remains an ambivalent figure; Bierce has yet to be properly enshrined. But the pulp magazines gave conventional critics a ready excuse to ignore or deprecate the weird tale.

Lovecraft was, regrettably, the victim of this prejudice. Endowed with a powerful analytical intellect that exhibited itself in wide-ranging philosophical, literary, historical, and political disquisitions (chiefly in his immense body of letters), at an early stage Lovecraft evolved a coherent theory of what he called "weird fiction" and produced work of a power, sincerity, and dynamism that simultaneously surpassed the hackneyed popular conventions of the pulp magazines and the timid literary horizons of standard publishers. Although a fixture in *Weird Tales*, he suffered the indignity of having some of his best and most pioneering work rejected by that magazine as well as by mainstream publishers such as Knopf, Putnam's, and Vanguard. Lovecraft paid the price of being ahead of his time, dying in poverty and obscurity.

Lovecraft's work was rescued from oblivion by the devotion of his friends August Derleth and Donald Wandrei, who in 1939 founded the publishing firm Arkham House and issued an immense collection of Lovecraft's work, *The Outsider and Others*. This small press, conceived initially for the sole purpose of publishing Lovecraft, gradually issued the work of other weird writers—mostly from the pulps—and became the leading publisher in the field, a position it retained until it finally became moribund in the early twenty-first century. Derleth in particular, although not having much genuine feel for the weird (as exhibited by the conventionality and mediocrity of his own horror tales), did much to promote the field and such other pulp writers as Clark Ashton Smith (1893–1961) and Robert E. Howard (1906–1936), both close friends of Lovecraft. In a sense, however, the dominance of Arkham House also contributed to the segregation of the terror tale from the mainstream, and in the course of time reviews of Arkham House books ceased to appear in standard newspapers and magazines.

For at least three decades after the death of Lovecraft, weird fiction in America was at a low ebb. The pulp magazines, whose readership rapidly declined with the onset of the paperback book after the Second World War, died out by the 1950s. Science fiction and detective fiction—both of which commanded, and continue to command, a far larger audience than horror fiction—flourished in both paperbacks and digest magazines, but horror fiction did not. Indeed, much of what we now consider the horror fiction of the 1940s, 1950s and 1960s masqueraded as science fiction, as the work of Ray Bradbury (1920–2012), Charles Beaumont (1929–1967), Richard Matheson (1926–2013) and Fritz Leiber (1910–1992) attests. Conversely, such a writer as Robert Bloch (1917–1994) wrote horror fiction under the guise of suspense fiction in such works as *The Scarf* (1947) and *Psycho* (1959). Bloch was a central figure in the development of psychological suspense, in which the probing of aberrant psychological states is carried out; some of his work of this kind actually falls into the supernatural, as in the celebrated tale "Yours Truly, Jack the Ripper" (1943). Meanwhile, the predominantly mainstream writer Shirley Jackson (1916–1965) produced a small but brilliant modicum of weird work, notably "The Lottery" (1948) and *The Haunting of Hill House* (1959). Jackson too was very skilful at psychological portrayal, but her quietly potent work has exercised little influence upon the field.

In England the situation was not quite so bleak. M. R. James had so perfected the supernatural ghost story that he seemed to give birth to the very different mode of the psychological ghost story, in which ambiguity is sustained to the very end of the tale as to whether the ghostly phenomenon is actually manifest or is merely the product of a disturbed mentality. Henry James had of course pioneered this mode in *The Turn of the Screw*, but such British writers as Walter de la Mare (1873–1956), L. P. Hartley (1895–1972), and Oliver Onions (1873–1961) carried it to great heights of subtlety, sophistication, and emotive effect. This trend reached its pinnacle with the powerful work of Robert Aickman (1914–1981), whose several collections of "strange stories" were virtually the sole instances of short horror fiction in the 1960s. (The endless array of occult novels by Dennis Wheatley [1897–1977] appealed only to the lowest levels of readership and are now achieving the oblivion they deserve.)

To be a reader or writer of horror fiction in the 1960s was, then, to be in a somewhat anomalous position. Most of the best work seemed to have been done decades in the past, and even much of this work was falling into obscurity. Such a reader would be forced to scour the used bookstalls in quest of elusive volumes by Machen, Blackwood and others for literary sustenance, and any writer choosing to work in this form would be compelled either to adapt his or her work into the neighbouring modes of science fiction or suspense fiction or to draw upon the great figures of the past. It was the latter course that Ramsey Campbell adopted when shocking the small world of horror fiction by issuing *The Inhabitant of the Lake and Less Welcome Tenants* at the age of eighteen in 1964.

It is a truism to say that Ramsey Campbell's upbringing seems to have predisposed him to the writing of horror fiction, especially his unnerving type of horror fiction that probes abnormal psychological states with uncomfortable intensity; but such flippancy masks what must have been an extraordinarily painful childhood and adolescence.

John Ramsey Campbell was born on 4 January 1946 in Liverpool, where he remained until well into his adulthood. Shortly after his birth, however, his parents became estranged; as divorce was then difficult and his mother was Catholic, the result was a very uneasy cohabitation. The marriage deteriorated from mere arguments to threats of violence by his father against his mother to complete mutual silence, as Campbell's father occupied the top floor of the house and Campbell and his mother occupied the bottom.[7] Campbell himself has etched the situation with painful honesty:

> For most of my childhood . . . my father was heard but not seen . . . I used to hear his footsteps on the stairs as I lay in bed, terrified that he would come into my room. Sometimes I heard arguments downstairs as my mother waylaid him when he came home, her voice shrill and clear, his blurred and utterly incomprehensible, hardly a voice, which filled me with a terror I couldn't define . . . If he was still in the kitchen

7. Many of the particulars of Campbell's life have been taken from an unpublished manuscript account, "Ramsey Campbell: A Summary," which the author has graciously supplied me.

when it was time for her to make my breakfast she would drive him out of the house—presumably it was unthinkable that I should share the table with him . . . In my teens I sometimes came home, from work or from the cinema, at the same time as my father, who would hold the front door closed from inside to make sure we never came face to face. Very occasionally, when it was necessary for him to get in touch, he would leave me a note, in French . . . Worst of all was Christmas, when my mother would send me to knock on his bedroom door and invite him down, as a mark of seasonal goodwill, for Christmas dinner. I would go upstairs in a panic, but there was never any response.[8]

It is scarcely any wonder that Campbell eventually shed his own Catholic religiosity and in later works would pungently satirise religion for its dogmatism and infliction of needless misery. His attendance of a Catholic primary school, Christ the King, with its customary doses of corporal punishment, did not help matters on this point. The miseries of school life are featured prominently in many of Campbell's stories and novels, and as late as *Midnight Sun* (1990) he seems still to be drawing upon them:

Soon Mr. O'Toole set about preparing the school for the festivities. When they opened their presents and ate their Christmas dinner, he yelled, they should be thinking of the child God sent to earth to suffer because people were so sinful that nothing less could make up for their sins. He dabbed spittle from his lips with a large stiff handkerchief and glared red-eyed around the assembly hall. "Have you no souls?" he demanded, his voice rising almost to a shriek. "File past that crib, the lot of you, and think of Christ's blessed mother

8. Ramsey Campbell, "At the Back of My Mind: A Guided Tour" (FD xvi–xvii).

having to see her only son whipped and crowned with thorns and nailed to a cross to die with vinegar to drink. I'll see a few tears before this assembly's over, or I'll know how to get them." (MS 39)

And yet, his mother nurtured his literary pursuits in general and his taste for weird fiction in particular. She herself had published a few short stories in a Yorkshire magazine before the Second World War and also attempted the writing of suspense thrillers; she also enjoyed horror and suspense films and took her son to see many of the now classic films of the 1950s and 1960s. Campbell's own interest in literary horror emerged at an early age. When he was six he saw an issue of *Weird Tales* (probably the British rather than the American edition) in a newsagent's window and felt that it was not only exactly the sort of fiction he wished to read, but the sort he wished to write. By the time he was ten he was reading science fiction and fantasy magazines (notably *Astounding Science Fiction* and remaindered copies of *Weird Tales*, which had ceased publication in 1954); and at fifteen he was collecting books published by Arkham House, since that firm had already achieved a kind of legendary status in the field.

In 1957, the year he enrolled at a grammar school, St Edward's College, Campbell began producing his first surviving literary work: an entire collection of twenty tales (most of them quite short but one as long as 6000 words), luridly illustrated by himself and entitled *Ghostly Tales*. With characteristic generosity, Campbell has allowed this work to be published, and it readily exhibits the influence of the writers he was reading at this time, chiefly M. R. James and Dennis Wheatley. Campbell actually submitted the volume to a publisher, T. V. Boardman & Co., and the director of the firm, Tom Boardman, Jr, wrote a surprisingly cordial and encouraging response, saying that the stories were "very well written and show real promise" (GT 2) and urging Campbell to continue gaining practice in writing.

Campbell did exactly that. He had already read some stories by H. P. Lovecraft in anthologies at the age of eight,[9] but did not come upon an entire collection of his stories until 1960. He read the book (*Cry, Horror!*) in a single day and promptly began writing pastiches of Lovecraft. In 1961, he sent some of these stories to August Derleth of Arkham House, who wrote a surprisingly long letter spelling out in detail the tales' literary deficiencies but giving sufficient encouragement for Campbell to feel it worth the effort to continue working. (It is evident that Derleth did not know of Campbell's youth when making his initial comments on the tales submitted to him.) Campbell's first professional sale occurred in 1962, when Derleth published "The Church in High Street" in the Arkham House anthology *Dark Mind, Dark Heart*. Derleth extensively rewrote the tale, but Campbell did not object to the procedure: he was thrilled by merely being included in a volume published by Arkham House, and moreover he learned much about the craft of writing from Derleth's revisions.

Derleth decided shortly thereafter to publish an entire volume of Campbell's Lovecraft pastiches, which appeared in 1964 as *The Inhabitant of the Lake and Less Welcome Tenants*. Other writers have testified to the amazement and envy they felt at seeing this book by an eighteen-year-old published by weird fiction's most prestigious small press. Campbell, however, felt that he had now said all he had to say in the Lovecraftian idiom and turned violently away to tales antipodally different.

Meanwhile Campbell's family situation was not improving. His mother had exhibited signs of clinical schizophrenia from Campbell's very early youth; and her increasing mania would make his adult life a living nightmare. His maternal grandmother had lived with the family from the time Campbell was a year old, but her

---

9. See Stefan Dziemianowicz, "An Interview with Ramsey Campbell," in *The Count of Thirty: A Tribute to Ramsey Campbell*, ed. S. T. Joshi (West Warwick, RI: Necronomicon Press, 1993), 7.

death in 1961 robbed him of a potentially stabilising force. He himself left school the next year, "having obtained passes in six subjects at O Level in the General Certificate of Education,"[10] and found work as a tax officer for the Inland Revenue. Four years later he changed jobs and began working for the Liverpool Public Library system. At this time, 1966, Campbell's mother went into hospital for an operation; but complications developed, and she became embittered at the hospital staff and attempted to sue the surgeon. Her lifelong paranoia waxed, as she became convinced that even her son was conspiring against her.

Campbell himself might have ended up much like his mother had he not met Jenny Chandler, the daughter of science fiction writer A. Bertram Chandler, in 1969 at a science fiction convention. (Campbell had briefly been engaged to a librarian and musician, Rosemary Prince, in 1967, but her parents broke off the engagement.) In 1970 Ramsey and Jenny met again and began seeing each other frequently. They married on 1 January 1971, and she and his children—Tamsin Joanne (born in 1978) and Matthew Ramsey (born in 1981)—have supplied the nurturing family life Campbell never received from his parents. And yet, shortly after he and Jenny returned from their honeymoon in the Lake District, Campbell was compelled to see his father face to face for the first time in twenty years: the elder Campbell had suffered a fall down the stairs and was seriously injured. A few days later he died.

By 1973 Campbell, dissatisfied with his library job, decided to plunge into full-time writing. His second collection, *Demons by Daylight*, had been published by Arkham House; and, although radically different in tone and style from his earlier work, it received positive reviews from several writers and critics in the field. In particular, T. E. D. Klein—himself later to become a distinguished writer of terror tales—wrote a glowing tribute,

10. "Ramsey Campbell: A Summary," 3.

"Ramsey Campbell: An Appreciation," which he sent to Campbell in 1974 (it was published in the small-press magazine *Nyctalops* for May 1977); Campbell found the essay enormously encouraging. He began writing great quantities of stories for magazines and anthologies, and his third collection, *The Height of the Scream*, appeared in 1976.

Campbell's American agent, Kirby McCauley, insisted that Campbell must write a novel if he wished to become an established figure in the field. It should be recalled that this was just before the horror "boom" of the late 1970s and 1980s. Ira Levin's *Rosemary's Baby* had appeared in 1967; William Peter Blatty's *The Exorcist* and Thomas Tryon's *The Other* jointly dominated the best-seller lists in 1971; but few writers had any notion of being able to write horror fiction full-time and make a career of it. Campbell had attempted the writing of novels (mostly science fiction or mystery fiction) from as early as his teenage years, but they had come to nothing; now he buckled down to the job, producing *The Doll Who Ate His Mother* in six months in 1975. It was published the next year, but sold poorly.

Campbell promptly turned to a second novel, *The Face That Must Die*. This unremittingly bleak story of a serial killer (written long before serial killer novels had become hackneyed excursions into bloodletting) had difficulty finding a publisher; several British and American firms rejected it outright as being too horrible and unpleasant—as if horror fiction should somehow be cheerful and uplifting. Finally it was published, with significant cuts, in 1979.

By this time Stephen King's first novels (*Carrie*, 1974; *'Salem's Lot*, 1975; *The Shining*, 1977) had appeared, achieving best-seller status; Peter Straub (*Ghost Story*, 1979) would shortly join him as a blockbuster writer. Campbell felt that he must deliberately write a popular novel of the sort that King, Straub, and a growing legion of imitators, hacks, and wannabes were producing. The result was *The Parasite* (1980; entitled *To Wake the Dead* in the UK). It was financially successful, and Campbell has continued with a steady

stream of novels, although they cater far less to popular taste. Perhaps his most substantial works in the novel form are *Incarnate*
(1983), *The Hungry Moon* (1986), *Midnight Sun* (1990), *The Long
Lost* (1993), and *The House on Nazareth Hill* (1996).

Campbell's concentration on the novel has resulted in a drastic
reduction in his short-story output. This is doubly regrettable,
since he is such a master of the short-story form and since horror
fiction still seems to work best in short compass. *Dark Companions* (1982) gathered many of the stories he had written in the late
1970s, but several subsequent collections—*Black Wine* (1986),
Night Visions 3 (1986), *Scared Stiff* (1986)—consist predominantly
of stories written in the 1960s or early 1970s. *Waking Nightmares*
(1991), however, is a substantial volume of his later tales, showing
that Campbell has not lost his mastery of the form.

In 1980 Campbell left Liverpool, the city with which he had
had such a love-hate relationship, moving across the Mersey to
Wallasey. Around this time, however, he was also having to tend
to his increasingly crazed mother. Although he had purchased a
house for her near his own so as to look after her more closely, he
would have bitter arguments with her: "More than once I grew
so frustrated that I ran at a wall of the room head first" (FD xxiv).
The situation continued to deteriorate, and Campbell has made
an appalling confession (but one that will ring true to those who
have had a falling out with someone they love): "Sometimes when
I took her for a drive I was tempted to leave her miles from anywhere; sometimes I thought of killing her, reaching across her on
a deserted stretch of motorway and opening the passenger door.
Perhaps she would leave the gas fire on unlit or finally wander
down into the river" (FD xxvi). At last, in 1982, she was taken to a
hospital and died.

By the mid-1980s Campbell, although never achieving the phe-
nomenal sales of King, Straub, and the new Liverpool writer Clive
Barker, had come to be acknowledged as perhaps the most literarily accomplished writer in the field. Robinson Publishing asked

him to select what he felt to be his own best stories, a volume published as *Dark Feasts* (1987). This selection was revised and expanded in 1993 into what may be a canonical volume in horror fiction, *Alone with the Horrors: The Great Short Fiction of Ramsey Campbell 1961–1991*. Fittingly, it was published by Arkham House.

Campbell has been the recipient of the horror fiction field's most prestigious awards. "In the Bag" received the August Derleth Award from the British Fantasy Society for best short story in 1978; that same year the World Fantasy Award was given for "The Chimney," and two years later "Mackintosh Willy" received the same honour. *To Wake the Dead* received the August Derleth Award for best novel in 1981. *Alone with the Horrors* won the World Fantasy Award and the Bram Stoker Award from the Horror Writers Association. Campbell, as mentioned before, was co-guest of honour at the World Fantasy Convention in 1986 and guest of honour at the 1995 NecronomiCon.

In the past two decades, Campbell has continued to generate impressive works of weird fiction. Much of his work has been in the novel form, and he has produced not merely some striking works of non-supernatural fiction (*Silent Children* [1999], *Secret Stories* [2005]), but an array of supernatural novels that continue to break new ground in the field while also drawing upon his own personal experiences: *The Overnight* (2004), *The Grin of the Dark* (2007), *Think Yourself Lucky* (2014), and his remarkable Daoloth trilogy, *The Searching Dead* (2016), *Born to the Dark* (2017), and *The Way of the Worm* (2018), which draws upon his earliest literary influence (H. P. Lovecraft) in a tapestry of cosmic horror that simultaneously portrays the course of his own life from vibrant youth to pensive old age. His output of short fiction has been relatively scanty, but has nonetheless allowed him to assemble several notable collections, including *Told by the Dead* (2003), *Just Behind You* (2009), *Holes for Faces* (2013), and *By the Light of My Skull* (2018).

Campbell has always felt the inclination to dabble in fields outside the realm of horror fiction. He has written a small body of science fiction (notably the novella *Medusa*, written in 1973 and published in 1987) and has even written several lengthy tales of the "sword-and-sorcery" type, also completing some story fragments by Robert E. Howard. In 1977 he published three novelisations of horror films—*The Bride of Frankenstein*, *The Wolfman*, and *Dracula's Daughter*—under the house name Carl Dreadstone, while in 1983 he published the horror novel *The Claw* (published as *Claw* in the UK and *Night of the Claw* in the United States) under the transparent pseudonym "Jay Ramsay." In 2010 he published *Solomon Kane*, a novelisation of a film based on a Robert E. Howard character.

In addition, Campbell has been an accomplished anthologist of horror fiction. His first anthology was *Superhorror* (1976), and it was followed by two volumes of *New Terrors* (both 1980). Arkham House asked him to edit *New Tales of the Cthulhu Mythos* (1980), a volume August Derleth had planned to edit prior to his death. *Uncanny Banquet* (1992) contains some very obscure items, including a nearly forgotten horror novel, *The Hole of the Pit* (1914) by Adrian Ross. With Stephen Jones, he has edited five annual volumes of *Best New Horror* (1990–94), generally acknowledged to be the best of the several competing anthologies of best weird tales of the year. *Meddling with Ghosts* (2002) is a worthy anthology of stories in the tradition of M. R. James.

Beyond the realm of fiction, Campbell has been a film critic for BBC Radio Merseyside since 1969. He has been a columnist for the *British Fantasy Society Bulletin* (1974–77), *Fantasy Review* (1984–86), *Necrofile: The Review of Horror Fiction* (1991–99), and *Dead Reckonings* (2007f.).

Ramsey Campbell celebrated his seventieth birthday on 4 January 2016, and he has been a dominant figure in the field for more than forty years. He is far from saying all that he wishes to say as a writer: such brilliant but very different works as the novella *Needing Ghosts* (1990), the comic horror novel *The Count of Eleven*

(1991), and a steady stream of short fiction all continue to forge new paths and remain ahead of the pack. Campbell himself does not know where he will end up; as he stated in an interview in 1991 when asked where he would be as a writer in five years' time:

> The serious answer to that question is I've absolutely no idea, and that's the good part, isn't it?
> I've got piles of notebooks and piles of notes in the books for ideas which I haven't yet used. Some of them may never get used.
> The great excitement is precisely that you don't know what you are going to do five years from now.[11]

The "horror boom" is now over: many publishers are scaling back their horror lines; magazines in the field are folding; and even popular writers such as King, Straub, Barker, Anne Rice, and Dean R. Koontz are remaining on the best-seller lists for shorter and shorter periods. Perhaps, then, it is time for literate writers such as Campbell, Thomas Ligotti, T. E. D. Klein, and Caitlín R. Kiernan, who have never depended on blockbuster sales to support their careers, to step to the forefront. It is their literarily substantial work that will survive long after the best-sellers have faded to merited oblivion. Ramsey Campbell, still at the forefront of modern horror writing, has not yet attracted the critical attention he deserves; but when the "Silver Age" of the horror tale during the latter half of the twentieth century is compared to the "Golden Age" of the first half, Campbell will be found worthy of the company of Machen, Blackwood, Lovecraft, and perhaps even of the Edgar Allan Poe who launched the entire tradition.

Campbell has spoken much about his aims and techniques as a writer. His actual practice of writing involves working initially

11. Stephen Jones, "*Weird Tales* Talks with Ramsey Campbell," *Weird Tales* No. 301 (Summer 1991): 51.

with a fountain pen in a notebook, the right-hand side of which he keeps blank during the first draft so that comments, additions, or corrections can be made upon it. He then types the draft (initially he used a typewriter; now he uses a word processor), doing further revision along the way. Very frequently he does much condensation: after reading the first chapter of his newest novel, *The House on Nazareth Hill*, at a convention, he reported that it would probably be reduced by a quarter or a third in its final draft. Campbell never actually writes more than one work at a time; although, during the writing of his novels, he may evolve ideas for short stories, he does not commence the actual writing of them until the novel is finished.[12]

Interestingly, Campbell has admitted that, after his first few novels, he no longer prepared elaborate synopses for his lengthier works, preferring rather to let them develop their own energy and direction. It is understandable that Campbell wrote no synopses for his short stories, which are usually focused intensely around a single incident or impression and its ramifications; but it is startling to learn that even so complex a work as *Incarnate*, although initially plotted very carefully, went off in unexpected directions after Campbell took the advice of his Macmillan editor, George Walsh, for a refocusing of some of its elements:

> Although what he said just seemed to be very minor, it virtually changed the entire book. And I thought, well, okay, what's suggesting itself now is even better than I had in mind in the first place, let's go with that. So quite early I discovered that I'd just thrown away the plot I had originally worked out . . . All that structural thing, I have to tell you, pretty well composed itself.[13]

12. Ramsey Campbell, reading *The House on Nazareth Hill* (then entitled *Nazarill*), NecronomiCon, Danvers, Massachusetts, August 1995.
13. Dziemianowicz, "An Interview with Ramsey Campbell," 16.

Of course, it is unlikely that such a seemingly extemporaneous manner of writing would have been successful in a writer who did not already have the years of experience Campbell had had or a clear sense of what he wished to say.

But what is Campbell specifically trying to achieve in writing horror fiction? It is difficult to find any single theme that unites the whole of his work, but an inkling of an answer comes in the following statement:

> I began writing horror fiction in an attempt to imitate what I admired and, as I learned some basic craft, to pay back a little of the pleasure which the field gave me. I've stayed in it because of its scope. So far it has enabled me to talk about any theme I want to examine, and I don't believe I've reached its boundaries by any means.[14]

What this suggests is that Campbell finds the horrific mode—whether it be supernatural or non-supernatural, and he seems equally comfortable in both—a vehicle both for expressing his views on human life and society and, in that hackneyed phrase, for exorcising his personal demons. Certainly Campbell draws upon his own life—his childhood, adolescence, and maturer years—for his work; but he also finds horror a sufficiently flexible medium for conveying any of his moods, conceptions, and images. Although his later work seems to be edging more and more towards what is conventionally called "mainstream fiction," Campbell himself believes that all his work remains within the parameters of horror fiction.

Campbell has always been vocal about the legitimacy of the horror story as an art form; he resolutely claims that it is far more than mere "popular fiction," and that it must have a literary dimension if it is to be worth the effort of writing or reading. In this he is very much like his erstwhile mentor H. P. Lovecraft, who wrote

---

14. "Ramsey Campbell, Probably," *Necrofile* No. 2 (Fall 1991): 16.

the treatise "Supernatural Horror in Literature" (1927) in large
part to demonstrate "the genuineness and dignity of the weirdly
horrible tale as a literary form."[15] Campbell has not written his
own treatise, but a number of shorter articles and columns have
served the same purpose.

Campbell realises that the horror tale has always been a kind
of poor relation to general literature (he has himself faced all too
often the naive query from general readers, "Why do you write
that sort of thing?"); but he maintains that this is exactly because
of its bold, confrontational nature: "Horror fiction is in the business of going too far, of showing the audience things they've
avoided seeing or thinking. Very much like humour, it's in the
business of breaking taboos, and it follows that once those taboos
are broken the fiction tends to lose power, to become 'safe.'"[16]
While this "definition" of horror may be close to Rosemary Jackson's conception of "subversion," Campbell does not wish to be
taken as wholly advocating the kind of over-the-top, in-your-face
horror that is associated with such modern writers as Clive Barker
and the "splatterpunks." Campbell has always gravitated toward
(and practised) "literary horror," and one of his most entertaining
polemics was an attack on Leslie Fiedler, who—with his devotion
to "popular fiction" and with staggering ignorance of the field—
asserted that nearly all instances of horror literature and film are,
and should be considered, schlock.[17]

In recent years Campbell has faced, both in articles and in his
fiction, a perplexing Scylla and Charybdis: on the one hand, the
proliferation of horror fiction and film whose gratuitous violence serves no aesthetic purpose, and, on the other hand, those

15. H. P. Lovecraft, *The Annotated Supernatural Horror in Literature*, ed. S.
T. Joshi (New York: Hippocampus Press, 2nd ed. 2012), 25.
16. "Dig Us No Grave," *Fantasy Review* No. 89 (March 1986): 36.
17. "Rebuttal: Fiedler on the Roof," *Fantasy Review* No. 71 (September
1984): 17–18.

self-appointed moral guardians of our society who wish to practise a mindless censorship that would indiscriminately ban all forms of horror (along with erotica and much else) on the grounds that it is "unwholesome" or that it directly induces violence. On these points Campbell has declared: "I'm less inclined these days to blame fiction for the reality it reflects, more inclined to suggest that fiction, even at its most extreme, expresses the emotions of its chosen audience rather than corrupting them."[18] It should be borne in mind that government censorship in England tends to be much more severe and arbitrary than in the United States; and Campbell has felt the need to respond to the outcry for censorship of "video nasties" after the Jamie Bulger tragedy, in which a two-year-old boy was killed by two ten-year-olds, even though it was never proven that the boys had watched any violent horror films. Campbell astutely remarked:

> ... since the effects of extreme imagery are still a matter of considerable disagreement, it may be more dangerous to censor these expressions of the collective unconscious than to let them regulate themselves, however tardily. Suppressing them will not make them go away, only fester—that's my argument, at any rate.[19]

Campbell may or may not wish himself to be the "conscience" of the modern weird tale, but as one of its most skilled practitioners he teaches by example the lesson that this mode can and should be regarded as literature in its best instances. And he will readily adopt a recognisable label in spite of its dubious connotations: "As for me, I just write horror fiction. I write horror fiction."[20]

18. "Beyond the Pale," *Fantasy Review* No. 82 (August 1985): 33.
19. "Ramsey Campbell, Probably," *Necrofile* No. 11 (Winter 1994): 14.
20. See note 14.

II. THE LOVECRAFTIAN FICTION

The reasons why H. P. Lovecraft's fiction has been so widely imitated and elaborated, especially after his lifetime, are not easily explicable. His self-styled disciples are nearly as numerous as those of Sir Arthur Conan Doyle, whose Sherlock Holmes continues to spawn pastiches, parodies, and takeoffs—some, indeed, from a Lovecraftian perspective. In the case of Lovecraft, both his life and his work were of a sort to attract fascination, devotion, adulation, and imitation, much of it sadly uncritical and inept. The gaunt, eccentric "recluse of Providence" (who, in fact, was anything but reclusive in his final decade, travelling up and down the eastern seaboard from Quebec to Key West) had become a figure of myth perhaps even before his death in 1937; while the "Cthulhu Mythos"—an invented body of myth upon which many of his later tales draw—was seized upon by the readers of *Weird Tales*, and by fellow writers, as something new and distinctive in weird fiction.

Lovecraft is only now coming to gain the recognition he deserves as both a master and a pioneer in the horror story. Early in his career, he was content to write relatively conventional tales of the macabre, inspired largely by Poe and the Gothic novelists;

although he produced several early triumphs, including the celebrated "The Outsider" (1921) and "The Rats in the Walls" (1923),
this apprentice work was perhaps of use only in allowing Lovecraft to develop the technique of documentary realism that would
hold him in good stead throughout the rest of his career. His discovery of Lord Dunsany's work in 1919 was critical, although the
shift in his literary work did not become evident for some years;
Lovecraft found Dunsany's notion of an imagined pantheon of
deities so striking that, beginning with "The Call of Cthulhu"
(1926) and continuing for the next decade, he fashioned his own
ersatz theogony. But there was a significant difference: whereas
Dunsany's gods operated in a decadent cosmos of pure imagination, thereby appearing less horrific than piquant, Lovecraft
boldly inserted his deities into the fabric of the real world, so that
they appeared as dim clouds of terror hanging over the very fate
of the human race and perhaps the entire universe. Also utilising
Arthur Machen's notions of dark cults lurking on the underside of
civilisation, Lovecraft fashioned a convincing series of tales that
embodied his philosophy of cosmicism. As he expressed it in a
1927 letter:

> Now all my tales are based on the fundamental premise
> that common human laws and interests and emotions have
> no validity or significance in the vast cosmos-at-large . . . To
> achieve the essence of real externality, whether of time or
> space or dimension, one must forget that such local attributes
> of a negligible and temporary race called mankind, have any
> existence at all.[1]

The keynote of Lovecraft's later work was, therefore, a union of

---

1. H. P. Lovecraft, letter to Farnsworth Wright (5 July 1927), in *Selected
Letters 1925–1929*, ed. August Derleth and Donald Wandrei (Sauk City,
WI: Arkham House, 1968), 150.

horror fiction with the developing field of science fiction, whereby the "monsters" he put on stage, originating as they did from the farthest reaches of space, appeared not so much to defy natural law as to obey natural laws very different from ours. He became, as Fritz Leiber has noted, a "Copernicus of the horror story": "He shifted the focus of supernatural dread from man and his little world and his gods, to the stars and the black and unplumbed gulfs of intergalactic space."[2]

The Cthulhu Mythos—never so termed by Lovecraft—is indeed a striking creation, but nearly all those who have sought to explicate it or add to it have missed its basic purpose: it was clearly a means by which Lovecraft expressed the core of his cosmic philosophy. The vast "gods" and forces who ruled the universe (Azathoth, the "nuclear chaos"; Nyarlathotep; Yog-Sothoth; Cthulhu) were designed as symbols for the eternal inscrutability of the boundless cosmos and the derisive insignificance of the human race within its parameters. Other elements of the Mythos—an entire library of mythical books of occult lore, chief among them the *Necronomicon* of Abdul Alhazred; a richly detailed imaginary New England topography, with such towns as Arkham, Dunwich, and Innsmouth in Massachusetts; and a subtle melding of real names, places, and books within the invented fabric, from Brown University to Margaret Murray's *The Witch-Cult in Western Europe* (1921)—are less central to the cosmic message, but have captured the imaginations of both Lovecraft's readers and his contemporary and posthumous disciples.

Imitations of Lovecraft's mythos began as early as 1928, when Frank Belknap Long published "The Space-Eaters" (*Weird Tales*, July 1928), a story that utilises some Lovecraftian themes and also includes a character clearly based on Lovecraft himself. Over

2. Fritz Leiber, "A Literary Copernicus" (1949), in *H. P. Lvecraft: Four Decades of Criticism*, ed. S. T. Joshi (Athens: Ohio University Press, 1980), 50.

the next few years such of Lovecraft's colleagues as Clark Ashton Smith, Robert E. Howard, Donald Wandrei, and Robert Bloch all began making their "additions" to the mythos—although in some cases these writers simply created their own gods, books, or places which Lovecraft would then co-opt into his stories. Indeed, the resulting stories were not so much pastiches as loose take-offs of Lovecraft's work in which certain invented terms would be dropped in a kind of cryptic allusiveness. Readers of *Weird Tales* were both puzzled and fascinated, many wondering whether Lovecraft and his fellow-writers were drawing upon some genuine but little-known body of myth.

It is, certainly, an exaggeration to say that Lovecraft actually encouraged these additions; but he made no attempt to curtail or repudiate them. As he wrote to August Derleth: "The more these synthetic daemons are mutually written up by different authors, the better they become as general background-material. I *like* to have others use my Azathoths & Nyarlathoteps—& in return I shall use Klarkash-Ton's [Clark Ashton Smith] Tsathoggua, your monk Clithanus, & Howard's Bran."[3] The first sentence is far more important than the second: what Lovecraft was really urging his friends to do was to write *their own stories*—that is, stories expressing their own moods, emotions, and conceptions of the universe—in which allusions to his myth-elements might be made for the sake of verisimilitude and evocativeness.

August Derleth, however, took it into his head to emphasise the second sentence, and the history of the Cthulhu Mythos after Lovecraft's death is largely the story of Derleth's elaboration—and, to be frank, perversion and misconstrual—of Lovecraft's basic conceptions. Derleth was, temperamentally, very different from Lovecraft: whereas the latter was secular, cynical, and cosmically oriented, Derleth was deeply religious, earnest, and earth-oriented.

3. H. P. Lovecraft, letter to August Derleth (3 August 1931); in *Essential Solitude*, 353 (emphasis in original).

He simply could not comprehend Lovecraft's notions of human insignificance, and so he twisted the Cthulhu Mythos to suit his aims. Whereas in Lovecraft's universe the cosmic entities (usually deemed the Old Ones) are supreme and toy with humankind as we might toy with ants, Derleth invented out of whole cloth a countervailing group of deities, the Elder Gods, who battled against the "evil" Old Ones on behalf of humanity. It would have been bad enough for Derleth to have employed this naive and simplistic framework for his own tales, as he indeed did in such works as *The Mask of Cthulhu* (1958) and *The Trail of Cthulhu* (1962); what was worse was that, in article after article, he attributed these views to Lovecraft, and his conception of the mythos was uncritically accepted by nearly all readers and critics, since Derleth had by this time established himself as Lovecraft's friend, publisher, and self-appointed spokesman.

Ramsey Campbell's early Lovecraftian work is surprisingly, and refreshingly, free from the misconceptions of the "Derleth Mythos," as it has been called, even though relatively little of it adopts—or, at any rate, adopts successfully—the cosmic perspective found in Lovecraft's greatest tales: Campbell's imagination does not seem naturally cosmic, and his most characteristic work probes the horrors to be found in human mentalities and human societies. Campbell has, however, clearly followed the breakthroughs in scholarship that finally dismantled the Derlethian conception of Lovecraft's mythos—breakthroughs that began in the 1970s with the work of Richard L. Tierney, Dirk W. Mosig, and others, and continue to this day—and his later Lovecraftian work is certainly more in tune with Lovecraft's own conceptions than his earlier work. What is more, Campbell has learned to insinuate Lovecraftian elements into tales and novels that outwardly owe little to Lovecraft and go far beyond mere pastiche; these works are fundamentally Campbell's own, infused with his vision and perspective and deriving only certain features or devices from his great predecessor.

The first allusion to Lovecraft in Campbell's work occurs in "The Hollow in the Woods," one of the stories in *Ghostly Tales* (1957/58). A man is asked by his friend, "Have you ever heard of a thing called a shoggoth?" He has not, and he promptly proceeds to look up the word in a dictionary (!), where he finds the following definition: "Shoggoth: evil spirit or demon in the shape of a tree with mouths scattered over its trunk" (GT 8–9). This is amusingly erroneous, since Lovecraft's shoggoth (as it appears in his short novel *At the Mountains of Madness* [1931]) is a huge fifteen-foot protoplasmic mass roaming the deserted city of the Old Ones in Antarctica. Campbell has, however, confessed to me that he derived the definition from Robert Bloch's "Notebook Found in a Deserted House" (1951), in which a shoggoth is indeed conceived as some sort of tree-spirit.

What this suggests, of course, is that Campbell had not read any of Lovecraft's own work at this time but only that of some of his imitators.[4] Campbell has admitted as much, stating that he had read only a few short stories in anthologies—"The Colour out of Space" in Groff Conklin's *Strange Travels in Science Fiction* (Grayson & Grayson, 1954); "From Beyond" in one of August Derleth's anthologies, either *New Worlds for Old* (Four Square, 1953) or *Worlds of Tomorrow* (Weidenfeld & Nicolson, 1954)—but, as mentioned earlier, he did not come upon a collection of Lovecraft's stories until, in 1960, he found a used copy of the luridly titled British paperback *Cry, Horror!* (World Distributors, 1959) in a second-hand bookshop.

In 1961 Campbell, on the recommendation of two friends, sent "The Tomb-Herd"—his first avowed Lovecraft pastiche—to August Derleth of Arkham House. His very first letter to Derleth, dated 16 August 1961, announced that "I have recently been

---

4. Most of the information on Campbell's early involvement with Lovecraft is derived from Campbell's essay "Chasing the Unknown," printed as the introduction to both editions of *Cold Print* (1985, 1993).

attempting a number of pastiches of the Lovecraft Mythos" and asked Derleth to read some of them (LA 3). By this time, "The Tower from Yuggoth" had already been accepted by a British fanzine, *Goudy*, edited by Pat Kearney, and it appeared in its second issue (1962). Derleth somewhat officiously responded:

> I should say at the outset that we had better see your pastiches of Lovecraft Mythos stories because a) the Lovecraft material is copyrighted and so protected and b) the approval of Arkham House is necessary before any copyrighted material can be released for publication. This is a necessary provision, of course, because if we did not enforce it scores of cheap imitations would flood the market, reflecting unfavorably on Lovecraft and his work. (LA 4)

Derleth's claims to ownership of the "Lovecraft Mythos" were largely fantasy, and he was unable to acknowledge that his own pastiches were themselves among those that "reflect[ed] unfavorably on Lovecraft and his work."

Derleth asked Campbell to send his stories in a group. It took some time for Campbell to type them, as they existed only in autograph manuscripts. He finally sent them on in a letter dated 10 August 1961, but this letter is clearly misdated and was probably written on 10 September. (A subsequent letter of 24 September noted that the stories were "on their way to you" [LA 11].) In his letter of 6 October 1961, Derleth reported having read two of the stories; he didn't specify which ones, but he did declare that "I do think them competent." But he went on to make the momentous suggestion:

> ...there is one alteration I think you should definitely make; ... and that is to remove your stories from the Lovecraft milieu. I mean, keep the Gods, the Books, etc., but establish your own place. This would give the stories vastly

more authenticity as an addition to the Mythos rather than pastiche pieces, and it might then be possible for us to consider their book publication in a limited edition over here.

What I suggest you do is establish a setting in a coastal area of England and create your own British milieu. This would not appreciably change your stories, but it would give them a much needed *new* setting and would not, in the reader's mind, invite a direct comparison with Lovecraft, for in such a comparison they would not show up as well as if you had your own setting and place-names for the tales. (LA 15)

Campbell quickly replied on 9 October, stating his eagerness to come up with a British locale for his tales: "it will, I should think, necessitate some research into the history and geography of the region I pick, and therefore some little time should pass before the revised version of the tales is completed" (LA 16). Campbell initially thought that the Devon-Cornwall region would be a possible locale, but he ultimately set his tales in the Severn valley.

In his letter of 18 October 1961 Derleth already all but accepted a volume of Campbell's tales: "I have finally found time to read your stories consecutively, and, without at this time making a firm commitment, I do think you have a potential Arkham House book here" (LA 18). Derleth repeated his criticism that Campbell should relocate his stories to England, and also that Campbell should do less summarising and more narrating. He then offered specific criticisms of "The Box in the Priory," "The Tomb-Herd," "The Tower from Yuggoth," and "The Horror from the Bridge." It is only in his letter of 22 October that Campbell told Derleth that he was only fifteen years old.

Of the tales Derleth read at this juncture, several do indeed betray the flaws that Derleth perspicaciously identified. "The Box in the Priory," a story about Byatis (an entity glancingly cited in Robert Bloch's "The Shambler from the Stars"), is set in Arkham; and, aside from a glancing citation (IL 180) of "Elder Gods"

(inventions of August Derleth, who wanted a set of "good" deities
to oppose the "evil" Old Ones), features a surprise ending—where
a "snake-like thing . . . as wide as a human body and impossibly
long, had been merely the face-tentacle of the abomination
Byatis" (IL 182)—taken either from Lovecraft's "The Shunned
House" (1924) or from his ghostwritten tale for Harry Houdini,
"Under the Pyramids" (1924; published as "Imprisoned with the
Pharaohs"), where what appears to be an entity of moderate size
proves to be only a tiny portion of an incalculably larger creature.

"The Tomb-Herd" is set in Kingsport (the Massachusetts city
that Lovecraft identified with Marblehead in "The Festival"
[1923]) and features a protagonist with the transparently Lovecraftian name Richard Dexter. Aside from a curious reference to
Zothique (IL 185)—a continent of the far future around which
Clark Ashton Smith wove an entire cycle of tales—the tale draws
from a number of Lovecraft stories, including "The Rats in the
Walls" and "The Call of Cthulhu." Even the throw-away line "I
read of what Azathoth had resembled *before* that monstrous nuclear
chaos had been bereft of mind and will" (IL 187) reminds us of
the line in "The Whisperer in Darkness" that reads: "I learned
whence Cthulhu *first* came . . . and I started with loathing when
told of the monstrous nuclear chaos beyond angled space which
the 'Necronomicon' had mercifully cloaked under the name of
Azathoth."[5] Campbell also errs in coming up with the implau-
sible-sounding name Asquith Place, which does not evoke New
England but rather the British prime minister H. H. Asquith.
And as for the conclusion of the tale, Campbell attempts to invest
the narrative with a kind of existential horror—"And I think of
those stains of which which I found at the last—*those stains on my
own face and hands*" (IL 191)—that not only evokes "The Whisperer in Darkness" again ("For the things in the chair . . . were

5. H. P. Lovecraft, *Collected Fiction: A Variorum Edition*, ed. S. T. Joshi
(New York: Hippocampus Press, 2015), 2.520–21.

the face and hands of Henry Wentworth Akeley"[6]—but also "The Shadow over Innsmouth," where the protagonist discovers that he is related to the hideous hybrid creatures in that decaying Massachusetts backwater.

"The Tower from Yuggoth" continues the excessively close pastiche of Lovecraft's stories by coming up with a narrator named Edward Wingate Armitage (derived from Edward Derby of "The Thing on the Doorstep," Nathaniel Wingate Peaslee of "The Shadow out of Time," and Dr. Henry Armitage of "The Dunwich Horror") and also by being set in the year 1929. (There are some chronological difficulties in the story, as it is declared that Armitage was born in 1879 [IL 221] and enrolled at Miskatonic University in 1916 [IL 223], at which time he is said to be eighteen years old [IL 225].) Once again a tissue of Lovecraftian elements, the story is a kind of mirror-image of "The Whisperer in Darkness": whereas in Lovecraft's tale the fungi from Yuggoth have come to the Earth to mine an element they cannot find on their native planet, here Armitage finds a tower, built by the fungi, that allows him to transport himself to Yuggoth. There are imitations of "The Dunwich Horror" as well as of *The Case of Charles Dexter Ward* (in the form of letters in archaic language found by Armitage).

"The Horror from the Bridge" may be of the the most interest among these very early tales. The story was based on entry 217 in Lovecraft's commonplace book: "Ancient (Roman? prehistoric?) stone bridge washed away by a (sudden and curious?) storm. Something liberated which had been sealed up in the masonry years ago. Things happen."[7] Set in the imaginary Massachusetts town of Healyville, it focuses on a character named Philip Wentworth. This name may have been derived from Derleth's "posthumous collaboration" "Wentworth's Day," in *The Survivor*

---

6. *Collected Fiction*, 2.538.
7. H. P. Lovecraft, *Collected Essays*, ed. S. T. Joshi (New York: Hippocampus Press, 2004–06), 5.233.

and Others (1957). Although the story is heavily indebted to "The Dunwich Horror," there is a major difficulty in reconciling it to that tale. Philip Wentworth is said to have been the "Miskatonic University librarian" (IL 209) in 1900 and appears to have retained that function in 1931; but if so, what happened to Henry Armitage, who was the librarian who defeated the Whateley clan in "The Dunwich Horror"? Campbell actually makes note of the fact that "1928 was a particular year of horror, with inexplicable occurrences in many places" (IL 211), but never cites Armitage.

Matters become more curious when we consider Derleth's similarly titled "posthumous collaboration" "The Horror from the Middle Span," which was based on the identical commonplace book entry but was manifestly written *after* Campbell's story. On 21 October 1965 Derleth told Campbell: "If I can find time I'll do another short Lovecraft tale from one of the HPL notes or dreams, but that depends" (LA 256). He did write the story sometime thereafter, including it in his anthology of original tales, *Travellers by Night* (1967); but he made no acknowledgement to Campbell that he might well have been inspired by Campbell's story to write his own.

Campbell asked Derleth why he had said nothing about "The Face in the Desert," to which Derleth responded somewhat opaquely on 25 October 1961: "I said nothing about THE FACE IN THE DESERT because I didn't need to say anything about it" (LA 24). By this Derleth meant that the story did not explicitly use Mythos trappings, even though its setting in the Arabian desert in the year 1930 clearly evokes Lovecraft's "The Nameless City." Once again Campbell attempts to invest the tale with existential horror out of "The Shadow over Innsmouth" when he has the narrator come upon a set of stone pillars in the desert, on the top of one of which "I glimpsed a loathsome and foetal replica forming at the centre of the translucent blub—a ghastly but recognisable likeness to my own face" (IL 198). Derleth, however, rejected this story for *Inhabitant*, remarking in a letter of 20 July

1963 that "it's just out of place here" (LA 127). In his letter of 25 July he added that it is "certainly the weakest story in the book" (LA 128). Weak or not, we may find that it is less irrelevant to the contents of *Inhabitant* than some other stories that made their way into that volume.

On 1 November 1961 Campbell announced the completion of a new story, "The Insects from Shaggai." He delayed sending it to Derleth until he had revised it several times, and he may not have sent it in until he mailed the entire manuscript of *Inhabitant* to Derleth on 11 March 1963. I cannot find a specific comment by Derleth on the story, but it is one of Campbell's stronger tales of this period, so presumably Derleth felt it worth keeping in the book. The title, of course, is derived from the title of one of Robert Blake's stories, "Shaggai," as cited in "The Haunter of the Dark" (1935). The first draft is set in Arkham and Ipswich (it is not clear whether, at this juncture, Campbell was aware that Ipswich was a real town in Massachusetts), but at least it appears to take place in the present day, if the mention of a "sports car" (IL 246) can be taken as a hint in that direction. The history of the insects from Shaggai found in the tale is manifestly an imitation of the history of the Old Ones related in *At the Mountains of Madness*.

Derleth expressed an interest in using a story by Campbell in his original anthology *Dark Mind, Dark Heart* (1962); but he made clear that such a story would not appear in Campbell's collection. By 22 January 1962 Derleth was expressing impatience with Campbell, stating that "If I am to see a story for possible inclusion in my new anthology of hitherto unpublished horror tales—DARK MIND, DARK HEART—I must see it posthaste" (LA 39). Campbell thereupon submitted a revised version of "The Tomb-Herd." Derleth, in his letter of 7 February 1962, said that he still found the story not quite satisfactory, but went on to say that he would use the story on two major conditions: 1) that the title be changed to "The Church in High Street"; and (2) that he be allowed a free hand to "alter and delete as I see fit" (41). Campbell naturally acceded to these requirements, for the prospect of appearing in an Arkham House volume at the age of sixteen was too good to pass up. Campbell, however, must have known that in England the common usage is not "High Street" (equivalent of "Main Street" in the United States) but "the High Street."

Campbell's version of the revised version of "The Tomb-Herd" does not survive, so all we have is Derleth's rewrite, which duly appeared in *Dark Mind, Dark Heart*. The one thing that can be said for it is that Derleth's revisions are relatively seamless, for it is difficult now to detect what the one author wrote and what the other. The story is, of course, now set in the Severn valley area that Campbell had chosen as the British equivalent for Arkham, Kingsport, Dunwich, and Innsmouth. Derleth himself had suggested this region in his letter of 18 October 1961, in reference to "The Horror from the Bridge," since the bridge in question was said to be of Roman origin. Campbell did not specifically reply to this suggestion, but on 19 November 1961 he reported:

I had some trouble inventing fictitious names for towns in the region, but finally came up with the following: Brichester, Camside, Temphill (originally 'Temple Hill', according to one of my tales), Severnhill and Goatswood (the last title may be good for the location of a tale about Shug-Niggurath, if ever I get round to it—there wasn't ever a story written about this deity by any author, was there?) I hope these all sound authentic. (LA 28)

"Severnhill," of course, was later modified to Severnford.

By this time Campbell was already revising the stories that would actually be included in *Inhabitant*. In this same letter he wrote:

I've completed the second draft of the BOX IN THE PRIORY, editing out the summaries, and also adding in

dialogue where possible. Since I didn't come across any references in my reseearch to priories in the Severn Valley region,
while I did find frequent ones to castles, I decided to play safe
and call the story, instead, THE ROOM IN THE CASTLE.
(LA 28)

The story, aside from being set in Severnford and (at Derleth's
suggestion) noting the existence of a copy of the *Necronomicon*
at the British Museum instead of at Miskatonic University in
Arkham, contains considerably greater dialogue than his earlier
stories—one instance of how Campbell took up Derleth's suggestion of telling instead of showing. But it still cannot be said that
the story is a notable success; aside from a citation of a "curiously-
figured star-shaped stone, which . . . would keep off the power of
Byatis" (IL 18)—an idea derived from Derleth's comical use of
these items (taken from *At the Mountains of Madness*) as talismans
against the Old Ones—we are regaled by the sight of the dreaded
god destroyed by gasoline (petrol), in the manner of the hydro-
chloric acid that the protagonists of "The Shunned House" use to
eliminate the psychic vampire in that tale.

"The Horror from the Bridge" is now set in Clotton, but still
takes place in the chronologically remote period of 1931, thereby
lessening its immediacy of effect. Here again we find a mention of
the "seal of the Elder Gods" (IL 33), and the tale remains heavily
reliant on "The Dunwich Horror." Instead of whippoorwills
serving as psychopomps, Campbell substitutes nightjars (IL 28);
and instead of the backwoods New England dialect that Lovecraft
used to good effect in his tale, Campbell introduces a character
who speaks in lower-class British dialect ("I was just goin' up to
bed w'en I 'eard these shots an' yells down be the river" [IL 39]).

"The Insects from Shaggai," now set in Brichester, remains
fairly close to the first draft. "The Mine on Yuggoth" is not notably different from "The Tower from Yuggoth," with the requisite
changes made to the name of the protagonist (now Edward Taylor)

to make it sound less obviously Lovecraftian, and to the setting (now Brichester). Derleth had been irritated that the original version of the story had been published in *Goudy*, which proved to be uncopyrighted, although the editor had informed Campbell that it would in fact be registered for copyright. When he got a copy of the magazine, Derleth fulminated (letter of 14 May 1962):

> I turned at once to your story, and I am sorry to say that THE TOWER FROM YUGGOTH is now in the public domain. The magazine is not under copyright, no sort of notice was published with your story that could be construed as a legal protection, and your story can now be lifted and reprinted by anyone who elects to do so. This is very foolish publishing, and I hope you will not again be so foolish as to permit such printing of a story without copyright. (LA 61)

But Campbell altered "The Mine on Yuggoth" sufficiently from its predecessor that Derleth felt justified in including it in *Inhabitant*.

Campbell stated in his letter of 26 April 1962 that he was "working on a new Mythos tale" (LA 57), "The Render of the Veils." A month later he asked Derleth if it would be all right to let Jack Chalker use the story in his fanzine *Mirage*; but Derleth, still angry over the *Goudy* matter, made pretty clear what his views were: "The book editor's point of view is simply this: why shd. I pay for the privilege of publishing this if the author can give it away to a fanzine?" (LA 64). It is not clear when Derleth actually read the story; he may have done so only when he received the full manuscript of *Inhabitant* from Campbell. At this time the collection was actually titled *The Render of the Veils [and Other Stories?]*; but Derleth, after reviewing the manuscript, declared that "the second most weak story is the one you have chosen for your title story, THE RENDER OF THE VEILS; so this must be altered" (LA 128). (The weakest story, which Derleth rejected outright, was "The Face in the Desert.")

And yet, "The Render of the Veils" has several points to recommend it. It may be the first Cthulhu Mythos story in which
Campbell does not seek to imitate Lovecraft's dense prose idiom.
There is a more contemporary tone to this tale than is present
in many of Campbell's earlier stories; and although it is based on
an entry in Lovecraft's commonplace book (no. 204: "Disturbing
conviction that all life is only a deceptive dream with some dismal
or sinister horror lurking behind"[8]) and features Campbell's
invented book of forbidden lore, *The Revelations of Glaaki*, the
story is much less of a Lovecraft pastiche than many other tales
of this period.

That cannot be said for "The Inhabitant of the Lake," the longest of Campbell's early Mythos tales. This novelette roughly
echoes "The Whisperer in Darkness" in its epistolary format, and
much information on *The Revelations of Glaaki* (which, we now
learn, extends to eleven volumes) and on the "god" Glaaki itself is
provided. Campbell leaves himself open to amusement at his own
expense when he depicts the baleful god as actually dwelling in a
placid-seeming lake in the middle of England; just as Lovecraft,
writing probably in a conscious parody of his own style and manner
in the ghostwritten tale "The Horror in the Museum," depicts an
explorer who brings back the actual god Rhan-Tegoth from the
frozen wastes of Alaska and locks him up in a large box in the
basement of a museum. There may be something of parody—or,
more precisely, a fairly obvious in-joke—in Campbell's devising of
a new "god," Daoloth, surely derived from the name of his correspondent and publisher. This entity was first cited in "The Room
in the Castle."

"The Plain of Sound" was conceived as early as late 1961:

I have another story waiting to be written after these have
been rewritten: the basic plot being about some shunned

---

8. *Collected Essays*, 5.232.

region in the Brichester-Camside area whence unplace-
able sounds are said to emanate. The sounds eventually are
discovered to be *beings* from some other dimension where
matter itself exists only as sound, and where matter of our
sort is known only as an odor. I think I could make something
worthwhile of this idea. (LA 30)

But he began writing it only in mid-July 1962. Derleth read it only
when he read the manuscript of Campbell's book, remarking:

As a general criticism, I have to point out that your endings
tend to fall down. THE PLAIN OF SOUND, for instance,
which is a good, interesting story, comes up with a weak
ending. "I saw what it took from its victims," as you have it, is
a let-down; it is simply not enough, at least, for this old pro;
we cannot imagine that "it" too anything sufficiently horrible
to drive Tony insane. (LA 128)

The basic thrust of the story is a novel one—"Sounds in this area
are equivalents of matter in another dimension" (IL 118)—and there
is nothing corresponding to it in Lovecraft's work. Campbell
does not seem to have altered the ending after receiving Derleth's
criticism, for the final line remains: "I saw what it took from its
victims! *I saw what it took from its victims!*" (IL 122), which could
indeed be subject to the criticism of excessive vagueness. And
yet, in some senses this ending echoes that of Lovecraft's *At the
Mountains of Madness*, where Danforth, seeing something that the
narrator (William Dyer) does not see as they are flying away from
the mountains of madness, utters all manner of cryptic phrases
evidently reflecting his apocalyptic vision. Campbell's protagonist does much the same: "He speaks of 'the snailhorns,' 'the blue
crystalline lenses,' 'the mobility of the faces,' 'the living flame and
water,' 'the bell-shaped appendages,' and 'the common head of
many bodies'" (IL 122).

"The Return of the Witch" is the most peculiar story in *Inhab-itant* in that, in spite of the citation of the *Revelations of Glaaki*, there is nothing notably Lovecraftian about it. Campbell dates the story to late 1962 (IL 288), although in his own bibliography he places it as the first story of 1963. He declares that the story is based on commonplace book entry no. 99 ("Salem story—the cottage of an aged witch—wherein after her death are found sundry terrible things"[9]), but in fact the tale focuses on a writer, Norman Owen, who moves into a house formerly occupied by a suspected witch, Gladys Shorrock; in the course of the story the soul of Gladys possesses the body of the writer, or at least coexists with his own soul.

Campbell has declared that he was struck by how similar the story was to Henry Kuttner's "The Salem Horror" (*Weird Tales*, May 1937), a story that Campbell had never read before its appearance in Derleth's anthology *Tales of the Cthulhu Mythos* (1969). It deals with a writer who similarly unleashes the spirit of a witch, Abigail Prinn, who had died in 1692, and is in fact a close pastiche of Lovecraft's "The Dreams in the Witch House." One detail in Campbell's story—where Norman finds that he has transported a wooden chest from a dream into the real world—echoes a similar detail in Lovecraft's story, where the protagonist, Walter Gilman, brings back a spiky image that, in a dream, he had broken off a railing.

"The Will of Stanley Brooke" is similarly only tangentially Lovecraftian, and perhaps not Lovecraftian at all. This story is also apparently not discussed in the Campbell-Derleth correspondence. Campbell dates it either to late 1962 (IL 289) or 1963 (*Core of Ramsey Campbell* 24). Here the idea is that Stanley Brooke, dying of cancer, makes a new will in which all his assets and effects are to be given to a man, William Collier, who proves to be his exact double. In the end Collier is killed by Brooke's lawyer. Are

---

9. *Collected Essays*, 5.225.

we to assume that Collier is the revived body of Brooke? More pertinently, where exactly is the Lovecraft influence? Campbell himself states: "The theme derives from Lovecraft's 'The Festival', although at the time I didn't realise it did" (IL 289). I am not certain of the purport of this remark, but my sense is that Campbell was (perhaps unconsciously) thinking of *The Case of Charles Dexter Ward*, where Joseph Curwen's colleague in alchemy, Simon Orne, departs from Salem and comes back as his own son, Jedediah, to deflect attention from the fact that he does not seem to age appreciably even with the passing of decades.

The final tale of *Inhabitant*, "The Moon-Lens," is set in Goatswood and fulfils Campbell's early wish to write a story specifically about Shub-Niggurath, which in his view had rarely been done. On 4 December 1961 he wrote to Derleth: "I don't recall stories solely about Shub-Niggurath, though I used him quite often in THE DWELLER IN DARKNESS" (LA 29). (The reference is to Derleth's story "The Dweller in Darkness" [*Weird Tales*, November 1944].) Campbell declares that the story was based on commonplace book entry no. 189 ("Ancient necropolis—bronze door in hillside which opens as the moonlight strikes it—focussed by ancient lens in pylon opposite?"[10]), and the story follows this plot-germ closely; but the scenario where the protagonist, wishing to get from Goatswood to Brichester, is tricked into staying overnight in a hotel is manifestly adapted from "The Shadow over Innsmouth."

We can now return to the issue of the title of Campbell's collection. As mentioned, he had wished to call it *The Render of the Veils*. His argument went as follows: "the story carrying this title is probably the best in the book, and the name of the collection might also be symbolic of my writing—'rending the veils' by the 'revelations' contained in the tales" (LA 79 [2 September 1962]). Derleth, even before reading the title story, expressed reservations:

10. *Collected Essays*, 5.231.

Our new bulletin is on press. In it I announced your book under the title of THE BOX IN THE PRIORY, which I have to confess I like as a title considerably better than THE RENDER OF THE VEILS, which isn't Lovecraftian but rather more like Bloch's THE OPENER OF THE WAY. There is still plenty of time in which to settle on a title. The RENDER is just a trifle too pretentious for my taste, suggests the mystic rather than the dreadful or terrible, and I should think we would want to avoid that and make its appeal more frankly Lovecraftian. (LA 99 [7 March 1963])

In my estimation Derleth is correct; Campbell, however, continued to defend his title. The book could not be called *The Box in the Priory* because Campbell had changed the title of that story to "The Room in the Castle," and this story was never considered as a potential title for the book. But, as we have seen, when Derleth actually read "The Render of the Veils," he felt that its weakness (in his judgment) disbarred it from being suitable for the title of the collection.

On 3 August 1963 Campbell suggested *The Inhabitant of the Lake* as a title, since it was "pretty Lovecraftian" (LA 132). Derleth was noncommittal, replying: "Well, we'll come up with something. It can be an inclusive title, needn't be taken from a story in the book. Something like UNWELCOME TENANTS or THE INHABITANT OF THE LAKE AND OTHER UNWELCOME TENANTS, which I like a little better than just the story title alone" (LA 134). Campbell expressed enthusiasm for the latter title, and that seemed to settle the matter. But then Derleth announced in a postcard of 4 February 1964: "Incidentally, because of my erroneous instructions to the artist for the jacket, the title of your book is now THE INHABITANT OF THE LAKE AND LESS WELCOME TENANTS, instead of OTHER UNWELCOME T." (LA 169). The artist in question was Frank Utpatel, who did not only the dust jacket art but also a map of the Severnford-Brichester area for the endpapers. It was only fifty years later, in his augmented edition of the book, that the originally agreed-upon title was restored. Campbell, who believed that the erroneous title was taken from Derleth's own forthcoming book, *Colonel Markesan and Less Pleasant Persons* (1966), has remarked dryly: "I felt few tenants could be less welcome than Glaaki" (IL 290).

Interestingly, as early as 12 October 1961 Derleth advised his young correspondent (LA 17): "Yes, I would advise signing your stories Ramsey Campbell—it's a good author's name, and it will avoid confusion with John Campbell" (i.e., the science fiction writer and editor John W. Campbell, Jr.). Derleth continued to press Campbell on the matter, especially when it came to the publication of "The Church in High Street" in *Dark Mind, Dark Heart*; but Campbell was insistent: "Unless you're really against it, I would prefer to retain the initial in 'J. Ramsey Campbell'. Without the initial the name sounds to me rather *bare*—and no other combination of my names sounds at all inspiring" (LA 46 [22 February 1962]). Only years later did Campbell feel that the "J." was unnecessary.

Campbell's early Cthulhu Mythos stories are not only heavily indebted to Lovecraft but, as he came to realise later, to Derleth. For the fact is that Campbell largely swallowed (as most other writers and critics up to that time did) Derleth's erroneous interpretation of the Lovecraft Mythos: in his view, benign "Elder Gods" were in a battle for supremacy against "evil" Old Ones (Cthulhu, Yog-Sothoth, etc.), with such ridiculous talismans as the star-stones cited in many of Derleth's stories. The bleak cosmic vision of Lovecraft's tales was largely beyond Derleth's comprehension; for him, Lovecraft's "gods" really were gods, and they could only be battled with the weapons of black magic—incantations, "forbidden" books, and the like. Campbell unwittingly adopted many of these Derlethian principles in his own Mythos tales, and it is a credit to his native talents as a writer that they remain as vigorous and entertaining as they are.

We have seen that several of the *Inhabitant* tales do display some faint and tentative signs of escaping from the Lovecraft influence; and tales that Campbell wrote just after completing *Inhabitant* go further in this regard. One of the most interesting is "The Stone on the Island" [1963], which Derleth included in his anthology *Over the Edge* (1964). It is certainly one of the best and most distinctive of Campbell's early Lovecraftian tales. Here, Michael Nash finds his deceased father's notes about a mysterious island near Severnford upon which, over the course of centuries, certain hapless explorers are found horribly mutilated. Travelling to the island himself, Nash returns uninjured but begins experiencing apparent hallucinations of an increasingly bizarre sort. At this point we can scarcely fail to think of Campbell's later work, in which the distinction between dream and reality becomes tenuous to the point of vanishment. As the tale progresses, it becomes focused more and more intensely upon Nash's psychology and perceptions, developing a weirdly hallucinatory atmosphere quite reminiscent of the *Demons by Daylight* stories that Campbell would begin writing the very next year. "The Stone on the Island," a fine tale in its own right, is a landmark story for Campbell's literary development.

But the two tales that fully embody Campbell's absorption of the Lovecraftian influence were written some years later. By the end of 1963 he was already writing tales that had little to do with Lovecraft, and such works as "The Reshaping of Rossiter" [1964; the first version of "The Scar"] and "The Cellars" [1965] testify to Campbell's declaration of independence from what had perhaps become the oppressive influence of the American writer. It was not long thereafter that Campbell produced two masterworks of Lovecraftian fiction, "Cold Print" and "The Franklyn Paragraphs."

"Cold Print" [1966–67] is set in Brichester, the central town in Campbell's fictional Severn milieu. Campbell makes the interesting admission that, by the mid-1960s, "My invented town of Brichester, originally intended as the Severn Valley equivalent of Lovecraft's Arkham, was Liverpool by now in all but name"

(FD xxi). We shall find this to be so in several of the *Demons by Daylight* stories that are set in Brichester but unmistakably evoke Campbell's hometown. Here, the seediness, grime, and slums of Liverpool—with their potential for explosive violence at every turn—are vividly etched as examples of urban decay very different from what Lovecraft did in, say, "The Shadow over Innsmouth," where the decline of that ancient city is attributed solely to the incursion of loathsome fish-frogs from the depths of the sea. Here, Brichester has caused its own degeneration by poverty, indifference, and lack of social cohesion:

> They crossed the roundabout, negotiated the crumbling lips of ruts full of deceptively glazed pools collecting behind the bulldozer treads of a redevelopment scheme, and onward through the whirling white to a patch of waste ground where a lone fireplace drank the snow. Strutt's guide scuttled into an alley and Strutt followed, intent on keeping close to the other as he knocked powdered snow from dustbin lids and flinched from back-yard doors at which dogs clawed and snarled. The man dodged left, then right, between the close labyrinthine walls, among houses whose cruel edges of jagged window-panes and thrusting askew doors even the snow, kinder to buildings than to their occupants, could not soften. (CP 301)

Sam Strutt, although not a native of Brichester, seems perfectly suited to the place. A man who relieves the frustration of his own wasted life by seeking out the most vicious types of sadomasochistic pornography (including such titles as *The Caning-Master, The Secret Life of Wackford Squeers*, and *Miss Whippe, Old-Style Governess*), he has come to Brichester because he has heard of a bookstore that caters especially well to his predilections. Strutt is perhaps the first in a long line of Campbell's paranoid characters: he "had a horror of touching anyone who was not fastidious"; he "felt abandoned in a tacitly conspiring, hostile world" (CP 299,

306). Although not written in the first person (Campbell, curiously, rarely uses first-person narration even in his Lovecraftian tales, even though it was Lovecraft's virtually exclusive narrative practice), all the events are seen through Strutt's eyes, and the reader is compelled to inhabit his harrowingly disturbed mind.

But Strutt finds more than he bargains for at the bookstore. He is offered *The Revelations of Glaaki,* here defined as "a sort of Bible written under supernatural guidance" (CP 309). At this point the tale lapses somewhat into pulpish luridness—the bookseller apparently proves to be the incarnation of the cosmic entity Y'golonac and dispatches Strutt hideously—but the atmosphere of dingy squalor is indelible; and Strutt goes to his death persevering in his paranoid delusions of conspiracy: "It wasn't playing fair, he hadn't done anything to deserve this . . . " (CP 314–15).

In *Visions from Brichester* (2015), a volume that supersedes both editions of *Cold Print* as the definitive volume of his Lovecraftian fiction written after the *Inhabitant* stories, Campbell has printed the original version of "Cold Print," titled "The Successor" [1964]. This story introduces us to the blandly named Derek Sheridan (a name far less evocative than "Cold Print's" Sam Strutt), who seeks out erotica from a dubious bookseller in Brichester. Specifically, he is seeking books published by "Sweden's Ultimate Press" (a stand-in for the Parisian publisher Olympia Press—many of which, as Campbell's correspondence with Derleth reveals, were banned in England, forcing Campbell to ask Derleth to order them for him, have them sent to the U.S., and then mail them on to him). Once again, even the titles of the books Sheridan seeks—*The Experiments of Youth; The Pleasures of Adam and Ryan*—pale in comparison to Strutt's chosen bill of fare, books that paint a much darker portrait of the psychology of Strutt. It is in such an environment that both individuals encounter the ultimate obscenity—the nine-volume *Revelations of Gla'aki;* but in "The Successor" Sheridan has a grotesque and unintentionally comical dialogue with the bookseller, who then metamorphoses into the god Y'golonac. (I am reminded of an analogous scene in Brian Lumley's disaster of a novel, *Beneath the Moors*, in which a character has a genial conversation with Bokrug, the water-lizard.) By contrast, in "Cold Print" the confrontation with the bookseller inexorably takes on more sinister overtones until the final revelation: "before he could scream out his protest his breath was cut off, as the hands descended on his face and the wet red mouths opened in their palms" (CP 315).

"The Franklyn Paragraphs" [1967] is an even more impressive accomplishment. First included in *Demons by Daylight* and then reprinted in the expanded edition of *Cold Print*, this tale is a masterful adaptation (and perhaps partial parody) of Lovecraft's "documentary style," in which letters, newspaper articles, telegrams, and the like are directly cited to augment a tale's verisimilitude. Campbell is himself a character, narrating the story in the first person and claiming to have established a correspondence with the horror writer Errol Undercliffe, who disappeared from his flat in Lower Brichester in 1967. Several real individuals—from August Derleth to Campbell's agent Kirby McCauley to J. Vernon Shea, a correspondent of and commentator on Lovecraft—are all cited by name in the tale; to complete the confusion, Robert Blake (a character in Lovecraft's "The Haunter of the Dark") is also mentioned.

Undercliffe has stumbled upon a very obscure volume, Roland Franklyn's *We Pass from View* (1964); and Campbell provides both the British National Bibliography catalogue entry for the work as well as a dismissive review of it from the *Times Literary Supplement*. On the surface, it appears to be the usual mélange of grandiosity and ominous prophecy that makes so many occultist works comical instead of frightening; but Undercliffe seems impressed with it and even joins a band of initiates once led by Franklyn, who has died. He seems to do so primarily as a lark, remarking flippantly, "I'd give a lot for a genuine supernatural occurrence" (DD 35). He gets his wish sooner than he expects. While looking at a

blank page of *We Pass from View*, he sees lines of print suddenly
appearing:

FEEL THEM COMING SLOWLY BURROWING
WANT ME TO SUFFER CANT MOVE GET ME OUT
SAVE ME SOMEWHERE IN BRICHESTER HELP ME
(DD 37)

It turns out that Franklyn was killed violently by his wife, a cir-
cumstance that has caused his soul to be trapped in his body and
to be ravaged by nameless "burrowers of the core" (DD 34).

This synopsis cannot begin to convey the richness of texture
and subtlety of execution that make "The Franklyn Paragraphs"
a masterwork of cumulative horror. The relationship between
writing and reality—a theme that dominates Campbell's work from
beginning to end—receives one of its most potent expressions
here. It might be thought that a horror writer would welcome the
actual experience of the supernatural, but in fact the reverse is the
case; as Franklyn's wife scornfully tells Undercliffe, "God! You'd
never write about it, you'd never write about anything again" (DD
42)—and this makes us realise why Undercliffe's last letter to the
narrator trails off in a fragment. The ultimate message of "The
Franklyn Paragraphs" is exactly that of Lovecraft's best work—
"No longer could I trust the surface of the world" (DD 44)—but
it is expressed in a mood and idiom that are entirely Campbell's
own.

Visions from Brichester also prints the early version of this story,
written in 1965. It is much less Lovecraftian than its revised
version and also commits the gaffe of placing its supernatural
dénouement at the beginning of the story. The basic motif of both
stories is again that of the "forbidden book," already well used
by Lovecraft himself and his disciples; by the time Campbell got
around to using it, something new had to be done. He did so—but
bunglingly in this first version. Here a character named Harvey

Shea (presumably derived from J. Vernon Shea, a correspondent of Lovecraft cited by name in the revised version) who comes upon a strange book by Roland Franklyn, *Magic, Legend and the Infinite Self* (a far less evocative title than the revised version's *We Pass from View*). But whereas in the later version the climax—the fact that the book begins writing words of its own accord in front of the narrator's eyes, as the spirit of Franklyn seeks to escape from the tomb in which his vindictive wife buried him—is placed well along in the story for maximum impact, in the early version it is matter-of-factly introduced toward the beginning. What is more, Campbell in the later version has incorporated his own persona into the narrative, presenting a series of letters from Roland Franklyn to himself and thereby radically enhancing (and in some senses subtly parodying) the "documentary style" so frequently used by Lovecraft to create verisimilitude.

Campbell has frequently admitted that, shortly after writing the stories in *The Inhabitant of the Lake*, he turned violently against Lovecraft "with all the obstreperousness of a fanzine contributor determined to make a name for himself at the expense of his betters."[11] One of the most notorious of Campbell's utterances on this subject is an article, "Lovecraft in Retrospect," first published in the British fanzine *Shadow* for September 1969. One paragraph will suffice:

> I cannot . . . accept the principle that one must suppress characterization in order to throw the horror into clearer relief. There seems no doubt that Lovecraft conceived this as a method because his characterization was incompetent; but even if, for the sake of argument, we discuss the inherent

11. Foreword to *Demons by Daylight* (New York: Carroll & Graf, 1990), n.p.

validity of the principle, I don't see that it can be justified artistically unless the "horror" is shown to be somehow profoundly meaningful in itself. But Lovecraft wasn't Conrad or Kafka (or Hitchcock or Franju, for that matter) and the only "statement" his horror makes is that the universe is vast, hostile, and inexorable.[12]

There is scarcely any need to examine this statement in detail: Campbell has already repudiated it in part, and in any event there is some grain of truth to it, for Lovecraft may well have been "incompetent" at characterisation because of his fundamental philosophical conception that "Individuals and their fortunes within natural law move me very little. They are all momentary trifles bound from a common nothingness toward another common nothingness."[13] By 1975, when he wrote the introduction to *The Height of the Scream* (1976), Campbell was a little more temperate but made the same basic point: "[Lovecraft's] minimal characterization and plot work because they are right for him; I had to find by trial and (much) error what was right for me" (HS x–xi). What this shows, of course, is that Campbell is seeking to escape from the Lovecraft influence and find his own voice as a writer.

Specifically, Campbell would seek to unify the cosmicism of Lovecraft with his own burgeoning sense of the complexities of human psychology. Campbell has, accordingly, gone on to write any number of additional stories in the Lovecraftian mode, although none are quite as successful as "Cold Print" and "The Franklyn Paragraphs." In "The Tugging" [1974] he attempts to

12. "Lovecraft in Retrospect" (1969), *NecronomiCon: Second Edition* (Danvers, MA: Lovecraft Society of New England, 1995), 8.
13. H. P. Lovecraft, letter to E. Hoffmann Price (15 August 1934), in *Selected Letters 1935–1937*, ed. August Derleth and James Turner (Sauk City, WI: Arkham House, 1976), 19.

mingle his own intimate, domestic horror with Lovecraft's impersonal cosmicism, but the result seems forced. Much better is "The
Faces at Pine Dunes" [1975], in which an adolescent boy comes
to the harrowing realisation that his parents are involved in a
witch-cult.

Campbell seems especially fond of "The Voice of the Beach"
[1977], remarking that it "was my attempt to return to Lovecraft's
first principles, to see how close I could get to his aims without
the encumbrances of the mythos . . . For my part, I believe it's the
most successful of these stories [in *Cold Print*]" (CP 18). There is
reason to question this judgment. To be sure, Campbell is correct in believing that too many imitators of Lovecraft are content
merely to create a new god or book but do not attempt to capture the intensity of vision that animates the best of Lovecraft;
and "The Voice of the Beach" is certainly refreshing in the total
absence of the now hackneyed citations of the *Necronomicon* or
Yog-Sothoth or what have you. But in its use of the equally hackneyed device of the harried narrator and his frequent ruminations
of the "had-I-but-known" sort, the story falls into a different kind
of cliché. Here again Campbell attempts to unite an intense focus
on individual psychology with Lovecraftian cosmicism, but the
former seems to work against the latter, which comes off sounding
contrived and unconvincing: "I seemed to be observing myself,
a figure tiny and trivial as an insect, making a timid hysterical
attempt to join in the dance of the teeming beach" (CP 497). Nor
are we ever given a true indication of what the cosmic force on the
beach is or how it is planning to overwhelm the world.

In 1994, after a long hiatus, Campbell returned to the Lovecraftian mode with "The Horror under Warrendown," written for an
anthology, *Made in Goatswood* (1995), consisting of other writers'
imitations of Campbell's early "Cthulhu Mythos" stories. This tale
may well be among the most successful of Campbell's pastiches
of Lovecraft—although, in a sense, that success is obtained at
the price of his partial suppression of his own individuality. The

story is quite similar in tone to some of Lovecraft's early tales, with their obsessive concern with the sensations of a first-person narrator (a rare usage in Campbell) as he is slowly drawn into the folds of an appalling horror. We are introduced to Warrendown, a "new" town in Campbell's Severn Valley. Graham Crawley persuades the narrator to take him there because he has evidently impregnated a woman and wishes to see how she and her child are doing. The narrator is at first repulsed by the overwhelming "vegetable smell"[14] of the place, whose humble cottages seem almost deserted; but as he becomes unwillingly enmeshed into his friend's plight, he finds himself pursuing Crawley into a seemingly abandoned church, descending a cavity at the altar (exactly reminiscent of a scene in Lovecraft's "The Festival"), and witnessing a hideous rite of worship:

> At first the dimness, together with shock or the torpor which had overcome my brain, allowed me to avoid seeing too much: only a horde of unclothed figures hopping and leaping and twisting in the air around an idol which towered from the moist earth, an idol not unlike a greenish Easter Island statue overgrown almost to featurelessness, its apex lost in the darkness overhead. Then I saw that one of the worshipping horde was Crawley, and began to make out faces less able to pass for human than his, their great eyes bulging in the dimness, their bestial teeth gleaming in misshapen mouths ... The earth around the idol swarmed with their young, a scuttling mass of countless bodies which nothing human could have acknowledged as offspring.[15]

This is very good pseudo-Lovecraft, as the narrator comes to

---

14. "The Horror uner Warrendown," in *Made in Goatswood*, ed. Scott David Aniolowski (Oakland, CA: Chaosium, 1995), 256.
15. "The Horror under Warrendown," 266–67.

realise that Crawley (whose very name symbolises a descent upon the evolutionary scale) has mingled with creatures who have so renounced their humanity as to become not merely bestial but half-vegetable. The conclusion—in which the narrator, in a now hackneyed Lovecraftian convention, distractedly ponders whether there may be more cults like this one around the world—is, if I may be pardoned a pun, a little too pulpish.

"The Other Names" (1998) is of interest in being a later story that utilises the god Daoloth, which Campbell invented in one of his early *Inhabitant* tales. One cannot help thinking that the author was making a not so subtle allusion to his early correspondent and mentor August Derleth, publisher of Arkham House. As for "The Correspondence of Cameron Thaddeus Nash" (2010), a story that Pete Crowther, publisher of PS Publishing, twisted Campbell's arm into writing for my first *Black Wings* anthology, it is a pungent tale that plays with the iconic figure of Lovecraft himself (Nash is a previously unknown British correspondent of the Providence writer). It is all great fun, and Campbell shrewdly uses Nash's increasingly abusive letters to highlight Lovecraft's excessively modest opinion of the merits of his own work.

Campbell is perhaps more successful at conveying the sense of the cosmic that is at the core of Lovecraft's work in tales that are not consciously Lovecraftian at all. One such example is "Snakes and Ladders" [1974], an early version of "Playing the Game" [1980]. To my mind this version is more successful than its rewrite, as it deals with a reporter who investigates a possibly fraudulent worker of magic in a seedy part of town and, after expressing scepticism, is pursued by some nameless force. Here Campbell deftly combines natural and supernatural horror (pursuit by hostile individuals in a suspect milieu and the suspicion of some vast entity just out of sight) and expresses as keen a sense of the cosmic as anywhere in his work. Is it possible, the story suggests, that we are all merely the playthings of appalling cosmic entities that toy with us as if we are pieces of some inscrutable game?

"The Pattern" [1975], although somewhat prolix, is powerfully cosmic in its presentation of a very bizarre horrific conception. A young couple, Tony and Di, move into what appears to be an idyllic rural milieu, only to be disturbed by strange screams that sound curiously like echoes. In true Lovecraftian fashion, Tony consults an obscure volume, *Legendry and Customs of the Severn Valley*, to examine the history of the region, finding it to have been "dogged by ill luck and tragedy" (DC 145) from remotest times. But what could be causing the screams? In a reprise of Lovecraft's fascination with the complexities and paradoxes of time, Tony learns that the screams are a kind of reverse echo of a tragedy from the future—the tragedy of Tony's own death: "He knew the pattern had reached its completion, and he was afraid. He had to close his eyes before he could turn, for he could still hear the scream he was about to utter" (DC 150). This story is in no sense a Lovecraft imitation, but it is a good example of how the Lovecraftian influence has been absorbed so as to lend substance to Campbell's own imagination.

"Dolls" [1974] is perhaps worth mentioning here. This historical tale of a witch coven that meets in the woods near Camside seems similar in tone to Lovecraft's evocations of the atmosphere of seventeenth-century New England Puritanism in such tales as "The Festival" and "The Dreams in the Witch House." Its sexual explicitness, of course, is very far from what the prudish Lovecraft could have imagined, and the tale presents several points of interest that make it worth studying in a different context.

Campbell has also attempted, at least indirectly, to reflect Lovecraftian conceptions in a few of his novels. While only a few of his novels can be considered "Lovecraftian" through and through, several of them present features that we have already found in some of his short stories—the use of mythical books, the notion of cults on the underside of civilisation, and, once again, the cosmic sense that reduces humanity to a minute and insignificant mote in the vortices of space and time. Two novels may be said to present such features most concentratedly, *The Hungry Moon* (1986) and *Midnight Sun* (1990).

The Hungry Moon takes us to the small town of Moonwell, evidently in the north of England, near Manchester. Into this apparently placid community comes Godwin Mann, an evangelist from California with a large band of unthinkingly devoted followers. Mann has chosen Moonwell as the seat of his conversion campaign because he takes umbrage at the citizens' continuance of a centuries-old (and now seemingly harmless) Druidic ritual that involves the decorating of a nearby cave with a figure made of flowers. Skilfully manipulating the townspeople so that they come to feel insufficiently pious, Mann eventually wins over nearly the entire town to his brand of narrow, dogmatic, fundamentalist Christianity. Only a few courageous and sensible individuals—notably a teacher, Diana Kramer, herself an emigrant from America—refuse to conform, and they are ruthlessly ostracised.

Diana, however, senses that there is more to the whole affair than merely the invasion of fundamentalism upon a previously tolerant community. Seeking out an aged and blind inhabitant, Nathaniel Needham, who had written a monograph on the cave (which is the entrance to a pit that seems immeasurably deep), she learns from him that the Druids believed that the ceremony of decorating the cave unwittingly kept at bay a monster lurking deep in the cave's pit—a monster that may have come from the moon, thereby explaining humanity's age-long fear of our satellite. Godwin Mann, therefore, is inadvertently blundering into a situation whose cataclysmic danger he does not even remotely understand; as one character states, "What's down there in the cave is older than Satan" (HM 112).

Mann nevertheless climbs down the cave so as to overwhelm the entity with his spiritual power. He goes down and then returns, but emerges strangely changed. Not long afterwards the entire town becomes blanketed with darkness. Telephones and clocks do not work; no papers or food are delivered into the place; and what is most harrowing, the outside world is seemingly forgetting about the very existence of Moonwell. People who attempt to drive out of the town encounter an impenetrable blackness that forces them to return. The inhabitants try to put the best face on things. First they blame the anomalous condition on the weather; then, when this proves to be untenable, they adopt a spiritual explanation, as one small boy notes: "The dark's the bad coming out of the cave, isn't it?" (HM 134). But while the town itself is swathed in darkness, a weird light—uncannily like moonlight—seems to be radiating from Mann himself.

Finally bizarre violence breaks out over the town. Father O'Connell—a Catholic priest who had refused to buckle down to Mann and whose own version of tolerant Christianity is rejected by the townspeople—is apparently killed by his own dog. Then a policeman is killed by three vicious dogs who seem to come out of nowhere. Can there be any relation between them and the three infernal dogs who, as Diana learns from Needham, accompany the moon-goddess Hecate? Even worse monsters begin to manifest themselves, including a loathsome spiderlike creature in the hotel room Mann is occupying. Craig Wilde, the father of one of the residents who has been caught in the town while visiting his daughter, sees the thing:

> It was naked. That shocked him so badly that at first it was all he could comprehend, and then he tried to deny what he was seeing. It couldn't really look like a gigantic spider crouching in the nest of the bed, thin limbs drawn up around a swollen body that was patchy as the moon. The patches resembled decay, but they were crawling over the bulbous body, over it or under the skin . . . The smallness of the hairless gibbous head in proportion to the body made the shape look even more like a spider. (HM 202)

Craig flees in horror when he finds that the face on the entity's body is Mann's.

Meanwhile Diana has been held a kind of prisoner in another person's house for trying to confront Mann and his evil. While there she has a strange vision as she looks intently at a picture of a moor bathed in moonlight. She appears to see the birth of the universe or the solar system, including a huge sentient entity on the moon whose goal appears to be to feed upon life on Earth. It was this entity that found itself caught in the pit near Moon-well, gradually losing strength over the millennia until revived by Mann, with whose body it has in fact merged. Diana senses that the creature will use the nearby nuclear missile base to overwhelm the earth.

But what can Diana do with her knowledge? How can she, a single small human being, battle such a cosmic entity? She realises that her only hope is merely to affirm her own humanity. She simply begins to sing in the town square:

And then the black sky burst into flames.

It was the sun, but it was like no dawn she'd ever seen. The orange light seemed to tear the blackness apart, to flood the sky like flames on oil, turning whiter as it claimed the sky, putting out the moon . . .

Daylight filled the square, and even the shadows it cast were welcome. The sun hung above the moors, a disk like blinding glass. The bloated thing was crouching low, the head with Mann's face searching the square for a refuge, the maggoty neck stretching. (HM 286)

The loathsome entity slinks off back to the cave; but although Moonwell is saved, many of the townspeople are blinded by the light.

Aside from Diana's consultation of Needham (a figure reminis-cent of Zadok Allen in Lovecraft's "The Shadow over Innsmouth," who is a repository of the town's loathsome secrets) and her reading of his pamphlet (another "mythical book"), perhaps the only genuinely Lovecraftian moment in *The Hungry Moon* is Diana's vision of the universe, specifically of the nebulous entity that seems to have taken up residence on the moon:

> The moon was already dead, she saw. Water and atmosphere had evaporated, and the globe seemed dry and hollow as a husk in a spider's web. Meteors still dug into the surface, causing it to erupt in huge volcanic craters. The bursting of the surface made her think of corruption, life growing in decay, hatching. But that wasn't what terrified her, made her struggle to draw back from the moon while there was still time. She sensed that however dead the globe was, it harbored awareness. The earth was being watched. (HM 214)

The deathly darkness that descends upon the town seems to echo William Hope Hodgson's *The Night Land* (1912), a powerful imaginative fantasy of the far future in which the earth and its few pitiful living creatures are similarly bathed in darkness after the death of the sun. In *The Hungry Moon*, of course, the darkness serves a symbolic function in suggesting the intellectual darkness of fundamentalism; Diana's comment at one point—that the dark "is a way of trying to reduce people to a primitive state" (HM 178)—has a similar connotation.

Campbell wryly undercuts the Christian fundamentalism by incidents clearly evocative of pagan myth. The three dogs that attack the policemen are reminiscent both of Hecate's attendants and of Cerberus, the three-headed dog that guards the entry to Hades, while the blinding of many of the inhabitants with the return of the sun makes us remember those many characters in Greek tragedy who blind themselves to blot out the horrible truth.

Some critics deprecated *The Hungry Moon* as too broad a satire on fundamentalism to be effective as a horror novel; but, firstly,

Campbell wisely lets the fundamentalists condemn themselves through their own utterances rather than attacking them directly, and secondly, the supernatural element is skilfully interwoven with the religious polemic in the course of the novel. Godwin Mann is already a threat to civilised society because of his dogmatism, intolerance, and fanaticism; but his possession by the moon-entity renders him a supernatural threat all the more difficult to eradicate. Perhaps the only true flaw in the novel is Diana's vision of the universe, an awkward contrivance that Campbell requires to convey the necessary information on the origin of the moon-entity. The dispatching of the moon-entity merely by the power of song may seem to some to lack a certain "punch"; but its simplicity, poignancy, and reaffirmation of humanity is more affecting than any blood-and-thunder climax could have been.

The Hungry Moon has a distinctive texture not found in any of Campbell's other works—a simultaneous sense of cosmic grandeur and human worth that he had not attempted save, in a very different way, in *Incarnate* and would not surpass save in one of his best novels, *Midnight Sun*.

In his acknowledgements to *Midnight Sun* (1990) Campbell refers to several modern writers (M. John Harrison, T. E. D. Klein, and Fritz Leiber) who are "keeping the tradition of visionary horror fiction alive" (MS [ix]). Campbell here mentions also the Arthur Machen Society, a small hand of enthusiasts in England and America devoted to that Welsh writer; and it is certainly Machen and Algernon Blackwood—the two writers who, along with Lovecraft, both have an acute sense of the cosmic and are capable of evoking the awesome power of the natural world—who are Campbell's chief influences in this novel.

The first part of *Midnight Sun*, entitled "The Seeds," opens with a young boy, Ben Sterling, running away from his aunt's home to visit the grave of his parents, who have just died in a car accident. Ben, a quiet, introspective boy, is soon brought back home, but continues pondering his past and that of his family. His great-grandfather, Edward Sterling, had written a book called *Of the Midnight Sun,* a collection of folk tales gathered from his explorations around the world. Ben is unusually interested in the book; but his timid and conventional aunt, fearing that the book might be having an unwholesome effect upon him, gives it away.

Some time later, during a Hallowe'en celebration, the young Ben tells a strange fairy tale when urged by the father of one of his friends. Only much later does he realise that this tale—involving the efforts of a remote people to keep the ice-spirits at bay by not letting the fire go out—is derived from Edward Sterling's book. Ben concludes the story with the fire being extinguished and ice overwhelming the world: "So that's one story about what happens when the ice comes out of the dark" (MS 36).

In the second part of the novel ("Things Overheard") Ben is now a grown man, married and with two small children, Margaret and Johnny. He is a writer of children's books and his wife, Ellen, illustrates them. The death of Ben's aunt—who had come into possession of the family's rambling house in the town of Stargrave, near Leeds—causes Ben and the family to go to the house. As Ben explores the house and the immense forest at the back of it, he becomes pensive and withdrawn; he grows gradually apart from his family and seems to be searching for something. One night he comes to the deserted house alone at night, sensing some great mystery in the forest. It is at this time that he learns that Edward Sterling had died in the forest: he had been found one day lying naked in the snow and ice. But Ben's children find the house delightful and plead with their parents to move there. In short order they do so.

In part three ("The Growth"), the Sterlings seem initially contented in the house, but Ben finds himself unable to write. He begins to haunt the forest, and he soon finds the grove where Edward Sterling must have died. At this point he comes up with a story idea, and he discusses it with his wife:

"Suppose that in the coldest places on earth the spirits of the ice age are still there in the snow and ice, waiting to rise again."

"Not much chance of that, the way the climate's going."

"It isn't the climate that keeps them dormant, it's the sun."

"I expect it would."

"The midnight sun, I mean. It shines so many nights each year that they can never build up enough power to leave the ice."

"So how do they, if they do?"

"They do, I promise you. I'm not quite sure how, but I know I've something in here," he said, tapping his forehead. "If I can just bring it out into the open . . ." (MS 155–56)

The winter, however, has turned harsh. An inexperienced traveller is found frozen to death in the snow on a crag. Later, the postmistress, Edna Dainty, is overcome by some nebulous ice-entity while attempting to restrain her dog in the forest behind the Sterlings' house. This is the first inkling we receive that some vaguely animate entity might perhaps be loose in the forest: "She had no words to fend off her sense of the presence which stooped to her, a presence so cold and vast and hungry that her blind awareness of it stopped her breath" (MS 179). Ben begins to sense that some concatenation of forces is causing these events: "Edward Sterling's death had been only the beginning. The forest concealed what his death had liberated—what had accompanied him beyond the restraints of the midnight sun" (MS 210).

Ellen Sterling now finds Ben himself to be unnaturally cold, even when they are making love. As the winter increases in severity, Ben ponders: "It would be here soon, and he mustn't be afraid" (MS 245). As Christmas approaches, Ben—who by now has become extremely preoccupied, distant, and vaguely frightening—urges his family to prepare themselves for some great change; but Ellen, finding that the children are becoming upset by the trend of this discussion, cuts it off abruptly.

Ellen now believes that Ben is psychologically disturbed. She decides to have the children spend the night at a neighbour's, since they seem to have become actually afraid of their father. But as they trudge in the bitter cold to the neighbour's house, they come upon an appalling sight as they look in through a window at the occupants: "Though their clothes were just identifiable beneath the coating of frost, she couldn't see their faces. Their bunched heads were visible only as a blur within the object which sur-mounted their shoulders—a globe composed of countless spines of ice" (MS 300–301).

Is it possible that the whole town is frozen? No one seems to be alive. Ellen and the children have no choice but to return to their home. Ellen attempts to start the car, but it too is frozen. Ben, meanwhile, is genuinely bewildered at these futile actions on the part of his family and continues to urge them to prepare for the "imminent transformation" (MS 313) that is to overtake them if they yield to the ice-entity. Ben now comes to realise that his return to Stargrave has reawakened the entity.

Then, suddenly, Ben has a change of heart as he sees that his own family is frozen. Incalculably huge as the entity he is con-fronting seems to be, perhaps there is a way to stop it. "The only light he wanted to see now, too late, was the light in Ellen's and the children's eyes" (MS 319). Shortly thereafter, however, he per-ceives the awesomeness of the force he is up against:

> The world and the stars had been less than a dream, nothing more than a momentary lapse in its consciousness, and the metamorphosis which was reaching for the world was infinitesimal by its standards, simply a stirring in its sleep, a transient dream of the awful perfection which would over-take infinity when the presence beyond the darkness was fully awake. (MS 323)

Nevertheless, he feels that some symbolic gesture might at least be worth the effort. He takes two containers of gasoline, goes into the middle of the forest, pours the gasoline over himself, and lights a match. His last thought as he is burning is a dim sense that the forest is perhaps trying to extinguish the flame.

In an epilogue, we learn the aftermath. Ben has died, and more than two hundred townspeople of Stargrave have frozen to death. Ellen and the children have survived and now attempt to carry on with their lives. The narrative suggests that she is by no means clear as to the nature of the whole affair or the causes of Ben's self-immolation; but it seems as if the ice-entity has been vanquished—or, at any rate, has retreated into itself—for now.

The critical issue in *Midnight Sun* is Ben's conversion at the end. Throughout the novel he has been, as it were, on the side of the ice-entity, which has perhaps possessed him; then, without much warning, he suddenly frees himself from its influence and sides with the human race again. In a perceptive review of the novel, Steven J. Mariconda charitably regards this conversion, and the novel's ending as a whole, as "inadequately motivated."[16] To my mind it is quite unmotivated, even if it is vaguely prefigured by the early story of the people who tend the fire to keep the ice-spirits away.

Midnight Sun bears some resemblance to a little-known novel by Algernon Blackwood, *The Human Chord* (1910). Here, a scientist summons four individuals who, by means of sound (the "human chord" they will sing), might loosen the very fabric of the universe. Toward the end, however, one character, Spinrobin, rebels from the plan because of the love he has come to feel toward another character, Miriam, a love that becomes inextricably tied to his yearning for the palpable realities of earth life. Picking up a handful of leaves, twigs, and earth, Miriam cries:

16. Steven J. Mariconda, review of *Needing Ghosts* and *Midnight Sun*, *Studies in Weird Fiction* No. 9 (Spring 1991): 33.

"We should lose this . . . there's none of this . . . in heaven! The earth, the earth, the dear, beautiful earth, with you . . . and Winky . . . is what I want!"

And when he stopped her outburst with a kiss, fully understanding the profound truth she so quaintly expressed, he smelt the trees and mountains in her hair, and her fragrance was mingled there with the fragrance of that old earth on which they stood.[17]

Blackwood handles this transition from cosmicism to earthly reality rather better than Campbell, but the two novels are quite analogous in this particular. It is, of course, unlikely that Campbell has been directly influenced by Blackwood; and, although Blackwood fascinatingly probes the mystical qualities of sound and music in this ethereal novel, *Midnight Sun* is on the whole a richer and more substantial treatment of the basic idea.

In spite of its possibly defective conclusion, *Midnight Sun* ranks close to the pinnacle of Campbell's novelistic output. Its quietly understated prose, especially in its first two sections, is as evocative of the throbbing vitality of Nature as any in his work, and the delicate character portrayals—which fuse the human and the cosmic, the inner and the outer, in an inextricable union—perhaps make Ben Sterling's transition a little more understandable psychologically even if it has not been sufficiently prepared for. This is a novel almost entirely devoid of horror in the usual sense, but rather full of the awe and wonder that Machen, Blackwood, and Lovecraft evoked in their most representative work.

Although Ben toward the end of the novel expresses the essence of Lovecraftian cosmicism, with its diminution of humanity to risible insignificance, Campbell is a writer for whom human beings matter; he can never adopt the blandly impersonal attitude of

---

17. Algernon Blackwood, *The Human Chord* (London: Macmillan, 1910), 306–7. See my discussion in *The Weird Tale*, 109–11.

Lovecraft (nor, it should be stated, did Lovecraft himself in his unfailingly generous and courteous dealings with his friends and correspondents), and it is clear that Ben's conversion is really Campbell's own. Perhaps, then, *Midnight Sun* in a sense represents Campbell's final declaration of independence from Lovecraft: he uses Lovecraftian cosmicism as vivid imagery, but comes down firmly on the side of humanity when all is said and done. The ice-entity that Ben Sterling wishes to usher into the world is the fatally alluring but chillingly remote cosmicism that Campbell has finally rejected.

Campbell came close to working in the Lovecraftian mode in a novel published in 2002, *The Darkest Part of the Woods*. Here he returns to Brichester, but this Brichester, far from being the implausibly archaic nexus of Lovecraftian horror that it was in the *Inhabitant of the Lake* stories, is a town fully enmeshed in the modern world, with its computers, cellphones, and televisions. And yet, Lovecraft is perhaps not far from Campbell's vision in this richly complex, meticulously crafted, and chillingly terrifying work.

We learn that Heather Price, struggling to support herself and her adult son, Sam, as a librarian, is the daughter of Lennox Price, a man confined in the Arbour, a nearby mental hospital. Lennox, the author of a scholarly work, *The Mechanics of Delusion*, has himself become unhealthily fascinated with the dense woods that surround Brichester, and on occasion he leads other inmates in conducting anomalous rituals in a clearing deep in the heart of the woods. He refuses to explain what he is searching for aside from uttering the curious name "Selcouth."

Matters are precipitated when Heather's long-lost younger sister, Sylvia, returns to Brichester after many years in America. Later she announces that she is pregnant, but refuses to reveal the father of the child. Sam, meanwhile, a man in his early twenties, finds himself unhealthily attracted to his young aunt.

The name Selcouth is finally elucidated (initially by an Internet site) as one Nathaniel Selcouth, a sixteenth-century magician who built a dwelling in the Brichester woods and sought to "create a messenger or servant that would mediate between him and the limits of the universe, both physical and spiritual" (DP 163). It is here that the Lovecraft influence manifests itself, and even more so when Sylvia discovers Selcouth's journal in an underground cavity deep in the woods. The echoes of *The Case of Charles Dexter Ward*, with Ward's discovery of Curwen's journal, are evident, and Campbell makes no secret of it: Curwen, it appears, "is known to have visited England in search of Selcouth's journals but failed to locate them" (DP 163). What follows are some of the most terrifying passages in all Campbell's work, as successive characters brave the depths of the woods either to carry out or to thwart the sinister plans of the ancient mage.

The Darkest Part of the Woods is, however, far from merely an exercise in shudder-coining. Campbell, at the height of his form in fluidity of prose, sensitivity in character depiction, and mastery of narrative pacing, has produced a novel that continuously and lovingly shapes his characters as on a potter's wheel; every statement, every gesture, even every moment of silence contributes to the etching of each distinctive personality. At the same time, the evocation of the terrors of the natural landscape, and the horrors that can emerge from the centuried past, supply a backdrop of cosmic horror against which the characters appear to struggle in vain. It is remarkable, in a novel of this length, to find not a single wasted word, not a single sentence or passage that does not in some way contribute to that "unity of effect" which Poe believed was solely the province of the short story.

The Last Revelation of Gla'aki (2013) brings us full circle, for of course the title alludes to the fictitious grimoire—*The Revelations of Glaaki*—that Campbell, in his first book, added to the groaning bookshelves of Lovecraft's Cthulhu Mythos. But to refer to this short novel as a pastiche in the manner of such crudities as "The Insects from Shaggai" or "The Mine on Yuggoth" would be little short of grotesque. What Campbell has done here is to reinterpret the "forbidden book" topos—a vital and ever-changing conception in Lovecraft's own work, but often rendered trite and hackneyed by some of his lesser imitators—in the light of his own immensely enhanced understanding of human nature and motivations. We are here focused on Leonard Fairman, an archivist at Brichester University, who ventures to the town of Gulshaw to secure a copy of the fabulously rare nine-volume work, *The Revelations of Glaaki*. (In a prefatory note, Fairman points out that, according to the redoubtable John Strong, the apostrophe in "Gla'aki" was dropped by Percy Smallbeam, the editor of the 1862 edition, "to make for ease of reading" [LR 6].) But as Fairman meets with Frank Lunt, the head of the Shaw Theatre in Gulshaw, he is disconcerted to find that Lunt has only one volume of the work. This begins an increasingly frustrating quest whereby Fairman is obliged to go from one inhabitant of Gulshaw to the next, each of whom hands him another volume of *The Revelations of Glaaki* while he continues to stay in a bizarre hotel in the town and consumes increasing quantities of the peculiar food he is given at various establish-ments. Meanwhile, Fairman is disturbed by the strangeness of the town's denizens, as in a home for the elderly he visits:

One old man was opening his mouth wide and circular to expose his greyish gums, and several of his companions joined in, as though they were competing to produce the roundest mouth. An old woman was dangling her arms on either side of her chair to touch the carpet, and Fairman might have thought her hands were too long for the arms. Outside the windows a number of apparently unsupervised residents were shuffling and wobbling about the grounds; several had gath-ered to stare through a gap in the wall into the ill-defined depths of the woods. (LR 67–68)

There is, quite frankly, not much of a climax to this short novel, but its chillingly cumulative sense of increasing unease is sufficient reward for any reader.

In 2017–18, Campbell published a trilogy of novels collectively titled *The Three Births of Daoloth*. The reference, of course, is to the entity Campbell cited in several of his early Lovecraftian tales, beginning with "The Room in the Castle." Conveniently for Campbell, this entity is generally mentioned in only the vaguest of terms in his early stories. The one clear elucidation of Daoloth's nature and purpose is found in "The Render of the Veils," where a character states:

> "Daoloth is a god—an alien god. He was worshopped in Atlantis, where he was the god of the astrologers. I presume it wsa there that his mode of worship on Earth was set up: he must never be seen, for the eye tries to follow the convolutions of his shape, and that causes insanity. That's why there must be no light when he is invoked—when we call on him later tonight, we'll have to switch out all the lights." (CP 140)

It is, however, not at all clear that, in his trilogy, Campbell is portraying Daoloth in accordance with this passage. Accordingly, the trilogy becomes less an homage to Lovecraft as a grand summation of Campbell's nearly sixty years of life and writing.

The first novel in the trilogy, *The Searching Dead* (2017), opens in 1952 and is told in the first person by Dominic Sheldrake, whose exact age is never specified but who appears to be in his early teenage years, living with his parents in Liverpool. Postwar rationing is still in effect, and parts of the city still remain devastated from German bombing. Our attention is arrested when a neighbour, Mrs Norris, tells Dominic's parents that the new church she has joined allows members to see the dead in the flesh; she, in fact, has spoken to her recently deceased husband. Dominic's father, Desmond, a strict Catholic, scoffs at this assertion as routine (and potentially blasphemous) spiritualism; but Dominic learns from Mrs Norris that it is his own teacher at the Catholic school he is attending, Christian Noble, who is the head of this new church, which calls itself the Trinity Church of the Spirit. This superficially Christian-sounding name clearly masks a much darker secret.

Dominic, who since childhood has teamed up with two friends, Jim Bailey and Roberta (Bobby) Parkin, in various adventures under the nickname of the Tremendous Three, believes something sinister is going on, and that Noble is behind it. Dominic had seen Noble in a nearby cemetery, pushing a pram; he now sees that Noble has a baby daughter, Tina, but Tina's mother, Bernadette, seems quite hostile to her husband. Noble now proposes to take some of the students on a field trip to World War I battlefields in France; his father, Jack Noble, tells the students hideous stories of life as a soldier in that war. The students go to France, where they come upon a field whose trees are all leaning away from it; could this be the "hungry place" (SD 70) that Jack Noble had mentioned? One night, Christian Noble sneaks out of the dormitory; Dominic and Jim follow him and see him perform some kind of ritual.

Later, when Dominic's and Jim's parents learn of the dubious church Noble has founded, they bluntly confront him: "Mr Noble, are you a Christian?" (SD 106). After various evasive answers, he finally admits, "Of course I believe. . . . In the three persons" (SD 107). Of course, he fails to specify which persons these are. By the beginning of the next school term, the students learn that Noble is no longer at the Catholic school. Soon thereafter, Jack Noble shows up at the school, revealing fear of his own son and making the astonishing statement: "The world would be better off without him" (SD 118). Jack hides a notebook of some sort in the gymnasium of the school, but Dominic has seen him do so and takes the notebook. It is manifestly a diary written by Christian Noble and addressed to his daughter, Tina, and it is full of cryptic and darkly terrifying hints of his plans for the future. He tells of his experiments in raising the dead ("Then I felt my mind catch hold of something more solid than the vision, and the plot of earth began to stir, quivering the flowers that leaned against the headstone" [SD 124]) and refers to Bernadette as follows: "Previously, I had found no use for her kind, but the time for your birth was approaching, and so I sought a suitable candidate without knowing why I did" (SD 128). He goes on to write: "My visit to the field in France whence I originated has revealed to me how many secrets we have yet to learn. He who lies beneath the field has gained strength from them, though centuries of searching for them has left him monstrously transformed" (SD 130). There is a later reference to "Daoloth, which is the name of that which rends the veils" (SD 130), an explicit nod to his early story. But Dominic is forced by school authorities to give back the notebook to Christian Noble.

But is Noble merely interested in resurrecting the dead? Something far more baleful seems to be at work, as a terrifying incident in a movie theatre suggests. When Dominic goes to the men's room, he feels a hand grab his neck. Initially he sees nothing in the mirror, but then he observes a "naked whitish hulking shape . . . pressing its hands or the approximation of hands against the glass" (SD 152). Dominic manages to flee, and when he brings Jim into the room, nothing is visible—but then they notice that there are fingerprints on the mirror, and that, incredibly, "They were inside the mirror" (SD 154). In a later discussion by the Tremendous Three with Jack Noble, he confirms that his son's church is "just a front for what he's planning" (SD 189). He also demands that the three take him to their parents, but they flee, and as he pursues them he perishes when he is hit by a tram and cut to pieces.

Dominic tries desperately to persuade his friends to take action against Noble and his church, but they are stymied by their parents' opposition to any such action. In a tense conversation with Christian and Tina Noble, the precocious Tina at last specifies who the members of the church's "Trinity" are: "The past and the present and the future" (SD 229). Even this apparent blasphemy does little to change his parents' minds; but then a newspaper reporter, Eric Wharton, who himself has infiltrated the church's membership, writes a column betraying hostility to the church. Dominic subsequently finds that the windows of the church have been broke and the interior of the church vandalised—apparently by shocked townspeople. In exploring the basement of the church, Dominic finds hundreds of potted plants on tables—are these the flowers planted on graves that Christian Noble believes have some occult power to raise the dead? Some of the flowers look exceptionally odd, like no flowers known to earthly botanists. Dominic systematically destroys all the plants, especially those that seem vaguely animate: "a bunch of swollen leaves groped to close around my wrist" (SD 261).

The Searching Dead is many things at once: a poignant tale of teenage life; an historical novel that tellingly speaks of the cultural and economic environment of post–World War II England; and, of course, a kind of prelude to the cosmic horrors to be found in the two subsequent novels. Even if the novel largely does little more than set the stage for the more explicit terrors to come, it does so in a masterful fashion, and its portrayal of the blandly enigmatic Christian Noble is a triumph. But even more effective is its loving characterisation of Dominic Sheldrake and his two young friends.

It is difficult to deny that Dominic embodies many of Campbell's own beliefs, and the passages discussing the rigid and religiously dogmatic Catholic school in which Dominic is an increasingly dissatisfied member surely reflects Campbell's own gradual shedding of his Catholic upbringing. At one point he states: "I was already on the way to elaving behind the belies I'd been taught, and now I could see no reason to keep hold of any of them" (SD 201). In this gradual evolution, Jim and Roberta play a critical role: Jim remains an aggressively devout Christian, but Bobby, influenced by her possibly atheistic parents, has already sloughed off much of the religious dogma of the society in which she finds herself. It is precisely because of this growing congruity of belief between Dominic and Bobby that he is so shattered when he sees Bobby and Jim kissing in a movie theatre when they believe he is not present—and this comes soon after Bobby had explicitly rejected going on a "date" with Dominic, fearing that it would negatively affect their friendship. This is one of the final scenes of the book, and its effect on Dominic is nearly as potent as the incident in the church, where he flees from the clutches of some nameless entity in the basement.

The Lovecraft influence is covert but telling in certain segments of the novel. The general scenario of a man begetting strange offspring with a human mother echoes both "The Dunwich Horror" and *The Case of Charles Dexter Ward*. In the former story, the huge, goatish Wilbur Whateley is ultimately revealed to be one of the twin sons of the hideous cosmic entity Yog-Sothoth and a hapless female member of the Whateley clan. In the latter tale, the preternaturally aged Joseph Curwen wishes to secure an advantageous marriage both to repair his standing in the community—he is regarded by his fellow citizens in Providence, Rhode Island, as a sorcerer and worse—and to secure an heir who will ultiately effect his resurrection. Curwen himself seems to be engaging in the revival of the dead, just as Christian Noble is; but, like Noble, Curwen has much bigger fish to fry. The notebook that Christian Noble has written is a clear nod to "The Dunwich Horror," where extracts of Wilbur Whateley's diary are presented to the reader.

As *Born to the Dark* (2017) opens, we have leapt thirty years, to the height of Thatcherite England in 1985. Bobby has become an investigative reporter, now partnered with a woman named Carole; Jim has become a policeman; and Dominic (now calling himself Dom) is married to a woman named Lesley, with a five-year-old child, Toby. He teaches film at the university. Our concern through much of the novel focuses on little Toby, who has apparently been subject to seizures from infancy. In desperation, Lesley enrols him in a facility called Safe To Sleep, which practises some kind of specialised sleep treatment. Initially, Toby seems to improve, but disturbing hints quickly emerge. Lesley tells Dom that Toby has "been scaring some of the children at school," stating that they may see "a giant face that lives in the dark" (BD 39) when they sleep. Toby himself describes some of his dreams about that face with unnerving naïveté: "It's like it's waiting for you to go to sleep so it can have your dreams to make a bit more of itself" (BD 40).

Dom, who has been sceptical of Safe To Sleep from the start, wonders if Toby has managed to read the extracts of Christian Noble's diary—which contain all manner of cryptically cosmic passages—that Dom had copied in an exercise book. Dom also realises that the name of one of the proprietors of the facility, a pediatrician named Chris Bloan, is a partial anagram for Chris Noble: could this be Christian Noble's daughter, whom he had referred to as Tina (i.e., Christina)? She herself has a son named Christopher (or Toph), an infant who seems incredibly precocious in numerous ways.

Dom's worst fears are confirmed when he sneaks onto the grounds of Safe To Sleep and sees the redoubtable Christian Noble himself come into the room where the children are sleeping. Noble, his daughter Tina, and her son Toph seem to be chanting the name Daoloth over and over again. It is at this point that Dom experiences a clutching moment of terror when he attempts to flee the grounds:

A wind that I couldn't sense was enlivening the foliage, which responded with a whisper unnecessarily reminiscent of the kind of hush you might address to a child who was unable to sleep. As the dangling carkins writhed they might almost have been striking to imitate the insects I saw everywhere I looked, squirming out of the trees but remaining embedded as if rather than nesting in the timber they might be extensions of the material. I was desperate not to touch them, especially those that reared up towards me, revealing how transparently gelatinous they were, as I tried to sidle past the trees. When a bloated tendril found my cheek it felt like a cold dead tongue, somehow animated. (BD 84–85)

It gets worse. When, later, Dom goes to the hospital where Tina Noble works, he sees her making strange hand gestures over the newborn babies—and he comes to the staggering realisation that she and her father have actually *induced* the seizures into Toby and other children so that her family can later gain control of them through their facility.

But horror and tragedy follow upon this revelation. When Dom frantically attempts to explain the situation to Lesley, she (perhaps rightly) believes that Dom is simply paranoid, a result of his boyhood encounter with Noble. She orders Dom from the house and immediately initiates divorce proceedings. (Lesley's sudden turning on her husband does not seem entirely plausible. They had been married for at least six or seven years, but her extreme reaction—even if it was motivated by a desire to protect her son from what she believed to be Dom's harmful behaviour toward him—is not wholly credible.) Dom comes to a dispiriting conclusion: "It looked as if I needed to protect Toby on my own, which left me feeling worse than isolated" (BD 105).

Things get worse for Dom before they get better. After confronting both Tina and Christian (both of whom appear to know who he is and what he has done in the past), Dom crashes his car near the facility after a hand-like object touches his face. He wakes up in the hospital with a serious head injury; his father, Desmond, is in the same place, suffering from the effects of an infection following a fall. And while Desmond is sympathetic to Dom's concerns about Toby and vows to take care of the matter, there is little Desmond can do; indeed, he dies shortly thereafter. At the funeral, Dom is disturbed when Toby makes the bland claim: "I don't think grandad's really gone" (BD 135). This may be nothing more than a conventional belief that Desmond is in heaven; but does it have a more sinister signification?

Dom may not be quite as isolated as he thinks. Perhaps the Tremendous Three can take up the matter. Bobby becomes interested in investigating Safe To Sleep, and she wants Dom to fax her the extracts from Noble's diary; but Dom is dismayed (a word, incidentally, that Campbell tends to overuse) to find the diary missing. Can Toby, under Noble's instructions, have taken it? Bobby nonetheless carries on her investigation; but when she meets Dom later at a pub, he is startled to find that she has become a convert to Noble's ideas. "Tina Noble's doing everything she can for the children," she says, adding even more ominously: "I've joined in" (BD 188–89). She actually advises Dom to try a sleep session at the facility; Dom agrees—but he has other plans in mind.

During the session, Dom manages to wake up and clumsily take Toby away in his car. Noble, incredibly, is fully aware of what Dom has done, but doesn't seem to care. In a brief confrontation he declares, "It matters much less than you imagine" (BD 209). Toby expresses a desire for his parents to be reunited, and Lesley drops her plans for the divorce. At a later stage Dom persuades Jim to conduct some private investigation of Safe To Sleep; but when they arrive there, they find the place almost entirely vacant. That, however, certainly does not seem to be the end of the matter; for in a dream Dom appears to hear Toph's voice saying: "You're ours when we want" (BD 279).

Born to the Dark is so powerful and skilful a novel that it is difficult to enumerate its virtues. For all that the first-person narration compels the reader to see events entirely through Dom's eyes, the portrayals of every other character—most notably the touchingly innocent Toby, but also the baleful and sinister Christian and Tina Noble—are razor-sharp. And if the novel is in one sense simply a bridge between *The Searching Dead* and the novel to follow, it is itself full of passages of both poignancy and terror that make it a gripping read in its own right. In particular, the cosmic reflections that come out of Toby's mouth, while fully in the language of an ordinary five-year-old, are extraordinarily potent:

> " . . . there's a creature that lives in the dark, only maybe the dark's what he is. Or maybe the dark is his mouth that's like a black hole or what black holes are trying to be. Maybe they're just thoughts he has, bits of the universe he's thinking about. And he's so big and hungry, if you even think about him too much he'll get hold of you with one of them and carry you off into the dark." (BD 180)

And the culminating scene, where Dom and Jim explore the deserted facility—especially its baffling cellar, where the floor appears to be twisting in a kind of vortex, like a shell—is a passage of quintessential horror fully equal to analogous passages in prior weird fiction, ranging from Lovecraft's *The Case of Charles Dexter Ward* (where Dr. Willett investigates the cellar of Joseph Curwen's laboratory) to Caitlín R. Kiernan's *The Red Tree* (2009). Campbell here is doing nothing more than expressing humanity's age-old fear of the dark—but he does so in a manner as plangent and chilling as anywhere in his entire corpus of writing.

But there is more to *Born to the Dark* than merely moments of terror. Even if only incidentally, Campbell has sharp words about contemporary culture clashes on both the right and the left. He makes no bones about the fact that Desmond Sheldrake is a religious and racial bigot. But Campbell is careful to suggest that Desmond's attitudes were common to the people of his generation. Campbell is also pungent in dealing with leftists—especially with a sort of curdled liberalism that takes quick offence at the most innocuous of remarks. Colleen Johns, the divorce lawyer Lesley has hired, becomes an infuriatingly smug figure, twisting Dom's words to what she fancies is her client's advantage. When Dom casually mentions his friend Bobby, the following colloquy occurs:

"Is this something else I ought to know about, Lesley?"
Colleen Johns said.
"Good God, you're eager for material, aren't you?" I pro-
tested. "She's a lesbian."
"Do you have some problem with that, Mr Sheldrake?"
(BD 169)

First, Colleen is slyly suggesting that Dom is having an affair with
Bobby, or at least is more than just friends with her; then, when
Dom denies it, she does a bait-and-switch and hints that Dom is a
homophobe! No wonder everyone hates lawyers. It later becomes
evident that Colleen is simply using Lesley's case to advance her
own anti-male agenda ("Every successful case is a blow struck
for all of us" [BD 217]—i.e., all women purportedly under the
thumb of patriarchy). Campbell's own position seems to be a sort
of middle-of-the-road sanity, eschewing the religious bigotry,
racism, and sexism of prior generations but not going so far as to
become a mindless captive of identity politics.

The one element where the novel may come up short is its purportedly Lovecraftian substratum. The references to Daoloth are
too slight and tangential to be fully comprehensible. What we are
led to infer, insofar as we can make any sense of the supernatural
manifestations involved, is the notion of astral projection—which
is certainly not a Lovecraftian conception. (Campbell refers several times to Rose Tierney, the protagonist of his earlier novel *The
Parasite* [1980], where astral projection is suggested.) The raising
of the dead might, as with *The Searching Dead*, be a nod to *The Case
of Charles Dexter Ward*, but it is so common a motif in weird fiction
that no specifically Lovecraftian implication need be assumed.

With *The Way of the Worm*, Campbell's cosmic trilogy comes to
a triumphant conclusion. We now reach the present day, where
Dominic in his seventies and calling himself by his full name, is
facing multiple trials and tribulations—not the least of them the
death of his beloved wife, Lesley. Toby is now married to a woman

named Claudine; and the moment we learn this we are alarmed, for Claudine was one of the children in a facility called Safe To Sleep organised by the baleful Christian Noble along with his daughter and grandson. We have seen that much of *The Searching Dead* and *Born to the Dark* was devoted to increasingly frenzied efforts by Dominic—as well as his compatriots Jim Bailey and Bobby Parkin—in exposing the nefariousness of the Nobles. Even though the latter novel ended with the apparent destruction of the Safe To Sleep facility, we are hardly reassured that the danger represented by the Nobles is in any way over.

And, indeed, it is not. Both Dominic and the reader are distressed to find that the Nobles are now the leaders of a church or cult called the Church of the Eternal Three—suspiciously similar to the Trinity Church of the Spirit whose building was destroyed in *The Searching Dead*. Christian Noble must now be incredibly old, but he and his daughter and grandson are still thriving. What's more, Toby and Claudine are now members of the church, as are many other former patients of Safe To Sleep; still more disturbingly, Dominic's son and his wife are even inculcating their five-year-old daughter, Macy, into the church.

But is it possible that the church is really benign? Toby does his best to persuade his father of that, and some of the keenest moments of tension in *The Way of the Worm* focus on intense discussions between Toby (who is clearly sincere in his belief that the church has benefited his family) and Dominic, who knows all too well that the Nobles are anything but benevolent. Campbell may well be underscoring the dangers of religious brainwashing here: he himself has long struggled with the Catholicism he was forced to absorb as a child, and there is a clear implication of his disapproval of any sort of indoctrination of the young before they are mentally and emotionally ready to decide matters for themselves. The fact that the names of both of the churches established by the Nobles have unquestionably Catholic resonances underscores this point.

What the members of the Church of the Eternal Three seem to
be engaging in is a series of deep meditation sessions—and what
could be the harm in that? When Dominic grudgingly agrees to
participate in such a session—which, to his alarm, takes place in
the very building, Starview Towers, where Toby and his family
live—he appears to dredge up memories of when he was a newborn baby. That is bad enough, but it is at this point that Dominic
learns that the church is led by one Christopher Le Bon—which
he easily recognises as an anagram for Noble. Later, Dominic
attends a sermon by the entire Noble family, where Christopher
delivers an ominous sermon about the imminent return of chaos
to the world:

> "Alliances are breaking up across the world. . . . Continents
> are separating into countries, and countries are splitting apart
> too. There are wars and rumours of more wars, and unseen
> armies fighting for no country are at large all around us. Reli-
> gions are reverting to their primitive states, and madness is
> loose on the streets, and ruling country after country. The
> climate is returning to its birth. Gender grows more fluid,
> and the minds of the masses are gathering in the space their
> computers and electronic devices create." (WW 70)

There is more, but this is enough to show how Campbell has
deftly weaved our current sociopolitical troubles into a tapestry of
supernatural menace.

The novel gains dynamism when Dominic uses his phone to
record a private conversation among the Nobles in which Chris-
tian essentially admits the appalling fact that he himself begat
Christopher through an incestuous union with his own daughter.
Dominic passes on the tape to Bobby, who writes a blog about it.
A furore erupts, and the Nobles are arrested. In a subsequent trial,
Christopher is found guilty of incest—but, to the astonishment and
dismay of Dominic and others, his ten-year sentence is suspended,

and the Nobles calmly walk out of the courtroom. This whole episode is narrated with such compelling intensity—including gripping cross-examinations of both Bobby and Dominic by the Nobles' attorney—that the reader comes to believe that Campbell could easily have excelled at courtroom dramas if he had not (thankfully for readers of weird fiction) chosen to work in another genre.

Throughout this whole segment, Dominic is pained by the obviously sincere disappointment of Toby and his wife at what he has done to the Nobles; Dominic, in turn, is crestfallen that his own son could be so indifferent to the Nobles' sexual irregularities, to say nothing of other, more anomalous dangers they present, of which he has first-hand knowledge. When Dominic accedes to another meditation session, he actually envisions his own death. Toby blandly remarks, "It's your future that's remembering" (WW 96).

But worse things are in store for Dominic. He is already battered by age, ill health, the death of his wife, and now an agonising estrangement from his own son and grandchild. When the Nobles are leaving the courtroom, Christopher comes up to him and states forebodingly, "You're starting to live in our world. . . . You will until you die. . . . And then so much more" (WW 147). Dominic realises he must take more decisive action to thwart the Nobles. Finding out where they live, he sees their house as he is travelling on a ferry: they appear to be "dancing rapidly back and forth . . . describing an intricate sinuous series of patterns with their entire body" (WW 156). And is it possible that their faces have all merged together? "A single face could never have filled all the windows of the house, glaring out at me with its six monstrously enlarged eyes, bereft of pupils but alive with darkness" (WW 158).

But others seem to do the work he had set out to do. A gang of citizens, outraged at the outcome of the trial, set the Nobles' house ablaze. The Nobles, apparently naked, burn to death: "I thought I saw their bodies start not just to melt but to merge into a single monstrous shape" (WW 165). But the entire course of the trilogy has led us to discount the possibility that the Nobles could be so easily dispensed with. Toby accuses his own father of complicity in the arson ("you've got rid of Christian and his family" [WW 172])—and he blandly takes over leadership of the church. He also posts online the pages from Christian Noble's journals that Dominic had copied out as a teenager. Dominic is disturbed by the parallels: on the one hand Christian, Tina, and Christopher Noble; on the other hand, Toby, Claudine, and Macy. When, after an argument, Claudine peremptorily declares that Dominic is no longer welcome in her house, Dominic seems to have reached the end of his rope.

There is much more to *The Way of the Worm* than the menace of the Nobles and the familial tension between Dominic and his son. Subsequent events, directly or indirectly engineered by the hideous entity that the Nobles have now become, cause Dominic to be bereft of nearly all his friends and family; and yet, even this is not the worst fate that befalls him. In a climax that melds otherworldly, cosmic horror with the distinctively intimate tragedy in which Dominic finds himself enmeshed, Campbell unifies his own worldview with Lovecraft's—and at the same time shows that richly detailed and loving characterisations of the human protagonists not only are not a barrier to the expression of cosmic insignificance, but can actually enhance it by rendering more poignant the fates of the hapless human beings who fall into the clutches of those forces (i.e., the Nobles) who symbolise cosmic dread.

One of the most striking elements of *The Way of the Worm* is the manner in which it features a pervasive sense of *unease*. Campbell recognises that *fear* is difficult to maintain over the length of the novel; it is too intense an emotion for the human psyche to endure for a prolonged period. But unease can be manipulated by the skilful writer in ways that become almost as unbearable as brute fear, but that can nonetheless be sustained almost without cessation. In this novel, Campbell also creates the novelty of *dialogue* that enhances the sense of unease, as featured in verbal sparring between Dominic and Christian Noble, among others. In the hands of lesser writers such colloquies can seem corny or contrived, but Campbell uses repartée not only to forward the plot but to underscore the deeply sinister threat that the Nobles constitute to the peace and safety of the world.

There is little doubt that Ramsey Campbell's trilogy—for the three novels must be regarded as a tightly knit unity—will take its place among the stellar accomplishments in the realm of weird fiction. I struggle to find any trio of novels in our field that could match its achievement—an achievement that extends not merely to its deft portrayal of numerous characters over six decades and the impeccable elegance and mellifluousness of its prose, but above all to the grimly terrifying nature of its weird manifestations. It is too early to say that this trilogy is the summit of Campbell's achievement, for he (unlike his protagonist, Dominic Sheldrake) remains a vigorous septuagenarian, with much more work to come in the future; but readers, critics, and literary historians will have little hesitation in regarding it as a landmark that few of his rivals could hope to match.

Ramsey Campbell learned much about the mechanics of horror writing from Lovecraft—more so than many other writers in the Lovecraftian tradition have done, content as they are to mimic their mentor's flamboyant externals without seeking to probe the essence of what makes his writing so powerful. In a contributor's note to *New Tales of the Cthulhu Mythos* (1980), Campbell wrote with characteristic modesty, "One of his ambitions is to write a single successful Lovecraftian story."[18] He can take heart that he

18. *New Tales of the Cthulhu Mythos,* ed. Ramsey Campbell (Sauk City, WI: Arkham House, 1980), 255.

has already done so on at least two occasions, with "Cold Print" and "The Franklyn Paragraphs."

But Campbell would not have felt the need to transcend the Lovecraftian influence if he did not have his own message to convey. Although he has returned to the Lovecraftian mode sporadically in short stories and novels, the bulk of his work is as different from Lovecraft's as it is possible to imagine. What is remarkable is that Campbell found his own voice so quickly after writing his early Lovecraft pastiches; and it is to those works—included in his landmark second collection, *Demons by Daylight*—that we now turn.

III. THE *DEMONS BY DAYLIGHT* PERIOD

I have noted that, almost immediately after writing the stories that would comprise *The Inhabitant of the Lake* and well before that volume was actually published in 1964, Campbell began to veer off in different directions, consciously repudiating the Lovecraft influence. "The Stone on the Island," the last of his early Lovecraft pastiches, already shows signs of independence, while "The Childish Fear" [1963], "An Offering to the Dead" [1963], and "The Reshaping of Rossiter" [1964] also suggest a search for new orientations. Several of these tales are, to be sure, not great successes, being by turns too obscure and too obvious, and failing to display the mastery of diction and tone that we find in the bulk of Campbell's work. Nevertheless, Campbell was clearly aiming for something new—and in the process he would help to usher in a new type of weird fiction, one that would still continue to draw upon older motifs but would otherwise be vigorously modern in its ability to address contemporary concerns about the interplay between the mind, the emotions, and the imagination, and the complex interaction of individuals with one another and with society. The first product of this new mode was Campbell's second collection, *Demons by Daylight* (1973), a volume whose importance—both in Campbell's own oeuvre and in the realm of weird fiction generally—cannot be overstressed.

Campbell himself was fully aware of the boldness of the new direction he was forging, and he has frequently admitted that he was not at all certain whether he was on the right track. But some timely encouragement by Robert A. W. Lowndes—a veteran of the field who had corresponded with Lovecraft and was the editor of a series of digest magazines in which one of Campbell's tales appeared in the late 1960s—gave Campbell the impetus to continue. Lowndes wrote a favourable review of August Derleth's anthology *Travellers by Night* (1967), in which he singled out Campbell's "The Cellars" as a notable piece of work.

And yet, why did nine years pass between the issuance of Campbell's first and second collections? He had finished nearly all the tales for *Demons by Daylight* by 1968, and the collection had been accepted by Derleth's Arkham House by no later than 1970. It was scheduled to appear in 1971, but Derleth's death in that year postponed the publication of the volume for another two years. Campbell had published relatively few of the stories he was writing during this entire period, and what stories he did publish in anthologies and magazines were very different from the *Inhabitant* tales. I recall hearing speculations in the early 1970s that Campbell had given up writing or was ill; in the United States, at least, little word about him was getting out.

Another reason for the delay, of course, is that Campbell rewrote many of his *Demons by Daylight* tales, so that in their final versions they are probably very different from their originals. A few of these originals still survive, although Campbell was so discouraged as to their quality that he did not even bother to type them or submit them to a publisher. The history of the writing of the fourteen stories that comprise the volume is as follows:

"Potential": written 1968

"The End of a Summer's Day": written 1968
"At First Sight": written 1968
"The Franklyn Paragraphs": first draft 1965; final draft 1967
"The Interloper": first draft 1963; final draft 1968
"The Sentinels": written 1968
"The Guy": written 1968
"The Old Horns": written 1968
"The Lost": written 1969
"The Stocking": written 1966
"The Second Staircase": first draft 1965; final draft 1968
"Concussion": first draft 1965; final draft 1967
"The Enchanted Fruit": first draft 1965; final draft 1968
"Made in Goatswood": first draft 1964 (as "A Garden at Night");
second draft 1966; final draft 1968

The matter is made more confusing in that, while Campbell has admitted that *Demons by Daylight* was conceived as a unity, the first edition of the published volume does not entirely embody his conception for it. It was originally to have included "The Cellars" [1965] and "Reply Guaranteed" [1967]; but the former was presumably dropped because Derleth had already used it in *Travellers by Night,* and the latter was excluded because a poet of Campbell's acquaintance, Alan David Price, thought it a poor story; Campbell substituted "The Lost" in its place.

What makes the *Demons by Daylight* stories so distinctive? First and foremost, it is their style—wondrously supple, atmospheric, dreamlike, even hallucinatory. Some seem like pure nightmares (the first three stories in the volume are in fact grouped under the heading "Nightmares"), while others seem like the effects of a drug-delirium (although Campbell's experimentation with drugs dates only to the early 1970s). Conjoined to this—and, really, scarcely distinguishable from it—is the tales' intense concentration on a single character's moods and sensations as he or she encounters the bizarre; combined with the first feature, the result is a frequent inability on the part of the reader—and, indeed, the characters—to distinguish illusion from reality or to determine whether the weird event has actually occurred or is merely in the mind of the protagonist. Thirdly, it is their forthright addressing of modern issues—class conflict, sexuality, gender confusion, the terror of random crime. It is this quality that made *Demons by Daylight* so revolutionary in the field and so different from the stale vampires and mad scientists of the enfeebled Gothic tradition.

Each of these features is worth discussing separately, although of course they frequently occur in combination in the tales; and it is their seamless fusing that renders the stories far more than the sum of their parts.

The very first story in *Demons by Daylight*, "Potential," exemplifies the hallucinatory approach perfectly. The tale is itself about drug-taking, and re-creates the atmosphere of the 1960s vividly with its portrayal of a "Be-In" in Brichester ("FREE FLOWERS AND BELLS!" [DD 3]). Interestingly, Lovecraft is actually mentioned in the tale, but in such a way as to suggest that (at least in the opinion of one character) he would, perhaps because of his incantatory style, be a good source for entertaining visions during drug-taking. One wonders whether the story was inspired by a passage in "The Franklyn Paragraphs" in which a tale supposedly written by Errol Undercliffe, "The Steeple on the Hill," is described: "a writer fond of lonely walks is followed by the members of a cult, is eventually drawn within their circle and becomes the incarnation of their god" (DD 30). In "Potential," the protagonist, Charles, leaves the "Be-In" in the company of a man named Cook who promises more interesting action at the home of a man named Smith. There, in the midst of stoned youths and weird music, Charles finds a young woman tied to the wall naked and is urged by Cook: "Let what is in you be you. Release your potential, your power" (DD 9). But we are far from some mundane ritual involving sex or violence: as the occupants kneel in front of Charles, a strange alteration overtakes him and he does indeed seem to become the reincarnation of a god.

"The Enchanted Fruit" may perhaps obliquely involve drug-taking as well. A man named Derek walks out of his Brichester flat a few hours prior to his housewarming party and wanders into a forest in Goatswood, where he comes upon a tree with strange-looking fruit. He eats a piece:

> Juice coursed from it; he threw back his head and drained the liquid spilling amber down his chin. In the shade his fingers were sticks of honey. He chewed and categorized. It was useless. He had tasted nothing to compare. Wine, fruit, meat—something of each, yet on another plane, something almost spiritual which was beyond eating, was the sunlight, shade, the open fields, the moment when one is truly alone and yet a part of all. (DD 130)

Returning to the flat, he finds that all other foods now have a sickly, rotten taste to them. He returns to the forest but cannot find the tree bearing the fruit. A doctor prescribes medicine for him, but to no effect. As Derek continues to degenerate, he even attempts to take communion, but the idea of swallowing the wafer revolts him. The story ends inconclusively with Derek clawing the ground in front of a tombstone.

The symbolism of "The Enchanted Fruit" is not easily understandable. Does the magical fruit signify Derek's pent-up imagination, which finds his boring friends (whose bland repartée at the housewarming party Campbell portrays with tart satire) and mundane life increasingly intolerable? In any event, the dreamlike atmosphere of the story is powerful enough in itself.

"The End of a Summer's Day" perhaps comes closest to pure nightmare. The seemingly simple events of the tale—a woman, Maria West, is led through a cave with her fiancé, Tony Thornton, and a party of tourists, but when they emerge, Tony is gone and a blind man is pointed out to her as her companion—are made bafflingly confusing by the narrative's concentration on Maria's increasingly neurotic perceptions and feelings. The tale is reminiscent of some of Shirley Jackson's similar pieces, notably "The Demon Lover" (in *The Lottery* [1949]); and the reader is left to ponder a variety of alternatives: did Tony (at least in the form he bore before entering the cave) ever exist, or did Maria's loneliness merely invent a handsome and manly lover for herself? Or was Tony supernaturally changed by entering the cave? Is the man's blindness a metaphor for Maria's own ignorance of her insecurity? Campbell wisely leaves the matter hanging in this curiously poignant vignette.

All the *Demons by Daylight* stories, in fact, tell relatively simple tales that, largely because of Campbell's oblique narration, become horrific even if nothing outwardly supernatural appears to have occurred. The poetically dreamlike atmosphere thus created— involving a melding of horror, pathos, and puzzlement—lends a unity to the tales in spite of the very different events they relate.

One of the chief reasons why *Demons by Daylight* was such a revelation in horror literature was the frankness with which Campbell confronted issues of sexuality and gender in his tales. Ira Levin's *Rosemary's Baby* (1967), William Peter Blatty's *The Exorcist* (1971), and Thomas Tryon's *Harvest Home* (1973) had certainly broached sexual matters, but in a somewhat more conventional way: in the first, impregnation of a woman by the Devil; in the second, the possession of a little girl by a demon who induces (among many other phenomena) sexual aberrations in her; and in the third, a primitive but non-supernatural ritual in a rural community whereby a sexual act is thought to symbolise fertility and renewal. Campbell's treatment of sex, while being as far as possible from the cheaply exploitative, confronts complex interpersonal issues with which we, as individuals and as a society, are still grappling.

The largest section of *Demons by Daylight*, comprising the last nine stories of the volume, is headed "Relationships." One story not included in this section is "At First Sight," which combines the nightmarish quality of the "Nightmares" section where it is placed with a rumination on the nature of obsessive relationships. In this tale, Valerie, a young woman recovering from an involvement with a man whom her parents forbade her to marry, finds herself attracted to a stranger who toasts her in a bar. The man tracks her down to her office and is clearly following her; Valerie admits to being frightened, but is also perhaps secretly pleased that a man is taking interest in her, however twisted that interest may be. Is she also resentful that her roommate, Jane, seems to be more successful with men than she is? The ambiguous ending to the tale—along with such other features as a calendar, given to Valerie by her ex-fiancé, in which each successive month reveals more and more of a woman's body with a man's hands gradually closing around it—all suggest the loneliness of Valerie's life that leads her to flirt with danger and death.

Rather similar is "The Stocking," which is Campbell's first avowedly non-supernatural tale. This story of sexual obsession involves nothing more than a man, Tom, who is clumsily trying to woo a co-worker, Sheila. Early in the story, during some mildly sexual horseplay in which Tom is tickling Sheila, he causes one of her stockings to run; in response to his request, she gives it to him. Later, increasingly frustrated at Sheila's resistance, Tom confronts her at the entrance to what appears to be an abandoned storage room, and it becomes clear to the reader that he means to strangle her with her stocking. The sexual tension generated throughout the story is remarkable—the more so when we realise that its author was twenty years old at the time of its writing.

Two stories, "The Sentinels" and "Concussion," are superb examples of how Campbell can utilise venerable supernatural tropes, and even some science-fictional elements, and refashion them for a contemporary audience by allusiveness of approach and the interplay of characters. In "The Sentinels" we are once again in Campbell's Lovecraftian topography. Somewhere near Brichester there is a place called Sentinel Hill, a name taken directly from Lovecraft's "The Dunwich Horror" (1928) (a subsequent mention of Exham [DD 57] is a clear nod to Exham Priory in Lovecraft's "The Rats in the Walls" [1923]). This hill seems to have a dubious myth attached to it: the stone figures there, the Sentinels, "are supposed to guard the hill against anyone who doesn't make a sacrifice to them" (DD 57). What could have been the hackneyed tale of an age-old curse becomes something much richer and more ambiguous as a pair of couples—Ken and Maureen, and Douglas and Barbara—go up to the hill and engage in a game whereby they must circle the sentinels and count them. There is anomalous difficulty in the process—are there seventeen, or eighteen, or nineteen?—and matters reach a climax when Maureen says quietly, "One of the figures isn't stone" (DD 61). But the secret of the tale's success is the portrayal of four clearly contemporary characters who, amidst their good-natured banter, refuse to take the hoary legend of the Sentinels seriously until faced with overwhelming proof.

Still more chilling—while at the same time reaching a level of poignancy that may make it the best tale in *Demons by Daylight*, if not in the whole of Campbell's work—is "Concussion." The extraordinarily oblique narration of the tale has raised considerable controversy over what actually happens in it; and, although a number of possibilities can be suggested, my understanding of the scenario is as follows. A woman, Anne, hits her head during an accident on a bus; during the week that she is in hospital recovering from a concussion, she somehow goes back in time fifty years and has a bittersweet romance with a young man, Kirk. In the present day (which, as various details at the beginning of the tale establish, is actually fifty years in the future), the now aged Kirk meets the still-young Anne on the same bus.

Stated baldly, the whole tale might easily seem ridiculous; but it is Campbell's skilful juxtaposition of the present and the past, and the abrupt transition between the two, that create the sense of strange reality in this story. Anne is perhaps especially susceptible to this sort of time-travelling because she is so fond of the past: "Sometimes when I'm going to sleep I think I'll wake up—oh, before I was born, when everything was lovely—well, not everything, there were the wars, but I don't know, the past seems awfully romantic" (DD 109). And Anne's remark that ghosts, if they are real, would probably be just like ordinary people certainly seems to hold good for herself, who is a kind of ghost from the past's future. As for the lonely Kirk, the one week spent with Anne not only seemed, as it did to her, like a dream, but also as if "they had wandered outside time" (DD 126). His life for the next fifty years is empty; and as he desperately confronts Anne in the bus and tries to convince her ("We met fifty years ago! You went back into the past somehow and we met on a coach . . . " [DD 127]), he causes the bus to crash. This, of course, is the accident that gave Anne the concussion.

However the actual events of "Concussion" are reconstructed, the tale's emotive richness resides in its delicate portrayal of bashful lovers slowly becoming emotionally bonded—something very new in a literature of horror that all too frequently has omitted affairs of the heart altogether or has depicted women as either voracious villains or helpless victims. The longest story in *Demons by Daylight*, it also unites its best features—dreamlike atmosphere, oblique supernaturalism, concentration on individual sensations and emotions—into a masterwork of mood and suggestiveness.

"Concussion" also provides an opportunity to examine the first and final drafts of the story so as to gauge Campbell's remarkable development in a matter of a few years.[1] The original version, dating to 1965, contains most of the basic incidents of the tale, but— aside from an opening paragraph noting how Kirk has caused the

1. I am grateful to Ramsey Campbell for permitting me to read the unpublished first draft of "Concussion."

bus accident—merely recounts, in a rather flat and atmosphere-less manner, the week-long romance between Kirk and Anne, then Kirk's subsequent confusion as he realises the time paradox that caused their involvement. This version is simply too obvious in its narration to convey the dreamlike delicacy and evocativeness of the finished draft. At one point Kirk ponders the matter:

> He had not been with Anne; but then, in their week together, when he remembered showing her Liverpool, where had he really been? Had he walked through crowds for days talking to the air? Or, more subtly disquieting, had he not visited those places where his memory located him? In the soft dark-ness and the muffled liquid sounds, he felt adrift.

It is exactly this kind of explicitness that Campbell eliminated in the final version.

Two other stories in *Demons by Daylight*, "The Lost" and "The Second Staircase," speak more ominously of how sexual tension and jealousy can cause trauma and psychosis. "The Lost" appears to be a non-supernatural tale whose simple premise—Don, travel-ling through Germany with an old friend, Bill, contrives to have Bill killed so that he can pursue Bill's wife, who was formerly Don's lover—is again masked by narrative obliquity. Unusually for Campbell, the tale is narrated by Don in the first person; and the evasive manner of his recounting of events suggests not only an attempt to deceive the reader as to his culpability in Bill's demise but also a kind of rationalising self-justification.

"The Second Staircase" is one of the strangest tales in the col-lection. We are initially introduced to a character named Carol, a film reporter; but Carol is not a woman but a man. Perhaps as a result of his unusual name, he feels the need to assert his man-hood: he sleeps naked as a "proof of his virility" (DD 97). But as the tale unfolds, what seems initially to be merely a certain excess machismo on Carol's part proves to be full-fledged misogyny,

perhaps as a result of his own gender confusion. He admits that
he has never had a girlfriend; and in a strange dream he seems
to wake up and reach for a vest, but puts on a slip instead. His
seeming concern for women—he complains that women are
always "degraded" (DD 98) by men in the sexual act—cannot conceal his own hatred of them, precisely because they have rejected
him ("Women—he hated them, their soft helpless bodies, passively resisting, unattainable" [DD 104]). In a bizarre conclusion
that could only have been effective in Campbell's hallucinatory
style, Carol finds himself somehow turned into a woman and
forced to undergo sex with the lascivious manager of a hotel. This
tale broaches issues of gender confusion that even the boldest of
today's drearily numerous "erotic horror" stories have not come
close to matching in intensity.

A whole range of stories in *Demons by Daylight* confront the
individual's place in a hostile and indifferent society. Although the
fictional Severn Valley topography that Campbell devised for his
Lovecraftian tales continues to be the setting for many of them,
the town of Brichester—which, as I have earlier noted, had about
this time become "Liverpool . . . in all but name" (FD xxi)—is very
different from the nebulous and faintly anachronistic place that it
was. Now it has its slums and its whorehouses, as well as its successful capitalists. Like Campbell himself, it has moved into the
contemporary world.

Perhaps the clearest example of Campbell's new social consciousness is "The Guy." Here again a relatively simple tale is
told. The ghost of a boy, accidentally killed in a bonfire during
Guy Fawkes' Day, comes back from the dead in the form of a
papier-mâché figure to exact revenge—not upon his father, who
had caused the accident, but his brother. Intertwined with this scenario, however, is a searing display of class snobbery:

Joe Turner was in the class next door to me; he'd started
there that term when the Turners had come up from Lower

Brichester. Sometimes, walking past their house, I'd heard arguments, the crash of china, a man's voice shouting: "Just because we've moved in with the toffs, don't go turning my house into Buckingham Palace!" That was Mr Turner. One night I'd seen him staggering home, leaning on our gate and swearing; my father had been ready to go out to him, but my mother had restrained him: "Stay in, don't lower yourself." She was disgusted because Mr Turner was drunk; I'd realized that but couldn't see how this was different from the parties at our house, the Martini bottles, the man who'd fallen into my bedroom one night and apologized, then been loudly sick on the landing. I was sorry for Mr Turner because my parents had instantly disliked him. "I don't object to them as people. I don't know them, not that I want to," my father had said. "It's simply that they'll bring down the property values for the entire street if they're not watched." (DD 64)

The narrator Denis's rumination as he begins telling the crux of the tale—"it was Joe who showed me injustice" (DD 65)—certainly has a literal meaning: Joe's death at the hands of his dead brother was a case of revenge being taken on the wrong person, although in some strange way Joe may have felt responsible for his brother's death and thereby contributed to his own. But the statement may also have a figurative meaning, as indicating how Denis's own family's response to the Turners showed the teenage narrator the cruelties of class distinctions. Simon MacCulloch further analyses Denis's remark:

> ...it was not justice of any kind that demanded Joe's grotesque demise, but the destructive power unleashed by the conjunction of three mutually compatible but explosive elements: Denis' suppressed imaginative craving for violence, a family in which the pattern of violence and guilt had become

ingrained, and a British folk ritual which celebrates violence masquerading as justice by making festival of the cruel public execution of a seventeenth-century terrorist. The explanation that eludes Denis lies in the nature of his own participation in the event.[2]

Three stories deal with religious conflict. We have seen how, in "The Enchanted Fruit," Derek's taste of the fruit has made him develop a violent distaste for all other foods. Derek is a Catholic, and at his housewarming party he engages in the following debate with his girlfriend, Janice:

> "As for me—well, of course we Catholics don't accept that animals feel pain. It would make nonsense of the whole religious analysis of pain."
> "God! Derek, have you ever heard a dog after a car's had its back legs?" asked Janice furiously. "I think you simply use religion as a shield. If you're confronted with something frightful you say it's the will of God. Can't you act instead of thinking?" (DD 132)

While there is an element of self-parody in this—all the members of the party show themselves to be shallow or archly sophisticated—it is an argument that Campbell would perhaps not disavow. And Derek's later revulsion at the prospect of swallowing the wafer at communion may perhaps suggest a conflict between conventional religion and the age-old paganism symbolised by the unpeopled forest and its strange fruit.

Such a conflict is at the very heart of "Made in Goatswood." Here again Nature is a symbol for paganism, which orthodox religion must always regard as its enemy. Terry Aldrich, an unbeliever,

2. Simon MacCulloch, "Glimpses of Absolute Power: Ramsey Campbell's Concept of Evil," in *The Count of Thirty*, 33.

buys some primitive-looking gnome-figures of grey stone to decorate the garden of his fiancée, Kim, a devout Catholic; Terry expressly states that the figures "ought to bring her garden closer to nature" (DD 142), while Kim's father declares indignantly, "It looks like a Druids' meeting-place" (DD 145). Kim accepts the figures with some reluctance, but as time passes she feels that she is being watched; she and Terry begin to have increasingly bitter religious disputes. On one occasion, as Terry is coming to Kim's house, he notices that the figures are gone; Kim is also missing. Have the figures come to life, and are they going to sacrifice Kim at a nearby grove? Terry encounters drops of blood, and then the figures themselves: he smashes them to bits. Later, as Kim is recovering from her experience, Terry makes the sign of the cross before entering her house.

This is, certainly, a somewhat peculiar ending for a lapsed Catholic like Campbell to have written. The whole tale ends up being a repudiation of atheism, a display of the evils of paganism, and an affirmation of religious faith. In this regard it is unique in Campbell's work. And yet, if nothing else, it is redeemed by one shuddersome moment when Kim senses the figures approaching her: "The grey stone silence inched toward her" (DD 151).

Somewhat along the same lines, although with a very different conclusion, is "The Old Horns." Here again a region called The Old Horns, a waste area separating the forest from the beach, leads to a dispute about the nature of paganism: one character, George, asserts that it represented emotional ecstasy and sexual freedom, while the first-person narrator declares violently, "It degraded the body. It didn't release you, it dragged you down into itself. It rotted you" (DD 72). As the young people in the tale play a game of hide-and-seek near The Old Horns, George vanishes and cannot be found. Later an anomalous figure is seen dancing madly and then falling into a pool in the forest. Have the pagan forces in The Old Horns seized George? The narrator's comment as he sees the figure—"It stood struggling still to dance; it threw

THE *DEMONS BY DAYLIGHT* PERIOD   99

up the arms of its open-necked shirt in a final gesture of joy" (DD 79)—suggests, however, that both his and George's conceptions of paganism were partial glimpses of the truth.

"The Interloper" is perhaps the most obviously autobiographical tale in *Demons by Daylight*. This is one of two stories in the section "Errol Undercliffe: A Tribute," and is presented as a tale by Undercliffe; the other is "The Franklyn Paragraphs," which relates Undercliffe's hideous end. A mad account of schoolboys' terror of authority figures, "The Interloper" involves the entry by two youths, John and Dave, into a deserted vaulted chamber where, amidst dust, cobwebs, and seemingly empty suits, a dubious figure is encountered:

And something appeared, hopping toward him inside the patched overcoat: long arms with claws reaching far beyond the sleeves, a head protruding far above the collar, and from what must have been a mouth a pouring stream of white which drifted into the air and sank toward Dave's face as he fell, finally screaming. (DD 51)

Dave is killed by the creature, but John escapes. Returning to school covered with cobwebs, John is horrified by one simple fact: a dreaded supervisor of teachers, nicknamed the Inspector, also has a few wisps of cobwebs adhering to his clothes.

This powerfully atmospheric tale viciously satirises the physical and emotional brutality inflicted upon hapless schoolchildren by embittered teachers. No doubt some details were taken directly from Campbell's own schooldays. School life will be featured in a number of Campbell's most powerful later stories.

Some consideration may now be given to the supposed unity of *Demons by Daylight*. Campbell never explicitly specifies the nature of this unity, and I believe it is more a matter of mood and texture than of plot or theme. As I have mentioned, the matter is further complicated by the last-minute switching of contents. The two stories omitted from the collection are similar in many particulars. "Reply Guaranteed" [1967] is set in Brichester and involves the ghost of a lecher who pursues a woman who whimsically answers his personal ad; perhaps its only flaw is slight verbosity. As for "The Cellars" [1965], this masterwork of atmosphere is perhaps the first tale set clearly in Liverpool; it speaks ominously of a man who lures a woman into the cellars under the city and is perhaps transformed by the fungus found there. The story mingles sexual tension and supernatural horror in a manner rarely excelled by any of the *Demons by Daylight* stories, and would have found a comfortable haven in that landmark collection.

Both during and slightly after the writing of the tales comprising *Demons by Daylight*, Campbell wrote a variety of stories that touch upon many of their themes and are narrated in a similar fashion. Some of these I will discuss elsewhere, but I wish to focus here on those several tales that mix sex and horror into a powerful unity. The statement by Yeats that Robert Aickman quoted at the head of one of his story collections, *Tales of Love and Death* (1977)—"I am still of the opinion that only two topics can be of the least interest to a serious and studious mind—sex and the dead"—could well be the leitmotif of these works.

One of the first stories Campbell wrote after finishing *Demons by Daylight* is "The Previous Tenant" [1968]. In this delicate tale, a married couple move into a flat previously occupied by a young woman who had committed suicide. The husband, an artist, is increasingly fascinated by the previous tenant, while his wife, sensing this, feels jealousy at her ghostly rival. She destroys a photograph of the woman and later throws away a glove belonging to her. Their marriage deteriorates, and the story ends abruptly with the husband murderously approaching his wife with a carving-knife. Campbell has remarked of the tale: "It's essentially 'The

Beckoning Fair One' done in miniature."[3] The reference is to Oliver Onions's classic story (included in his collection *Widdershins* [1911]) about a man who falls in love with the ghost of a woman in a flat into which he has moved. Campbell's tale further broaches the notion of the difficulty of reconciling artistic creation and domestic existence.

"The Void" [1968] is a bizarre tale, bringing "The Second Staircase" to mind. The premise—a man and a woman have both received organs from the same donor, thereby establishing a curious bond between them—may seem a little contrived, but the secret of the tale is its rapid switching of narrative voice between the two characters, Tim and Edna, to the point where we are frequently unsure who is speaking or whose thoughts and sensations we are reading about. Another story along the same lines, and one that also brings "The Lost" to mind, is "Second Chance" [1970], in which a man, Gerald, changes his outward form so as to look like his friend Terry because he longs for Terry's girlfriend.

Campbell has published a volume of seven stories under the title *Scared Stiff: Tales of Sex and Death* (1986), containing works written between 1974 and 1986. Several of the earlier tales were commissioned for various original anthologies compiled by Michel Parry, some of them being sex-horror volumes that Parry edited under the piquant pseudonym Linda Lovecraft (a combination, of course, of H. P. Lovecraft and the erstwhile porn queen Linda Lovelace). One of these, "Dolls" [1974], I have already discussed briefly. It is one of the few instances in which Campbell has set a tale in the past; here we appear to be in the eighteenth century. The story is a variation of the voodoo motif. A member of a witch coven, John Norton, has created a wooden devil-figure used in the sexual rituals of the cult; but it seems to bear a strange symbiotic relationship with him, for it first becomes supernaturally animated, then, when it is destroyed, John himself is killed. The rich

3. Dziemianowicz, "An Interview with Ramsey Campbell," 12.

texture of the tale, vividly re-creating the historical period while also etching each character distinctly and portraying the blasphemous sexual rites, is further enhanced by an ambiguity sustained almost to the end about the exact nature of the wooden figure: could John be actually inside the life-size doll? No, for when in anger the woman who has had sex with it pulls off both its right arm and its penis, she finds that they are merely of wood and that the figure is empty; but later John is found with his right arm and penis torn off . . .

Just as powerful in a very different, and very modern, way is "The Other Woman" [1974]. Here an artist, Phil, who is forced for monetary reasons to paint lurid paperback book covers, many of them depicting violence toward women, imagines what it might be like actually to strangle a woman; for some reason he endows this imaginary woman with one blue eye and one brown eye. Later he dreams of raping and murdering the woman, and then he finds himself unable to make love with his wife, Hilary, unless he continues to indulge his sadistic fantasies. On one occasion while in bed with Hilary, he even envisages himself engaging in a kind of necrophilia with his imaginary sex-slave. In the end he rapes his own wife and kills her; appalled by the act, he is still more horrified to find that his wife now has one blue eye and one brown.

The partial inspiration for this story may have been Poe's "Ligeia," that masterful account of a dead wife whose will to live was so strong that she impressed her features upon those of her husband's second wife. Campbell's tale can be read as a variant of his own "The Previous Tenant": here Phil finds that his art suddenly gains in power as he continues to envisage violence toward his imagined woman; but his wife, noticing his occasional bouts of impotence, begins to wonder whether he is seeing another woman. Campbell exhibits the ugliness of sexual violence unflinchingly:

> . . . suddenly she was struggling beneath the full length of his body. She was trying to drive her knees into his groin, but

his thighs had forced her legs wide. His elbows knelt on her forearms; her hands wriggled as though impaled. His hands were at her throat, squeezing, and her eyes welcomed him, urging him on. He closed his mouth over hers as she choked; her tongue struggled wildly beneath his. He drove himself urgently between her legs. As he entered her, her genitals gave the gasp for which her mouth was striving. He drove deep a half-a-dozen times, then was trying to hold back, remembering Hilary; too late, too late. He bit the pillow savagely as he came. (SS 29–30)

The other stories in *Scared Stiff* are less satisfactory than these two, being at times overly obscure and failing to deliver on the promise of their suggestive plots. Perhaps the last story in the book, "Merry May" [1986], written specifically for the collection, is the best of them. Here a man named Kilbride (whose name is immediately suggestive) becomes increasingly fascinated with the idea of having sex with schoolgirls. He is lured to a remote village in Lancashire by a group calling itself Renewal of Life, arriving just before May Day; then a May Queen is picked—a fourteen-year-old girl. The man gradually realises that he will be expected to have sex with her, and still later he realises why: a local factory has apparently done something to the men to cause them all to be impotent; he is therefore needed to "renew the life" of the community. He indeed has sex with the girl in the church, but just afterwards he mentions her name—a serious violation of the ritual. He thinks the men will kill him, but instead they merely drive him into the woods; and he becomes gradually aware that they will castrate him and use him as their own May Queen for Old May Day, to be celebrated ten days later.

One story Campbell considered including in *Scared Stiff* but decided to omit is "The Limits of Fantasy," originally written in 1975 and significantly rewritten in 1989. In this tale, a photographer in the pornography trade, Syd Pym, finds himself fascinated with a woman whom he sees, and photographs, undressing in the building across the street from his. Developing the photographs, Pym uses some sort of sex magic with them to indulge his fantasies of spanking the woman. On several subsequent occasions he sees her walking stiffly and painfully; when he meets her on a bus and offers her his seat, she awkwardly refuses. Becoming increasingly obsessed, Pym pursues her on the street, but the woman falls into a lake and drowns. Appalled and guilt-ridden, Pym walks home past a display of magazines depicting women holding whips. Somehow these images come to life and Pym is drawn into a realm where he will suffer what he imagined performing on the woman of his fantasies. Here again the supernatural supplies an added dimension to what might otherwise be a mundane study of sexual obsession.

Campbell's boldness in depicting sexual situations in the *Demons by Daylight* stories and other tales of the period is only one of the features that make this body of work dynamic and revolutionary. Its other features—allusiveness of narration; careful, at times even obsessive focusing on the fleeting sensations and psychological processes of characters; an aggressively modern setting that allows commentary on social, cultural, and political issues—all conjoin to make *Demons by Daylight* perhaps the most important book of weird fiction since Lovecraft's *The Outsider and Others* (1939).

It would certainly be an exaggeration to say that Campbell ushered in the modern horror movement single-handedly with this one volume. Campbell did indeed have a few significant predecessors who contributed to the updating of the genre. Stephen King has remarked in an interview that "my idea of what a horror story should do [is that] the monster shouldn't be in a graveyard in decadent old Europe, but in the house down the street,"[4] and

4. Tim Underwood and Chuck Miller (ed.), *Bare Bones: Conversations on Terror with Stephen King* (New York: Warner, 1988), 94.

goes on to mention Ray Bradbury, Shirley Jackson, and Richard Matheson as significant precursors in this regard. These authors are certainly noteworthy, but Bradbury's and Matheson's influence was largely restricted to the fantasy/science fiction field, while Jackson was considered a rather peculiar mainstream writer, and her work has had regrettably little impact on horror fiction. The systematic work of bringing the horror tale into the contemporary world was, then, accomplished by Campbell in *Demons by Daylight* and its successors.

Indeed, it might be said that a substantial number of Campbell's works utilise well-known topoi of the horror story (vampires, ghosts, hauntings, psychic possession, and the like) and endow them with surprising freshness by subtlety of execution and a clearly contemporary ambiance in setting and characterisation. Such works, which range from his earliest to his most recent writing, will be addressed in the next chapter.

IV. THE TRANSFORMATION OF SUPERNATURALISM

One of Campbell's greatest strengths is his ability to transform the conventional tropes of supernaturalism, lending them new vitality by allusiveness of approach, innovations in narration, and modernity of setting, tone, and character. While it would be unjustly limiting to Campbell to say that he has done nothing but revivify the themes and modes of a superannuated Gothicism, he has certainly supplied a surprising freshness to venerable motifs, especially in stories and novels of the late 1960s and 1970s. And yet, it might well be said that these works, while distinguished in themselves, are in fact merely the stepping-stones to the still more innovative works of the 1980s and 1990s.

One of the most recognisable features in horror fiction is the monster, whether it takes the form of a vampire, zombie, werewolf, witch, mummy, or some more eccentric creature. The monster can be non-human, super-human, or sub-human, and as such—beyond any mere threat to our species—it presents an intellectual challenge by its mere existence; for such an entity, obeying laws of

Nature very different from the ones we know, reveals an appalling deficiency in our conceptions of the universe. The monster, therefore, is of interest not so much in itself as in its symbolism; and beyond its overriding suggestion of the impenetrable mystery of the universe, it can serve as a metaphor for a variety of intellectual, social, political, and other concerns (the vampire as cultural outsider, for example) in accordance with the author's wishes.

Old-time Gothic fiction did not, curiously, employ monsters to any great degree, except the ghost; its chief motif was the haunted castle. Many of the most popular and common monsters are of comparatively recent vintage. The vampire received perhaps its earliest literary treatment in John William Polidori's "The Vampyre" (1819), and Bram Stoker's *Dracula* (1897) certainly raised the motif to canonical status, even if that novel itself is only intermittently effective. In reality, it was horror films that both canonised Stoker's novel and made the vampire a ubiquitous horrific icon. Witches certainly have appeared regularly in literature since Shakespeare's *Macbeth* (1606), but there has been a surprising dearth of truly distinctive treatments of them, with such notable exceptions as Fritz Leiber's science-fictional *Conjure Wife* (1953). As for the werewolf and zombie, they have to this day received no truly canonical treatment, although many worthwhile stories and films involving them have been produced. In spite of the familiarity of these standard monsters, then, the field was still open for someone like Campbell to make them anew.

One of the chief means by which Campbell achieves this effect is by modernity of setting. We have already seen that one of the earliest innovations in his Lovecraftian tales is their placement in Campbell's own time, rather than Lovecraft's. This is a dominant quality in the whole of his work; his treatment of modern urban life is so distinctive as to merit separate discussion. Here we can point to such a tale as "Night Beat" [1971], in which a policeman investigating a series of murders proves to be the murderer himself: he is transformed into a werewolf by the moon or (as he finds when he enters a museum) when he stands near anything from the moon, such as a lunar rock. The story is effective not only because it etches keenly the mundane dangers that have become so common in urban life—

He felt profoundly what his superiors wearily accepted: that violence surrounds us all. His first beat had led him through both suburbia and slums; and if each broken bottle outside a pub hinted terror to him, equally he felt the presence of violence in quiet suburban roads behind the ranks of sleeping cars, knew instinctively which set of patterned curtains concealed shouts of rage, the smash of china, screams.[1]

—but because the transformation of the policeman (which simultaneously transforms the tale from one of natural to supernatural horror) is saved till the final paragraph:

Sloane felt his mouth forced open from within. His skin ached as if a million needles were being forced through. But they were hairs; and his shoulders slumped as his hands weighed down his arms, formed into claws, and dragged him at last to stare down at the unconscious caretaker.[2]

Somewhat similar is "The Change" [1976], in which a man writing a book on lycanthropy in modern life sees signs of increasing savagery all around him; but he is unaware that he is himself gradually and insidiously becoming animalistic.

The *Doppelgänger* or "double" motif is frequently used by Campbell; some of the most interesting instances occur in several tales involving dolls, although I wish to study these elsewhere. A pure instantiation of the motif—distinctive because it is enmeshed

1. "Night Beat," *Haunt of Horror* 1, No. 1 (June 1973): 117.
2. "Night Beat," 120.

in an evocation of the gritty atmosphere of the city—is "The Scar" [1967], a rewriting of a crude early tale, "The Reshaping of Rossiter" [1964]. The setting is Brichester, but it is the Brichester that is virtually identical with Liverpool or, more generally, with any large city where members of differing social classes mingle. Lindsay Rice, the brother-in-law of Jack Rossiter, informs Jack of a man whom he saw on a bus who could be Jack's double except for a scar on the side of his face. Later Rossiter finds himself in a dark alley, and is then assaulted—slashed in the face—by a dimly seen man who identifies him by name. Jack survives, but as the weeks pass his demeanour is strangely changed; and his humour is not improved by the burgling of his jewellery shop (something that was predicted by his assaulter: "I'll be visiting your shop soon" [HS 8]). Jack becomes moody and mistreats his wife, Harriet: it is manifest that he has been replaced by his double. When Lindsay takes "Jack" to a ruined house from which he recently saw "Jack" emerging, they encounter the real Jack naked and bloody in the basement. Lindsay kills the impostor, but then finds looming in front of him another man—his own twin.

"The Scar" is a grimly atmospheric tale that is full of tart anticipations of the role-reversal ("That doesn't sound like you at all, Jack," Harriet says early on [HS 5]; later she says in apparent innocence as he is going to work, "Come back whole, darling" [HS 6]). But it also becomes clear that Jack is terrified of losing his social standing (while strolling through the lower-class section of Brichester he ponders that "it reassured him to think that here was a level to which he could never be reduced" [HS 7]), so that his replacement by his aggressively violent duplicate is just about the worst fate he can envisage.

Another means by which Campbell renovates an old topos is a novel narrative perspective. In the 1970s he wrote several tales utilising second-person singular narration, a rarely used form but one that was put to great effect in at least one classic horror tale, Thomas Burke's "Johnson Looked Back" (in his *Night-Pieces*

[1935]). Campbell perhaps overused the device, but he produced one memorable tale in "Heading Home" [1974]. In this story about how "you" are trying to recover from some apparently severe injury at the hands of a rival and are crawling up the basement stairs, the reader does not understand the true state of affairs until the very end: the "you" is merely the severed head of a scientist that is cumbersomely returning to its laboratory to wreak vengeance upon a man who is having an affair with his wife. The title, of course, becomes a pun, and indeed the whole tale mingles the comic and the horrific inextricably. "Conversion" [1974], however, strains credulity by its second-person narration: here we are asked to believe that a man who has become a vampire fails to remember his identity or his recent "conversion" to vampirism when he returns home.

"Jack's Little Friend" [1973] uses second-person narration to account supernaturally for the heinousness of Jack the Ripper's murders (as Robert Bloch did earlier in his memorable tale, "Yours Truly, Jack the Ripper" [1943]). A man in the present day finds a box with the dates of Jack the Ripper's murders carved on the lid but with nothing inside except, apparently, a thin coating of what looks like saliva. It is later suggested that some anomalous entity (the "little friend" of the title) may perhaps reside in that saliva and compel individuals to murder, as the protagonist finds to his cost.

"A New Life" [1976], although narrated in Campbell's habitual third-person singular, is nonetheless intensely focused on the dazed and confused central character, who proves to be Frankenstein's monster. The tale is only of interest in that it was probably inspired by Campbell's work on the novelisation of *The Bride of Frankenstein* [1976], written earlier in the same year. In both works Campbell is keen on emphasising the pathos of the monster's fate by viewing events from his perspective.

"Jack in the Box" [1974] returns to second-person narration and forces us to envisage ourselves as a vampire or zombie attempting

to escape the "box" or coffin in which we find ourselves. The
zombie theme is also found in "Rising Generation" [1974], but
the story—involving children who enter a cave and somehow turn
into zombies there—lacks plausibility. The whole topos is reduced
to parody in a later story, "Seeing the World" [1983], in which
it gradually becomes clear to the reader that a couple who have
returned from a vacation overseas have turned into a pair of zombies. The couple's neighbours discover how a boring evening of
seeing vacation slides slowly turns into something far worse:

> The next slide jerked into view, so shakily that for a moment
> Angela thought the street beyond the gap in the curtains
> had jerked. All three Hodges were on this slide, between two
> ranks of figures. "They're just like us really," Deirdre said,
> "when you get to know them." (AH 430)

Angela frantically wants to believe that the reference is to Italians,
but we understand that Deirdre is talking about zombies in the
catacombs.

Parody may be the object of an earlier story, "The Whining"
[1973], involving a very eccentric monster: the ghost of a dog. The
dog had, in life, proved especially pestiferous in its attentions to a
man, who had finally wounded and then killed it. Haunted by the
creature, the man wonders how on earth one is to get rid of such a
creature. "'You realize it's impossible to exorcise an animal? They
don't understand English, never mind Latin'" (HS 30).

Voodoo is the focus of several stories. "Missing" [1973] employs
a diary form to tell of a man who becomes involved with a strange
woman who may be the avatar of a voodoo murderess, while the
man himself appears to be the avatar of the woman's husband,
whom she murdered. The tale, however, is marred by an excessively oblique narration. "Dolls" [1974], as we have seen, is a fine
story involving voodoo. "It Helps If You Sing" [1987] uses voodoo
to probe the issue of religious fanaticism. A priest, angered by his

Haitian wife's return to her native religion, vows to use his enemies' methods to defeat them. As the protagonist, Bright, discovers, this involves the use of strange, sexless-looking fanatics who barge into people's houses and leave a cassette, presumably of their master's teaching. Bright pricks his finger on a piece of the cassette; and he later realises that it contains a drug that immobilises him while the fanatics re-enter and plan to castrate him, since they believe that "Neither men nor women shall we be in the world to come" (WN 242). The fear of sex, and of women ("Man was made to praise God, and so he did until woman tempted him in the garden" [WN 240]), so prevalent in evangelical religions is laid bare here.

Even beyond tone and setting, Campbell rarely features monsters in their conventional guises. Mercifully, the vampire—which has lately been the focus of such a prodigious array of hackneyed treatments that its symbolic function must surely be exhausted—appears in very few stories, including the peculiar, half-flippant "The Sunshine Club" [1969], about a vampire who seeks a remedy for his condition with a psychoanalyst. "Wrapped Up" [1974] is an entertaining but relatively predictable tale of a mummy's revenge. Witches appear in startling forms in a few of Campbell's works. Perhaps one of the most striking is "Baby" [1974], in which a derelict kills a harmless-seeming old woman but then finds himself pursued by whatever is inhabiting the perambulator she used to wheel about in life. This vivid modernisation of the legend of a witch and her familiar succeeds because, in our socially and economically polarised society, an old woman who seems nothing more than a bag lady pushing all her belongings about in a baby carriage can all too often strike us as something alien and nonhuman.

Campbell uses the standard ghost in relatively few stories, although, as we shall see in a later section, several memorable instances occur in his tales of hauntings. Here we can discuss "The Ferries" [1978], in which a man's uncle is continually fearful of something from the sea; one night he seems to drift away on a ghost-ship. Later, the man himself is haunted by the ship—and in the end he is found in his office, drowned. The imagery of the ghost-ship—

> It seemed to be the colour and the texture of the moon. Its sails looked stained patchily by mould. It was full of holes, all of which were misshapen by glistening vegetation. Were its decks crowded with figures? If so, he was grateful that he couldn't see their faces, for their movements made him think of drowned things lolling underwater, dragged back and forth by currents. (AH 314)

—seems to be a subtilisation of some of the imagery found in the classic tales of William Hope Hodgson, a master of sea horror who in "The Voice in the Night" (1907) exhibits loathsome funguslike creatures on board a ship.

Campbell's monsters can frequently be of highly peculiar nature, refusing to fit conventionally into any of the standard tropes evolved by old-time Gothicism. Consider "Midnight Hobo" [1978]. This story seems on the surface nothing more than an account of radio DJ, Roy, fascinated against his will by a derelict dwelling wretchedly under a bridge; and certainly the socioeconomic distinction between the two characters is clearly at the forefront. But why does the hobo never leave his lonely haven? Is it that he absorbs animate creatures who come into his range and takes on distorted versions of their shapes? And does this fate overtake Roy's rival Derrick? As with so much of Campbell, the gradualness and insidiousness of the supernatural incursion make this tale a masterwork.

The motif of psychic possession might perhaps be considered somewhat antiquated in the present day, for—at least to sophisticated readers—it inevitably suggests certain religious and philosophical conceptions (specifically the existence of an immaterial soul and its survival after death) that have now become

difficult to accept. The motif is, of course, capable of a psychological interpretation; and, indeed, a variety of psychological theories
have been put forward to account for old tales of demonic possession. In horror fiction, the idea gained new life with *The Exorcist*
(1971), in which William Peter Blatty, a devout Catholic, seriously
maintained that a little girl's aberrant behaviour could only be
explained in terms of possession by a devil. Later works have been
forced to be somewhat more oblique and less orthodox in their
presentations of psychic possession; and, of course, as stories from
Lovecraft's "The Thing on the Doorstep" (1933) to Anne Rice's
The Tale of the Body Thief (1992) attest, the conception is capable of
being expressed in an entirely secular mode. Three of Campbell's
novels involve psychic possession in varying degrees, although
none of them can be said to be among his strongest.

Set in present-day Liverpool, *The Doll Who Ate His Mother*—
Campbell's first novel, written in 1975 and published in 1976—is
a mixture of the supernatural with psychological suspense. Clare
Frayn, a schoolteacher, suffers a car accident when a strange-
looking man darts out in front of her car. She herself is not
seriously injured, but her brother is killed in a horrible manner:
his arm is severed by the abrupt closing of the car door after he
had attempted to get out of the car. Still worse, his arm vanishes—presumably stolen by the strange man. Shortly afterwards,
she encounters Edmund Hall, a writer of true crime books who
believes that the person responsible for the accident is a man he
has long been tracking—an old schoolmate of his named Christopher Kelly, who had exhibited cannibalistic and other loathsome
tendencies in school. Later George Pugh, a theatre owner, joins
them in the belief that the man who had killed his mother is the
same Christopher Kelly, while a street theatre performer named
Chris Barrow completes the quartet of informal detectives: he
believes Kelly had killed and partly eaten his cat.

The bulk of the novel is involved with the various characters'
attempts to locate Kelly. His mother is dead, and he was largely

raised by his grandmother, who scarcely relished the task. She herself had declared on one occasion, "You're a child of the Devil" (DM 85)—a remark that coincides with that of a neighbour, "He wasn't born human" (DM 83). Are these remarks to be interpreted literally? Campbell, in a flashback, presents Kelly's own ruminations on the matter: " . . . one night, he had realized there was no God . . . If there was no God, there could hardly be a Devil. But then he wasn't a child of the Devil. He wasn't a monster at all" (DM 86). To be sure, this may simply be Kelly's rationalisation for his hideous acts, but perhaps we are to detect a kernel of truth in it as well.

The point seems confirmed when the searchers track down a doctor who had known Kelly's mother. Although he had not delivered Kelly himself, he had delivered the baby of another woman who, like Kelly's mother, had become involved in a mysterious cult led by one John Strong. Strong had warned that if this woman did not turn her baby over to his control, he would cause the baby to be born "monstrous" (DM 106). This indeed seems to have happened, as the doctor relates chillingly: "It couldn't have lived . . . It was nearly two feet long" (DM 112). Kelly's mother, fearful that the same thing would happen to her, acquiesces and lets her baby come under the influence of Strong.

What, exactly, is Strong after? It is, regrettably, never made entirely clear. He has written a book, *Glimpses of Absolute Power*, which Clare reads in a library:

> I have undertaken this work late in life, for it was no part of my design. The truly great man confides his wisdom to a single pupil and companion, rather than publish it to the paws of the mass.
>
> But the truly great man is always at bay. Perhaps the mass may claim a petty victory in robbing me of my intended pupil; though it shall come to pass that my power rescinds that theft. Yet I shall set my knowledge down, in the certainty

that it speaks to none save him who will dare to test it. Perhaps, among the mass that fumble over these pages, one may
read who, glimpsing my way dimly, will set himself to follow.
(DM 147)

This passage—in which we are to infer that the "pupil" is meant
to be Kelly—suggests the influence of Lovecraft's *The Case of
Charles Dexter Ward*. In that novel, Joseph Curwen, a seventeenth-
century alchemist, needs to find a successor who will discover the
"essential saltes" of his remains and resurrect him so that he may
continue his demonic activities in the present day; and it happens
that Charles Dexter Ward, a shy and scholarly youth, proves to be
Curwen's unwitting successor. But whereas Curwen's purpose and
motives are relatively clear—he wishes to gather up the remains
of the dead so as to extract knowledge from them that might lead
to his rulership of the world and perhaps the universe—Strong's
motives are never at all clarified.

In any event, two-thirds of the way through the novel Campbell produces a startling revelation: Chris Barrow, the engaging
young man to whom Clare is more than a little attracted, is in fact
Christopher Kelly. To first-time readers of the novel, this revelation is shocking and effective. It might be thought, however, that
Campbell has telegraphed his punch and rendered the rest of the
novel an anticlimax. In fact, the reverse is the case: since none of
the characters knows Barrow's true identity, suspense is actually
enhanced when they continue to deal with him as an ally rather
than as their foe. The novel concludes with a tense scene in the
basement of the house John Strong occupied, in which Clare does
not learn until almost the last minute that her friend Chris is in
fact the perverted killer they have been pursuing.

The Doll Who Ate His Mother is clearly a first novel, and in some
senses almost a practice work. The development—especially for
one who has come from reading the best of Campbell's compact
short stories—is leisurely almost to the point of tedium, and the

rather flat, atmosphereless style (perhaps an attempt to render
the work more commercially marketable) is a disappointment
to those who relish the hallucinatory prose of Campbell's short
stories. It can also be wondered whether the supernatural component of the novel is well integrated into the work, or is even
necessary. Christopher Kelly's dreary upbringing might be sufficient in itself to have turned him into the monster he has become
as an adult; and the supernatural motif—Kelly's coming under
the "control" of John Strong—renders him in a sense morally
blameless, since his derelictions could be interpreted as merely
the result of Strong's manipulation. And yet, *The Doll Who Ate His
Mother* is an able piece of work, and far superior to the hundreds
of routine supernatural thrillers that have followed it; only when
judged by the rest of Campbell's own novelistic work does it fall
short.

Much better is *The Parasite* (titled *To Wake the Dead* in England),
written in 1977–78 and published in 1980. Campbell has admitted
that this novel was written explicitly with market considerations in
mind: "I tried to do what appeared to be the perceived model of
the contemporary horror story, which is characters in an ordinary
environment and something out there is attempting to get them
for whatever reason."[3] Campbell himself, as a result, feels that the
novel is quite unsuccessful; but although it is by no means a distinctively original work, it is also far from contemptible.

The Parasite opens with a harrowing prologue in which an
unnamed ten-year-old girl participates somewhat unwillingly in a
séance with some older children at a deserted house in which a Mr
Allen had died. The little girl is accidentally locked into a room
alone, and before she can be rescued something grabs her from
behind: "They must be hands, for they had fingers, though they
felt soft as putty—far softer than putty, indeed, to be able to do to
her what they began to do then" (P 10).

---

3. Jones, "*Weird Tales* Talks with Ramsey Campbell," 49.

As the novel moves to the present day, it becomes clear that Rose Tierney—who lives in Liverpool and writes popular books on film with her husband Bill—is the girl who had suffered the strange experience in the deserted house. Although traumatised in youth by it, she seems to have recovered well enough. On a trip to New York, however, she is mugged and, shortly thereafter, has the first of several out-of-body experiences that severely unnerve her. In one such experience—another séance conducted by her Liverpool neighbours, Colin Hay and his mother, Gladys—she seems to be drifting uncorporeally to a house where a group of people are involved in some occult gathering; perhaps, indeed, they themselves had somehow summoned her spirit.

Things come to a head in Munich, where Rose is finally cornered by a bald-headed man whom she thinks she has seen dimly on several occasions. He seems, incredibly, to know of her childhood experience in the deserted house, and in fact says to her that she was "infected" (P 96) at that time; but she exercises some sort of power that drives him away before he can tell her some further revelation about herself.

Meanwhile a woman named Diana, whom Rose had come to know in New York and who is interested in the occult, tells her increasingly bizarre stories about the nature of out-of-body experiences. In particular, Rose learns that Peter Grace—a vaguely evil figure who lived in the early decades of the century and who is the subject of book called *Astral Rape*—believed that he could attain immortality by transferring his spirit into another body, perhaps that of a baby. Adolf Hitler, who was interested in the notion of reincarnation and had apparently had out-of-body experiences himself, was intrigued by Grace; and there are dim suggestions that Hitler somehow survived the death of his body in 1945 by the method Grace had outlined. Grace himself was apparently killed by disgruntled ex-followers who sensed the danger of his plan of action.

Rose scarcely knows what to make of all this, but then she

receives a pamphlet on astral projection and, somewhat unwisely, goes to the Manchester address whence it originated. There she is confronted again by the bald man and others—perhaps the same ones who may have summoned her spirit months before. Again she escapes by exercising some inner power:

> Just let her intuition take over, believe that it could do so, just let it move one muscle and the rest would follow, before the gray things emerged, dropping their bodies like discarded clothing, and dragged her out into their midst—just let a cry reach her throat, a cry of outrage that would give her strength, just let her mouth suck air into her lungs, let her throat which was drowning in saliva form the sound, let her cry out, oh please—
> But when the cry came, it was not from Rose. (P 164)

At long last, Rose's parents—encouraged by her husband Bill, whose relations with Rose have been steadily deteriorating as a result of her occult experiences and his disbelief in them—tell her about the childhood incident, which she had almost entirely repressed. And when Rose learns that the house where the incident had occurred is a place Peter Grace had known, she fears the worst. Is she herself merely the carrier of some supernatural parasite—the spirit of Peter Grace?

> She felt the presence which was watching over her come clear. It was only one. It was neither of her relatives, but she knew it all too well. It was old and sly and utterly ruthless, and had deceived her effortlessly . . .
> But its physical form, whatever that might be, was no longer trapped in the walls. The séance had set it free. She had touched it through the dusty sheets of the bed, a thin flabby limb. Perhaps her touch had awakened it fully, for it had got out of the bed. (P 231)

Events now rapidly reach a climax. Rose is again attacked by the bald-headed man, who turns out to be Hugh Willis, the author of *Astral Rape*. He seems to know that Peter Grace's spirit is lodged within Rose's body and he wants to destroy both it and her. But she is saved by her husband Bill. Shortly thereafter, however, Colin and Gladys Hay kidnap her: they are in fact part of a sect that wishes the return of Grace. Willis tracks them down, but he is captured by the sect. Suddenly Rose feels tremendous pain and then a sense of utter deflation: the spirit of Grace has left her and apparently entered Willis's body. Then Bill bursts in and, in an attempt to rescue Rose, kills Willis. To her horror, it seems as if Grace's spirit has entered Bill. Shortly thereafter some cosmic presence enters the place and seems to bear off Grace's spirit, apparently resolving the matter happily.

But perhaps some traces of Grace have remained. About a year later Colin Hay, who was thought to have died in a car accident while escaping from the police but has clearly survived, confronts Rose as she is about to give birth to a child. He tells her: "Nobody Grace touches is ever free of him . . . You least of all." The implication is clear: Grace has entered the body of her unborn child. She believes she has only one course of action: she drowns herself in the river.

The Parasite is, to be sure, not a masterwork of the weird; but it is much more than a routine shilling-shocker. In spite of its flamboyance, especially at the conclusion, its rather hackneyed incorporation of occultist elements, and the implausible nod to Hitler (whose atrocities were all too humanly generated), *The Parasite* is a compelling read for its vivid characters and its smooth-flowing prose. Precisely because it is told entirely from the point of view of Rose Tierney (a narrative feature Campbell believes limits the novel's effectiveness), she becomes the intense focus of the reader's interest; her pursuit by a variety of shadowy figures whose intentions remain unclear almost to the very end produces a keen suspense that powers the novel to its cataclysmic conclusion. Also noteworthy is Campbell's careful etching of the slow estrangement of Rose and her husband Bill, who is appalled at what he believes to be her credulousness in the occult and who acts with manifest sincerity but a clumsy lack of sympathy in attempting to rid her of her supposed delusions. When even her parents seem to take Bill's side in the issue, and Colin and Gladys prove to be enemies rather than friends, Rose seems appallingly alone in having to deal with a very real supernatural threat.

The Influence (1988) is the third of Campbell's novels to involve some sort of psychic possession, and indeed it features it in its purest form, as an old woman dies but is so tenacious of life that her spirit persists and occupies the body of her own grand-niece. But I wish to study this novel elsewhere, since its supernatural premise is relatively conventional but its treatment of childhood poignant and evocative.

The theme of supernatural revenge is an age-old one in horror fiction and has remained popular up to the present day. The reason for this ubiquity is not difficult to find: it satisfies a rather naive moral prejudice that, in spite of all evidence to the contrary, good will triumph and evil will get its just deserts. The corpse that returns from the dead to avenge its murder; the ghost that haunts some morally culpable individual—these and similar tropes have been utilised over and over in the literature of terror, and much of the work of such popular writers as Stephen King and Clive Barker continues to cling to this hoary moral fantasy. Campbell has, fortunately, rarely used the theme in a straightforward way, since he is far too aware of the triumph of evil in the real world— or, rather, that good and evil are merely fruits of perspective and are found in inextricable combination in any given individual or society.

"Dead Letters" [1974] is a clever story in which a pair of couples who play with a kind of ouija board find that, apparently of its own accord, it suggests that someone has been or is being murdered by slow doses of poison; only then does the narrator realise why his friend Bob, who has been drinking heavily, looks "white and sweating as if from a death battle with the Pernod" (TD 219) and the significance of the fact that his wife Louise is a nurse. "Only the Wind" [1974] tells the chilling tale of wind that seeks revenge upon a builder of shoddy houses.

I have no idea whether "In the Trees" [1983] should be studied here; but it is such a bizarre tale that I cannot forbear to comment on it. This harrowing story of a man who finds himself lost in a forest whose trees have been shaped in the form of carved, quasi-human figures suggests, on the whole, a dichotomy between Nature and civilisation, specifically the hostility of Nature to mankind (the man in question is a book salesman, and perhaps the trees sense, as he himself does—"his vanload of books, pulped wood on the way to be pulped again" [WN 66]—that much of his product is rubbish) and the feebleness of our "domination" of Nature. The tale, however, is not capable of easy explication, and several points remain nebulous (are the carved figures made by human beings at all, or did they in fact grow in that way?); but the atmosphere of strangeness is unexcelled:

Twigs scraped his skin, the touch of dank leaves on his face made him shiver. Twigs hindered him as he gasped and struggled backward out of the thicket, which felt all at once like a trap. He hadn't seen the body of the figure, only its face grinning at him, the eyes bulging like sap. He hadn't time before he recoiled to be sure, and couldn't make himself go back to determine, that the carved face bore a distorted, almost mocking resemblance to his own. (WN 74)

Allied to the notion of supernatural revenge, and perhaps an offshoot of it, is the venerable idea of magic wishes. In horror fiction this trope has been embodied in W. W. Jacobs's very well-known

and still effective "The Monkey's Paw," but its overtones of fable
have nearly banished it from adult horror fiction altogether.
Campbell has used it in at least one story—"Old Clothes" [1983],
about an impoverished man who finds an old raincoat in a dead
spiritualist's house and, when he reaches into its pockets, finds
coins, diamonds, and other valuables, although later he begins
to discover such unnerving objects as items his dead parents had
worn—and in one novel, *Obsession*, written in 1983–84 and published in 1985.

Obsession begins in 1958, when the teenager Peter Priest, living
in the small coastal town of Seaward, receives a strange package
from an anonymous source in London announcing simply: "whatever you most need I do" (O 26). He responds both for himself and
for three of his friends—Jimmy Waters, Steve Innes, and Robin
Laurel—who all face a variety of adolescent troubles, mostly concerning their families. In reply, Peter receives a simple form to be
filled in and with a seemingly innocent "price" to be paid for what
each of them most needs: "The price . . . is something that you
do not value and which you may regain" (O 33). Although all the
young friends are sceptical of the ploy, they nevertheless fill in the
forms—but before they can be mailed, the forms fly off into the
sea. There the matter seemingly ends.

Very shortly, however, it becomes clear that the eventuality
each youth wished for is being realised: a co-worker who had been
harassing Robin's mother is seriously injured by a car and leaves
the town; Jimmy's father, an inveterate and unsuccessful gambler,
wins the football pools; Steve's nemesis, a schoolteacher named
Gillespie, suffers a stroke. All this makes Peter wonder fearfully
whether the thing he most needs—that his grandmother, who has
moved in with his family and is creating severe tension with her
domineering ways, be put "out of the way"—will transpire, and
how. He is momentarily relieved when his grandmother decides
to leave and reside with a friend, but he is so anxious that no harm
come to her prior to her departure that he causes her to become

jittery and fall down the stairs. She dies, and Peter is overwhelmed with guilt.

Twenty-five years pass, and we now see what appears to be the fruition of the wishes. Robin, now a doctor, faces her increasingly neurotic mother, who gradually becomes convinced that her daughter is dealing in illegal drugs; Steve, although in youth a communist, has taken over his family's real estate business but is losing out to a competing agency; Jimmy, now a policeman, is devastated when his wife Tanya suffers a serious injury in an abandoned theatre (a property managed by Steve's agency) and eventually dies, leaving Jimmy a widowed father of two small children; and Peter, a social worker, faces increasing pressure in his job, especially with regard to a man, Roger Marvle, who is fanatically overprotective of his sister Hilda. All these events make Peter wonder whether the "prices" that the old wishes had exacted are now being collected: Robin, as a child without a father, had previously been heedless of her reputation, and now she herself is losing her reputation as a good doctor; Steve, who had not cared for private property, is losing many of his properties; Jimmy had not liked girls as a boy, and now he has lost his wife; and Peter, who had tried to mask his timidity by a bluff exterior, is now being forced to face up to the manifold fears and worries in his life, in addition to the gnawing guilt he still feels at causing the death of his grandmother. Peter now begins seeing the ghost of his grandmother, who ominously warns him: "You'll pay . . . just as your friends are paying" (O 89). What is worse, it appears that others see her also. Later he even sees the ghost of Roger, whom he had quite consciously killed when Roger began harassing him and Hilda more and more relentlessly.

All that Peter can do is to hope that the "price" that is being exacted will somehow be regained, as the old form had declared. But, as he finds things becoming worse and worse for himself and his friends, he comes to believe that this was a lie and a deception:

It had taken him in. It must have, for killing Roger to have seemed any kind of a solution, let alone for Peter to have done so. He ought to have known that a power which could kill his grandmother when all he'd ask for had been for her to be out of the way, could offer nothing except suffering and temptations that led to greater suffering. He could almost sense its feeding on his distress, though he had no idea of its form or where it was. (O 175–76)

Peter becomes obsessed with finding the address—a London post office box—whence the form had originated, and believes Jimmy to have this information, although Jimmy himself, scarcely thinking the twenty-five-year-old matter worth bothering about, cannot take the trouble to look for it. Peter then conceives a wild plan to kidnap Jimmy's children so as somehow to force Jimmy to look for the address, but things go very wrong: although he fabricates the existence of two men who had supposedly kidnapped the children, he realises that the crime will in fact be pinned on him, and in despair he kills himself.

Before this happens, however, things seem to have worked out rather providentially for his friends. Robin, distraught over the increasingly erratic behaviour of her mother, nearly kills herself with an overdose of sleeping pills; while she is in hospital, her mother herself breaks down and, after a hospital stay, finally realises the need to be placed in a rest home. When Steve attempts to calm Robin's mother at her office, he finds a critical piece of information among her files: Gillespie, the old teacher on whom Steve had wished harm, had had his stroke two days before Steve had made his wish. Clearly Steve had had no involvement with Gillespie's malady, and the wishes had meant nothing. This fact is confirmed when the old address in London is found to be a non-existent post office box.

The novel at this point seems to have collapsed into a purely non-supernatural story of guilt (the title reflects Peter's obsession with the wishes and his frantic effort to escape their apparent influence); but Campbell leaves in a few tantalising elements of the inexplicable. We have noted that several individuals aside from Peter have apparently seen the ghost of Peter's grandmother. What is more, Tanya had wandered into the abandoned theatre because she thought she had heard a child's voice there; and one of her children nearly comes to harm when he almost jumps overboard from a boat because he heard his name being called from the water. In the end, these touches of supernaturalism are merely a kind of escape-hatch to keep the novel within the realm of the outré; in other respects, *Obsession* is the closest Campbell had come up to this point to writing a purely mainstream novel.

Although far lesser in scope than its predecessor, *Incarnate*, *Obsession* nevertheless is distinguished by its crisp and vivid characterisation and its skilful blending of the diverse narratives of four very different individuals. This latter point may well have been derived from Campbell's similar success in maintaining a multitude of narrative threads in *Incarnate*, and the result here is just as successful on this smaller canvas. In particular, Campbell's depiction of Jimmy and Tanya's innocent and engaging children, Francesca and Russell—who seem clear reflections of his own children, who were about the same age at the time—makes them virtually the leading protagonists of the latter part of the novel, at least in terms of the reader's sympathy. It is scarcely to be denied, moreover, that Campbell's searing depiction of Robin's increasingly demented mother—and of Robin's own increasing despair at finding any solution to the problem—is yet another reflection of Campbell's own mother.

The deflation of the supernatural in *Obsession*, at least as regards the matter of the wishes, does not lead to disappointment, for this elimination of a supernatural "out" for the various characters' problems only underscores the point the novel has been making all along: that guilt can be as harrowing a pursuer as any vengeful ghost. Peter, in large part the focus of the novel, exemplifies this point. The anguish he feels at seeming to cause the death of his grandmother is reflected in (apparently genuine) spectral manifestations on her part. Her first emergence is chilling, and later, when Peter thinks he has banished her by taking charge of his own life, her sudden reappearance is still more so:

> Perhaps she was one of his cases; her grasp felt urgent enough. The sun was in his eyes, and at first he couldn't see her face clearly, had time to tell himself that he was mistaking what he thought he saw. He lowered his head, his scalp burning under the toupee, and saw how dusty her eyes were now. Perhaps there was nothing but lumps of dust in the sockets.
>   He was shuddering so violently that he couldn't even pull free of the tattered grasp on his arm when she opened her crawling mouth. "You can't get rid of me that easily," she said in a voice that came and went like the wind. "It's only just begun." (O 154)

It is hardly to be wondered that, after seeing such a spectacle, he resorts to the desperate expedient of kidnapping his friend's children in the wild hope of putting an end to his victimisation.

The haunted house or castle is, as mentioned previously, perhaps the oldest trope in Gothic fiction. Although the haunted house frequently lodges supernatural entities (specifically the ghost), the question focuses not so much on the nature of these entities as on the causes for their existence in such a locale. Is it a murder or other heinous act committed on the spot that compels a lost soul to haunt its former residence? The Gothic castle, with its abundance of secret passageways and unused halls, provided a ready-made locus for the spectral; in modern horror fiction, the haunted house must be presented far more subtly and more in accordance with present-day realities.

One of Campbell's earliest triumphs, following his Lovecraftian period, is "Napier Court" [1967]. A young woman named Alma Napier learns that the house she occupies was once owned by an eccentric man who rarely stirred from the place and later committed suicide, expressing the odd wish to "fade into the house, the one possession left to me" (DC 21). As time passes, Alma is increasingly aware of a presence in the house, until it finally manifests itself:

When the figure formed deep in the mirror she knew that all was over. She faced it, drained of feeling. It grew closer, arms stretched out, its face inflated gray by gas. Alma wept; it was horrid. She knew who it was; a shaft of truth had pierced the suffocating warmth of her delirium. The suicide had possessed the house, was the house; he had waited for someone like her. "Go on," she sobbed at him, "take me!" The bloated cheeks moved in a swollen grin; the arms stretched out for her and vanished. (DC 31)

Alma herself is incorporated into the house.

But the key to the story is that phrase, "someone like her": for this story is in fact a psychological portrait of Alma, and it sets out to show why she had to meet the fate she did. Her weakness of will (early in the tale it is remarked that her mother's overprotectiveness "threatened to erase her completely" [DC 18]); her longing for a man like her ex-lover Peter (whom her parents had forbidden her to see) to lend meaning and substance to her life; her fruitless attempts to find solace in books and music—all these things make it clear that she was just the sort of victim the house was looking for. "Napier Court" is a superb example of how the portrayal of character can be enhanced by the use of the supernatural.

Few of Campbell's other "haunted house" tales are as powerful, although many are quite successful in their more limited scope: "Ash" [1969], in which a house is afflicted with an anomalous quantity of ash, emerging supernaturally from the remains of a woman murdered in the place and burnt in the furnace; "Cat and Mouse" [1971], a story that, although superficially about a house haunted by the ghosts of cats, also becomes (like "The Previous Tenant") an account of tensions between husband and wife; "The Proxy" [1977], a striking tale about the ghost of a house; "Drawing In" [1977], a combination of the haunted house and vampire motifs; "Down There" [1978], about the hideous things that haunt the basement of a building where a madman had stored an immense quantity of food; and "Second Sight" [1985], in which an elderly man's new flat is haunted by presences from the trauma of the war years.

The House on Nazareth Hill—written in 1994–96 and published in 1996—might seem on the surface merely an artfully executed haunted house novel, but it proves to be much more. This work is indeed a triumphant return to the supernaturalism that had seemed to be becoming increasingly rare and attenuated in Campbell's recent novels, but it is also as searing a portrayal of domestic tension as any in his entire body of work.

The novel opens with a prefatory chapter in which Oswald and Heather Priestley and their eight-year-old daughter Amy walk by a house on a hill named Nazarill (short for Nazareth Hill), overlooking the small town of Partington in northern England, near Sheffield. The place was built centuries ago but, after serving as offices in the nineteenth century, is now a deserted ruin. Amy has long been fascinated and vaguely terrified by the site, referring to it as "the spider house." Oswald, in a clumsy attempt to rid her of her fears, boldly takes her to a ground-floor window of the house and, placing her on his shoulders, urges her to look inside; but she becomes frightened at some obscure entity she seems to see in the place, and in the ensuing confusion she actually tumbles into the room. She is pulled out hastily and brought home, where eventually she calms down. But that night she has a nightmare in which her father says to her grimly, "Your mother's dead, and you're mad; and you're staying here in Nazarill" (HNH 25).

As the novel proper opens, Amy is nearly sixteen. She seems in many ways a typical teenager—playing loud heavy-metal music, wearing an array of metal ornaments in various pierced parts of her body, and having a boyfriend, Rob Hayward—but we quickly learn that her mother had died years before in an automobile accident, and that she and her father have actually moved into Nazarill, which has been refurbished and rented out as flats. Amy and Oswald also have what appear to be no more than the disagreements to be expected of a somewhat rebellious teenage daughter and her ageing father.

Things seem placid enough until one day the cat of a fellow tenant of Nazarill, Teresa Blake, is found hanged on an ancient oak tree in the yard. Later Oswald seems to see spiders lurking in the corners of his own flat. Another tenant, a photographer named Dominic Metcalf, takes a group shot of the occupants of Nazarill in the yard; but, when he develops the picture, he finds that a strange face has appeared in the photograph, looking out of the window of his own flat. Shortly thereafter he is killed by some hideous skeletonic creature.

Amy, meanwhile, is increasingly obsessed with the history of Nazarill (especially in what it may have been before it was a set of offices) and also increasingly troubled by what she takes to be her father's overprotective and dictatorial behaviour, almost as if he were her jailor. Shortly after Christmas, Amy finds a Bible that had been somehow trapped in the huge oak tree outside the house that had recently been cut down. It appears that someone has used it as a diary, writing in a crabbed handwriting in the margins of the pages. Amy then learns more things about Nazarill. It was apparently a hospital of some sort centuries ago, and there is also a rumour that the Partington witches—assuming they existed at all—used to dance upon the hill before Nazarill was built. Oswald, attempting to put an end to what he believes to be Amy's delusions, resolutely takes her through the now entirely unoccupied ground-floor flats of Nazarill to convince her that there is nothing there. But as she is in the Roscommons' old flat she sees a skeleton figure in a windowless room. Her father, however, does not see the figure and, as he is about to turn on the light, the creature shatters the light bulb and flees through a door "where no door should be" (HNH, 204) to the adjoining flat. Returning the keys to the housing agent, Oswald asks whether there is in fact anything odd about the history of the place. The agent grudgingly mentions that Nazarill was a mental hospital in the seventeenth and eighteenth centuries and that it had been gutted by a fire that had killed all the inmates and the staff.

Amy has in the interim virtually come to this conclusion herself through her reading of the diary in the Bible, which is clearly the work of a female inmate in the erstwhile asylum. The diary tells of the horrible maltreatment of the occupants by the staff, but also suggests that the asylum housed the very witches who were said to have practised their rites on the spot. Meanwhile Oswald has discovered the diary and thinks that Amy herself has made the marginal notes. During a confrontation between Amy and Oswald, Rob regretfully confesses that he also believes the diary to be in Amy's handwriting, since it tallies with the latter portions of a transcript she had made in a notebook. Baffled and enraged, Amy breaks off relations with Rob.

Relations between Amy and Oswald deteriorate rapidly. Left alone, Amy looks out of the peephole of her flat and thinks she sees some loathsome creature outside. She feels she must leave Nazarill at once. As her father leaves for work, she creeps downstairs, but finds all six doors of the ground-floor flats slightly ajar. A bony hand emerges out of one door; worse, the entity actually speaks to Amy. As she mutters to herself, "I never wanted to live here in the first place," the other replies: "None of us did" (HNH 286). Then the creature reveals itself:

The grey wispy coating of the skull was certainly not hair. The figure still had some of a face, or had somehow reconstructed parts of one, which looked in danger of coming away from the bones, as the scraps of the chest were peeling away from the ribs to expose the withered heart and lungs, which jerked as though in a final spasm as Amy's gaze lit on them. (HNH 287)

Could this be one of the witches interned in the asylum? Then a smaller creature (the witch's familiar?) emerges and chases Amy back to her own apartinent; but she cannot find her key, since Oswald had taken it from her bag. As she is hacking at the lock with a metal comb, Oswald returns in rage and hurls her into the flat. The other figures have disappeared.

As if the supernatural incident which Amy has just experienced—one of the most terrifying moments in the whole of Campbell's work—is not enough, a perhaps even more wrenching domestic conflict follows. Oswald threatens Amy, and she locks herself into the bathroom and takes the cordless phone with her. She tries to leave a message for Rob, but Rob's mother answers and brusquely declares that Amy is mentally disturbed and should seek medical help. At this point Oswald rips the phone housing from the wall. The confrontation continues and, exactly as in her dream, Oswald says to Amy, "You're mad, and you're staying here in Nazaril" (HNH 302); then he punches her full in the face, knocking her out.

Amy comes to and finds herself locked in her room, as Oswald has fitted a bolt on the door. Amy attempts to unscrew the hinges with her metal comb, but only manages to loosen a few screws before the comb breaks. Then she looks in her mirror: instead of seeing the reflection of her own room, she sees a brick-lined cell with a dim figure lurking in it. Meanwhile, some strange transformation has been overtaking Oswald. During his confrontation with Amy he had used the word "wronghead"—a word found in the Bible diary. He also seems to be unaware how to use the intercom in answering the doorbell. Throughout the rest of the novel he continues to speak with antiquated diction: has he been possessed by the spirit of Nazarill, specifically its brutal hospital staff?

Oswald, in his continuing attempts to subdue Amy, shuts off all the electricity in the flat. In the darkness Amy again thinks she sees figures in the mirror; then, when she touches the wall of her room, she feels moist brick rather than plaster. At this point Amy feels she has no other weapon than to terrify Oswald into letting her out. She talks constantly of the spiders that might come down upon him, saying that he can only escape them by letting her out and fleeing the place. In rage and fear Oswald bursts into her room and, in what must be one of the most vicious incidents in the entirety of Campbell's work, cuts out his own daughter's tongue.

This is, however, not the end but only the beginning of the horror for Oswald. He falls asleep, but his dreams are obsessed with spiders. Waking up, he sees spiders everywhere in his flat. He opens the window and calls for help, but no one is there. He sets fire to the old Bible and torches a spider that had woven a web over the latch of the front door. Entering the hall, Oswald is petrified to see the entire corridor lined with spiders. An explosion in the kitchen fells him. The gas oven has gone up in flames, and fire lands on his arms, then races over his entire body. In a last fit of remorse he attempts to free his daughter, still locked in her room and having fainted from loss of blood, but he cannot reach the door before the fire consumes him.

Meanwhile Amy wakes. Emerging from her room, whose door has fallen to ashes, she finds Nazarill a gutted ruin. In an atmosphere that becomes progressively dreamlike she is led down to apparent safety by a strange creature; but she realises that she no longer feels her footsteps as she is descending the stairs. She meets with some misty figures on the lawn who take her hand and ascend to the crown of the hill. The final chapter informs us of the truth: Amy and Oswald perished in the fire, and it is her spirit that has joined those of the Partington witches.

The House on Nazareth Hill, one of the longest of Campbell's novels, will certainly not be long in taking rank as one of the finest haunted house novels in literature, rivalling even Shirley Jackson's masterful *The Haunting of Hill House* (1959). Readers will welcome it as a return to supernaturalism, which was absent in some of Campbell's recent novels, such as *The Count of Eleven* (1991) and *The One Safe Place* (1995); but more than that, it is an adept fusion of the intense supernaturalism that we find in his short stories with the wrenching domestic conflict we have seen in his later novels, along with the gripping depiction of paranoia (in the figure of Oswald, who becomes a crazed religious maniac in the latter stages of the work) found in such an early novel as *The Face That Must Die.* In essence, *The House on Nazareth Hill* is a summation of the best of Campbell's many-faceted work.

Campbell provides no explicit account of the supernatural phenomena in the novel, and the solution must be inferred from various hints scattered throughout the work. Specifically, an old song found in a book that Amy's mother had given to her as a child—a song that Amy uses to terrify Oswald at the end—speaks of a madwoman named Mother Hepzibah who declares:

We'll dance through the fire, we'll dance into the sky.
The power of the hill means none of us shall die . . .

(HNH 351)

The hill, then, contains some occult force that allows the spirits of the witches to perpetuate a half-material existence to the present day. There is still less explanation for the change that overtakes Oswald; and we must assume that the spirits of the asylum staff— who, in their vicious treatment of their charges, may have been as mad as the inmates—overwhelm him and cause his maniacal behaviour.

The inevitable question that the student of Campbell's work must raise is the degree to which the novel is autobiographical. At the time of the novel's writing, Campbell's own daughter, Tamsin, was exactly Amy's age, while Oswald appears to be in that period of middle age in which Campbell found himself. Speculation on the point is of course useless in the absence of evidence, and the likeliest theory is that Campbell used his imagination to exaggerate what might be the customary disputes between teenagers and their parents—loud music, body piercing, personal untidiness—into a Grand Guignol of supernatural and domestic horror. It is, certainly, of interest that the narrative urges the reader to sympathise largely with Amy rather than with Oswald, who is depicted—even before his supernatural transformation—as a somewhat overprotective parent. Oswald, however, is not lacking in sympathy himself at the beginning, since his plight in raising a headstrong teenage girl in the absence of his beloved wife is an affecting one. And yet, one wonders how we are to interpret Amy's perception of her father at one point:

> She gazed at him . . . and saw a furtively anxious old man in an out-of-date grey overcoat and black scarf. His face seemed to have devoted its recent years to producing more of itself, its lower cheeks bellying on either side of the jaw and pulling down the corners of the mouth, while the underside of the chin had settled for adding itself to the throat. His eyebrows had always been prominent, but their greyness made them appear heavier, and to be weighing down his eyes. (HNH 171–72)

However much this may or may not tally with Campbell's own impression of himself, it emphasises a point that many of Campbell's novels have made: the difficulty of dealing with change, specifically change of character. Oswald's change in outward appearance from the vibrancy of young manhood is later echoed by a psychological transformation that makes Amy feel that the father she once knew is no longer even present, but has been replaced by some hideous gorgon whom she refuses to recognise or acknowledge.

For such a lengthy novel, *The House on Nazareth Hill* is remarkable for having, basically, only two central characters, Amy and Oswald. Even Rob Hayward, although significant to the evolution of the plot, remains a minor figure. The alternations in narrative focus come at critical junctures: the death of Dominic Metcalf is seen through his own eyes, as are the encounters of Hilda Ramsden and Donna Goudge with the ghostly entities. These scenes allow the reader to be fully aware of the supernatural nature of the phenomena, and also bring further sympathy to Amy, whose own glimpses of the weird are seen to be unmistakably genuine and whose frantic attempts to convince sceptics like Rob and her own father of their reality only lead to her demise. The alternations of narrative perspective between Amy and Oswald in the latter stages of the novel are also psychologically telling, in that they clearly delineate both her own fears (of the creatures hovering around her as well as of her demented father) and Oswald's crazed rationalisations of his abuse of his daughter.

The House on Nazareth Hill testifies that Ramsey Campbell was at the peak of his form in his fourth decade of writing. With this novel he unified the many themes of his earlier work—pure supernaturalism, exploration of social and domestic trauma, chilling portrayal of psychosis—in a seamless fusion. The work certainly infuses new life into the most venerable motif of weird fiction—the haunted castle—but is by no means merely an exercise in antiquarianism, as its searing displays of social and family conflict attest. *The House on Nazareth Hill* shows that readers can look with confidence to Campbell's continuing innovations in the multifaceted modes of horror fiction.

The Overnight (2004) is a slight variant of the haunted house motif; it is also a perfect embodiment of the adage "Write what you know." In the spring of 2000, as he announces in a brief preface to the novel, Campbell began working fulltime at a Borders bookstore in Cheshire Oaks. I am sure I was not the only one to be astounded and dismayed when I heard at the time that the leading horror writer of our generation felt the need to take on this work to help support himself and his family; one thinks of Lovecraft toiling away at poorly paying revision work (and even, on one occasion, securing temporary employment as a ticket-taker at a movie theatre) to make ends meet, or Machen grinding out reams of vapid journalism before he received his Civil List pension. Even though Campbell's bookstore stint lasted only a few months, it seemed to reflect badly on a number of facets of contemporary society—the state of horror publishing, especially in the UK (Campbell no longer has a major commercial publisher to issue his works in his native land); the inequities of a capitalist system that consistently fails to reward excellence but only rewards popular appeal—even though it reflected supremely well on Campbell himself in his willingness to make sacrifices for his art and his family. We should therefore not be surprised that, in a few years' time, Campbell transmuted his reasonably pleasant descent into wage-slavery in the crucible of his imagination, the result being *The Overnight*, a supernatural novel that ranks high among the achievements of his long and varied career.

We here encounter—in a present-tense narration that Campbell has used relatively infrequently for long works, most notably in the novella *Needing Ghosts* (1990)—a succession of workers at a bookstore, Texts, in a small shopping plaza (Campbell calls it a "retail park") in the Manchester/Liverpool area. A setting less promising for the incursion of the superatural would seem difficult to imagine, but Campbell manages it through shifting narrative perspectives—each chapter is seen through the eyes of a different bookstore worker—and the extraordinarily subtle accumulation of bizarre details.

Texts is run by an American named Woody, whose attempts at introducing a kind of brash, cheerful efficiency are not well received by his largely British staff of young professionals. Inter-personal tensions also add their weight of unease to the narrative: one employee has just left his partner (a fellow employee) and taken up with another coworker; another employee named Agnes (she pronounces it Anyes) is harried by overprotective parents; another, a gay man named Jake, is predictably harassed by an intolerant bigot named Greg. But these emotional complications are only the unnerving backdrop to increasingly harrowing supernatural manifestations that eventually become too plain to be ignored. A constant and ever-thickening fog seems to hover around the retail park; computers develop minds of their own, failing to correct typographical errors even after repeated proofreading; elevators malfunction; books continually seem to get misshelved; and, most disturbing of all, small grey animate objects are half glimpsed skulking around shelves, in the stockroom, or in the workers' staffroom. What could be the cause of these manifestations?

It is here that *The Overnight* might perhaps be criticised for excessive reticence. Campbell does not wish to spell out the matter in an obvious way, but the hints that are sprinkled throughout the narrative—hints based upon the sinister history of the region as a focal point of violence and death for centuries or millennia—seem just a trifle too vague and imprecise to account for the horrors on display. It also takes a pretty large leap of faith to assume that such age-old horrors—many of which are exhibited during an all-night shelving session that Woody insists upon, lending the book its title—could have the wherewithal to affect the most sophisti-cated paraphernalia of modern life, from computers to electronic elevators to the very essence of contemporary published books, whose text and illustrations hideously melt into an amorphous mass before one horrified worker's eyes.

But this cavil seems insignificant in contrast to the many deft images of terror and bizarrerie, as well as the gripping sense of cumulative horror that envelops *The Overnight*. As the novel develops, such seemingly innocuous words as "gritty," "grimy," "fog," and even "smile" take on appalling overtones. The novel may also be open to the flaw of introducing too many characters (we encounter such bookstore employees as Woody, Madeleine, Jill, Connie, Wilf, Geoff, Greg, Jake, Gavin, Ray, Angus, Agnes, and Nigel, along with cameos by the authors Brodie Oates and Adrian Bottomley), few of whom seem sufficiently different from one another to take on distinct personalities of their own. But there is a certain perverse fascination in seeing each of these characters killed off one by one toward the end of the novel, in scenes that are narrated by the doomed workers themselves as they encounter a fate they strive haplessly to avoid.

The Overnight also reveals Campbell's finest melding of humour and horror since *The Count of Eleven* (1991). Aside from some moments of extraordinary wordplay, the novel features moments of pure hilarity that in some inexplicable way only augment the horror of the general situation. One scene in which the relentlessly cheerful Woody strives to encourage his reserved British under-lings to greet their potential customers with grinning smiles and a robust "Welcome to Texts!" is a comic vignette that Wodehouse could not have surpassed. And Campbell has also developed an enviable skill at portraying the finest shades of emotional nuance in the interpersonal exchanges between his characters. All apart from its merits as a supernatural novel, *The Overnight* can be read with pleasure as a dissection of the societal and personal complexi-ties of life in the twenty-first century. And the manner in which Campbell successively shifts the narrative voice to exactly those characters whose actions or sensations carry the story forward is a remarkable feat of literary architecture.

Still another adaptation of the haunted house motif occurs in *Thieving Fear*, written in 2006–7 and published in 2008. The novel begins with a prologue: the brothers Hugh and Rory Lucas and their cousins, Charlotte Nolan and Ellen Lomax, are camping at Thurstaston Cliffs on the Welsh coast. One night Charlotte wanders away from the others and stumbles upon a trapdoor near the edge of the cliff. She almost falls over the cliff, thinking she had heard her name called from the pit revealed by the trapdoor—and perhaps a hand reaching up to her.

Ten years later, Charlotte is an editor at Cougar Books in London; Ellen has just been fired (perhaps unjustly) for apparent derelictions concerning her work at a retirement home; Hugh is having trouble with his coworkers at Frugo, a supermarket; and Rory is a concept artist who has just created a large sculpture made out of tin cans. They all sense strange presences around them, Charlotte in particular. Ellen, who has ambitions to be a novelist, outlines the plot of a horror novel: "Four people share some kind of magical experience but they don't realise till years later when it starts to affect all their lives" (TF 58).

Further investigation of the site in Wales reveals that there had once been a house on the cliff owned by Arthur Pendemon. He was apparently an occultist who had some nebulous relations with Peter Grace (whom readers will recall from *The Parasite*). As all four continue to have various difficulties, they begin to realise that they are each being afflicted by their worst fear or phobia: Hugh becomes disoriented and cannot find his way to the simplest location; Rory goes temporarily blind and has a bad auto accident; Ellen believes she has become hideously fact, when in fact she is alarmingly thin; and Charlotte is increasingly claustrophobic. They come to believe that these phenomena are all connected with Pendemon and his house. Their subsequent exploration of the house—which lies *beneath* Thurstaston Cliffs—confirms their suspicions.

The novel has resonances not so much with *The Parasite* (Peter Grace in the end plays a very small role in the narrative) but with *Incarnate* (the idea that different people are afflicted by the same supernatural phenomenon) and perhaps also *The Long Lost* (the notion that the supernatural causes one's own fears to become manifest). *Thieving Fear* is rich in chararcterisation, as all four principal characters are vividly and distinctively etched.

"Digging Deep," collected in *Just Behind You* (2009), is the delightful half-comic terror tale that Campbell read at the World Fantasy Convention in Saratoga Springs in 2007—the tale about a man who is buried alive but who happens to have his cellphone (or mobile) with him. His frantic and seemingly unsuccessful efforts to convince the police that he is not a prankster but is really and truly buried alive would be bad enough—but the grim twist at the very end is much worse. Nothing can surpass Campbell's own reading of the tale, and some media company could do well by issuing an audiotape of such readings.

There are two other stories in *Just Behind You* about cellphones, although by far the best one—and perhaps the best in the whole book—is "Breaking Up." This magnificently haunting tale of the terrors that can lurk in the bitter cold of a snowstorm features a cumulative build-up of horror that is well-nigh unsurpassed. Consider the care with which the following paragraph fuses overt description with sinister implication:

> Despite her glove, the rail felt like a handful of ice. To her right, lumps of snow had been gouged out of the crests of the hedges for snowballs or by someone's desperate clutch. Beyond the hedges on both sides of the road, pale figures no more shapely than a child's first drawing appeared to mark her progress. She might almost have fancied they were watching her, even those that had least with which to do so. When a phone jangled, she was near to imagining that it related to a dim hunched shape with the sloughed remains of a face. The sound was in the house belonging to the snowman. She hauled herself past it in a rage at her nerves. It fell silent, and her phone rang. (JB 124–25)

"Peep" (HF) conveys, in twenty pages, the complex social ties that an old man struggles to deal with—both an aunt whose strange behaviour had disturbed him as a boy and the daughter and grandchildren whose affection he strives to retain. Does the ghost of the aunt return from the dead at the end? We never know for certain.

"The Decorations" is told from the perspective of a boy who senses that his grandmother is for some reason afraid of a plastic figure of Santa Claus placed on the roof of her house. The grand-mother dies—but does she too come back from the dead?

He saw at once that she'd become what she was afraid of. She was draped with a necklace of fairy lights, and two gut-tering bulbs had taken the place of her eyes. Dim green light spilled like slimy water down her cheeks. She wore a long white dress, if the vague pale mass wasn't part of her, for her face looked inflated to hollowness, close to bursting. Perhaps that was why her mouth was stretched so wide, but her grin was terrified. He had a sudden dreadful thought that both she and the worm were inside the shape. (HF 117)

Here again, every sentence, every word is made to count; and the passage, without the least violence of diction or image, conjures up—or, more precisely, allows each reader's imagination to con-jure up—visions of unthinkable horror.

Thirteen Days by Sunset Beach (2015) returns to the venerable theme of vampirism, but adds a few twists along the way. The novel recounts the two weeks spent on the Greek island of Vasilema by an extended British family: the elderly married couple Ray and Sandra Thornton, their adult children Doug and Natalie, Doug's wife Pris, Natalie's second husband Julian Banks, and a trio of chil-dren and teenagers, Tim (son of Doug and Pris), Jonquil (Natalie's daughter by a previous marriage), and William (the five-year-old son of Julian and Natalie). Soon after reaching their hotel on the island, they discover that a nearby area of bars, restaurants, and shops called Sunset Beach is frequented by noisy young people who seem to enjoy partying all night. During the day, the place is practically deserted.

Campbell lets the cat out of the bag quite early on, when Sandra discovers that she has been bitten on the neck, presumably by an insect. This telltale suggestion of vampirism is enhanced by countless details in Campbell's oblique narrative. Soon thereafter, Tim and Jonquil also find themselves having been bitten on the arm. A clerk at a grocery tells the Thorntons that the people who come to Sunset Beach are "not like us" (SB 21).

Disquieting details continue to accumulate—and then the Thorntons make a gruesome discovery. As Ray is exploring a cave off the beach, he comes upon a rotting corpse:

> The shape had once been much more human, but now it seemed to sum up age an decay. It looked as withered and contorted as the husk of a spider's victim. The man's head was thrown back as if it had been paralysed in the act of uttering a final cry, which had shrunk the lips back from the teeth in a tortured grimace. The hands might have been lifted to fend off or deny his fate, unless a convulsion had raised them. (SB 55)

After Ray and Julian—who also comes upon the body—report the find to the authorities, the police inform them that the corpse was that of an English tourist who had gone missing some weeks before. Later they are stunned to discover that the tourist, a Mr Ditton, was quite a young man, perhaps a teenager.

It had already become evident, through subtle hints, that Sandra is gravely, perhaps terminally, ill; and we are not surprised when Sandra confirms that she has cancer and may be dead by Christmas. And yet, her stay on the island has seemingly rejuvenated her: she has much more vigour and her appetite is robust.

Ominously, she new states that she feels as if "I've had some kind of transfusion" (104). Ray is both encouraged and disturbed by this apparent change in his longtime wife's health.

One day the Thornton clan decide to explore a monastery lying in ruins on one part of the island. They are struck by the apparent fact that it and the neighbouring forest has been damaged by a recent fire. Some family members seem to detect shadowy presences here and there, but it is Ray who sees the most hideous sight:

> The legs came first—eight of them creeping around the far edge of the entrance to the cell. In a moment, though by no means a reassuring one, Ray saw that they weren't legs at all; they were scrawny fingers clutching at the rock. As he struggled to breathe they brought their owner forth into the corridor. It was bent low with age or stealth, and entirely bald. Although it was naked, the whitish body was so withered that he couldn't guess at its sex. It twisted its thin head towards the light, and Ray glimpsed a face like a flimsy paper mask moulded to a skull. (SB 120–21)

But no one else sees this loathsome entity.

Ray finds, in a crudely written and printed book on the Greek islands, a poorly (or ambiguously) written account of a local legend: the "Vampire of Vasilema." This account relates to the arrival at the monastery of a traveller named Proskynitis ("pilgrim"), who then decides to stay and adopt the name Brother Skiá ("shadow"). He wishes to embrace eternity, "but eternity needs life to feed on" (SB 128). Increasingly disturbed both by this opaque legend and by the harrowing things he has seen, Ray becomes convinced that his family members have been afflicted by the vampirism that he believes to be rampant throughout the island. He desperately tries to persuade his sceptical family that "he [Brother Skiá] used people to feed on his behalf, and then he fed on them. You know what it means by feeding, don't you? Drinking their blood" (SB 174). And, in Ray's judgment, Brother Skiá is still doing it.

In a gripping final scene, Doug and Natalie accompany Ray back to the monastery, largely to convince him that his beliefs are pure fantasy—or perhaps a paranoid reaction to his beloved wife's imminent death. When Natalie twists her ankle, Doug remains with her while Ray descends down some steps, reaching the cave where he had discovered the body of Mr Ditton. On the way back, he ses a "swollen bulk" (SB 214) in an alcove:

> The face was a man's, or had been. Now it resembled a bloated mask, almost engulfed in a mass of flesh so pallid it might never have been touched by the sun. The nose resembled a colourless tuber, and the thick broad lips were just as white. It was impossible to judge what expression the face bore, not just since the lips appeared to have swelled together in an immobile straight line but because the eyes had atrophied, puckering so deep that they'd sucked the lids inwards. (SB 215)

Ray realises this is Skiá. He scares off the creature by using the flash on the camera of his cellphone. Returning to Doug and Natalie, he is not entirely surprised to find that the image of the creature does not show up on the photograph he had taken of it. At the end of their vacation, the family leaves the island without incident. Sandra, Tim, and Jonquil appear to be recovering, but Ray wonders if they will be inexorably drawn back to Vasilema some day.

Thirteen Days by Sunset Beach is one of Campbell's most meticulously written novels, but there is at times an almost excessive reticence or indirection in the conveyance of the supernatural threat in which the Thorntons find themselves. A great majority of the hints of vampirism and other aberrant phenomena are conveyed by the Thorntons' frustrating conversations with the Greek townspeople, whose command of English is either poor or deliberately opaque. As with many of Campbell's later works, so much attention is paid to the complexities and ambiguities of language that overt episodes of terror are reduced to a minimum. The novel comes across as largely a series of teasing references to vampirism without anything explicit occurring. Only at the very end do we come upon the source of the supernatural phenomena; and that climactic scene, effective as it is, does not provide an adequate catharsis to the extremely gradual build-up of hints and allusions.

Campbell largely adheres to the standard elements of the vampire myth. While the afflicted persons (Sandra, Tim, and Jonquil) are not absolutely unable to appear in sunlight, they do find it preferable to be out and about when it is overcast or at night. Their images appear in mirrors, but those images are wavering or flickering. At one point Ray has anomalous difficulty photographing the trio. And they seem to exhibit no desire to afflict others with their vampirism.

While being far from a failure, and exemplifying to a remarkable degree the extent to which Campbell makes every word count in even a full-length novel, *Thirteen Days by Sunset Beach* will probably be regarded as one of his lesser works for not quite delivering on its promise as an exhaustive treatment of the vampire myth. Perhaps its greatest triumph comes not in its supernatural premise but in its character portrayal, notably the ageing Ray Thornton (in part a stand-in for himself, as he and his wife have taken frequent vacations to Greece and Turkey over the years), harried by the thought that his wife of many years will be taken from him, and especially of Julian Banks, an insufferable prig whose every utterance reveals him as self-righteous, domineering, and sanctimonious, and yet oddly defensive in his realisation that, as a second husband, he has not been fully embraced by his family and in particular by his own stepdaughter. Other characters—Sandra, who has quietly reconciled herself to her fate; the rebellious teenagers Tim and Jonquil; and the lively youngster William, whose blunt utterances unwittingly suggest oddities and terrors of which he remains unaware—are also well portrayed. For these features alone, *Thirteen Days by Sunset Beach* will prove a satisfying read.

V. DREAMS AND REALITY

We have seen that, in *Demons by Daylight*, the focus on the fluctuating perceptions of a possibly disturbed individual rendered the stories akin to dream-narratives, although none of them was in fact presented unambiguously as such. While they figure in a number of Campbell's stories, dreams—and their possible intrusion into the mundane realities of daily life—are, in different ways, at the centre of two of Campbell's most powerful works: *Incarnate*, one of his finest novels, and *Needing Ghosts*, a separately published novella.

Incarnate—written between 1981 and 1983 and published in 1983—opens with an experiment on dreams conducted in Oxford by Stuart Hay and Guilda Kent. Five individuals participate, all of whom have confessed to having dim precognitive faculties. The nature of the experiment is not elucidated, and it ends abruptly with possibly traumatic psychological results for some or all of the participants.

The novel then takes up the story of the five individuals eleven years after the experiment. It is at this point that Campbell begins an extraordinary tapestry of narration in which the lives of the five individuals—who have not had anything to do with one another

in the interim—become insidiously intermingled. For the purposes of analysis, it will be necessary to pursue the threads of each
character's activities before examining how their fates become
enmeshed.

Joyce Churchill has become the head of a small old folks' home
that is now threatened with closure by the local government. One
day her husband Geoffrey, a dealer in stamps, thinks he sees some
entity like a huge baby—"naked and fat and doughy white" (I 64).
Later an ancient woman shows up at their doorstep, and Joyce
naturally feels sympathy and wishes to take care of her. While
Joyce tries to marshal her elderly charges to protest against their
eviction, the old woman staying with them appears to be inducing
strange dreams in Geoffrey. Some change has come over Joyce
also: she believes that she has found a new home for her people,
but it later turns out that she has imagined the whole thing and
has in fact been wandering the streets for days or weeks. The
distinction between dream and reality is breaking down both for
her and for Geoffrey. Later Geoffrey dies in trying to escape the
house and the anomalous old woman.

Helen Verney is attempting to carry on with her life after the
break-up of her marriage. She moves into a flat in London with
her young daughter, Susan, who strikes up an acquaintance with a
little girl named Eve. While at first she likes her, Susan gradually
finds Eve—who also encourages Susan to dream—more and more
peculiar. Helen, however, takes to Eve fervently, perhaps finding
in her a more satisfactory daughter than her own. Eve moves in
with Helen and Susan, and in a haunting episode Eve somehow
locks Susan into some huge dark space in the apartment and takes
on Susan's outward form.

Danny Swain is a working-class young man who still lives with
his parents and has a poor job working in a cinema owned by a
friend of his father's. Paranoid, full of rage and resentment, he
blames both Dr Kent and Molly Wolfe (one of the other members of the experiment) for the shabbiness of his life. One day

Dr Kent runs into Danny in Soho and takes him to a decrepit little office she has set up, called Know Yourself Ltd. She baits him, chiding him for purchasing pornographic magazines, and he leaves hastily and angrily. Later it appears he has developed the power to change reality: while he sits in his home watching a well-known movie on television with his family, the film changes from what it had always been. Shortly thereafter Danny lures Dr Kent into the cinema where he works, sets the doctor aflame, and burns the whole cinema down. But not long afterwards Dr Kent shows up at Danny's home, unharmed but with the smell of burning clinging to her: her face blackens before his eyes. He flees from the house.

Freda Beeching is another of the dreamers who is trying to lead a normal life. She is particularly disturbed because her friend Doreen is shattered by the loss of her husband Harry. One day, in a deserted amusement park in Blackpool, she meets a mysterious man named Sage, who claims to predict the future. Freda finds herself fascinated by this tall, gentle, and quiet-spoken man; but her friend Doreen is even more overwhelmed. Later Sage moves in with Doreen, and she achieves a dreamlike state of ecstasy because Sage appears to have brought Harry back from the dead.

Incarnate, although simultaneously telling the lives of these four individuals, is focused largely on Molly Wolfe. She now works for a television station in London, and falls quickly in love with a visiting American documentary director, Martin Wallace. Wallace one day receives a home video showing a black man, Lenny Bennett, being beaten to death by police while in a jail cell. Wallace persuades Molly's television station to broadcast the video, but both she and Wallace are disgraced when it is proved conclusively that the film is a fake. Molly is then taken in for questioning by the police and is humiliated and roughed up by Inspector Maitland, who had been accused of the Bennett killing, and a loutish assistant named Rankin. But, to her amazement, the entire incident proves to have been a dream, as Maitland was without doubt in church at the time Molly says the incident took place. Has the distinction between dream and reality broken down for her? Later she sees the other policeman, Rankin, on the street—the very man she had seen in her "dream" but whom she had never seen in reality. She is convinced that the "dream" is somehow a reflection of reality; in that case, the police killing of Bennett must also be real. She follows Rankin home and worms her way into his flat; there she sees a bracelet owned by Bennett. Although Rankin initially threatens her, Molly uses some sort of inner power to overwhelm him and make him confess that he and Maitland in fact killed Lenny Bennett.

At the opening of the novel each of the members of the dream experiment had received a letter from Stuart Hay, asking in apparent innocence whether the dreamers have experienced any unusual after-effects. Molly tells Wallace of the experiment, and they feel that Hay must be looked up and questioned. Finding him, they ask where his colleague Dr Kent is. He informs them that she is at a mental hospital in Norfolk—not as a doctor, but as a patient. Although diagnosed with acute paranoid schizophrenia, she seems rational enough, but she is harried by the weight of some monstrous conception. "The dreams are getting stronger," she states. "My dreams and everyone else's. We've allowed them to grow stronger by trying to explain them away, don't you under-stand?" (I 424). She continues: "Dreaming isn't a state of mind, but we scientists have lulled people into thinking it is . . . It isn't a state of mind, it's a state of being" (I 425).

But if we have attempted to ignore dreams and explain them away by a feeble rationalism, where is it that dreams "go"? Kent calls it "The dream place, the collective unconscious . . . I call it the dream thing. It's alive, I'm sure it is. It wants to feed on what we call reality, feed on it so it can take its place. We've given it that strength, we even helped it gain a hold. That time at Oxford let it break through" (I 427). How was that possible? Kent believes that the dreamers undermined reality, this reality, the one we take for granted. What do you think holds reality together if not our shared perception of it? They shared a perception of something else and made it stronger . . . I'll tell you something I've never told anyone else, because I think you'll see it's true if you give it a chance. I don't think our subjects at Oxford foresaw the future—not always, anyway, and not all of them. I think sometimes some of them made it happen by dreaming of it. (I 427)

The mysterious Sage proves to be a supernatural being who is assisting in this process of dreams taking over reality: it was he, or various embodiments, who infiltrated the lives of all the other dreamers (in the form of the old woman coming to the Churchills, Eve coming to Helen Verney, and the pseudo–Dr Kent coming to Danny Swain) and caused them to come together; for it is by their combined dreaming that reality will be overwhelmed. In one of the most harrowing and bizarre sequences in modern horror fiction, the dreamers find themselves at Doreen's home, with Sage. In attempting to flee Sage, they wander out of the house but find everything changed: in fact, London is being replaced by a dream of their own making. Molly seems to be the unwitting leader of the band, but she scarcely knows what to do to end the horror and return the waking world to its rightful place. Somehow she comes to the realisation that she must simply renounce the dream so that the real world can return; she does so after tremendous mental effort, and the dream collapses upon itself. The real world is restored.

Incarnate, one of the longest of Campbell's novels, is likewise among his best. The complexity of the plot, the intricate interweaving of narratives and narrative voices, the suppleness and richness of the prose, and the harrowing nature of the central horror—dreams that are so real that they not only are taken for reality but actually replace it—all fuse into one of the finest weird novels of the second half of the twentieth century. One of the major difficulties with "horror novels" is that they are frequently mere works of suspense or melodrama with horrific interludes interspersed at random intervals; many lack a genuinely weird conception sufficiently extensive to serve as the basis for a full-scale novel. And while it is true that in some sense *Incarnate* achieves its complexity merely by multiplying the number of characters, these characters are nonetheless affected differently—in accordance with their own temperament—by their dreams, and it is their coming together toward the end that creates the novel's powerful concluding tableau: individuals wandering confusedly through a twilight world of their own minds that is insidiously replacing the real world whose familiarity and stability they desperately seek to regain.

Incarnate can be thought of as an exact reversal of the technique utilised in the *Demons by Daylight* stories: instead of a narrative whose dreamlike nature renders the real world a dream or nightmare, here dreams have the crystal clarity that we normally expect from the real world. Certainly the most jarring moment in the novel's earlier sections is the discovery that Molly's being roughed up by the police was "merely" a dream; but her loss of the distinction between dream and reality had already been prefigured in an earlier sequence:

An arctic wind had left the streets deserted. Under the streetlamps the slushy pavements were shivering. Alone in bed, she wished she had stayed with Martin. She woke in daylight, orange through her eyelids, and wondered if Martin had left by now. She stretched out her arm and bruised her knuckles against a bony object that shouldn't have been there beside the pillow. Her eyes sprang open. She wasn't in her flat, she was in the four-poster bed.

It was as though she'd dreamed herself back into Martin's flat. The place was too quiet; it felt like the times when sounds withdrew from her ... So she had only dreamed that she'd gone home; she realised now that she hadn't felt her steps. Nevertheless the flat and its antique furniture seemed unreal, a museum exhibit she had strayed into by mistake. As she used the shower, she wondered when exactly she had started dreaming. (I 126–27)

Understandably for so lengthy and complex a novel, Incarnate seems to have a few flaws and loose threads. The central puzzle is the figure of Sage: what exactly is he, and what does he want? Perhaps Campbell is wise in not specifying Sage's physical nature; but one might have wished further clarification on his motives in desiring the replacement of the real world by dream. It is true that he anticipates the conclusion when he remarks: "Many are cut off from their night side, but that only makes it stronger. It cannot be denied now. The doors are opening" (I 225). But what does he stand to gain? Even at the end, when he takes the form of Eve (who herself has reshaped her appearance to look like Susan Verney), we receive no clear indication of his purpose.

But this is perhaps a minor point, and it scarcely affects our appreciation of the novel as a whole. If we are thrown off guard when we discover that various events that seemed so real to Molly Wolfe were dreams, how can we react when we find the dreams of other characters affecting others and shaping what they believe to be reality? The moment when Danny and his parents are watching a film on television and find that it is changing before their eyes is particularly chilling:

The scene wasn't meant to go on like this. He was making it happen somehow. His parents frowned at it and shifted resentfully in their seats as Maureen O'Hara brought Brazzi a cane, and Danny knew what Dr. Kent had done: by reminding him of Oxford she'd weakened his hold on things so they could change. He knew that when the pleading girl raised her face to the camera it would be Dr. Kent's or Molly Wolfe's. He was seized by a suffocating fear that his mother would realize he was making the film change. He staggered up from his chair, though his penis almost jerked him back into it, and switched off the television. (I 301)

And then there is the moment when the figure of Dr Kent, supposedly burned in the cinema fire, comes back to visit Danny:

"Is it how I look that's bothering you, Danny?" Dr. Kent pointed at the side of her face. "A woman's secret, that's all. We both know I don't really look like this."
Danny ground his knuckles into his lips. Her face was blackening, her eyes had started to glaze and swell, first the left and now the right. He didn't know if his mother was able to see this, but even if she wasn't, she would soon know what he had done. He would have to tell her everything once he began to scream. (I 362)

But *Incarnate* succeeds not by these individual moments of weirdness and grue, but by its overall conception, its crisply realised characters, and its cumulative intensity. Lengthy though it is, it is one of those rare novels that one does not wish to come to an end.

A very different type of work is *Needing Ghosts*, written in 1989–90 and published in 1990 in a series of separately published novelettes issued by Legend/Century. Campbell had rarely experimented with the novella form—which, from Le Fanu's "Carmilla" (1872) to Algernon Blackwood's "The Willows" (1907) to H. P. Lovecraft's "The Whisperer in Darkness" (1930) to T. E. D. Klein's "Children of the Kingdom" (1980), has been particularly felicitous in the creation of horror—and some of his previous attempts, such as the science fiction tale *Medusa* [1973], cannot be considered among his most successful works. But *Needing*

Ghosts proves to be perhaps the most quintessentially weird work in Campbell's entire output, an unclassifiable item that melds humour, horror, grotesquerie, and paranoia into a baffling fusion.

Needing Ghosts opens with a man who awakens from an apparent sleep not knowing who he is. The unusual narration—third-person singular, but in the present tense and intensely focused on the protagonist—creates an atmosphere of dream or hallucination that does not abate even as the last word is read. As he leaves the house in which he has found himself, the man boards a ferry and then a bus, which takes him to the centre of some large city. Wandering into a bookstore, he finds a book, *Cadenza*, by Simon Mottershead—and the picture on the back cover, although taken many years ago, is unmistakably his own.

Mottershead now begins to remember certain things. In particular, he realises that he is scheduled to lecture at a writers' group that day at a library. A surly taxi driver takes him to a shopping mall that, incongruously, houses the library. Blundering into a room there, he gives a fragmentary lecture to a largely unreceptive audience. As he is attempting to leave, a bald man—who, Mottershead now perceives, has been following him for some time—accosts him and says he wishes to talk with him. Fleeing, Mottershead dashes into a bookstore, where, in an apparent effort to confirm his own existence, he looks for a copy of *Cadenza* (the previous copy, which he had purchased from the other bookstore, he had left in his rucksack in the library). Although he finds a number of child pornography volumes by someone named Mottershead, he cannot locate the book or any others he may have written. Another bookstore also proves to have nothing by him.

Mottershead now encounters the bald man again. In a bizarre confrontation, Mottershead plucks out the man's false teeth and hurls them into a tree. He then strolls into a park when all of a sudden he remembers that he has a family—a wife, a son, and a daughter—and that they live nearby. With difficulty he follows a path through some woods and comes to a house that he believes is his; but it is now an old folks' home. He then takes a ferry back to his house—perhaps the house he woke up in earlier in the day. There he is met by his wife and children, who urge him to take rest. He finds a videotape containing an interview he had once given, which establishes that he had previously had a nervous breakdown. Shortly thereafter he enters a room and finds his family all killed—books are lying across their throats, with knives impaling them. The story ends inconclusively with Mottershead wondering whether he is either mad or dead.

The attempt to summarise the plot of *Needing Ghosts* is still more futile than it is for Campbell's other works, for a summary can scarcely begin to convey the nightmarish quality of the tale. Its incidents defy clear elucidation, and the atmosphere of surreal fantasy is unabated. There has been considerable disagreement as to even the most fundamental points of plot in the novella. What, in essence, is Mottershead's state? Is he mad, dreaming, or dead? Steven J. Mariconda believes that it is

the story of Simon Mottershead, a horror writer who has gone mad, murdered his family, and then turned the knife on himself. The events of the story, told from the perspective of Mottershead after his death, are a surreal series of episodes that lead to his realization of the murders. The entire narrative, Campbell hints at the end, is—somehow—simply a dream of the dead author.[1]

While Mariconda makes a compelling argument for this view, I believe an alternative interpretation is as or more likely: Mottershead has *fallen into his own fictional universe.* Many points in the narrative seem to point to this conclusion. The frequent citations of books, bookstores, and the like suggest that we—and Mottershead—are somehow in a work of fiction rather than the

1. Mariconda, review of *Needing Ghosts* and *Midnight Sun*, 33.

real, waking world. And what of the fact that *Cadenza* begins with the same words—"He knows this dark" (NG 27)—that opens *Needing Ghosts* itself? Some of the remarks Mottershead makes at the writers' club lecture are also indicative: "Writing won't leave you alone ... When it comes to life ... it's like dreaming when you're awake" (NG 34). Later in the narrative Mottershead wonders, "Perhaps one day he'll be able to derive a story from all this ... but hasn't he already written something of the kind?" (NG 52). Perhaps the clinching point is the videotaped interview seen at the end, in which the plots of some of Mottershead's stories seem uncannily like *Needing Ghosts:*

In one of his stories a man who's obsessed with the impossibility of knowing if he has died in his sleep convinces himself that he has, and is dreaming. Another concerns a man who believes he is being followed by a schizophrenic whose hallucinations are affecting his own perceptions, but the hallucinations prove to be the reality he has tried to avoid seeing. The reader is left suspecting that the schizophrenic is really a projection of the man himself. (NG 73)

In the end, however, perhaps my interpretation and Mariconda's are not so far apart, and can even be fused together. Mottershead may indeed be dead, and has thereby entered his own fictional world. Whether he is responsible for the deaths of his family is a question that must be left unanswered; I see no textual evidence for such an assertion.

It would not be going too far to say that *Needing Ghosts* has the potential of becoming a modern *Turn of the Screw*, with several, perhaps many, competing interpretations being offered even as to its basic scenario, let alone its overall philosophical message. What indeed is that message? Again, Campbell is deliberately vague on the point, and many features of the narrative seem to resist clear symbolic or metaphoric interpretation; but perhaps the overriding conclusion we are to take from *Needing Ghosts* is the danger of failing to distinguish between fiction (dream, hallucination, madness) and reality—or, rather, the dangers that the inherent difficulty of distinguishing fiction and reality can engender. And yet, it may be best simply to enjoy the atmosphere of twisted lunacy in the work. Steven J. Mariconda has put it best:

> This is a Campbell *tour de force*—nearly surreal, a juxtaposition of reality and unreality, with nothing to guide the reader on his terrified journey . . . *Needing Ghosts* is a masterwork, one that only Campbell could have penned. It has a dreamlike illogic; multiple levels of meaning—a horror story about a horror story writer's stories—resonate powerfully, folding back upon each other. Outside of Campbell's own work, there is little else to which we can compare it—imagine Lovecraft's "The Outsider" written by Franz Kafka.[2]

A more recent novella, *The Pretence* (2013), features some of the same sense of unease, discomfort, and vague disturbance found in *Needing Ghosts*. In what seems like the simple narrative of a man, Paul Slater, coming back from some unspecified island (where he had been visiting his ailing mother, who is presumably in a hospice) to his home in Liverpool, we find an increasing array of unsettling details. For example, who are the Finalists? Are they a cult that has predicted the end of the world, and has this cult gained a worldwide appeal? Has their prophecy, apparently having something to do with the failure of the sun to rise in the morning, already come true? The greyish-white sky that Slater encounters the morning after he returns is as peculiar as the bland but subtly menacing encounters that Slater has with the police and others. Toward the end Slater reflects: "He couldn't recall when he'd last seen a colour" (Pr 76). In prose whose crispness is matched by its

---

2. Mariconda, review of *Needing Ghosts* and *Midnight Sun*, 33–34.

poeticism ("the stones and the trees [in a cemetery were] deep in a secret colloquy like silence rendered solid" [Pr 68]), Campbell leads the Slater family, and the reader, to an ambiguous conclusion where they scale a mountain in an apparently fruitless effort to see the sun. Almost every utterance in the tale is a double entendre, usually with some sinister undercurrent. This novella may not be quite as bizarre as *Needing Ghosts*, but it is a reminder of the effortless skill that Campbell can marshal in the evocation of weirdness.

From the tenuous distinction between dreams and reality it is a small step to the equally problematical distinction between art (the distillation of dreams) and reality. In Campbell's work, all forms of art—writing, painting, sculpture, music, film—come into play, introducing their distinctive worlds into commonplace reality and perhaps subverting or replacing it. The whole issue of writing and, more broadly, language is worth a separate section; other aspects of art can be dealt with here.

Campbell, an enthusiast of film from youth (he has admitted that he initially became a prodigious moviegoer to escape his tense family situation, although in those teenage years he would frequently go with his mother [FD xvii]), has found the "virtual reality" effect of film powerfully suggestive. So early a tale as "The Childish Fear" [1963] deals with the anomalies to be found in dark theatres. The story itself is mediocre, being of interest only as an early attempt by Campbell to break away from Lovecraftian pastiche. Far more successful is "After the Queen" [1969], a hauntingly baffling tale dealing with the intermingling of film and reality: a man finds himself sitting alone in a cinema seeing a film of a man sitting alone in a cinema . . .

The topos reaches a pinnacle in two exceptionally bizarre stories, "Boiled Alive" [1986] and "The Worst Fog of the Year" [1990]. In the former, an accountant with the odd name of Mee is subject to repeated wrong numbers because his telephone number was used without his permission in a cheap horror film, *Boiled Alive*. Gradually Mee loses the ability to discriminate between film and the real world:

> The idea of living in a film wasn't entirely unappealing. If it had been a better film he might even have been flattered. Being able to repeat favourite moments and speed up the boring parts was certainly tempting, not to mention the ability to say of bad times "it's only a film" or to have a hidden voice explain things when he looked at them. But how much control would he have? About as much as one generally has of one's life, he thought. (AH 482)

This entire mad story must be read to understand how keenly Campbell has exhibited the degree to which the artificial reality of films has overtaken the generally mundane lives of most of us, to the point that when any unusual thing happens we are inclined to say, "I feel as if I'm in a movie."

"The Worst Fog of the Year" is peculiar both in itself and in its genesis. It was first written in 1970 and submitted to a magazine that folded before it could publish the story; the magazine also lost Campbell's manuscript. Twenty years later Campbell found the first draft of the story in a notebook and rewrote it. The tale concerns a film reviewer, Gaunt, who falls asleep while watching a B-movie and, when he awakens, finds himself in the movie. Dazed and confused, he is threatened by a man with a hideous face: "It was crushed and discoloured. It might almost have been a mask shaped of mud and insufficiently baked" (TD 250). He grabs at the man's arm and tears it loose from the shoulder—it is nothing but wires and metal rods. He does the same thing to a woman in the room. In a magazine appearance of the story Campbell ended with Gaunt awaking abruptly in the theatre; but in a reprint he preserved the sense of bizarreness by keeping Gaunt in the film— which has now become his reality—and facing a loathsome end:

"He felt he walls and floor and his sense of himself begin to give way to the dark" (TD 251).

The film topos is treated most exhaustively in the novel *Ancient Images*, written in 1987–88 and published in 1989. Although perhaps lacking the intensity of some of Campbell's other novels, it builds to a powerful and satisfying conclusion and probes the curious way in which film can perhaps reveal dark truths lurking hidden behind the facade of ordinary life.

Ancient Images opens in 1988, when a film researcher named Graham Nolan, working for a British television company, realises a long-held dream by tracking down what may perhaps be the only surviving print of a horror film, *Tower of Fear*, made in England in 1938 and starring Boris Karloff and Bela Lugosi. Directed by Giles Spence, who died shortly after the film was completed, *Tower of Fear* was somehow suppressed when the negative and the rights to it were purchased by an anonymous source. Prior to giving it a private showing in his London flat, however, Nolan dies by jumping off a neighbouring building—either as a suicide or in the midst of hunting down (or perhaps fleeing from) the person who took the film. The whole matter is highly puzzling; as a policeman remarks, "He could hardly have been running away from an old horror film" (AI 21). His flat is in a shambles, and only a small, ragged clip of the film remains as evidence of his find.

Sandy Allen, a friend who had been invited to the showing and had actually seen Nolan jump to his death, feels obliged to pursue Nolan's research, especially when Nolan's lover Toby gives Sandy the notebook containing the leads that ultimately directed Nolan to the film. She and a friend, Roger Stone, begin retracing Nolan's footsteps by interviewing—or attempting to interview—many of the individuals cited in the notebook. As they begin their travels all across England in search of actors and production workers on the film; they find that nearly everyone connected with the project—including Karloff and Lugosi—had very mixed feelings about it. Roger, a writer on film, had himself talked with some individuals about the film:

> "Maybe you know Lugosi's doctor said Lugosi ended up on morphine because he used to be so anxious. [Ed] Wood told me Bela once admitted to him that it was a movie he made in England that caused him the most grief . . . [Peter Bogdanovich] didn't get much out of [Karloff] about this film except that he really didn't want to talk about it at all or even about the director, Giles Spence." (AI 42–43)

A variety of "accidents" and vandalism had occurred on the set of the film, and even some strange presences:

> "Billy was convinced there were people on the set who shouldn't be, for one thing—we assume he meant people. He ruined more than one take because he said someone made a face at him round the scenery, and he got more nervous when the director asked what kind of face. Then there was something about a smell when they were in the last week of filming. They couldn't trace it, they thought it had to do with some plumbing nearby, and so they did their best to forget it, all except Billy. He kept insisting it was something dead." (AI 127–28)

A stuntman in the film falls from a tower because he sees what appear to be dogs—"The dogs with a man's face, and things growing in their eyes" (AI 137).

Gradually the plot of the film becomes known to Sandy: it concerns an ancestral curse upon the land as a result of some accidental death. Another clue reveals that Lord Redfield, the owner of the land on which the film was being shot, had given a thunderous speech in Parliament condemning the "horrorific" film in general and *Tower of Fear* in particular, saying that it would cause a decline in the morals of the people who saw it. Redfield's speech seems unusually vehement, and Sandy looks up the present Lord Redfield, grandson of the man who made the speech. A suave, debonair nobleman, he gives her the history of the region: shortly after the Battle of Hastings, an army led by one of William the Conqueror's nobles came to the area and killed every human being on the land. Sandy discovers other disturbing things. Spence himself had died in a car accident on Redfield land, shortly after Lord Redfield had attempted to stop the film because Spence had included a parody of the Redfield coat of arms in one scene. In the churchyard, Sandy notices a pattern of violent deaths that seem to have occurred to selected individuals in a nearly unbroken pattern every fifty years going back to 1438; Spence's death in 1938 takes on a more ominous significance, and the fact that the present year is 1988 is still more unnerving.

While Sandy is in Redfield, Roger is attacked by "someone wearing a mask or with something wrong with their face" (AI 223). Not long thereafter, Sandy finds that a print of *Tower of Fear* is still in existence. Obtaining the film, Sandy watches it and finds it highly disturbing. But she senses that the sources of the horror are beyond merely what is shown on the screen. Herself dogged by nameless presences that lurk just out of sight, she develops the impression that the people of Redfield have perhaps unconsciously carried out a kind of scapegoat ritual whereby the land—known for the rich flavour of the bread made from its wheat—is nourished with blood every fifty years. Moreover, she believes that "the land was able to send something to hunt victims on its behalf" (AI 286), and this lends a foreboding significance to the fact that a ragtag force called Enoch's Army, which repudiates civilisation and yearns to return to Nature, has been invited by Lord Redfield to remain on their land. Sandy, who felt keenly the hostility of the townsfolk of Redfield toward strangers and had been forced to escape from the town by guile, fears that the tension between Enoch's Army and the townspeople will lead to unthinkable violence:

Enoch's Army mustn't go to Redfield. She had barely tasted the hostility that lay in wait there for strangers, but if anything was capable of releasing the violence that drowsed beneath the contentment of Redfield, it would be a convoy of scapegoats. Fifty years, her mind intoned like a refrain, and she wondered if the scale of the violence she foresaw could be what the land and its token bloodlettings had been waiting for. (AI 252)

Having picked up the print of the film, Sandy drives rapidly to Redfield in an attempt to head off Enoch's Army; and it is at this time that the entities spawned from the land finally reveal themselves openly:

Though they were on all fours, they weren't animals . . . Their heads looked swollen, too large for their naked scarecrow bodies. Grayish manes that might be hair or vegetation streamed back over their sticklike necks, over their ribs where gaps were encrusted with shadows of earth . . . She saw how their grayish manes grew out of ragged eye sockets, from one of which a clenched flower dangled as if it had been gouged. (AI 287)

One of the creatures approaches her car:

Its mottled limbs looked both lithe and horribly thin. Its torso had shrunk around its ribs, its greenish penis had withered like a dead root. Almost worse than all this, she recognized the face. Perhaps she was recognizing that the eyes, when it had had eyes, had been set so wide as to make the forehead

seem lower than it was, but the vegetation that patched the
skull had grown into a misshapen parody of the face that had
once been there—the Redfield face. (AI 288)

But when Enoch—who feels close to the land and its natural
forces—finally arrives in Redfield, he senses something amiss and,
after a tense stand-off with the townsfolk, withdraws. He is, however, seriously injured by a creature that lunges at him, but Sandy
manages to drive him away to a hospital, where he eventually dies
but at least not in Redfield. Later it proves that the entity that had
attacked him was Lord Redfield's grandfather.

Ancient Images is a supernatural detective story, as Sandy and
Roger pursue leads and finally piece together the nature of the
mystery. In the end, the film does not play a central role in the
plot except insofar as Sandy's pursuit of it leads her to the age-old
curse on the Redfield land. The idea of such a curse is, of course,
a venerable one in horror fiction, and the detail whereby the creatures pursuing Sandy and others have the Redfield face on them
may have been taken from Lovecraft's "The Dunwich Horror"
(1928), where the twin offspring of a cosmic entity, Yog-Sothoth,
and an ignorant farm girl, Lavinia Whateley, both have the Whateley features: one of the twins, Wilbur, is more or less human
in appearance, but the other, his unnamed twin, is spectacularly
bizarre in outline but still retains the Whateley face surmounting
the ropy tentacles that form his huge body.

In a sense, *Ancient Images* is a disappointment for failing to
probe the many profound issues it raises. It is, moreover, deliberately deceptive: there is a suggestion, maintained for much of the
novel, that the film itself is a kind of supernatural phenomenon,
or that something supernatural went into its making. The actual
state of affairs is that the director, Giles Spence, had perceived the
truth of the situation at Redfield and had attempted to capture it
on film, only to perish for his troubles. Nevertheless, in spite of
its lack of depth, *Ancient Images* is a thoroughly entertaining read

and contains all those features—sharp characterisation, polished diction, and a cumulative horrific climax—that we have come to expect of Campbell's novels. Perhaps it is meant to be no more than an affectionate tribute to the classic horror films of the 1930s that fascinated Campbell in his youth.

Perhaps the only significant point broached in *Ancient Images* is the conflicting views offered on the nature of horror film and literature as art forms. On the one side there are the fulminations of Lord Redfield in Parliament about the moral unworth of the horror film; although purporting to have been uttered in 1938, they ring true in today's climate of hostility toward an art form that, at its best, can reveal a variety of unpleasant truths about ourselves:

> It is heartening to observe that our nation recognises the snares of libertarianism for what they are, and that there have been public outcries against the exhibition of such films. I am relieved to learn that a certification is shortly to be introduced that will bar children from viewing films that are judged to be too mild in their gruesomeness to be banned outright from our shores . . . (AI 156–57)

On the other side, however, are those individuals who thirst for horror fiction and film—the more violent and misogynist the better—as a transparent means of satisfying their own aggressive tendencies. In a tart satiric vignette, Sandy visits the writers of a small-press horror magazine:

> It was a stapled bunch of duplicated typed pages called *Gorehound.* She thought someone had spilled coffee on it, until she realized that the stain was meant to illustrate the title. "I should have thought the film I'm looking for wouldn't do much for you after the kind of thing you watch."
>
> "Some films were pretty good even then," John disagreed.

"Lugosi bursts a blind man's eardrums in *Dark Eyes of London*, and that was before the war."

"And before that, in *The Raven*, he cripples Karloff's face," Trantom added eagerly, "and locks him in a room full of mirrors."

"And in *The Black Cat* he starts ripping his skin off," Minihin offered.

"If your film was banned it must be good," Trantom said. "If it's horror we're interested. We can never get enough."

"No fucker tells us what to do." (AI 72–73)

Another novel about film is *The Grin of the Dark*, written in 2004–5 and published in 2007. The novel is the first-person nightmare of Simon Lester, a recently graduated film student newly out of a job when the controversial critical magazine he writes for is sued. Simon is wasting his days pumping gas and freeloading in an apartment off of his girlfriend's disapproving parents when he is approached by his former university advisor and asked to start writing film studies for a newly endowed university publishing program. For his first book, Simon's advisor strongly advocates an expansion of his thesis on forgotten stars of silent film, with special attention to Tubby Thackeray, a former music-hall comic turned silent film star whose career ended prematurely and ignominiously in scandal.

Tubby, it appears, produced a movie that, for reasons never entirely clear, caused viewers to riot in the streets after screening. He tallied twenty-three films between 1914 and 1920, all of them bearing bizarre alliterative titles such as *Tubby's Terrible Triplets*, *Tubby's Troublesome Trousers*, and the like, and in each he was a grade-A mischief-maker, given to pranks that play out in surreal, almost supernatural fashion, and that invariably drive those caught up in them to the brink of insanity.

Known details of Tubby's life are spare and spotty, and copies of his films are surprisingly hard to come by. That his last movie was

never released suggests that his film legacy may have been deliberately suppressed. A dedicated researcher, Simon applies himself
to exploring Tubby's history and the myustery of his eccentric art.
A rare video anthology Simon buys that features the one generally available snatch of a Tubby movie on it scrambles itself after
a single sowing. (Later, the only known archive of all of Tubby's
movies burns to the ground.) A series of unsettling mishaps in
Simon's personal life dovetails with the frustrations and dead ends
in his film research, making them seem not entirely coincidental.
Simon's discovery that Tubby was a professor (whose real name
was Thackeray Lane) of mediaeval studies in the years before his
stage and screen work sends him to Manchester University, where
Lane's few remaining class and lecture notes are peserved. There,
he uncovers research Lane was undertaking into the ancient
pagan rituals that celebrated—and actively promoted—the fundamental chaos of existence. The truths that Simon uncovers both
make perfect sense of all the comically cruel misfortunes that have
beleaguered him and brilliantly prepare the reader for the ending,
one of the more audacious and effective in Campbell's body of
work.

Other forms of art also find their way into Campbell's work. In
particular, the doll motif is very frequently utilised from his earliest to his most recent work. As mentioned previously, this motif
is chiefly used to embody the *Doppelgänger* theme, but it always
has overtones implying the incursion of art or artistic creation into
reality. "Cyril" [1968] is a chilling tale in which a woman, Flora,
attempts to seduce a naive young man, Lance: she persuades him
it is too late to leave her house, so that he must spend the night
there. She becomes, however, irritated by his lack of initiative, as he
remains sleeping in the front room while she lies in her bed. Flora
then finds that a doll, given to her by Lance, whom she has named
Cyril has come to life and is making loathsome sexual advances
on her. Has the doll been animated by her own desires? And has
it also developed some unnatural relationship with Lance? When,

in anger, she throws it into the fire, she hears a scream from the front room . . .

Other stories of dolls or puppets are perhaps too insubstantial or opaque for analysis, but "The Puppets" [1978]—in which there is a suggestion that a man is somehow manipulating events in his entire village by the use of his puppets—and "Little Man" [1978]—in which wooden figures in an arcade show avenge their destroyers—can be noted.

Music becomes the focus of several stories. We have seen that Campbell has stressed the horrific potential of music and sound as early as "The Plain of Sound" [1962]. "The Dark Show" [1971] tells of a rock band and its attempt to break down the distinction between performers and audience; but does their elaborate stage show, involving evocative music and flashing strobe lights, actually cause the audience to become a single, drugged entity? In "Hearing Is Believing" [1979] a man hears increasingly odd sounds coming out of his stereo: first rain, then the tramp of some large creature, then a kind of terrified chanting. Later he falls into the realm from which these sounds are proceeding.

Even radio can inspire horror. "Broadcast" [1969] is a chilling tale in which two boys accompany their teacher, Mr Rolands, to the radio station where he works in the evenings. A malfunction occurs, and Rolands is asked to continue speaking into the microphone, even though it is not broadcasting. What is happening to the stream of words he is uttering? Why is he saying that the microphone is "draining me away" (BW 34)? Later, when one of the boys frantically asks him where he is, Rolands responds feebly: "I don't know where I am. Am I at all?" (BW 37). This story keenly hints at the dangerous paradox that must be faced by all performing artists. To what degree can they be distinguished from their performance? Are they—to the audience, at any rate— anything but the sum total of their performances? Is it not the case that, in a sense, a recording of Toscanini is more "real" than Toscanini himself?

Campbell's recent novel *The Wise Friend* (2020) is focused on pictorial art—specifically, the later paintings of a well-known artist, Thelma Turnbill, and their possibly supernatural impetus. As the novel opens, Thelma is already dead: she had either fallen, jumped, or been pushed from a tower block in the Liverpool area. The first-person narrator, Patrick Semple, is her nephew; and he has already been experiencing difficulty maintaining a connection with his fifteen-year-old son, Roy, following his divorce from his wife, Julia (who has custody of Roy). When Roy becomes fascinated with Thelma's paintings, just as Patrick had been when his aunt was alive, there seems to be the possibility of a tightening of bonds between father and son; but things take a very different turn as the novel progresses.

We receive only fleeting glimpses of Thelma's later life, when she divorced her longtime husband, Neville, and took up with a "companion" named Abel who became her "inspiration." We are also not given full particulars of the nature of Thelma's late work, aside from a passage early on that speaks of "how the intense lyricism of her early landscapes had grown hallucinatory before advancing into a highly personal form of surrealism, where enigmatic elements recalled the magical suggestions of Leonora Carrington, Thelma's favourite painter."

When Patrick and Roy begin visiting the places where Thelma had received inspiration for her paintings—especially Third Mile Wood, where they become momentarily lost and have difficulty finding their way out—the frequency with which disturbing details accumulate becomes unnerving. Consider this description of the wood:

> Already the trees looked flatter than they ought to be, more like a painting that could render us just as motionless. If they came to life I was afraid it might be a wrong kind. Perhaps they would start to dance where they stood, unless they scurried on their knuckly roots to clasp one another's branches

before forming rings everywhere around us in a ritual dance. The holes fallen branches had left in the tree trunks looked about to gape if not to burst into song, to surround me with the lyric I'd heard last time we were here.

This proves to be a dream that Patrick had after his first visit to the wood, but it points to how the natural world, and the terrors it may conceal and then reveal, are really the focal point of the entire novel.

Things take a still more disturbing turn when Roy takes up with a girl, apparently of his own age, named Bella. At first, both Patrick and Julia are encouraged to see their son developing this relationship with a member of the opposite sex, but it is not long before Patrick finds this slight, enigmatic female (if indeed she is female, or even human) alarming and even terrifying. This sense of dread, nebulous at first, is substantially augmented when Patrick's parents die in a suspicious auto accident (Patrick was actually on the phone with them when the accident occurred) and, later, when a woman who had seen Thelma jump or fall off that tower block also dies mysteriously.

Meanwhile, Roy is becoming obsessed with Bella as only a fifteen-year-old can, and his father's objections only strengthen his resolve to stick with her. Patrick can only watch helplessly as Bella leads Roy to the various sites that Thelma had painted, collecting samples of earth just as Thelma herself had done (she had thrown them off that tower block just before her own death). And what of the fact that Bella's parents seem to be nowhere in sight, and that she apparently lives in an abandoned and derelict hotel? Patrick's own obsession with Bella—and his fervent desire to break her hold over his son—cause increasing tension with his son and his ex-wife, who makes the appalling suggestion that Patrick is sexually interested in her. But a book on witchcraft that Thelma had read—and that Roy and Bella had also pored over—tells Patrick more than he wants to know about who, or what, Bella really is.

The deceptively simple, even bland title of *The Wise Friend* masks one of the quiet triumphs in Campbell's novelistic output. With scarcely any overt horror until the concluding chapters, the novel incrementally creates a sense of *unease* that at times becomes almost unbearable. Patrick's wanderings through the wild, rustic areas that his aunt had painted lead his acute senses to discern the hideous possibility that the vegetation surrounding him has suddenly become sentient. His increasingly hostile dealings with Bella lead to sharp exchanges where every utterance augments the tension and dread. Early on, in a discussion of print books and their electronic counterparts, Bella states: "That's the way with old things. They come back in another form." Is she really talking about books here? In portraying her relationship with Roy, she says, "We're helping each other grow." Patrick and the reader suspect that there is far more to this than a trite expression of self-actualization.

Toward the end, when Patrick has unmasked Bella's true nature, she issues the ominous warning: "Expect me any time." Sure enough, Patrick now seems besieged—both at his home and his office, and all along the journey from the one to the other—with grotesque presences that she may have summoned up or that are various forms of her own identity. In an ambiguous conclusion, Patrick appears to have triumphed and saved his son—but we are left wondering if the horror is truly eliminated.

There is a great deal more to *The Wise Friend* than merely an excursion into age-old horror. I am particularly impressed at how Campbell has incorporated classical music—from Monteverdi to Britten—into the narrative, using these compositions at key moments to enhance the unnerving scenario. And Campbell's mastery at character portrayal is once again on display in his depiction of the increasingly frazzled Patrick, the naïve but headstrong Roy, and the embittered Julia, whose discussions with her ex-husband lay bare the contempt and loathing she feels for him. But it is Campbell's portrayal of the inscrutable Bella, who is clearly more than—or entirely different from—the fifteen-year-old girl she appears to be, that makes this novel the masterwork that it is.

We also must single out Campbell's richly textured, smooth-flowing prose. After more than fifty years of writing, Campbell has honed his prose idiom into a formidable weapon that can, with seeming effortlessness, say exactly what he wishes to say. Here, in a remarkable expansion of Poe's "unity of effect" to novel length, every single word has some bearing on the overall thrust of the narrative, and he can express fine shades of emotional resonance with the deftness of a Henry James without that author's occasional verbosity and turdigity. Campbell also has a bit of fun every now and then with contemporary usage, particularly the problematical use of "they" in the singular—which here causes all manner of ambiguities and confusions, just as it does in real life.

The Wise Friend may not have quite the spectacular horrific imagery of, say, *The House on Nazareth Hill* or the psychological intensity of *The Face That Must Die*, but it easily stands as a signal contribution to Campbell's oeuvre. Ramsey Campbell has already left nearly every other weird writer, past or present, in the dust; and this new novel only cements the lofty reputation he has achieved through a lifetime of stellar work.

It is scarcely surprising that a writer like Campbell, so given to niceties of style and to fashioning horror not so much by overt incident as by manipulation of narrative, should develop a sense of the awesome, perhaps horrific, power of language. The number of writers in Campbell's novels and tales is substantial; and in several tales he has directly addressed the relationship of language and reality, and of how the former can interpenetrate the latter.

Several earlier tales on the subject cannot be deemed entirely successful. An uncollected story, "Writer's Curse" [1970], tells of two men, the narrator and his friend Dunn, both of whom are

horror writers. The narrator states that Dunn's stories are deriva-
tive of his own, and in an altercation Dunn shatters an inkwell and
causes the narrator's arm to bleed. Later, a new story by Dunn
evokes more horror than the narrator expected—to the degree
that he sees monsters outside his window. We are then given to
understand that the monsters are a result of the narrator's blood
that Dunn used in his ink. The tale is somewhat marred by excessive obliquity and a flippant conclusion that turns the story into a
kind of black comedy.

Similarly unsuccessful is "The Words That Count" [1973],
although Campbell retains an inexplicable fondness for it. Here
the basic premise of the story is that the first word of every
paragraph consists of the Lord's Prayer recited backwards—a
monumental sin in the eyes of devout Catholics, evidently. What
Campbell does not perceive is that such a story will have no effect
on anyone else. In any case, the whole structure and narration of
the tale become highly unnatural as a result of this verbal trick.

Rather cleverer is "Out of Copyright" [1977], in which an
unscrupulous bookseller and editor reawakens an ancient curse
when he corrects a typographical error in a story. When corrected,
the initial letters of the opening paragraphs of the story read *E
mortuis revoco* ("From the dead I summon thee"); and sure enough,
some "grey blotch" (AH 268) descends upon the hapless narrator
as he reads the all too correctly printed tale.

In later works Campbell returns repeatedly to the complexities,
bizarreries, and anomalies of words, and in particular to their effect
upon those neurotic individuals whose grasp of reality is weak
to begin with. Of course, this cannot be called a recent concern
in any sense; recall Campbell's admission that among the many
changes inflicted upon his novel *The Face That Must Die* [1976–77]
when first published was the "taking out [of] most of the paranoid
puns, which still seem to me to ring truer than almost anything
else in the book" (FD xiii). But certainly the tendency has become
pronounced in his more recent work.

"End of the Line" [1991] deals with a man in the telemarketing business, Roger Speke (his last name is clearly significant), who experiences a variety of bizarre telephone exchanges and finally goes mad: is he being haunted by the voices of his deceased ex-wife and child? The bare outline of the plot is the least significant thing about this story, which fluctuates wildly from outrageous humour (Speke can scarcely resist making horrible puns when speaking to unresponsive individuals on the phone) to psychological horror as Speke descends into insanity.

Then there is "McGonagall in the Head" [1991], about a man who runs the births, deaths, and marriages department of a local newspaper and who is so haunted by a wretched piece of doggerel designed as a death notice that he is compelled to speak in rhyme.

"The Word" [1993] is an intensely strange story that features dark ruminations on the power of language. Told in the present tense by the jaundiced, possibly mentally disturbed editor of a fan magazine, Jeremy Bates, the story deals with the improbable rise to fame of a wretched hack, Jess Kray, who first produces the obligatory trilogy of windy fantasy novels, then achieves even greater success with *The Word*, an immense novel that achieves notoriety because it is deemed blasphemous by both Christian and Muslim fundamentalists. The work seems to affect every reader profoundly, and Bates can only marvel that people are so fatuous as to be taken in by Kray's rubbish. Yearning with maniacal fervour to expose Kray, he manages to worm his way on to a televised panel discussion with Kray, in the course of which he rips out Kray's throat and then kills himself.

"The Word" carries a multitude of messages: the ignorance of the reading public, unable to distinguish merit from hackwork ("It almost makes me laugh to find I didn't want to be shown that people are as stupid as I've always thought they were" [TD 331]); the pomposity of literary critics (one critic opines: "I think the core of this book may be the necessary myth for our time" [TD 331]); and the fanaticism of religious fundamentalists who seek to suppress what they fail to understand. Indeed, toward the end the story metamorphoses from a meditation on language to a religious allegory, as Kray's death is explicitly compared to that of Jesus Christ. Is Kray (as his very name suggests) the second coming of Christ, and does his book embody Christ's true teachings, as the hypocrisy of modern Christianity fails to do? "The Word," mingling the misanthropic satire of Ambrose Bierce with the existential angst of Franz Kafka, is one of Campbell's most disturbing tales.

"Out of the Woods" [1994] was initially issued on an audiotape of Campbell's stories, *Twilight Tales from Merseyside* (1995). Campbell states in an introductory note that he was asked by a Finnish publisher to write a story about wood, paper, or a Finnish legend; Campbell obliged by writing a single story about all three. A publisher of children's books scorns a book manuscript delivered to him by a strange man. The book proves to be made merely of leaves and twigs. As the publisher hurls the book out the door into the yard, he finds that the books stored in his warehouse have suddenly disintegrated. Later he is pursued by some wooden totem figure and is overwhelmed when he flees into a nearby forest. The story's fundamental message is of Nature's revenge on humanity, and the tale develops a powerful atmosphere of horror as its climax approaches. To hear it read by Campbell himself increases the listener's shuddersome pleasure.

In *The Seven Days of Cain* (2010) Andy Bentley works in a Liverpool photography studio, Bentley & Son, established by his parents, Brian and Hazel Bentley. Andy's wife Claire works for an organisation called Home From Home, which provides temporary housing for homeless people until they can get back on their feet. Claire is having trouble getting pregnant, and doctors cannot seem to identify any cause. Andy begins getting odd e-mail messages alluding to an incident related in the first chapter, where a man brutally killed a woman named Serena Paz. Two other, seemingly unrelated, incidents are causes for concern: an eccentric customer calling himself Max Beyer proposes collaborating with Andy on a book, and Claire meets a man named Tim Battle, an out-of-work actor who claims to have been a schoolmate of hers.

As Andy continues to receive disturbing messages, both by e-mail and by phone, the reader wonders whether Andy could himself have been involved in the Barcelona incident. Claire, for her part, wonders if Andy is being unfaithful to her. Finally Andy explains the matter to Claire: Years before, Andy had wished to become a writer, and he found a website that claimed to assist him in building characters: the site (which evokes the name of Roland Franklyn, author of *We Pass from View*) encouraged users to imagine a life for seven characters (each of them representing a distinct quality in oneself), complete with identity numbers, blogs, and so on. Andy had devised six characters—and these are the ones that he is now hearing are being killed. Could these characters have come to life somehow? And are they being killed by the seventh character, whom Andy had never finished creating?

Andy goes to Birmingham and looks up Adam Caboodle (a pseudonym), who had designed the website, but learns little from him. Then a neighbour suggests a disturbing possibility: Max Beyer and Tim Battle (who has managed a remarkable resurrection in his fortunes and is becoming increasingly attentive to Claire) might be the same person. And this person may in fact be the killer of Andy's characters. What does he want with Andy and Claire? Andy is further disturbed by coming upon a book by a local writer, Mick Pocus, titled *Clare's Tale:* its lead character's upbringing (especially in regard to the death of her parents) seems very similar to what Claire has told Andy about her past. Is Claire herself a product of Andy's imagination? Claire invites Tim into her house, and Andy comes home to confront them—with consequences that no one can predict.

The novel is one of Campbell's most unnerving, in suggesting that the line between reality and fiction can never be clearly drawn, and that what we take for reality may be fantasy. The novel also confirms Campbell's innovative use of modern technology to create a sense of terror, as e-mails, the Internet, cellphones, and other tokens of contemporary life are at the heart of the narrative.

VI. HORRORS OF THE CITY

R amsey Campbell is the poet of urban squalor and decay. His Brichester and Liverpool (which, as we have seen, had already become interchangeable by the late 1960s) evoke the filth, noise, decadence, and smouldering class tensions that typify much urban life, and this is another way in which Campbell has radically modernised the horror tale, which had previously been content to seek horror in the remote wilderness (Machen, Blackwood) or in the small villages of England (M. R. James) or America (Ambrose Bierce). Lovecraft was, to some small degree, a forerunner, for, aside from a few stories that etch his detestation of the megalopolis of New York, his New England cities, real or imagined, certainly have a meticulous realism of a kind. But that realism emphasises the loathsomeness that may emerge from antique structures or dubious history ("witch-haunted Arkham") rather than the social pressures that can make daily life a hell for so many urban denizens. Clearly Campbell has drawn upon his own experiences in Liverpool, a city with which he has maintained a love-hate relationship even after moving out of it in 1980.

We have already seen that the evocation of the seediness of the urban landscape—slums, pornography, prostitution—made "Cold

Print" [1966–67] far more than a simple pastiche of Lovecraft. An earlier story, "The Cellars" [1965], is in fact Campbell's first tale to be set in Liverpool, drawing upon an actual subterranean location for a tale of supernatural horror. A description of a walk through the city sets the stage for terror:

Fewer feet splashed through the dirty puddles at the end of Church Street. They skirted the cloaked black figure among the Victoria Monument's pillars and hurried down the line of parking meters like hooded cobras. On either side the discreet life insurance buildings with their golden nameplates mounted to wild turrets. Vic led the way below the regimented windows and cream rain-striped walls of Exchange Flags; scattered men and women, dwarfed by the ebon figures chained below a maritime motto, ran from the scything rain. Here Julie lost her way; they wandered through a maze of streets whose sides descended to unlabelled blackened doors, past makeshift bookstalls cloaked in drooling oilskin, between opaque windows and boarded doors. Very far away, it seemed, a steamer blew its nose. Then, when she was least expecting it, she was led through a gaping arch between two silent storage houses into an inner court, across the slimy cobbles to a railing which boxed in a heavy long trapdoor, hooked back to show treacherous stone steps burrowing into rectangular darkness. (HS 101–2)

That "maze of streets" through which Julie "lost her way" is critical to the fantastic enterprise: what seems like a meticulous, if somewhat impressionistic, description of a real topography must veer off into the mysterious if it is to allow room for the inexplicable to enter.

"The Other House" [1969], although otherwise a rambling and undistinguished tale, supplies good evidence of the sharply etched vignettes Campbell uses to portray the urban landscape:

I splashed cold water on my face. Finding no towel, I stood on the woven ironwork of the balcony and gazed across the baked brown chimneys to the green foreheads of the fields beyond. On Milton Street the grey porous house still absorbed the sunlight . . .

The infrequent bookshops seemed to stock mainly *Private Eye* and *Rubber News*. Children threw tyres on a pale orange fire on a bomb-site. Two girls carried piles of records into a second-hand shop. An old man swayed beneath a bottle on a doorstep. A couple embraced in a cemetery, watched by a movie camera and a bored clapper-boy with a Coca-Cola. Halfway down a street of disembowelled houses, I read a pencilled sign in a curtained window: "We still live here." (BW 72–73)

Each sentence, so seemingly simple, embodies a multitude of resonances, in some cases evoking an entire socioeconomic portrait of impoverished lives struggling against hopelessness to survive.

In Campbell, horror can be found anywhere. "Litter" [1972] finds it in an outdoor market or mall. Again, the setting is Brichester, but it is not the Brichester of the early Lovecraft imitations. Modern but nevertheless eerie in its nightly desertion, the mall causes one character to remark: "This place is about the least haunted I've ever encountered, and it makes me uneasy" (HS 136). Why is the litter that is the unavoidable accompaniment to so many urban vistas so copious here? Why does it seem to attack the narrator?

It consisted largely of paper: old grey newspapers, paper bags puffed up like lungs, tendrils of receipts, scraps like leaden moths. As the wind tore it from the pillar and threw it at me, the mass resembled a hulking attacker swooping from concealment; it was almost my height, and for a moment gave the impression of a similar build, and of a sort of faceless

impersonal aggression. Then it flew apart, scattering on the
floor, pasting itself to the walls and to me. (HS 139)

This would be bad enough, but read what follows: "I brushed it
off furiously, my heart pounding, and hurried away. Or began to,
for I hadn't taken three paces when I heard a fluttering behind me.
I turned and saw the litter falling from the walls into a heap and
reforming" (HS 139). One wonders whether there is a subtle nod
to Lovecraft's "The Call of Cthulhu" (1926), in which an extrater-
restrial entity is rammed into by a ship and bursts into pieces but
moments later recombines itself into its original shape. In "Litter"
there is, moreover, a suggestion that the narrator's own fear is ani-
mating the garbage.

Later stories begin to explore the varieties of social and other
distinctions—rich and poor, old and young, men and women—
that the city seems to exacerbate by simple juxtaposition. "The
Sneering" [1975] is a bizarre but poignant tale in which the sneers
that an elderly couple receive from youths seem symbolic of the
cynical, modern attitude they cannot understand. "The Brood"
[1976] finds terror in a lonely old woman who collects stray animals—but is she fully human, and is she perhaps using the animals
for food? The anonymity that it is possible to preserve in a popu-
lous city allows a variety of horrors to be carried on behind closed
doors.

Perhaps the single most frightening story Campbell has ever
written is "Mackintosh Willy" [1977], which tells of a derelict who
terrorises a group of boys both in life and in death. He seems to
live in a bus shelter, and the thoughtless boys plague him with the
mercilessness of their kind:

> We were too young for tolerance—and besides, he was intol-
> erant of us. Ever since we could remember he had been there,
> guarding his territory and his bottle of red biddy. If anyone
> ventured too close he would start muttering. Sometimes you

could hear some of the words: "Damn bastard prying inter-
fering snooper . . . thieving bastard layabout . . . think you're
clever, eh? . . . I'll give you something clever . . . " (AH 282)

In life he is variously compared to "an injured spider" (AH 282)
and "an old grey sack" (AH 283). Then, when he dies in the shelter,
he is likened to an "old bag of washing, decayed and mouldy" (AH
284). With heedless disrespect, one of the boys places bottle-caps
on his eyes. Some time later a man is noted in the shelter, wearing
some strange kind of spectacles. It is in fact Mackintosh Willy,
who now seems like "a half-submerged heap of litter" (AH 294).
He hideously avenges the desecration of his corpse by killing the
boy who placed the bottle-caps on his eyes.

"Mackintosh Willy" is a masterwork because of the insidious
gradualness with which the tale unfolds and the cumulative horror
it achieves. Intermingled with the purely supernatural component
is the sensitive story of the narrator's slow maturation as he relates
to his friends and parents, has his first girlfriend, and goes through
the other customary stages leading from adolescence to adulthood. But in the end it is the horror of the tale that remains in
our memory, as Mackintosh Willy exacts revenge on the narrator's
friend in a pond:

> When I tried to raise him, I discovered that he was pinned
> down. I had to grope blindly over him in the chill water,
> feeling how still he was. Something like a swollen cloth
> bag, very large, lay over his face. I couldn't bear to touch it
> again, for its contents felt soft and fat. Instead I seized Mark's
> ankles and managed at last to drag him free. Then I struggled
> towards the edge of the pool, heaving him by his shoulders,
> lifting his head above water. His weight was dismaying. (AH
> 296–97)

"The Depths" [1978], which features one of the most original premises in Campbell's entire work, provides a kind of philosophical rationale for his tales of urban horror. Here, a writer, Jonathan Miles, moves into a house where a man had murdered his wife in some hideous way. Miles is himself writing a book on murder and feels that the atmosphere might give him inspiration. It does more than that. He begins having horrible nightmares, later writing them down for sheer relief, even though he is ashamed of their vile content. Shortly thereafter Miles notices that if he does not write down his loathsome dreams, the events they depict will happen in real life. It is clear that Miles is serving as a kind of focus for the collective repressions of a society that would prefer to ignore the very existence of crime and its sources:

> No wonder they [his dreams] were so terrible, or that they were growing worse. If material repressed into the unconscious was bound to erupt in some less manageable form, how much more powerful that must be when the unconscious was collective! Precisely because people were unable to come to terms with the crimes, repudiated them as utterly inhuman or simply unimaginable, the horrors would reappear in a worse form and possess whomever they pleased. (AH 352)

This conception reminds us of the basic premise of *Incarnate*, although here the idea that dreams wish to replace the real world is given a pointedly social dimension.

We have seen that Campbell's investigation of class conflict emerged in so early a tale as "The Scar" [1967]; in "The Alternative" [1990] it achieves a striking culmination. Here a man named Highton, a successful accountant, has a recurring dream in which his wife has become aged and broken, his teenage daughter a whore, and his teenage son a drug addict. The dream takes place in a slum area not far from where he lives, and one day he drives there in an attempt to rid himself of the obsession; instead, he finds that a particular flat tallies uncannily with the setting of his dream. Out of a bizarre sense of guilt he stuffs £100 into the letterbox of the flat.

The dreams, however, continue, and now Highton dreams that his son found the money and apparently ran off with it, for who knows what purpose. Highton vows to give the occupants of the flat more useful items—a television, his son's computer—in another attempt to relieve his guilt; but as he is staging a burglary in his own house so that he can take the items away, his wife and children return unexpectedly and catch him. Later he dreams that his son bought a television and computer with the £100 he found. Highton reflects: "Life at the flat had started to grow hopeful because life at the house had taken a turn for the worse" (GGT 49). In a dreamlike conclusion, Highton goes to the flat, sets fire to his Jaguar, and goes into the flat to await his family.

This poignant tale simultaneously touches upon the nebulous distinction between dream and reality as well as the shuddering guilt felt by many of the middle class at the existence of grinding poverty, especially in cities where the propinquity of rich and poor makes it all too obvious. The opening of the story relates Highton's dream of his decline in socioeconomic status, but Campbell does not make it evident that Highton is in fact dreaming: the point, of course, is to show how the members of the middle class can so easily envisage themselves falling into such a state. The rest of the story pointedly cites the necessary luxuries of middle-class life—an expensive car, a microwave, a computer, a house with a spacious garden and patio—that can only be a dream to those who dwell in the slums.

The majority of Campbell's novels are set in the urban milieu; indeed, only six can be thought of as taking place in towns, villages, or the wilderness (*The Claw*, *Obsession*, *The Hungry Moon*, *Ancient Images*, *Midnight Sun*, and *The House on Nazareth Hill*). Liverpool is the setting for *The Doll Who Ate His Mother*, *The Face*

That Must Die, The Parasite, The Influence, and *The Count of Eleven*.
London is largely the setting for *The Nameless* and *Incarnate*, and
The Long Lost is based in Chester. *The Parasite* also features a vivid
tableau of New York. In several of these works we are far from
the cheerless slums that are found in Campbell's short stories, as
this poetic description of London as seen from a roof in *Incarnate*
testifies:

> A silenced crowd streamed homeward along Kensington
> High Street, and the muted brass of traffic drifted up. The
> rooftops were a different city—weathercocks dozing for
> the moment among the turrets and highbrow windows and
> rooftop greenhouses; flags stirring among the shrubbery of a
> roof garden. Beyond the sunset roofs, Chelsea looked carved
> out of amber. A breeze lifted a hint of bells from the spire of
> St. Mary Abbot's. (I 103)

But of course, London has its seedier side, and it is called Soho:

> Lights chased around the borders of neon lights in Old
> Compton Street, cards bearing women's handwritten names
> were tacked above doorbells in shabby alleys. Spiky rubber
> penises stood in shop windows, masked women brandished
> whips on glossy covers, women bared breasts like a baby's
> dream, improbably muscled young men looked made of
> bronze or chocolate. Women with faces that made sure
> nobody thought Soho had anything to do with them were
> hurrying home through the narrow crowded streets. (I 77)

All these novels certainly provide telling glimpses of both the
thriving life and the social ills of the metropolis; but it is *The One
Safe Place*, written in 1993–94 and published in 1995, that portrays city life and class conflict in an especially bitter and searing
fashion.

The novel opens with a prelude in Florida, where twelve-year-old Marshall Travis is threatened by a gang of rowdy youths, one of whom may have a gun, but manages to elude them. The tone is set for the novel's exploration of lawlessness and violent youth, even though the scene shifts to England, where the Travis family—Marshall and his parents, Susanne, a professor, and Don, a bookseller—have settled. Initially, however, a vignette is offered of Darren Fancy, a teenager from a working-class section of Manchester. We quickly learn that Darren is repeatedly beaten by his parents and that his father, Phil, has grudgingly made room in his ill-kept house for his sick and senile father, whom Phil's wife Marie can scarcely be bothered to look after.

In another early chapter Susanne finds herself the source of ignorant abuse when she participates in a televised town meeting on violence in society. She teaches a class at the university on representations of violence, and her understanding of the complexity of the issues is overridden by the simple-minded views of the locals, who are quick to recommend blanket censorship as well as corporal punishment as easy solutions to the problem.

Don seems to be doing better in his book business, which is what brought the family to England in the first place. But as he is driving home from his shop, he becomes involved with a man in a black Peugeot who is driving recklessly and who then corners him in a dead end and pulls a gun on him. The man leaves only when he notices that a witness has seen the entire incident. This individual proves to be Phil Fancy.

Phil is incensed when an unflattering identikit sketch of him appears in the paper after Don reports the incident to the police. He skulks at the Travis house and, when Marshall comes home from school alone, he forces his way in. When Don arrives, there is a scuffle and Phil breaks his ankle. After a short trial he is sentenced to eighteen months in jail, and the Travises are satisfied that justice has been done. But their lives are further disrupted when the police raid their home and confiscate all the videos that

Susanne uses to teach her course, as well as videos belonging to Marshall. Some of these are banned in England, and in any event none of them—even harmless films like *Singing in the Rain*—have a British censor"s certificate. They are taken, one and all.

At a party, a novelist friend of Don's had quietly offered to arrange for him to secure a gun, skirting Britain's very strict laws on the possession of weapons. Don initially scuttles the idea as needless, but then, when the Fancy family—nearly all of whose members are involved in a variety of criminal activities—threatens the Travises at the trial, Don has second thoughts. At a seedy bar he pays £300 for a small handgun.

Matters turn worse for the Fancy family. One of their relatives, Jim Fancy, dies in a car accident while fleeing the police. Ken and Dave Fancy, Darren's uncles, vow revenge against the American family whom they blame for their troubles. They confront Don in front of his bookshop; Don pulls the gun on them, and they momentarily retreat, but they quickly learn that the gun is not loaded, so they pummel and kick Don to death while a busload of commuters watch.

At their trial Ken and Dave are found guilty, not of murder, but of manslaughter, since Don had been threatening them with the gun. They must serve no less than five years in prison. The Fancy family objects even to this sentence, while Susanne is stunned by what she feels is an appalling miscarriage of justice; she is widely quoted in the newspapers as saying the killers would have been very differently treated by an American jury. Marshall tries as best he can to deal with the loss of his father and the subsequent brouhaha of the trial. On the way to school one day, however, he sees a newsstand with a notice flamboyantly quoting (or mis-quoting) Susanne's reaction to the verdict ("SEND KILLERS TO FLORIDA" [OSP 184]); enraged, he tears it up. The incident is reported to the offensively stuffy headmaster of Marshall's school, who takes little account of Marshall's emotional state and upbraids him for his "vandalism." Marshall abruptly leaves the school at midday and heads for the cemetery where his father is buried. Increasingly upset and disoriented, he is shocked and dismayed to find that his father's headstone has been broken into pieces. He goes home, changes out of his uniform and into a track suit, and leaves again, not even having any clear idea where he is going. He finds his way into a shopping mall, where he buys a soft drink. If at any point in the novel, it is here that an element of fantasy enters. Consider this description of a derelict as seen by Marshall:

> . . . he almost tripped over a figure seated against the wall under the window of a clothes shop—a man dressed in a sack or an old coat, which he'd pulled up over his head and draped around a grey dog on his chest. The animal must be dead, because it was grey with dust, and so was the stubble covering much of the man's caved-in face. Were his eyeballs coated with dust, or were his eyes shut? The head fell back, the face began to move, which ought to mean he was alive, except that it appeared to be coming to pieces. (OSP 206)

Only much later do we learn that this and other hallucinations were engendered by some LSD secretly slipped into his drink by an individual who ran into him at the mall—none other than Darren Fancy.

Fancy then accosts Marshall, calling him by name. Marshall, now quite dazed, thinks he may be a friend. Darren takes Marshall home, intent on harming or even killing him. He hides Marshall in his filthy room and, when Marshall—now scarcely aware of his surroundings—asks for some medicine, Darren gives him one of his mother's birth control pills. Darren does not wish to let anyone know that Marshall is there, especially when other members of his family, who have just committed a large burglary, hide a great quantity of money and valuables in the place and tell Darren not to let anyone know about it.

At this point Darren's mother sees Marshall and peremptorily tells her son to get rid of the boy. Darren and Marshall play Russian roulette with a revolver that has a single bullet in its chamber. Marshall thinks it is just a game, and he pulls the trigger six times in succession after spinning the chamber (he has learned to sense where the bullet is lodged). Then, when Darren is asleep, Marshall turns on the television and puts a video on—the one he chooses happens to be pornography (*A Bitch and Her Mate*) about a woman and a dog. At the end of the video Marshall is puzzled to find a taped news report of himself and his mother standing in front of Don's bookshop.

Meanwhile, Susanne is frantic about the absence of her son. The school knows nothing; he is not at any of his friends' houses. Finally she calls the police (who have, partially in consideration of her series of misfortunes, dropped their prosecution of her over the videos). Nothing turns up until a security guard not only remembers seeing a boy matching Marshall's description but believes that the boy with him bore a striking resemblance to the identikit picture of Phil Fancy. The police, with Susanne, immediately head for the Fancy residence.

Darren, seeing a motorcyclist driving repeatedly by the house, thinks it is a policeman, so he comes up with a plan: he persuades the still confused Marshall to hide in Darren's grandfather's room and bark like a dog. When the police arrive, the plan incredibly works. Susanne, however, thinks she sees Marshall's track suit in Darren's room, but it proves to be a British make belonging to Darren. The police, having no evidence, have no recourse but to leave.

Susanne, in despair, then remembers something of possible significance: when she thought she had identified Marshall's track suit, she had perceived a guilty look momentarily flash across Darren's face. She is convinced Marshall is in fact at the Fancy house, but she does not think she can convince the police of that; so she goes there herself. Just as she is getting out of her car, she hears a gunshot.

What has actually happened in the Fancy house is this. The motorcyclist whom Darren thought was a policeman was in fact Barry, a criminal associate of the Fancys who had seen the police arrive and was worried about his stash of stolen loot. Barging into the house and learning of Marshall's identity, he vows to put an end to the boy himself. Marshall, meanwhile, manages to get hold of the revolver with its single bullet. Barry jeers at him, thinking either that the gun is not loaded or that Marshall will be unable to pull the trigger. As Marshall walks out into the yard, he aims the gun at Barry. Barry seizes Darren and holds the boy in front of him. Marshall, still thinking Darren a friend, orders Barry to let him go, but Barry refuses. Just as Marshall pulls the trigger, Barry lifts Darren up and covers himself with the boy: the bullet shatters Darren's skull and also penetrates Barry's neck; both die.

In a rapid conclusion, Campbell skips over the subsequent trial, indicating that Marshall was exonerated because he had been drugged by Darren. Susanne and Marshall feel that they have no alternative but to leave England and return to America. On the plane ride back home, however, Marshall begins reflecting on events. He is determined to grow up and become a police officer; or if not, at least he will own a gun and, unlike his father, keep it loaded.

The One Safe Place, one of the longest of Campbell's novels, is as relentlessly cheerless a work as any he has written, *The Face That Must Die* not excluded. After the death of Don Travis, who in life cracked his share of jokes (as many of Campbell's later characters do), the novel becomes almost unbearably depressing. To say this, however, is only to praise the powerful atmosphere of gloom in the work and its ruthless display of the tragedy of wasted lives. The character portrayal is particularly fine. Campbell etches the differing socioeconomic status of the Travises and the Fancys largely by their speech; the latter can hardly utter a sentence without monotonously lacing it with profanity, and their scornful references to the police ("the filth") and women (who are all "tarts") betray their attitudes far more than their actions.

But the depiction of the Fancys, while harsh, is far from being uniformly contemptuous. Campbell is careful to show that Darren in particular is merely the product of his environment and upbringing. Brutalised since youth by both his father and his mother, raised in a filthy, impoverished home where the only money comes from crime and where his mother blandly takes to prostitution to raise money when her husband goes to jail, Darren can scarcely be expected to be other than he is—ignorant, ill-tempered, smouldering with hatred and resentment, and thirsting for the violence of which he himself has been the victim. "He wasn't going to let her [his mother] see how much she was hurting him, he was saving it up until he could pass it on to someone else" (OSP 315): this single sentence laconically exposes the unending cycle of violence engendered by domestic abuse.

As for the Travis family, almost to the end they desperately maintain that their coming to England was not a mistake, even though Don has died, Susanne is outraged at the lack of freedom of expression, and Marshall is confused by British ways and British English. The fact that they are Americans is significant: having come from a country where violence has become endemic and gun ownership a supposed right, they are scarcely prepared for the level of violence they face in a land where the murder rate is a fraction of what it is in the United States.

How are we to read Marshall's concluding resolution? How else but as the final capstone of horror in the novel? Those many individuals in the United States who feel that guns are the solution to everything—or anything—will no doubt agree vigorously with Marshall's change of heart; but what has he done except to become just like the Fancys he so despises? The interior monologue Campbell presents as Marshall reflects upon owning a gun is full of exactly the obscenities ("Let George S. and his cronies try to fuck with him then") and cold-bloodedness

("'Always make sure your gun is loaded,' he whispered" [OSP 373]) that we found so prevalent in the Fancy clan; and we are merely left to wonder whether Marshall will turn from killing in self-defence to killing for vengeance, perhaps himself being killed in the process.

The censorship issue is perhaps the one facet of the novel that disappoints, for its sudden resolution when the police decide not to prosecute Susanne seems something of a cop-out. An American readership might be very interested to pursue the legal ramifications of the matter in a country where there is no First Amendment. In particular, Campbell has no discussion of the university's position in the whole situation, even though Susanne hopes and believes that it will support her contention that the confiscated videos are educational in nature. Campbell had treated the issue previously if glancingly in *Ancient Images*, and perhaps he wishes here to do no more than to draw attention to the general problem: on the one hand, the possible effect of actual pornography (as in the bestiality videos owned by the Fancys) on impressionable people; and, on the other hand, the arbitrary nature of government censorship—supported by perhaps a majority of unthinking individuals in the society at large who find in "nasty" videos a simple answer to the difficult issue of crime and its causes. Campbell is, of course, manifestly on the side of freedom of expression, even though he has delivered a warning to the purveyors of explicit horror fiction that cannot be ignored: "I think it is high time some of them considered that they may be producing something more deplorable and more pernicious. The best I can hope is that their work, with the tedium of its excesses, destroys nothing but itself."[1] But in *The One Safe Place* he somehow fails to come to grips with the issue.

The overriding question in regard to the novel, of course, is whether the work is within the realm of horror fiction at all.

1. "Ramsey Campbell, Probably," *Necrofile* No. 11 (Winter 1994): 15.

The question is only of interest for purposes of classification
and can scarcely affect one's evaluation of the work itself. Not
only is *The One Safe Place* non-supernatural, but it is not really
even a suspense novel with horrific interludes (as, say, the novels
of Thomas Harris are): only the passage involving Marshall's
wandering out of school and falling into the hands of Darren
can be said to be remotely outré. *The One Safe Place* is a mainstream novel, pure and simple. There is one rather meretricious
instance where Campbell attempts to inject horror artificially
into the scenario, when he suggests that the gun has actually
gone off as Marshall is playing Russian roulette; but beyond this
there is nothing in the entire novel to engender the sensation
of fear or horror. One other passage—in which Susanne dreams
that she is driving around the neighbourhood at night looking
for Marshall—approaches the surreal impressionism of some of
Campbell's short stories:

> He hadn't been any of the boys who had clustered around
> the Volvo to offer themselves to her and to anyone else who
> might be in it, some of them at least as young as Marshall but
> with faces several times that age. He hadn't been among the
> children running away from an Indian jewellery store which
> had been set on fire. She'd thought she recognised him out-
> side an all-night pharmacy until the small figure had turned,
> catching a neon gleam on the syringe in his arm. Nor had
> Marshall been the child she'd seen dragged, screaming like an
> injured animal, into a car which had screeched away before
> she could read the number-plate. His hadn't been the body
> sprawled in the middle of a road, the blue pulse of an ambu-
> lance insistently blackening its spillage of blood. He hadn't
> been in any of the piles of newspapers in shop doorways,
> though each of the piles to which she'd stopped had poked
> out at least one head, and she hadn't found him among the
> inhabitants of a gap between the houses of a derelict street,

people crowding so closely around a fire that their clothes
had begun to smoulder. (OSP 281)

But in reality, perhaps only Marshall's concluding reflections allow
the novel to end on a genuinely chilling note.

And yet, it is difficult to deny *The One Safe Place* a high standing
in Campbell's work overall, however anomalous it may be and
however puzzled many of his devotees may find themselves upon
reading it. It is an unpleasant novel that leaves a bad taste in one's
mouth, but that is its intent. It lays bare the culture of criminality
and violence that is ripping apart the fabric of both English and
American society and is leaving no one, however exalted in social
or economic rank, unscathed. It offers no hope and sees no solution to the problems it exposes; and if this be deemed a flaw, it is a
flaw with which society as a whole is afflicted.

Creatures of the Pool (2009) is set entirely in Campbell's hometown. The "pool" of the title refers generally to Liverpool—and,
perhaps more specifically, to the pool of water, the Mersey, around
which Liverpool grew. For this novel is nothing less than an
attempt—and a highly successful one—to draw upon history as a
source of terror. *Creatures of the Pool* may be Ramsey Campbell's
ultimate tribute to the hold that the city has exercised on him
his entire life, even though in 1980 he moved across the Mersey
to live in neighbouring Wallasey. In this novel Campbell enlivens
both the topography of Liverpool (the published edition actually contains several splendid historical photographs of the actual
locales described in it) and its history by suggesting both literal
and metaphorical depths of which most of its hundreds of thou-
sands of citizens are mercifully unaware.

Much of the novel is a delightful fusion of the (historically)
real and imaginary. The first of several epigraphs is a couplet
from a *Description of Liverpool* (1802) from an obscure poet, William Colquitt. This person is a real individual, although his poem
is not a self-standing work but a contribution to his volume of

Poems (1802)—and I imagine that some of the lines of poetry scattered throughout the text are in fact of Campbell's, not Colquitt's, devising. The technique naturally reminds one of Lovecraft, who, even when citing real works—such as Remigius' *Daemonolatreia*—creates the impression that they are invented for the occasion. Campbell continues this pattern by repeatedly citing John Strong's *Glimpses of Absolute Power*, an imaginary work he had originally invented for his first novel, *The Doll Who Ate His Mother* (1975)—and the remarkable advances that Campbell has made since the writing of that novel thirty-odd years ago are no more clearly evident than in the highly disturbing and inscrutable passages by Strong scattered throughout *Creatures of the Pool*, so different from the rather crude and bombastic occultism of the analogous passages in *Doll*.

The first-person narrator of *Creatures of the Pool* is Gavin Meadows, who runs the Liverghoul Tours—tours of locales in the city where murders have occurred. His father, Deryck, is increasingly obsessed with the secret history of Liverpool, thinking that there is a vast conspiracy of silence that hides something baleful behind—and beneath—the city's bustling streets and plazas. Deryck runs a website devoted to the subject. Gavin finds his father's brusque and abrasive manner rather mortifying, especially in one instance where Deryck had demanded to be allowed to see some unpublished papers that the public library was supposed to house, but which the librarians (including Gavin's girlfriend Lucinda, who works there) denied owning. Things take an alarming turn when Deryck disappears—and Campbell effects a striking juxtaposition of past and present by the fact that Gavin delves simultaneously into Liverpool's past and hears sporadically from his father by means of curiously misspelled text messages on his cellphone. Gavin also develops something akin to his father's obsession as he continues his explorations around, and under, the city.

And yet, *Creatures of the Pool* is not quite the success that one might wish it to be. Campbell's prose has never been so scintillating and crisp, and the omnipresent rain that Campbell depicts throughout the novel—augmented by Gavin's anomalous thirst, which compels him to consume enormous quantities of water whenever the occasion allows—is harrowing; and, although there is a compelling climactic episode in which Gavin seeks to track both parents (for his mother has also by now disappeared) through the (real) tunnels of Liverpool, in the end we are not given quite the climax we are expecting. There is really no adequate explanation for the range of bizarre incidents scattered throughout the novel, so that the whole work becomes a kind of tease. I am not giving anything away in saying that Lovecraft's "The Shadow over Innsmouth" hangs heavy over the novel—even though Campbell, in his afterword to *Just Behind You*, seeks in part to deny its influence.

Recent stories continue the focus on urban blight and squalor. Consider this passage from "Becoming Visible" (1998):

I let my bicycle off its chain on the cold sweaty pipe in the Gents and carry it down the worn concrete stairs and out of the side door. A puppy or a rat scuttles down the alley, away from the bins outside the Chinese restaurant, where the kitchen is full of jabbering not much more alien than the talk that surrounds me every day. Above the senseless assortment of roofs the clouds are a slab of grease, holding down the heat of all the drudges who tramp the streets at lunchtime. They've gone home now to pretend they've lives worth living, only some have changed into this season's uniform and are swarming to the lights of clubs and pubs. I pedal past couples stuck together by their hands and imitating dummies in shop windows, past people who've given up pretending that a home is worth the effort and are nesting in the doorways of dead shops. Then there are buildings that are being smashed and burned, and a park with a lake that litter is soaking up and trees that move about so much I have to keep my curtains

shut. I cycle through, past two children undressing each other
in a shelter, and then I'm where I try to live. (TD 115–16)

This entire scene evokes the urban paranoia of *The Face That Must
Die* (1979/1983), the first and greatest of his non-supernatural
novels. "Agatha's Ghost" (1997; TD) comes close to equalling it in
its cheerless portrayal of an elderly woman who believes herself to
be haunted by her dead nephew.

In "Passing through Peacehaven" (HF), we find an older man
seemingly alone at night in a strange train station, unable to make
out the muffled announcements over the PA system and dimly
aware of vague threats, both physical (there is a deserted factory
nearby) and spiritual. The sense of isolation, helplessness, and
vulnerability this story evokes is unmatched even in the bulk of
Campbell's own work. Somewhat similar is "Recently Used" (HF),
where a man seeks with increasing alarm to locate his wife in a
hospital, and finally finds her—with ominous results.

"The Rounds" (HF) tells of an elderly man on a subway train
haunted by the prospect of a young Muslim woman who appears
to have left a suitcase (or a bomb?) on the train. "Chucky Comes
to Liverpool" (HF) is a pungent story of a woman so obsessed
with banning what in England are called "video nasties" (films
portraying extreme violence) that she fails to notice that her own
teenage son is turning into a delinquent.

The separately published short story *The Long Way* (2008)
features many of those elements that have made his work immediately recognisable—an unflinching portrayal of urban blight
and decay, a meticulous attention to prose that results both in
the crisp etching of character and a powerful sense of cumulative
horror, and a careful imprecision in the nature of the supernatural
phenomenon that tantalises without lapsing into vagueness or
obscurity. We are here confronted with a suburban development
named Copse View (the pun on that first word is not overlooked),

where a "figure . . . leaning on sticks" (4) is seen inside an abandoned house. How the teenage narrator deals with this, and with
his increasingly querulous handicapped uncle, is the double thread
that Campbell weaves in this glittering gem of supernatural terror.

VII. PARANOIA

On a psychological level, one of the most severe effects of modern urban life in Campbell's work is paranoia. We have already seen his fascination with the complexities of human psychology in the tales of the *Demons by Daylight* period—tales that featured an intense, almost stream-of-consciousness focusing upon a given character's mental state as he or she became insidiously enmeshed in the bizarre. In many cases, we learned, it was not immediately clear—and sometimes remained unclear to the end—whether the supernatural in fact came into play or whether the perceived anomalies were merely the result of an aberrant consciousness.

Campbell's later novels and tales in some senses follow and develop this pattern, but a significant proportion of them display characters whose extreme paranoia is itself the source of horror, with no supernaturalism even suggested. In recent decades many works of this kind have been written by various hands under the guise of horror fiction, but such a classification becomes problematical in many cases because these works so closely tread the borderline between horror and the mystery/suspense field, many times crossing over it.[1] Many critics—H. P. Lovecraft among them—have maintained that the horror story must be supernatural, because only in this way can it convey the metaphysical fear that the universe itself has suddenly become an appallingly mysterious place, something far different from the mundane fear of being murdered or maimed that mystery/suspense fiction generates. If there are vampires; if people can rise from the dead; if there can be such an entity as Cthulhu or Gla'aki—then it means that we have somehow misconstrued the true nature of the cosmos, and our place in it has now become tenuous indeed. Can the witnessing of even the most severe psychosis, and the crimes it may engender, achieve this level of metaphysical frisson? Clearly not; and yet, it would seem difficult—from Campbell's work alone, if not that of Ambrose Bierce, Robert Bloch (*Psycho*), and many others, going back even to some of Poe's tales ("The Man of the Crowd")—to exclude all non-supernatural works of psychological suspense from consideration as horror tales. No simple rule can be applied, and each such work must be judged on an individual basis; and one significant criterion might perhaps be, not so much the number or even the grisliness of the crimes committed by a psychotic mind, but the degree of aberrance of that mind and the intensity of its portrayal. By this criterion, few of Campbell's non-supernatural tales of paranoia would be denied a place in horror fiction.

Campbell's most chilling treatment of paranoia is the novel *The Face That Must Die*, written in 1976–77, published in truncated form in 1979, and issued in a restored text in 1983. It was his first major work of non-supernatural horror; but three earlier

1. See, in general, my chapter "Killing Women with Robert Bloch, Thomas Harris, and Bret Easton Ellis," in *The Modern Weird Tale* (Jefferson, NC: McFarland, 2001), 175–88.

tales—two of which are supernatural—anticipate that baleful
triumph.

"Through the Walls" [1974], one of the lengthiest of Campbell's
earlier short stories (it was published as a chapbook in 1985), is the
story of a man, Hugh Pears, who comes to harbour evil designs
on his own family, developing in particular an incestuous desire
for his ten-year-old daughter. Seen entirely through Pears's point
of view as he goes about his mundane activities with his wife, son,
and daughter, the tale gains exceptional power as Pears's reason
inexorably gives way:

> He stared emptily at the encroaching fog. He wasn't going
> mad, he wasn't. But he couldn't bear to think that what he'd
> been experiencing was real. Yet if he were going mad the
> horror was himself, dragging him deeper, saving its worst
> until all his defences were down—not yet even hinting at its
> worst. He thoughts slithered, eluding him. (GGT 100)

Toward the end he fails even to recognise his daughter:

> The presence of the young girl disturbed him most of all.
> She was his greatest danger. There was something in her he
> must destroy; her freshness was deceitful, her soft plumpness
> was a snare. She was like the walls of the house, whose cor-
> rupted cores oozed now, thick with evil. Her innocence was
> disgusting, intolerable, false. He'd make sure her body could
> never again lure anyone. (GGT 107)

This is, of course, a textbook case of transference—the attribution
of one's own psychoses or guilt to another. Pears cannot face up to
the horror of his unwholesome desires, so he must attribute them
to his daughter as a defence mechanism.

The tale, however, is not simply one of obsession. It ventures
into the supernatural in its suggestion that Pears's psychosis is the

result of powerful drugs that are somehow seeping through the walls of his house from the flat of his next-door neighbours. And what of the blood that Pears sees repeatedly appearing on those walls? Is it symbolic of the blood his daughter might shed were he in fact to have intercourse with her—or kill her?

Then there is "The Little Voice" [1976], a poignant tale of an embittered schoolteacher named Edith who is increasingly unnerved by what appear to be the sounds of a baby coming from the house next door, where only an old man lives. These sounds—nothing more than *la, la, la,* repeated unremittingly throughout the story—continue even after the old man dies. Can there be an abandoned child in the place? Or is it, in fact, a ghost—the ghost of the child Edith had aborted years before? "The Little Voice" is another example of Campbell's utilisation of an old supernatural trope as a metaphor for a disturbed psychological state.

Perhaps the closest analogue to *The Face That Must Die* is "Looking Out" [1974]. This non-supernatural tale of a psychotic old man, Nairn, is told entirely from his point of view, as he repeatedly sees figures within his flat when he is standing outside but never finds anyone, then comes to believe that his landlord is employing these figures as a means of frightening him out of the place. Nairn's wretched life is etched in a few brief pages: alone, his beloved wife dead, he feels wronged by the entire world—his landlord, the police, his neighbours, even a girl at the supermarket checkout counter. Although Campbell does not declare explicitly that the figures seen by Nairn are a product of his imagination, the implication is that they are hallucinations produced by Nairn's descent into paranoia.

This short tale, however, could scarcely have prepared us for the exhaustive treatment of a diseased mind that we find in *The Face That Must Die*. Not only is it a quantum leap in quality from Campbell's first novel, *The Doll Who Ate His Mother*, written only the year before, but its relinquishing of the supernaturalism upon which he had largely relied to convey his message up to this point makes it an experiment that was by no means assured of success. The source of its success—aside from Campbell's own developing skill at character portrayal and the novel form—was, as he later admitted, very close to home.

The Face That Must Die introduces us to John Horridge, an embittered and disturbed man in middle age dwelling in a dreary tenement in the Cantril Farm area of Liverpool. As we follow Horridge on his comings and goings, seeing the world almost exclusively through his jaundiced eyes, we learn many things about him. One of the first to be brought to our attention is his prejudice against gay people: "You mustn't do anything to upset homosexuals," Horridge thinks resentfully to himself. "Homosexuality was the most natural thing in the world: at least, that was what the government and the media . . . would like everyone to think" (FD 45). Correlated with this is extreme misogyny, especially against women who do not outwardly conform to "feminine" ways ("She tucked her hair beneath a black wool cap, as though she didn't want to look like a woman" [FD 13]). Gradually Campbell reveals some of the sources for these attitudes. As a boy Horridge had been warned by his father against any involvement with girls, and he was accordingly derided by his peers as being a "queer" himself. As a result, Horridge had developed a loathing of all forms of sex.

Horridge is, in addition, an unashamed racist and anti-Semite. He is prejudiced against those on the dole, thinking them laggards, but only later is it revealed that he himself is on the dole because of an injury to his leg that presumably prevents him from working. That injury—which Horridge finds deeply humiliating—was caused inadvertently by his own father when Horridge as a youth was climbing a ladder.

The events of the novel commence with Horridge noticing a police sketch of an individual suspected of committing the murders of two homosexuals. On a bus ride home Horridge is convinced that he has identified the murderer, a man in a nearby block of flats named Roy Craig. He supplies an anonymous tip to the police and experiences rage when the police, after interviewing Craig, appear to apologise for bothering him. At this point Horridge supplies one of the first instances of prototypical paranoid behaviour by pondering: "Was the whole world mad?" (FD 45).

Horridge decides to take matters in his own hands. He boldly goes to Craig's block of flats, which he manages to enter by claiming to another tenant, an artist named Fanny Adamson, that he is a private detective. While in Fanny's flat he contrives to make an impression of the keys to the building in a lump of clay.

Matters quickly come to a head. Following Craig home one evening, Horridge brutally kills him with a razor. This incident, however, is only the beginning of the events. Fanny had painted a portrait of Horridge, and her friend Cathy Gardner, who lives in the building, recognises him as a man who frequents the library where she works. Meanwhile, Horridge realises that he has left fingerprints in Fanny's flat and feels the need to remove his traces. He breaks into the flat but is caught by Fanny, so he decides he has no choice but to kill her.

A peculiar incident now ensues. Cathy, believing from a discussion with Fanny that Horridge is a detective, sees him one foggy afternoon and seeks to question him. Horridge, however, knowing that Cathy lives in the building where he has now committed two murders, believes that she is pursuing him, and he flees as rapidly as his bad leg will allow. Cathy chases him and considers the whole situation a rather absurd lark, not realising that Horridge is on the verge of turning around and killing her as well. But Cathy loses him in the fog, and nothing comes of the encounter.

Horridge feels that he must flee, and thinks of going to his old home in Wales. But then he notices that he has somehow lost the payment book that allows him to collect his disability benefits. With no money he will not get far; so he comes up with a plan. He enters Fanny's room again and makes a sound. This entices Peter Gardner, Cathy's husband, to investigate. Once in the flat, Peter is confronted by Horridge, who demands that he drive him to Wales. But Peter can't drive—the van that they use is driven exclusively by Cathy. So they wait until Cathy arrives, and Horridge forces both of them into the van, threatening to cut Peter with his razor if Cathy does not take him to Wales.

The tense drive seems to last an eternity, but finally they stop late at night at a remote quarry. Horridge forces Cathy and Peter out of the van. He tells Cathy to walk forward in the dark, and Cathy nearly falls into the quarry; but she clings precariously to the edge. There are sounds of a scuffle, and presently Horridge approaches, with the intention of kicking her over the edge. But Peter has injured him with a rock, and in a daze Horridge himself falls over the edge, screaming "You bitch" (FD 206). Peter and Cathy are saved; and, although the police find no trace of Horridge in the quarry, they assume that he is dead.

But an unexpected epilogue to the novel now follows. Months have passed, and Peter and Cathy seem to have made good progress in recovering from the awful ordeal: they have purchased a small house and Cathy is pregnant. But she is tense and nervous, and has now herself developed a limp from the fall in the quarry. Then a peculiar letter comes from the tenants occupying their flat in Liverpool, saying that a man had called and wanted Cathy and Peter's address, and they had given it to him. Peter finds this letter but tears it up; when Cathy asks if anything important came in the mail, he remarks blandly—or distractedly—"Nothing worth bothering about" (FD 213).

It is no wonder that *The Face That Must Die* was deemed almost unbearably dismal and cheerless by nearly all readers and reviewers—including, let us recall, the several publishers who rejected the novel when it was submitted to them. The view of the world as seen through Horridge's eyes is indeed twisted and paranoid; and the most appalling thing is that Horridge believes that he is the only sane one while all the rest of the world is mad. In abstract terms, some of Horridge's views may perhaps not be entirely off the mark: when he sees a graffito scribbled on a wall

("KILLER"), he ponders on the seeming amorality of modern youth and concludes, "Television had a lot to answer for" (FD 57). There is some grain of truth to the remark, but it is a facile and superficial account of a complex social problem. What all this suggests is that Horridge is not as far from other seemingly "normal" individuals as we would find it comforting to think: but for the accidents, physical and psychological, of his upbringing, he might in fact be "normal"—and, conversely, had we experienced what Horridge had, we might be very much like him.

Campbell, in his introduction to the 1983 edition of the novel, admitted that Horridge was based largely upon his mother—with, one hopes, some suitable degree of exaggeration. Actually, Campbell never states directly the connexion between Horridge and his mother; but his detailed account of his mother's descent into psychosis can scarcely have any other *raison d'être* than to suggest the sources of Horridge's similar mental aberrations.

Indeed, as events in the novel progress, other characters seemingly develop a milder case of the paranoia that Horridge exhibits in its extreme and violent form. Cathy, when she and Peter are visiting his parents, finds the atmosphere so tense and potentially explosive that she begins to suspect her mother-in-law's motives ("She was treating Cathy as she might have treated any visitor—in order to avoid hearing her thoughts about the argument?" [FD 109]); and later it is remarked, "Her question must have made him [Peter] paranoid for some reason" (FD 175). It is as if Horridge's mental unbalance is a kind of contagion that is spreading to whomever he has come into contact with.

Cathy also serves a key structural function in the novel. Several chapters are seen through her eyes, and they not only provide a certain modicum of relief from the oppressiveness of Horridge's perspective but also supply a more "objective" picture of Horridge than Campbell could have derived if he had kept the narrative point of view strictly on the lunatic. Cathy's very first impression when she sees Horridge in the library, early in the novel and well before he has committed any crimes, is telling: "Never before had she seen such intense distrust peering from anyone's eyes" (FD 34). This is no doubt one of the reasons why Campbell chose to narrate the novel in the third rather than the first person.

Campbell, however—as I have remarked in passing previously and as I shall discuss in greater detail later—uses first-person narration relatively rarely; and in *The Face That Must Die* he has an added reason for avoiding it. In this novel he utilises for the first time a technique that I call *double narration*. This is a device whereby we see an incident or set of incidents first through one character's eyes, then through another's. In chapter 11 Campbell narrates how Craig is relentlessly hunted down by Horridge, as he is cornered in the foyer of his building and brutally killed. Then, in chapter 12, Campbell goes back and shows these same incidents from Horridge's point of view. This chapter is particularly excruciating because we know the conclusion to which the incidents are leading, although of course Craig does not until the very end; and we also witness the twisted fantasies of self-justification that Horridge conceives to vindicate his actions. Campbell uses the same technique when he narrates the death of Fanny, first from her point of view, then from Horridge's. The peculiar chase scene involving Horridge and Cathy is narrated in an interlocking chain of double narrations: one chapter is seen through Cathy's eyes, and narrates events up to a certain point; the next chapter backtracks partially and shows events as seen by Horridge, and moves the scene a little farther along; and the next chapter again backtracks and switches to Cathy's point of view, presenting the conclusion of the episode. Campbell uses double narration in several later novels, but he has never done so as effectively as here.

The "surprise ending" to *The Face That Must Die* is perhaps a trifle contrived, as it seems implausible that Horridge would have survived the fall from the quarry; but it is an appropriately grim conclusion to a novel that offers no hope or redemption: no hope to Cathy, Peter, and all the rest of those like them who are trying to lead normal lives in a violent world, and no redemption for Horridge, who remains mad and unrepentant to the end and is still stalking his perceived enemies with unabated fanaticism. *The Face That Must Die* is by no means Ramsey Campbell's most popular novel, even among his followers, but in its concision and its unrelenting intensity it must rank high in his novelistic output. More importantly, it shows that a work that wholly lacks supernatural elements can still remain within the domain of horror by the unflinching display of a diseased mentality.

A tale that might provide a transition between Campbell's two serial killer novels is "See How They Run" [1990], which appears to draw upon some of the conceptions of *The Face That Must Die* as well as employing the *Doppelgänger* motif. In this tale a man named Foulsham serves on the jury of a murderer, Fishwick, who confesses to committing hideous crimes: he slashes his victims' leg or arm muscles so that they are helpless, then draws sketches of them before finally dispatching them. Like Horridge, Fishwick had experienced an abusive childhood in which his father not only discouraged his artistic efforts but may have caused a broken leg that resulted in Fishwick's having a limp until he finally overcame it through exercise. Foulsham feels a strange connexion with the defendant during the trial; after Fishwick is found guilty and sentenced to life imprisonment, Foulsham is shocked to hear that Fishwick later killed himself in prison by gnawing at the veins in his arms and bleeding to death.

Thereafter Foulsham begins to develop some of Fishwick's characteristics. A painful cramp causes him to limp, and at several other points Foulsham feels an unnatural unity with the dead murderer. Finally, as he confronts another juror at her shop (it is about to close and is therefore empty), he is somehow compelled to injure her fatally with a pair of scissors. The tale ends with Foulsham planning to hunt down more of the jurors.

An ambiguity is maintained to the end as to whether Foulsham
has been possessed by the spirit of Fishwick or whether he has
simply become obsessed with the murderer and is thereby led to
follow in his footsteps. Whatever the case, "See How They Run"
is a concentrated bit of venom that packs all the horror and paranoia of *The Face That Must Die* into a short story.

Comparisons between *The Face That Must Die* and *The Count of
Eleven*—written in 1990–91 and published in 1991—are inevitable
in that they both focus on a serial killer; but in many ways the
comparisons are inapposite and even grotesque, as *The Count of
Eleven* has been explicitly declared by its author to be a "comic"
serial killer novel. Some background is perhaps needed to explain
the very notion of such a seemingly paradoxical idea.

In the nearly fifteen years that elapsed between the writing
of these two novels, fiction about serial killers was produced in
great quantities both by respected writers in the field and by the
usual array of hacks, opportunists, and wannabes. The models for
many of these works were two best-selling novels by the American
writer Thomas Harris, *Red Dragon* (1981) and *The Silence of the
Lambs* (1988). Far from being potboilers, these novels are skilfully crafted and competently written studies of psychosis and its
origins; but it was their popular success, not their psychological
insight, that so many other writers yearned to duplicate. As a
result, the whole subgenre of the "serial killer novel"—a branch
of psychological suspense, which for a time in the 1980s was fool-
ishly thought to be the eventual replacement of the "outmoded"
genre of supernatural horror—came into disrepute. Campbell,
then, might well have written *The Count of Eleven* as the ultimate
twist on a hackneyed trope: his novel would not only be comic in
abstract terms, but it would force the reader to sympathise with a
character who would ordinarily elicit horror, loathing, and facile
moral condemnation.

The Count of Eleven centres on Jack Orchard, a genial but
somewhat bumbling owner of a video rental store in a suburb of

Liverpool. Throughout the novel Jack frequently evokes images from Laurel and Hardy, and a whimsical statement he makes on the very first page—"Got to laugh, haven't you?" (CE 1)—becomes a leitmotif of the entire book. Through no fault of his own, Jack becomes involved in a series of unfortunate and, in some cases, comic disasters that end up leaving his life, and that of his family—his wife, Julia, and his teenage daughter, Laura—in a shambles. A friend, Andy Nation, who was doing construction on the store had left a blowlamp on the premises. This instrument results in the burning down of the shop when a senile old man from a nearby old folks' home blunders in and raises havoc that is explicitly compared to "slapstick comedy" (CE 18). Shortly thereafter, other bad news emerges: Julia's credit card is stolen and the thieves empty the Orchards' bank account; Jack, who had been counting on getting insurance money from the burned store to start a new business, learns that his ex-partner had cut off the insurance policy shortly after leaving the business; and the stingy bank where Jack has asked for a loan gives him only a very small amount, and that grudgingly.

Jack—whose parents, it is fleetingly mentioned (CE 37), had been numerologists—has in the meantime become fixated on the number 11. He has long been playing a game whereby he assigns an ascending numerical value to the letters of the alphabet, and he finds that his name adds up to 11—at least, it adds up to 92, which when added together becomes 11. He begins to find references to 11 wherever he looks—and it becomes gradually clear to the reader that Jack can play with numbers in such a fashion that he can contrive to find 11 at almost every turn.

In the course of his run of bad luck Jack had received an anonymous chain letter instructing him to pass on the letter to thirteen other individuals if he wishes to have good things happen; conversely, bad things will happen if he does not pass on the letters. (Thirteen becomes a secondary talisman of good or bad luck, according to Jack's fancy.) Jack had initially dismissed the letter as nonsense, but then, feeling that anything is worth a try in his current situation, he sends the letters. His luck, however, does not immediately change, and Jack comes to believe that he must make sure the letters have reached their destinations and are themselves sent on by their recipients; Jack maintains that, without these assurances, the bad luck of not passing the letters on would rebound back to his own family.

Jack thereby begins redelivering the letters, this time personally. He had chosen the recipients randomly out of a business directory, so he knows exactly where to go; and his new job as a librarian allows him to drive his van around the area in search of individuals who have failed to return overdue books—a good cover for his impromptu mailing activities. In the first case he confronts a woman who had received his previous letter but had not passed it on; when Jack hands her the new copy of the letter, she tears it to pieces in front of him. Jack, enraged, later burns the pieces of the letter and stuffs them into her house when she is gone; the place goes up in flames.

Just then, Laura is roughed up by some local boys who had been trying to steal her bicycle; she is saved from worse harm by a passerby, who recognises the boys. But because the passerby had not witnessed the beginning of the conflict, the police feel unable to press charges, as they have no independent witness for the conflicting tales told by Laura and the boys. Jack feels that he must continue his letter-delivery to turn his luck. The next recipient he confronts speaks to Jack with a tirade of insults and abuse; Jack finally crosses the line from mere arson to murder by killing the man with his blowlamp.

And yet, Campbell manages Jack's transition from klutz to killer with superb skill. In the first case, Jack's arson caused no personal injury. In this second case, we had already become prejudiced against Jack's victim by his verbal assault on Jack ("I'm afraid your daughter's got a liar for a father, if you've even got a daughter" [CE 115]) and for the obnoxious racial and social views he holds.

Perhaps, after all, this fellow deserved to die . . . Moreover, we do not see the murder being committed, as the chapter ends ominously, "Jack . . . came roaring out of the van; or something did" (CE 116). Then, as Jack reflects on his crimes, he adduces a perfectly admirable reason for his actions: "He'd done what he had to do for his family" (CE 141). In other words, we continue to *like* Jack even after he has become a murderer.

But as bad luck continues to plague his family, Jack feels he must continue his delivery of letters and, perhaps, kill once more ("Not again," he laments to himself [CE 156]). Another hostile encounter with an abusive individual leads to another murder. Shortly thereafter Jack begins calling himself the Count of Eleven—a pun, clearly, on the two possible meanings of "count." He also ponders his own situation: "When people felt themselves to be meaningless, he thought, they were capable of anything" (CE 185). Does this refer to his numerology or to his murdering? Perhaps both: the number-mysticism Jack engages in is a way of supplying "meaning," however contrived, to his life; and his murders seem to him the next logical step to change his fortunes.

As Jack confronts yet another letter recipient, he commits his most heinous murder, although even this one has elements of buffoonery. A man is resting near a canal, and as the confrontation escalates he falls into the canal in an attempt to escape Jack's blowlamp; but he cannot swim, nor can Jack, and Jack—who actually tried initially to rescue him—feels no choice but to shut the man up by torching him. Even though the whole episode has a kind of Three Stooges quality to it, there is probably no more hideous scene in all Campbell's work than the slow death of this hapless individual:

> [Jack] trained the jet of flames on the largest target within reach, the top of Foster's head. In a very few seconds the man's hair hissed and withered, and he was both bald and piebald. During these seconds he emitted an almost inarticulate

crescendo of sound—"Mmmur"—and Jack had the dis-
maying impression that he was crying out for his mother.
His hands were convulsively slapping the water and keeping
him afloat, so that he was unable to move out of range of the
flame. His scalp was peeling by the time shock or helplessness
or a yearning for the cool water caused him to sink. (CE 199)

About this time Jack's luck does indeed seem to turn: the boys
who had attacked Laura are arrested for burglary; and his family
wins a holiday to Greece in a raffle sponsored by a restaurant
owned by his friends. And yet, Jack continues his campaign: he sets
fire to a garage, and the owner dies inside; he torches a dentist's
office after having bludgeoned the dentist unconscious, leaving
him to die in the blaze.

Then, suddenly, startling news comes from two fronts: it was
Andy Nation who had sent the chain letter to Jack as a lark; and
the restaurant owners, knowing of Jack's ill fortune, had pur-
posely let the Orchards win the prize holiday. Jack is shaken:
have his actions had no effect at all on his changing luck? And
what of Julia, who—reading about the serial killer now labelled
"the Mersey Burner"—remarks, "I didn't want to admit I came
from anywhere that could produce such a monster" (CE 298)?
It is at this time that Jack commits what appears to be his worst
crime. In previous instances, Jack had some slim justification
(at least in his own mind) for murder from the abusive treatment he received at the hands of his letter-recipients; but what
of the young single mother, Janys Day, whose house Jack sets
afire while she is out shopping but her baby is inside? Campbell tantalisingly postpones the revelation as to the baby's fate,
but eventually we learn that it was not in fact killed, but was
saved by a neighbour. And yet, it could easily have been killed,
and it is Julia's response to this act that causes Jack profound
disquiet and, finally, a sense of self-loathing. On their holiday
to Greece, Jack, consumed by guilt and fearful that his family

will eventually learn of his actions, hurls himself into the sea and puts an end to his life.

The sensations we feel as we read *The Count of Eleven* are to some degree similar to those evoked by Patricia Highsmith's five novels about Tom Ripley. Especially in the first two novels, *The Talented Mr. Ripley* (1955) and *Ripley under Ground* (1970), Ripley presents himself as a man who kills, to be sure, and for quite selfish motives, but who wins the reader over by his geniality and such unusual traits (for a criminal) as gardening and playing the harpsichord. As in Campbell, the reader experiences an intense moral conflict in liking Ripley but disapproving of his murders. *The Count of Eleven* is even more wrenching precisely because Jack Orchard, aside from being a bit of a buffoon whose pratfalls, puns, and wordgames make one groan with sympathetic laughter, is guided chiefly by an overwhelming desire to aid his struggling family—a goal in every way admirable except in so far as Jack uses appalling means to satisfy it. In extreme contrast with *The Face That Must Die*, it is only toward the end that we finally, and grudgingly, admit that Jack is seriously disturbed mentally. In this sense he is even more of a "normal" character than Horridge; we can so easily imagine ourselves behaving exactly like him.

The "comic" elements are most prominent toward the beginning, and make the novel seem like anything but a work of horror or even a tale of psychological suspense. Jack, bothered by a cold, tries to talk on the phone with a man who thinks his store sells camera film:

> "Wrog dumber," Jack said, trying to keep down yet another sneeze, some of which escaped with a sound like stifled mirth. "I'b a libry. If you like old filbs—"
>
> The voice interrupted sharply, vibrating the earpiece. "I didn't care for April Fool pranks as a boy and now I like them even less. I hope you don't think you convinced me with your imitation of a cold. I'm a doctor."

"So was Henry Jekyll," Jack retorted . . . (CE 3)

But of course the greatest comic moment in *The Count of Eleven* is the burning of the store. The entire episode must be read to appreciate its exquisite humour, as Campbell weaves alternately between slapstick farce and a keen sense of the real danger of the fire and the disastrous effect it will have on Jack's economic future.

A variety of subsidiary issues are touched upon in the novel. One wonders whether the consistently hostile or abusive responses Jack receives from individuals to whom he delivers his letters is a reference to the decline of civility in modern society. Joel Lane, an English reviewer, sees a still wider social commentary:

> The problems faced by the Orchard family are synonymous
> with Thatcherite economic culture: the slick, cold mecha-
> nisms of banks, employers, insurance agents, estate agents.
> Life becomes a lottery, a numbers game in which survival
> depends on "chancing." Jack Orchard takes this value dis-
> tortion literally, reducing people to numbers and placing
> absolute trust in luck.[2]

The impotence—or cowardice—of the police in not pursuing Laura's attackers infuriates not only Jack and Julia but the reader, and Campbell conveys well the sense of frustration that many now feel as helpless victims of irrational violence. Ironically, Jack's victims are in exactly the same situation, and the fact that he manages to escape detection by the police with relative ease also signals the imminent breakdown of a law-abiding society into a group of vigilantes. As Jack himself says at one point, "Forget the law, we don't need it" (CE 134).

Campbell's complex portrait of Jack Orchard—a clumsy,

---

2. Joel Lane, review of *Waking Nightmares* and *The Count of Eleven*, *Studies in Weird Fiction* No. 11 (Spring 1992): 33.

good-hearted, family-oriented, and intelligent arsonist and murderer—is such a success that we feel keen poignancy at his death.
We hope against hope that he may be able to stop killing and
reform himself, but—in a final display of his own humanity—
Orchard finds that his guilt is so overwhelming a burden that
self-destruction is the only solution. Even here he arranges his
death in such a way as to look like an accident, so that his wife
and child will—with luck—never learn either of his criminal acts
or of the fact of his suicide. Literature has rarely offered a more
winning villain than Jack Orchard.

If *The Face That Must Die* and *The Count of Eleven* are Campbell's
most substantial works of psychological suspense and at the same
time his most exhaustive treatments of paranoia and psychosis, it is
a later novel that deftly fuses the supernatural and the psychological in an inextricable union, with the result that each emphasises
and elucidates the other. I refer to the enigmatic work entitled *The
Long Lost*, written in 1991–92 and published in 1993.

In *The Long Lost* David and Joelle Owain, on holiday in Wales,
decide to explore a small island just off the coast and find an old
woman lying all by herself in a seemingly deserted house. At first
thinking her dead, they find that she is indeed alive, and shortly
thereafter David learns to his amazement that she is Gwendolen
Owain, "a long-lost relative" (LL 32): a photograph of David's
mother as a child is found in the house, with Gwen in it.

Gwen seems a little disoriented, and many of her utterances
are cryptic. No one in the village seems to know of her, even the
minister, who also knows of no one living offshore. David and
Joelle seem to have no choice but to bring her back to their home
in Chester, where Gwen is at first startled by various mechanical
devices—a burglar alarm, an answering machine, even a washing
machine—that we all take for granted.

Gwen decides to settle in an old folks' home nearby, proffering as payment a large bag of coins that prove to be so old as not even to be legal tender, but which turn out to be highly prized collectibles that net her a considerable sum. By this time the alert reader knows Gwen's true function: one of her first utterances, in response to a seemingly innocent query, was, "I'm used to eating what's put in front of me" (LL 37), and things become clear—to the reader if not to David—when she says, "I doubt you'll meet anyone who believes in sin more than I do" (LL 71).

David and Joelle give a barbecue for their friends, and Gwen is eager to contribute: she will make cakes for the occasion. The party goes well enough, but several people have too much to drink, and many find Gwen's cakes to be somewhat curious-tasting. And yet, Gwen herself experiences a tremendous sense of relief after the party: "Nothing . . . can touch me any more" (LL 125). It is at this point, however, that a variety of ills descend upon the people who had attended the barbecue—or, more precisely, who had actually sampled Gwen's cakes.

Herb Crantry, the driver of a commuter train, has found himself emotionally devastated after his wife Mary left him for another man. He learns that this man, Victor Harper, rides the very train he operates; and one day he contrives to have Victor as the sole occupant of his train, after which he drives it off the rails and smashes it into a brick wall, killing both himself and his rival.

Bill Messenger, a television comedian, wanders into a bar in a rough area of town and, during an awkward confrontation with an elderly crippled man, has his face slashed by the man's son. Profoundly shaken by the attack, he becomes a hermit in his home and refuses to see any of his friends.

Terry and Sarah Monk have become friends with an American couple who have settled in England, Jake and Henrie Lee. Terry has an affair with Henrie prior to the barbecue. Sarah learns of it when Terry awkwardly confesses that Henrie is pregnant. Sarah, who is childless, develops a wild plan of pressuring Henrie to give up her baby and let Sarah raise it, but is overcome with grief when she learns that Henrie has already aborted the foetus. Sarah suffers a nervous breakdown.

David himself is unwholesomely attracted to Angela, the fourteen-year-old daughter of his lawyer friend Doug Singleton. While doing construction work on Doug's aunt's house, he finds himself in several awkward situations with Angela, who seems to be actively urging David on in his attentions. David reaches a state whereby he can no longer perform sexually with his wife unless he thinks of Angela. In addition to this, Doug Singleton becomes the prototype of the heartless lawyer by claiming that David is doing poor or needless work on his aunt's house and threatening to take him to court.

Joelle then runs amok. She had been very disturbed by her friend Hayley Pinnock's ill-treatment of Hayley's infant son, Rutger. Joelle devises a crazy scheme to kidnap the baby and raise it herself (she and David cannot have children), only to be caught by Rutger's father. Although the Pinnocks do not press charges (perhaps afraid of being found guilty of child abuse), Joelle is shattered and humiliated by the experience.

But the worst fate is reserved for Richard Vale, his wife, Judith, and their adolescent children, Olga and Simon. Richard runs a computer store that is doing very poorly, and he encounters repeated misfortunes: a school that had initially asked him to supply computers abruptly withdraws the offer; the city council then decides to terminate the lease on Richard's store. Going to Doug Singleton for assistance, Richard learns that Doug's law firm believes nothing can be done against the city council, and adds insult to injury by charging Richard an enormous sum in legal fees. Richard, at the end of his rope, feels he has no option: he must kill himself and his family.

In one of the most harrowing tableaux in the whole of Campbell's work, the Vales spend what seems to be a perfect day by the river while Richard secretly ponders his plan. Repeatedly his wife makes innocent-sounding statements—"One day like this won't kill us, will it?" (LL 298); "Come on before we lose them [the children]" (LL 298); of Henrie's affair with Terry, "I don't believe anyone is that ignorant of what the person they married is up to" (LL 299)—that do nothing but twist the knife in Richard's heart. But he is determined. As the family comes home after a wonderful but exhausting day, he insists that they have hot chocolate as a bedtime drink and inserts two full bottles of sleeping pills into the drinks. He somehow manages to get them all to drink the ill-tasting chocolate, and he goes to bed thinking that all their troubles are permanently over. But only horror is in store for him: he himself had not drunk enough of the chocolate, and he awakens in the dark to find his wife and children dead. Overcome with horror and self-loathing, he first swallows a bottle of bleach, then tries to slit his throat on the glass of a broken window, then hurls himself out of the window, then finally puts an end to his wretched life by dashing in front of a bus.

David, appalled by this series of misfortunes that have descended upon his friends, wonders at the cause. Could Gwen somehow be involved? He then remembers an astounding fact: the picture he had seen on the island in Wales was not of Gwen as a child, *but as she is now.* How is this possible? He cannot find the picture to confirm his fears, but feels he must confront Gwen. However, in the middle of the night Gwen comes to David's house and asserts that she must now "go back to where I came from" (LL 357)—whether that be Wales or somewhere else. David decides to take her in his car and attempts to interrogate her; but she baffles him with enigmatic responses. The truth finally dawns upon him: she is a professional sin-eater, and she has been carrying on her activities for decades or even longer, eating the sins of the dead and taking the coins proffered for the act; but she had become so frightened of dying with those sins on her soul that she prolonged her life unnaturally as a way of escaping death. In giving her cakes to others she had finally freed herself of these sins and can die in peace. She does exactly that, leaving David's car as dawn approaches and ascending a steep hill:

> It wasn't just her cry, in which triumph and terror were inextricably mingled, that halted him. He'd craned his neck back at the sound in an attempt to find her, and for a breath he did. The cloud had sailed away all at once as though to expose her to the sky, and David glimpsed her silhouette. Perhaps it was the distance and the onslaught of light which made her limbs look thin and blackened as spent matches, but that was as much as he saw. Then her cry disintegrated as if her mouth had turned to dust, and she collapsed like a figure composed of sticks and vanished beyond the peak. He felt her merge with the blaze wider than the world or be engulfed by it, and he tottered against the sodden grassy wall of the bend in the path to support himself. (LL 374)

Just prior to this she had fed David the last of her cakes—and perhaps she has transferred her sin-eating capabilities to him: "He would go wherever his instincts led him. Just now he felt capable of taking away the sins of the world" (LL 375).

In *The Long Lost* Campbell has reduced the element of the supernatural almost to the vanishing point; but the novel is, of course, supernatural in the anomalous longevity of Gwendolen Owain and, by implication, in the cakes that she feeds the guests at the barbecue. The exact nature of those cakes is never clearly stated by Campbell, but perhaps he need not have done so. They embody the "sins" that Gwen internalised when she ate the cakes from corpses as a sin-eater; but the puzzle is in exactly how the "sins" are manifested. It seems—and this is the reason for studying this novel here, in juxtaposition with two other clearly non-supernatural novels—that the cakes' principal function is in exacerbating the "sins" or psychological maladies already evident in nebulous form in the various characters. Campbell has not, however, in every instance provided sufficient indications that the characters were predisposed to the actions that cause their misfortunes or deaths prior to their eating the cakes. There is, for example, no indication that David had any secret hankering for under-age girls, and we are left to infer that his interest in Angela is simply a result of his sharing a cake with her.

There is also some perplexity in explaining how and why the effects of the cakes finally wear off. Doug Singleton, the lawyer, is apparently the first to come around, but his sudden reformation at the funeral of the Vales does not seem well accounted for. In fact, aside from those who die, we hear nothing of the later fates of the characters. Has Bill Messenger recovered from the physical and psychological effects of his attack? Has Jodie become reconciled to her childlessness? What of the intertwined couples, Terry and Sarah Monk and Jake and Henrie Lee? Perhaps the fact that we hear of no further bad luck befalling them—or, rather, nothing bad of which they themselves are the authors—suggests that Gwen's cakes have dissipated over time; and Campbell is certainly not obliged to provide neat conclusions to lives that will no doubt go on with the usual mixture of good and ill that is our common lot.

The figure of Gwendolen Owain is a triumph of characterisation, no less than that of John Horridge or Jack Orchard. She is in no sense an "evil" figure, some old witch who has woven a curse around innocent people for vengeance or spite; rather, she is a tenuous, inscrutable, almost intangible presence, as ghostly in her psychology as her pale white skin makes her look in appearance. Her utterances are, in almost every single instance, *double entendres*, seeming to answer some innocent question but in reality reinforcing the heavy burdens of her ancient occupation. Toward the end, David comes to believe that her actions—chiefly the willed prolonging of her life and the supplying of the cakes—are largely a result of fear, a fear that she will suffer eternal damnation if she dies with her accumulated sins weighing upon her soul. She then becomes a tragic and pathetic figure: yes, she has apparently caused—or, at least, helped to trigger—the deaths of several individuals, including an entire family; but, as with Jack Orchard, we derive no sense that with her death some great evil has been obliterated from the world. Rather, her death is a kind of release—both for herself and for her sins.

The quietly modulated prose of *The Long Lost* somewhat resembles that of *Midnight Sun*, which purely on the level of diction remains Campbell's finest novel. In a sense, the novel presents as great a difficulty in genre categorisation as *The Count of Eleven*, although from a very different direction. In the latter novel the elimination of the supernatural and the liberal inclusion of humour made its classification as a work of "horror fiction" problematical. In *The Long Lost*, we certainly have a tenuous but pronounced incursion of the supernatural, but the actual events are less horrific than poignantly tragic. Perhaps only the appalling episode of Richard Vale's killing of his family and himself causes the novel to accept the label of "supernatural horror," where both words receive equal weight. *The Long Lost* is a delicate, ethereal, elusive work—a work so far outside the realm of conventional horror fiction that only Ramsey Campbell could have had the courage to write it and the skill to make it a success.

Secret Stories (2005) features one of the most ingenious openings in contemporary horror fiction. We are plunged into the narrative of a nameless male protagonist who comes to the assistance of a young woman being victimised by a gang of surly men on a subway train in Liverpool. But the man is not content to act as the woman's rescuer; he himself pursues her, perhaps hoping for some reward beyond mere thanks—and in the end pushes her on to the train tracks, where she is killed by an oncoming vehicle. Only gradually do we learn that this is in fact a short story written by the central figure of the novel, Dudley Smith, a young man who, although working for a living (at a job assistance bureau), still lives with his mother. He calls her by her first name, Kathy, but it

quickly becomes evident that her seemingly benign overprotectiveness has smothered and infantilised him.

Actually, the above narrative is the second chapter of the book;
the first chapter—consisting of a single sentence ("' . . . Dudley,
there's something I haven't been telling you,' she said, and at
once he was terrified that she knew" [SS 3])—is similarly puzzling until we learn that Kathy has surreptitiously submitted the
story, entitled "Night Trains Don't Take You Home," to a newly
formed magazine, the *Mersey Mouth*, which is sponsoring a contest for unpublished writers. But why would Dudley be "terrified
that she knew"? What is it that he fears she knows? This, too,
is something we learn only gradually. When Dudley's story wins
the contest, a staff writer for the magazine, Patricia Martingale, is
assigned to write a piece on Dudley to accompany the story. She
interviews several of Dudley's friends and colleagues, including a
schoolteacher who had disapproved of Dudley's early writings for
reasons he does not make entirely clear: Is it that these stories—all
involving the killing of women—are too graphic? Is it that they
seem to be based on actual occurrences? The teacher, Mr. Fender,
wonders, "I should want to ascertain how fictitious the stories are"
(SS 133), and later: "Smith was wholly devoid of imagination"
(SS 133). It is not entirely unusual for a writer to base his tales
on actual events; but what are we to make of the remark about
Dudley by Walt Davenport, the owner of the *Mersey Mouth:* "I've
never met a writer who was closer to his creation" (SS 66)?

Slowly the truth dawns on us: Dudley has actually committed
the murders about which he is writing.

This revelation, coming relatively early in the novel, colours
our perceptions of all the subsequent events, and furthermore
turns virtually every statement made by the central characters
into a kind of *double entendre*. Patricia, when first meeting Dudley
after having talked with Kathy, remarks: "I hope you don't mind,
but your mother has been letting us into your secrets" (SS 45). At
this point, Dudley does not know how much Kathy knows about

his activities. When, a little later, Kathy protests against staging Dudley for a photograph holding a knife, commenting, "He's a writer, not a murderer" (SS 49), we are already sensing that she is merely engaging in a pitiable wish-fulfilment fantasy.

Dudley is initially offended that his mother went behind his back in submitting the story, but gradually he comes to look forward to appearing in print. But things begin insidiously going wrong. First, the insufferable boss at his office, Mrs Wimbourne, expresses doubts about whether Dudley can even allow the story to be published and accept the prize money, for this would constitute "competing employment" that might be prohibited by the conditions of his employment. Campbell is brilliant at portraying the petty office politics that make Dudley's life there a slow-burning hell. Then follows the incident with Shell Garridge. She is a comedian with a ferocious and aggressive feminist streak; as a columnist for the *Mersey Mouth*, she had cast a vote against Dudley's story and continues to protest its publication. At a club one evening she provides what proves to be a telling psychological portrait of Dudley:

"Tortured animals when he was a kid. Scared of women. Hasn't got a girlfriend. Likely brought up by a single mum. I'm not dissing him, but she'd have kept telling him how he was better than everyone else, treating him like every time he farted somebody should bottle it and sell it. Only deep down he'll know he's nothing and hate her for not stopping him knowing. That'll be another reason he's got it in for women even more than most men have. So whenever he's feeling more than usually knobless, because I don't reckon he'll have much to play with and anyway he won't be able to get it to salute, he goes creeping after women on their own so he can pretend he's worth knowing about. Most of the time he can't catch them, because women aren't as stupid as him. Just now and then one of them's unlucky, thinks he's so pathetic he has to be harmless." (SS 69–70)

Shell has spoken better than she knew; for she proves to be Dudley's first victim—or, rather, the first victim whose gruesome murder Campbell allows us to see.

But if Shell, through her cruel verbal abuse of Dudley, seems a not entirely sympathetic victim, Patricia Martingale is very much otherwise. As things continue to go badly for Dudley—the family of the woman who had died in the train station, having heard of the imminent publication of Dudley's story, protests against it and forces the magazine to withdraw it, although they promise to publish another of his stories; a short film that was to be based upon his story is similarly protested by the friends and family of the dead woman; Dudley finally walks out of his job, having come increasingly close to losing his hold on reality—he comes to blame Patricia for his troubles, and in the end kidnaps her, ties her entire head, along with her hands and ankles, in package-sealing tape (he refers to her as the "package," a classic dehumanising gesture), and confines her in his bathtub. Her struggles to escape provide fodder for the story Dudley is now writing.

Secret Stories ranks high among Campbell's output for the deftness with which the central figure is drawn, and his gradual but unremitting descent into paranoia and madness. The slightest of touches—as when Kathy wipes Dudley's mouth at dinner, with Patricia present—conveys how Kathy has unwittingly kept her son tied to her apron-strings and prevented his maturation into a healthy adult. Nearly every one of Dudley's utterances comes across as juvenile and sophomoric. Campbell's final, poignant comment on his protagonist—"he looked like a child outraged and terrified by the unfairness of the world" (SS 410)—perfectly encapsulates the boy that Dudley has remained into manhood. And yet, Dudley is far from being the only vivid character in the book: Kathy, Patricia, Shell, and others come to vibrant life under Campbell's hands.

But it would be unfair to *Secret Stories* to suggest that it features the unrelieved gloom of *The Face That Must Die*. Indeed, one of the best-kept secrets of Campbell's writing is the degree to which he has, especially in later years, become a comic writer. To be sure, this novel does not seek to reach the levels of grotesquerie found in *The Count of Eleven*, but clever touches abound. My favourite, perhaps, is when Dudley sits down at breakfast to eat a bowl of Sticky Rotters. Kathy's unsuccessful attempt to make a pie is described as follows: "Kathy brought out of the oven a pie so collapsed that it seemed bent on negating its own shape" (SS 151). Whole scenes—as when Dudley is beaten up by the brother of a woman who claims Dudley insulted her at his office, or when Kathy, staying at a hotel to keep out of Dudley's way, makes the acquaintance of a seemingly normal man who in fact is a masochist and wants Kathy to whip him—are full of comic buffoonery. But they do not counteract the prevailing mood of grimness, even tragedy, that hangs as a pall over *Secret Stories*.

Ghosts Know (2011) is one of the most compulsively readable of any of the novels that Campbell has written in recent years—and that is saying much. It concerns Graham Wilde, a radio talk show host in Manchester who, firstly, becomes involved with a reputed psychic, Frank Jasper, whom he hopes to debunk, and, secondly, with the death of a teenage girl, Kylie Goodchild, who proves to have been murdered. The first-person account by Wilde is hypnotic, revealing Campbell's seemingly effortless skill at character depiction and in worrying out the smallest nuances of meaning and emotion by means of dialogue. Jasper becomes Graham's apparent enemy when the latter claims on the air to know revealing details of Jasper's past by psychic means, when in fact he had known him in school. Graham himself finds Kylie's body in a canal drain, and it is later revealed that she had come to the radio station on the night of her death, evidently seeking to talk to

Graham for some unspecified reason. Suspicion naturally turns to Graham himself as a possible murderer—a suspicion that Jasper augments in a speech at Kylie's funeral.

Throughout the text, we sense that Graham is seething with barely suppressed rage, and Campbell deftly traces this to incidents in Graham's past, especially to his relations with his parents. When Graham is pressured into taking a lie detector test on his own radio program—and, more disturbingly, when the person administering the test finds many of his responses "inconclusive," perhaps because Graham's rage was distorting the polygraph machine—things look bleak for him. Is he an unreliable narrator who in fact killed Kylie but is keeping vital facts from his readers? Does his increasing paranoia see enemies where none exist? There are no simple answers to these questions; and even when many of the central issues of the scenario are resolved, the novel ends without full resolution.

My only reservation with this gripping and consistently unnerving novel is its title. It manifestly suggests the supernatural, but there is nothing supernatural here. Even some of the chapter titles bear the word "ghost" or "ghosts" in them, but I am apparently too dense to ascertain their precise meaning or relevance. But this is the only flaw in the novel, if indeed it is a flaw.

The remarkable feature of *Think Yourself Lucky* (2014)—one of the most compelling of Campbell's recent novels and certainly among the best novels he has ever written—is that it cleverly and poignantly fuses the two modes of supernatural and psychological horror into a single unclassifiable amalgam.

The novel introduces us to David Botham, a mild-mannered, perhaps overly self-effacing man who works at a travel agency in Liverpool. But Botham is, in a sense, periodically obliterated in the course of the narrative by the intrusion of another figure—whose presence is indicated by a different typeface and first-person narration, as opposed to the third-person narration of the passages about Botham. This person seems like a typical representative of

the anger-filled, alienated youth that populates big cities everywhere ("I'm glad my rage hasn't deserted me, but then it never
does" [TYL 13])—but this individual acts upon his rage by causing
the deaths of any number of individuals, but always in such a way
that the victims appear to have died by accident. And what is even
more horrible is that these deaths frequently happen to individuals who superficially seem to *deserve* to die—or, at the very least,
are morally and socially culpable in some way. An overweight man
who munches a hamburger and French fries on a commuter train
(and heedlessly litters in the process!) is dispatched in an elevator;
another fat man who continually gets in the way of the killer in a
movie theatre is loathsomely killed in the theatre's toilet.

But what possible connexion can there be between the placid,
somewhat inhibited Botham and this vile murderer? David reveals
something of his past to his current girlfriend, Stephanie, when he
tells her that as a child he had created an imaginary playmate who,
unlike him, was able to do bad things and get away with them. He
had called this creature Lucky, then later given him the surname
Newless. He also admits that he had taken an unknown drug at
college—could this somehow have caused Lucky to come to life?
Whatever the case, the incident allows Campbell to indulge in
some fine prose-poetry as he relates the hallucinatory effect of the
drug:

The old buildings of the university had glowed like bones in
a fire, but he'd seen that the new blocks lit by white globes
on stalks were fossils of the future. As he crossed a road, the
cars that glared at him with their great eyes had seemed
poised to multiply their speed the instant he stepped off the
kerb.... Despite the January chill, he'd felt his sweaty feet
squelch at every step. At last he'd come into the open on
the far side of a stile, which was as cold as metal and transformed his hands on it into wood. The electric amber sunset
of the town had faded from the sky he'd left behind him, and

eventually he'd lain down in the middle of a field that frost had turned into enormous spiky half-buried ribs. He'd felt the skeleton splinter beneath him, and then he'd been aware of nothing except the sky, where the moon had sharpened the edges of clouds as it crept from behind them. (TYL 52)

David is now horrified to find that a person calling himself Lucky Newless is writing a blog (the title of which, "Better Out Than In," David had invented) in which the murders are spelled out in painstaking detail.

This extraordinarily ingenious premise—supernatural in the sense of an imagined entity coming to life, but psychological in multiple senses, in that Lucky may represent the rage and frustration that David himself feels but is unable to act upon, and also in that the deaths that Lucky contrives are all too plausible and grimly realistic—engenders a remarkable sense of unease in the reader. For long stretches of the narrative we are unsure whether anything supernatural has actually happened: David himself wonders whether he himself is writing the blog without being aware of it—and he is also unnerved by the realisation that he has encountered many of the individuals who are so callously rubbed out by what may or may not be a creature of his imagination. Lucky engages in contriving increasingly grisly deaths for his chosen victims, as when he causes a disabled man in a scooter to be hit by a truck in the street: "I'm diverted to see how many ways metal and cloth and meat can be torn apart and rearranged together" (TYL 74).

Campbell enlivens the scenario by exhibiting the very real social and personal tensions under which David, and others around him, are compelled to live. David's superior at the travel agency is Andrea, a woman who was his former lover—and their tense conversations, with so many hidden meanings lurking under their superficially bland words, are almost enough to create terror in themselves. David's mother, a social worker, tells of a particularly disturbing case that is troubling her—one Benny Moorcroft, who for a time the reader is led to believe may be the killer, until it becomes clear that he himself is one of Lucky's victims. David manages to look up a man whom Lucky did not manage to kill but only injure seriously: this person, who is in the intensive care unit, can barely manage to speak, but he sends a chill in David (and the reader) by saying that he did see the person who caused him to fall from a ladder: "Somebody that's got your face" (TYL 125). Later, a security guard who has followed both David and Lucky states ominously: "I might have mixed him up with you if I wasn't careful" (TYL 140).

In a sense, *Think Yourself Lucky* is a vast expansion of Campbell's story "The Depths" (1978), where a true-crime writer finds that if he does not set down his hideous dreams of murder and mayhem, they happen in real life. In the story, the writer serves as a kind of focus for the collective repressions of a society that would prefer to ignore the very existence of crime and its sources. In the novel, Campbell employs the *Doppelgänger* motif—the influence of Poe's "William Wilson" seems particularly strong here—to suggest that the horrors are the result of David's own repression of his anger at the seemingly endless annoyances of life in the twenty-first century.

Indeed, *Think Yourself Lucky* is only the latest and perhaps most pungent of Campbell's ventures into satire—and, in this case, satire of an engagingly misanthropic sort. All manner of contemporary absurdities are held up to ridicule: the Internet, which has made possible the dreary proliferation of writing by all manner of people who shouldn't be engaging in it; the excessive use of euphemisms in a frantic effort not to cause the slightest offense to anyone; the tortuosities of office politics, where subtle forms of one-upmanship are constantly indulged in; and much else. An exquisitely hilarious passage relates how Lucky walks into a bookstore and compels a sales clerk to look for the several literary classics that have a certain politically correct word in the title, until finally she is forced to utter the name of a celebrated novel by Joseph Conrad: *"The En Word of the Narcissus."* As Lucky sagely comments, "You can't suppress words. . . . It doesn't make the thoughts go away" (TYL 202).

As always, Campbell puts on stage a wide array of crisply realised characters, each rendered distinct in the most compact possible manner, chiefly through their speech. The dialogue Campbell places in their mouths is, in all frankness, quite artificial: it is difficult to imagine normal people engaging in the kind of tit-for-tat repartée that we find throughout this work. But what this usage signals is Campbell's increasing awareness of the baffling complexity of language—a complexity that can lead to all manner of misconstruals, double entendres, and subtle insults or denigrations that suddenly open a window on the character of the persons making the utterances. But, in contrast to some of his recent works, this intense focus on the ambiguities and overtones of everyday language does not in any way hinder the progression of the narrative or make it any less of a page-turner in proper bestseller tradition.

Think Yourself Lucky is Ramsey Campbell at his very best. No one in the entire range of supernatural fiction can evoke terror in a single sentence, or depict gruesomeness without the slightest coarseness or violence of diction, or generate an atmosphere of appalling, cumulative horror as well as he. After more than fifty years of writing, his work remains fresh and vivid, to be read as much for its insight into our troubled psyches as for its expositions of horror and weirdness.

The separately published novella *The Booking* (2015) may be worth studying here, as it similarly fuses supernatural and psychological horror. The setting is a bookstore, although a very different one from that in *The Overnight*. This is emphatically a used bookstore of the sort that used to be common before the advent of online bookselling—one in which cobwebs are omnipresent and there seems to be no order to the books on the shelves

aside from the idiosyncratic tastes of the bookstore's owner, Mr
Alfred Brookes. The very name of his bookstore—Books Are
Life—is enough to arouse unease in the reader. Bowing to the
inevitable, Brookes hires a young man, who gives his name only as
Kiefer, to set up a website for the bookstore. Kiefer loses the key to
his girlfriend Cynthia's flat, and Brookes generously offers to put
him up temporarily at the store, where he himself lives. The plan
proves a mixed blessing for Kiefer, for he finds that Brookes is not
only highly suspicious—to the point of paranoia—of computers,
the Internet (which he thinks is "a mind looking for somewhere to
live" [39]), and other tokens of contemporary technology, but he
is also displeased that Kiefer has, on his own initiative, sold some
books to a customer while Brookes was away. It is almost as if
Brookes does not want to sell any of his stock. Kiefer is unnerved to
find that the three books he sold have apparently returned to their
shelves. Is it simply that Brookes had duplicates of these books, or
did he secure the return of the books from the customer—perhaps
by nefarious means?

As Kiefer conducts increasingly unsatisfying conversations
with Cynthia via his computer, he seems to be developing the
same kind of paranoia as his employer ("Kiefer had begun to feel
interrogated. Certainly Brookes would think that was the case
if he could hear" [59]). Kiefer now finds evidence that Brookes
has not been mailing out the books that have been sold online;
confronting his boss on the matter, he is not surprised to hear
Brookes confess, "Maybe I can't let them go. It's like giving away
bits of my mind" (76). In a climactic scene, Kiefer, sensing that
Brookes himself may have taken the key to Cynthia's flat as a way
of keeping him on the premises, pursues his boss through the
upstairs storage rooms of the bookstore, where the books seem to
be "inching towards" (79) him. This scene is gripping, but then
it is suddenly revealed that Cynthia is not Kiefer's girlfriend but
his daughter. There is in fact no Mr Brookes—or, rather, the two
are a single person, Kiefer Alfred Brookes. This jack-in-the-box

PARANOIA   237

revelation is not entirely satisfactory, and it is unclear whether all
the previous events of the story can be fully reconciled to it; but
The Booking nonetheless is a powerful tale of the mountainous
weight of the information contained in the countless number of
books published over the centuries, as well as a rumination on
the problematical status of online information and communica-
tion. Campbell may or may not be wedded to the old-fashioned
print medium, but he is fully aware that there is something not
quite real or healthy in our devotion to cellphones, computers,
and the Web. The paranoia that Brookes directed toward these
phenomena in the early stages of *The Booking* may perhaps not be
entirely irrational.

It is not entirely clear whether Campbell's most recent novel,
Somebody's Voice (2021), should be discussed here; suffice it to say
that you've never read a book by Ramsey Campbell like *Somebody's Voice*. You've never read a book by anyone like *Somebody's
Voice*.

In this scintillating, obsessively readable novel, this veteran
of more than sixty years of writing tackles some of the most
sensitive issues of our time: sexual abuse of children, gender
transitioning, the perils of social media, and others. From the
first page to the last, it is as unputdownable a book as Campbell
has ever written.

At the outset we appear to be dealing with Carla Batchelor, who
claims she was abused by her stepfather, Malcolm Randall, after
her own father died tragically in a car accident when she was a
little girl. Carla's account is searing, although Campbell's elliptical
narrative spares his readers any explicit details of the abuse; let us
simply say that, although it was not quite as horrific as it could
have been, it was bad enough.

Campbell's account keenly and painfully etches how Carla
became increasingly isolated, especially from her own family. Her
mother, Elaine, profoundly grateful that Malcolm rescued her
from a life of poverty, refused to believe that her new husband was

anything but the emotional and financial saviour she perceived him to be, and she constantly chastised her daughter for not being sufficiently grateful to Malcolm for all that he had done for the family. Carla found herself unable to discuss the matter with her few close friends; and to add to the horror, when she attempted to confide in her priest, Father Brendan, he not only dismissed her story but then took the opportunity to abuse her himself.

Carla later underwent a gender transition and became Carl. He then decided that his story needed to be told; he approached Tiresias Press, and its editorial director designated Alex Grand, a struggling crime writer (who had just published a novel that partly addressed some of these same issues), to be a ghostwriter. Working with Carl, Alex wrote the book, which was published (with a joint byline) under the title *When I Was Carla*.

The novel takes an unexpected turn when a woman gets in touch with Alex, announcing herself as Hilary Wilson. She claims to be the daughter of Malcolm and Elaine. In *When I Was Carla* Carl had maintained that Elaine had suffered a miscarriage, so if her account is to be believed there should be no such person as Hilary; but Alex discovers that she is in fact who she says she is, and this casts much of Carl's account into doubt. Hilary claims that her father never abused Carla at all and that Father Brendan, although in jail for pedophelia, was never known to have molested girls, only boys.

In the midst of the controversy now surrounding the book, Alex is further troubled by issues with his own family. His father, Gordon, a noted English professor, appears to be developing dementia—and he bizarrely accuses his son of writing *When I Was Carla* as a veiled attack on himself. Alex's mother does her best to make peace between her husband and her son, but to little avail.

If all these fraught issues aren't enough, Campbell also engages in keen and bitter satire on identity politics and on the viciousness of social media. Once some of the apparent errors or inconsistencies in Carl's book are publicised, Alex's Twitter account is bombarded with anonymous posts lambasting him and actually advocating violence against him. And there is the figure of ToM, a person who has transitioned from a woman to a man and is now a strident advocate for his cause.

And the stink of religion hangs over the entire work. Malcolm in particular is evilly adept at hypocritically summoning his God as a bulwark for his own loathsome actions, and Carla (assuming her account is true) finds anything but comfort or protection from the religious authorities she appeals to for help.

This novel may seem leagues away from Campbell's customary work in weird fiction, but there are elements of continuity all along the line. From the very beginning of his career—so early as *The Face That Must Die* (1979/1983)—Campbell has ventured into psychological terror, and in other such works as *The Count of Eleven* (1991), *The Last Voice They Hear* (1998), *Silent Children* (1999), and several others, he has dealt poignantly with issues of class distinctions, gun violence, the victimisation of children, and other social ills. And while it can be said that *Somebody's Voice* is as close to a mainstream novel as any Campbell has written, this is merely a matter of genre categorisation, not a qualitative judgment. Indeed, in the latter portion of the novel the focus is on Alex's own increasingly deteriorating mental state, very much along the line of Horridge in *The Face That Must Die* or Jack Orchard in *The Count of Eleven*.

Campbell's writing in *Somebody's Voice* has never been better. Every word, every sentence contributes to the overall effect. The dialogue is particularly fine, as each utterance crackles with a sinister undercurrent that emphasises the hideous moral and sexual depravity that fuels the narrative. And the novel really is unputdownable. I have never been convinced that this is a vital or lofty goal for writers, since it can be found in any number of forgettable potboilers in the mystery, suspense, or horror genres; but here the hypnotically compelling hypnotic nature of the scenario urges the reader on absorb chapter after chapter. The narrative is skilfully arranged by alternately recounting Carl's story and the events of Alex's life; and even if Carl disappears toward the end and a few issues remain unresolved, Campbell reserves one final cataclysmic revelation to the end, bringing the novel to a suitably cheerless conclusion.

VIII. THE CHILD AS VICTIM AND VILLAIN

Ramsey Campbell has always been fascinated by childhood—both his own and, more recently, that of his two children. His anomalous upbringing surely led to some of the bizarre stories involving adolescents in the *Demons by Daylight* period (notably "The Interloper"), and in more recent novels and tales children are often the focus of natural or supernatural attacks. What is it about childhood that intrigues Campbell? Does he find children peculiarly vulnerable to the strange—or, conversely, peculiarly resilient to its violent incursions? Is a child's perspective inherently more fantastic than that of an adult, closer to those dreams and fancies which, as we have seen in other works, can dislodge the real and substitute nightmare in its place? Campbell has no monolithic view of children: they can be both helpless victims and singularly evil villains; they can yield passively to the weird and boldly combat it. And while several works clearly draw upon his own childhood experiences and those of his family, in many novels and tales he touches upon fundamental issues regarding children and their relationships with adults and with society at large that resonate far beyond his personal traumas.

Two key stories of the 1970s get to the heart of Campbell's attitude toward children, connecting also with his conceptions of urban horror and age-old evil. "The Man in the Underpass" [1973] is a magnificent tale narrated entirely from the perspective—and in the language—of an eleven-year-old working-class girl, Lynn, in Liverpool. Amidst the all too familiar hazards besetting children in a rough neighbourhood, Lynn attempts to carry on as best she can, retaining some of the naïveté that is her birthright as a pre-adolescent but also becoming prematurely hardened simply in order to survive. Lynn and her friends—in particular a girl named Tonia—become interested in a pedestrian underpass, noticing that it contains a crude drawing of a man whom some adults have identified as Aztec. Is it possible that the underpass is still being used in connexion with the vicious midsummer sacrifices of the Aztecs, in which they would tear out the hearts of their still-living victims? Lynn reveals, without being aware of it, that Tonia has learned some Aztec rituals and is teaching them to smaller children; and at the end we are given to understand that Tonia has been impregnated by an Aztec god.

This bare summary cannot begin to convey the subtlety and gradualness of the successive revelations as they emerge unwittingly from the lips of a small girl. The whole story might perhaps be thought of as an updating of Arthur Machen's "The White People"—in which a girl writes a diary that clearly (but, to her, unknowingly) betrays her indoctrination into the witch-cult and her later impregnation by some hideous entity—and Campbell catches the tones of childhood bantering perfectly:

"Oh, it's only that stupid thing on the wall," June said. "No, it isn't," Tonia said. "There's a real man down there if you look." "Well, I don't want to see him," June said. "What's so special about him?" I said. "He's a god," Tonia said. "He's not. He's just a man playing with his thing," June said. "He probably wouldn't want you to see him anyway," Tonia said. "I'm

going down. You go home." "We'll come with you to make
sure you're all right," I said, but really I was excited without
knowing why. (AH 87)

And, of course, "The Man in the Underpass" speaks harrowingly
of the sexual victimisation of children, something we have already
seen in such a story as "Through the Walls."
    Still more chilling is "The Chimney" [1975]. As we read this tale
of a boy who has a vision of a charred Father Christmas coming
down the chimney and is thereafter terrified of what might emerge
from that orifice, how can we not think of Campbell's own childhood, in which his father lived upstairs and was rarely seen, only
heard as his footsteps padded across the floor above?

    . . . I heard the slithering in the chimney.
    Something large was coming down. A fall of soot: I could
    hear the scattering pats of soot in the grate, thrown down by
    the harsh halting wind. But the wind was emerging from the
    fireplace, into the room. It was above me, panting through its
    obstructed throat.
    I lay staring up at the mask of my sheets. I trembled from
    holding myself immobile. My held breath filled me painfully
    as lumps of rock. I had only to lie there until whatever was
    above me went away. It couldn't touch me. (AH 160–61)

Campbell has admitted that Christmas was the worst period in
his tense family situation, which no doubt made the conception of
"Father Christmas" even more anguished for him. It need hardly
be remarked that "The Chimney" does not at all depend upon a
knowledge of Campbell's autobiography for its effectiveness; but
such knowledge lends the story an added poignancy. The story
as a whole captures that peculiar isolation and vulnerability that
children can feel in a confusing world run by adults.
    Another tale of this kind is "Bedtime Story" [1980], in which

a boy is terrorised by his grandmother, who disapproves of his being illegitimate. A story she tells him—about children going to a witch's gingerbread house—in order to keep him from playing with the oven frightens him so much that he begins to see a curious figure in the mirror of his bedroom. Later it is suggested that the figure comes to life, possesses the boy, and causes him to kill his grandmother. Here the psychological damage that can be caused by brutal and unthinking behaviour by adults is suggested.

Several other stories of the period bring "The Man in the Underpass" to mind, notably "The Trick" [1976], similarly told from the point of view of an adolescent girl whose friends are fascinated by a witchlike figure and ultimately burn her, only to suffer the revenge of her familiar; and "Eye of Childhood" [1978], in which a young girl reads a witchcraft book and casts a spell that summons up entities that look like four-year-old boys who kill her teacher. Again, it is the modern urban settings of these tales, as well as Campbell's allusive narration, that update and enliven what might otherwise be stale and hackneyed supernatural conceptions.

Campbell summed up many of these early tropes in the novel *The Nameless*, written in 1979 and published in 1981. It begins, as often in Campbell's early novels, with a sinister prologue. Here a Doctor Ganz, claiming to be a psychiatrist, comes to Alcatraz to interview Frank Bannon, who has committed a gruesome murder. After a lengthy interrogation in which he seeks to ascertain Bannon's motive in committing the crime, Ganz seems to receive the answer he was seeking. Bannon tells him: "Well, I feel somehow I was doing it for someone else" (N 9). Ganz assures Bannon harrowingly: "You are not the first to ask me such a question . . . You are not alone. If it is a consolation, there are others driven by the same forces as you" (N 9–10).

As the story proper begins, we see Barbara Waugh, a successful literary agent in London, trying to overcome the loss of her daughter Angela, who had been kidnapped from nursery school at the age of four. (Barbara's husband, Arthur, had died on the very day of their daughter's birth.) Later the body of a girl, believed to be Angela, is discovered. So the matter apparently rests, until Barbara receives a phone call from someone identifying herself as Angela, who would be about thirteen years old if she had lived. Barbara is incredulous but wants desperately to believe that it really is her daughter. It appears that the girl is being kept against her will in a house off Portobello Road by a cult whose purpose is unclear but who have no names, either as individuals or as a group. When Barbara comes near the house to investigate, she encounters another woman, Margery Turner, who claims that her daughter Susan had been kidnapped by the cult. The two women plan to explore the house together, but Margery loses patience and goes alone, only to die at the hands of some obscure entity:

> Of course a draft might have shifted the gray mass from the doorway, and perhaps a draft was making it, or something like it, come flopping down the stairs toward her. In the ground-floor room she had been reminded of an animal, but this looked hardly formed, a fetus covered with cobwebs and dust or composed of them. It was so quick that it had swarmed up her body and was almost at her face before she began to scream. (N 101)

Coming upon the scene a little later, Barbara finds a sketch, probably drawn by Susan, of a figure who looks uncannily as Angela would look if she were still alive.

A reporter, Gerry Martin, had learned something of the cult, and with Barbara's encouragement seeks to infiltrate it. She is, however, captured—but not before she catches sight of a girl who is probably Angela. Later, another phone call leads Barbara and her friend Ted Crichton to go to Scotland to hunt down the cult. Ted had tried to dissuade Barbara from the enterprise, thinking that she is being duped, but grudgingly accompanies her. But then he is captured by the cult. Although he is released shortly thereafter, it is clear to the reader (but not to Barbara) that he has been drugged or hypnotised. He successfully persuades her to leave Scotland.

On a business trip to New York, Barbara stumbles upon more information on the cult. It is apparently headed by a man named Jasper Gance or Kaspar Ganz, who has been investigating the psychology of murder since at least the Second World War. The worst part of the matter, as far as Barbara is concerned, is that the cult kidnaps children and indoctrinates them into its twisted beliefs; these children are "initiated" (N 258) in their thirteenth year—exactly Angela's age. After a harrowing experience in a deserted house in Glasgow—one of the cult's previous headquarters—Barbara makes her way to Glasgow Airport, where Angela (according to Ted) had told her to meet. Sure enough, both Ted and Angela are there. We as readers, of course, do not by any means feel any comfort in this reunion, given our lingering suspicions of Ted, but Barbara is overjoyed. Upon their return to London, however, the truth becomes known: both Ted and Angela are full-fledged members of the cult.

The cult members capture Barbara and take her on a speedboat to some unknown destination. During the trip Barbara tries in vain to plead with Angela to repudiate the cult. Then Ted somehow snaps out of his hypnosis and battles against the members. In the ensuing struggle Angela herself seems to experience a change of heart; and because she seems now to be the actual leader of the cult, the other members flee in horror. Barbara hopes faintly that she, Ted, and Angela might return to a normal life; but after she and Ted step off the boat, Angela suddenly takes it and drives it away. She is so appalled at her involvement with the cult that she sets herself ablaze with her own occult powers.

There are many problems of conception and execution in *The Nameless*, which cannot rank very high in Campbell's novelistic output. The whole work really does not hold together. As with several previous novels, Campbell is attempting to mingle psychological suspense with supernatural horror, to the detriment of both. The actual motives of the cult are never clearly spelled out, and all we learn of Kaspar Ganz's theory on murder is the following:

He believed that the worst murders were inexplicable in terms of the psychology of the criminals. One of the criminals he'd interviewed had described a sense of being either close to something or part of something which the act of torturing had never quite allowed him to glimpse—a sense that he was trying to assuage a hunger which was larger than he was ... Perhaps the crimes formed a pattern over the centuries, or perhaps they were stages in a search for the ultimate atrocity. (N 253–54)

This is not very helpful, and in the end does not amount to much.

Moreover, the relation of the supernatural element—the cobwebby monster that kills Margery and almost kills Barbara—to Ganz and his theories is never clarified or even addressed. Is it somehow the cause of all horrible crimes, from Gilles de Rais and Jack the Ripper to the present? Who can say? This entity seems to exist for the sole purpose of providing a supernatural shudder.

The conclusion of the novel is very weak, and both Ted's and Angela's conversions are highly implausible psychologically. If Ted's emergence from hypnosis might be marginally acceptable because he has not long been inculcated into the cult, Angela's turnabout—after nine years of indoctrination, and merely as a result of seeing the other cult members seeking vengeance on Ted in their struggles with him in the boat—strains credulity to the breaking point. Campbell has frequently had difficulty with the endings of his novels, and rarely has it been more apparent than in *The Nameless*.

Even the symbolism of namelessness is not examined coherently or in detail. The root notion may have had its source in a sword-and-sorcery tale, "The Changer of Names" [1976]: "He'd heard of name-changers, who by hypnotism or drugs would take a man's name and the whole of his life, then rename him. The practice disgusted Ryre: how could anyone be so disloyal to himself as to give up his name, whatever he might have done? It was the ultimate weakness" (FAN 34). If this is not very compelling, the conception as evolved in the novel is still less so; in fact, the significance of namelessness is never even addressed, and it seems merely a device for the cult to elude detection.

The Nameless is dedicated to Campbell's own daughter, Tamsin—"who helped without even knowing." Although only a year old at the time Campbell wrote the novel and therefore not the literal model for the adolescent girl it features, she is clearly a symbol for parents' love of their children and the terror they would feel at their death or abduction. Certainly the most moving and genuine portions of the novel are Barbara's conflicting emotions as she hopes against hope that her daughter is still alive and still vaguely like the little girl she knew; and these portions lend the work whatever poignancy it has.

Three years after writing *The Nameless*, Campbell wrote another novel that, while not exclusively focusing on children, keenly probes the terrors of an isolated child whose parents become more and more unrecognisable. *The Claw*, written in 1980–81, was published in 1983 under the pseudonym Jay Ramsay. It is the only one of his novels, aside from the Carl Dreadstone books, not to appear under his own name; and it caused a certain flurry of controversy at the time. Was Campbell somehow implicitly repudiating the novel by the use of the pseudonym? Was it an early work that he did not feel came up to his standards? All this speculation now seems a trifle hyperventilated; for *The Claw* (which only recently has been published under its proper title) was issued under the pseudonym only because Campbell's publisher was about to release *The Nameless* and *Dark Companions* and did not wish Campbell to compete against himself. The novel, while by no means his best, is a creditable piece of work, largely for its portrayal of childhood.

The Claw opens in Nigeria, where an anthropologist, David Marlowe, contrives to have writer Alan Knight take an artefact—a ferocious-looking but beautifully crafted metal claw—back to England with him. Later Knight is startled to learn that Marlowe, the father of a young girl, killed himself shortly thereafter. Knight had been instructed by Marlowe to give the claw to the Foundation for African Studies; but since the foundation informs him that the matter is not urgent, he lets the claw remain in his house in Norwich.

Alan's writing, however, does not go well. A crime novelist who had gone to Africa for background for his next novel, he finds himself unable to put his experiences on paper. Meanwhile Alan's six-year-old daughter Anna finds herself uncomfortable around the claw, and his wife Liz thinks she sees a bloody-faced man near the house. Seemingly because of his writing difficulties, Alan increasingly loses patience with both Liz and Anna.

Things turn still uglier when Joseph, a soft-headed local youth who had previously never exhibited any violent tendencies, is found tearing a goat to pieces with his bare hands. Later it is learned that, on a visit to Alan's house, he had inadvertently scratched himself with the claw. Had he been infected with a nameless taint? Joseph himself seems to think so: "Joseph stared back over his shoulder, crying: 'He [Alan] brought it here!' until his captor shoved him into the back of the van" (C 96).

Alan himself, faintly sensing that the claw has some inimical quality, is now anxious to take the object to the foundation. Reaching the foundation's offices, he learns from its director, Dr Hetherington, that the claw belonged to a secret society in Nigeria called the Leopard Men. Not only are these men cannibals, but they are initiated into the cult by a particularly horrible ceremony: each must kill his own daughter. Hetherington explains:

"Each man had to give his young daughter to the cult before he could be accepted—a girl child of his own or his wife's

blood. They would send the child running down a path
through the bush at night. When they caught her they would
tear her to pieces and eat her." (C 106)

Shuddering, Alan opens his briefcase so as to hand the claw
over—but realises that he has somehow failed to bring the claw
with him. He suspects that this is no simple matter of forgetful-
ness on his part; and his fears in this regard are confirthed when,
upon returning home, he learns that the claw has been stolen by
someone.

Isaac Banjo, an African colleague of David Marlowe's, is familiar
with the claw and its properties. He calls Alan and informs him
of its evil nature, claiming that the originator of the talisman,
according to legend, would try to influence whoever owned it and
"would appear in the form of a naked man covered with the blood
of all his feasts" (C 148). Isaac tells Alan to come to Africa, for the
only way he can be cured of the evil effects of the artefact is to kill
the man who had given the claw to Marlowe. Alan catches the next
flight to Nigeria, and he and Isaac undertake an arduous journey
through the African jungle in pursuit of the few remaining members of the cult of the Leopard Men. As they trudge through the
rain and wilderness, Alan comes to a loathsome realisation: he will
not only have to kill the Leopard Man, but he will have to eat
at least a token portion of his body. Finally they come upon the
individual, a feeble, aged man lying in a hut. But the man shows
surprising agility, leaping viciously upon Isaac and tearing out his
throat before Alan can kill him with a gun. With great revulsion
Alan then boils pieces of the man's buttock and eats them, vom-
iting them up immediately.

Meanwhile, in Norwich, Liz finds herself growing more and
more irritated with Anna. On one occasion Anna, utterly dismayed at the change that has come over her mother, runs away
from home and goes to the house of a neighbour, Jane, where she
sees a horrible sight:

The figure at the window was the man she could never quite
see, the man who was too red. She could see him now, grinning down at her with his sticky crimson teeth. She could
see now that he wasn't a person after all, not with that face
as long as an animal's, not with those eyes and teeth. (C 240)

Later it is learned that Jane had for some reason killed her baby,
Georgie, by smashing its head against the wall. Liz comes to believe
that Jane took the claw, but she seems unaware of its baleful effects.
Her impatience with Anna continues, and it reaches a point where
she wishes to do actual violence to her own daughter. Just as she
seems on the brink of doing so, Alan's mother Isobel shows up, and
shortly thereafter Alan himself arrives. Isobel, who had noticed Liz's
strange behaviour for weeks, does not wish to leave Liz with Anna,
but she has no choice: she must take Alan, who is on the brink of
nervous collapse, to the hospital. Anna, unable to endure being with
her mother, runs away; Liz gives chase but in the tumult is struck by
accident by Isobel's car. Alan himself then gives chase to Anna; but
although he is now cured of the influence of the claw, Anna is too
frightened to notice and continues to flee. She heads to Jane's now
deserted house and hides in an upstairs cupboard, where she finds
the claw; she flings it into the room. Alan, coming there, sees the
claw—but, in a significant gesture, kicks it away. Anna recognises
that whatever had been affecting her father is gone, and she comes
with him to see her mother in the hospital; Liz has also emerged
from under the influence of the claw.

One last task remains, however. Alan takes the claw and hurls
it into a vat of liquid nitrogen. Only at this moment does the
"follower of the claw" (C 365)—the bloody figure that has been
lurking just out of sight—come out into the open; but as the claw
is thrust into the nitrogen, an incredible transformation overtakes
the entity:

[Alan] saw the naked figure jerk to a halt a few feet away from

him, jerk and contort like metal under intolerable stress. All
at once the crust of blood broke open in a multitude of places,
and then the scrawny flesh did as its own thin blood boiled
out. The figure collapsed as if age and death and its aftermath
had seized it all at once, yet for an instant Alan thought he
saw a kind of relief, almost gratitude, in its eyes. (C 367)

The Claw is, to be sure, somewhat pulpish in its supernatural
premise, although the scenes in Nigeria, which could easily have
become hackneyed displays of primitive savagery, ring true with
crisp, telling details:

> . . . he manoeuvred onto the road to Lagos. Misshapen buses
> bounced over the potholes, battered taxis dodged through
> the traffic, their wing mirrors turned end up to give their
> drivers more room to scrape by, and that was all there was
> until Lagos closed in. Then they were hours in the go-slow,
> the city's daily eighteen-hour traffic jam. Today was an even
> day of the week, when only cars with even-numbered plates
> were allowed onto the island, yet the go-slow seemed even
> more sluggish. (C 144)

But, of course, the novel gains greatest poignancy in its depiction
of the hapless Anna facing a mother and father whom she finds
increasingly unlike the loving parents she once knew; as Campbell
wrote in the afterword to a 1992 reprint of the novel, "everyday
domestic savagery can be blacker and more dangerous than any
magic."[1] Incredibly, Campbell has admitted that an early draft of
the novel featured no chapters told from Anna's point of view;
but he must have quickly realised that the girl's perspective would
augment the emotive effect of the work, and it is in many ways
these chapters—rather than the somewhat flamboyant episode

1. "Afterword," *The Claw* (London: Warner Books, 1992), 372.

of Alan's trudge through Nigeria to find the Leopard Man—that
represent the true horror in *The Claw*. Some of these scenes are
excruciating:

> "You're hurting me." Anna began to cry. "You're hurting
> my arm." But mummy didn't let go until she'd dragged her
> back to the car, all that way through the crowds. Anna's arm
> hurt dreadfully, worse than when she'd fallen off the top of
> the climbing frame at the nursery. The worst thing was the
> way people laughed as they saw mummy dragging her along,
> as if that was the proper way to treat her. They didn't know
> that mummy was never like this. (C 202)

In *The Claw*, then, the supernatural premise is only a rather
makeshift excuse for the display of increasing tensions between
adults and children; and Campbell's decision to examine the issue
from both perspectives, with both sets of individuals attempting to
justify their own actions and feelings, gives *The Claw* an emotional
resonance exceptional in his work.

Campbell's short stories of the 1980s continue to address the
distinctive vision of children and their interaction with a world
that can frequently seem confusing and hostile. The traumas of
school life are the subject of several tales, forming a reprise of such
older stories as "The Interloper" and "In the Bag" [1974]. This
latter tale is told from the point of view of an adult, a school principal named Clarke, who as a ten-year-old had killed a boy, Derek,
when, during a game, he had put a plastic bag over Derek's head.
For the rest of his life Clarke is haunted by anomalous rustling
sounds; at the end Derek returns from the dead to kill Clarke's wife
and son. Again this bald summary fails to do justice to a brooding,
atmospheric tale whose denouement is loathsomely prefigured by
Clarke's noting that his wife's and son's heads "gleamed faintly"
(AH 125)—from having plastic bags put over them.

"The Other Side" [1985] is similarly told from the point of

view of an adult, a man named Bowring, who teaches in a school in a dismal section of some unnamed city but who resides across the river in a better section of town. His encounter with an odd prancing figure who is attacking children ends abruptly when he confronts the figure, chops him up with an axe, and—as he sees that all the pieces of the curiously bloodless body have his face on them—eats the pieces. This surreal *Doppelgänger* story is not so much a tale of childhood as it is a social commentary, suggesting Bowring's attempt to distance himself from the social decay of the region around his school.

"Apples" [1984] returns to a child's perspective. A group of girls and boys frequently steal the apples growing in the garden of an old man. One day he pursues them with a pair of shears, clearly seeking to do far more than scare them; but he ends up dying of a heart attack. The narrator, a girl, remarks significantly as she sees him lying dead, "He looked as if he'd gone bad somehow" (AH 445), suggesting some anomalous identification with his apples. This suggestion is augmented when, in addition to child pornography, piles of rotten fruit are found in his house. A year later, at a Hallowe'en party, the children are bobbing for apples when a figure enters the room. The children think it is merely the mother of one of their number, dressed up in a costume; but it is the old man, returned from the dead and seeking to carry out vengeance. In a rare instance of boldness in the face of the supernatural, one child gains the courage to set fire to the figure, dispatching him a second time. Is Campbell saying that children are better able to come to terms with horror than adults, whose excessive rationalism might paralyse them in a similar situation?

One of Campbell's most exhaustive treatments of childhood in his later novels is *The Influence*, written in 1986–87 and published in 1988. The novel opens with the death of Queenie, an embittered, domineering old woman who was virtual dictator of her house, where her niece Alison resides. Queenie had snobbishly scorned Alison's husband, Derek, an electrician, and had taken an intense interest in their young daughter Rowan. Queenie's will to live was so strong ("I'm never going to die," she had said in the past [I 50]) that when Alison and her sister Hermione examine the upstairs room where Queenie lies dead, Hermione—who herself has chillingly keen memories of being terrified of Queenie—is convinced that her aunt is only feigning death: "Look at her . . . She's listening to us, can't you see? God help us, she's smiling" (I 16). At the funeral, Hermione is still more agitated by the fact that Queenie is being buried with a locket that contains a lock of Rowan's hair.

Queenie had, with unusual generosity, left the house—in a seaside town not far from Liverpool—to Alison. Not long after the funeral, Rowan encounters on the dunes a little girl with strangely mature mannerisms and speech-patterns who says her name is Vicky. It will not take the reader very long, from the moment this name is mentioned, to deduce that this is the spirit of Queenie lodged in another body; only much later does Campbell note that Queenie's given name was Victoria (I 85).

As the friendship of Vicky and Rowan grows, both Hermione and Alison's disturbed cousin Lance (who had previously been institutionalised for taking an interest in under-age girls) develop a dim sense that Vicky is in fact Queenie reincarnated. But Lance dies horribly by seemingly jumping on to a train track while a train is approaching. It appears as if a little girl had somehow induced him to his fatal action. Meanwhile, another convenient accident—an electrician who had underbid Derek for fixing the school's wiring system is found dead of electrocution—allows Derek to get the job instead and thereby remain in Queenie's house.

Hermione is now convinced of Queenie/Vicky's evil intentions with regard to Rowan and believes that two things must be accomplished to foil Queenie's plans: first, Rowan must be removed from the baleful influence of Queenie's house, and second, the locket with Rowan's hair must be removed from Queenie's coffin. Hermione manages to persuade Alison and Derek to let Rowan stay with her for the weekend, but she is denied her request to

exhume Queenie's body. Increasingly unbalanced, Hermione frantically goes to the cemetery and digs up the corpse herself, only to
discover that the locket is no longer there. She also finds horror:

> ... the moving shape wasn't Vicky, nor was it beside Rowan.
> It was much closer to Hermione, which was why she hadn't
> been able to focus at once. It was a hand, a shriveled hand
> piebald with earth. Though it was jerky as a puppet's hand, it
> was able to close around the back of Hermione's neck.
>
> She flinched convulsively away from its touch, and tried
> to scream as if that would help her twist out of reach. But
> a pain deep in her innards had sucked breath into her, pain
> that bowed her over herself and sent her sideways into the
> coffin. She was still gripping the flashlight, which thumped
> the lining of the coffin and showed her Queenie's grinning
> head. The head was rising from its nest of hair.
>
> The hair stuck to the lining. It tore free of the gray scalp
> as the corpse sat up stiffly, a bald grinning doll with no eyes
> worth the name. Perhaps it was mindless as a puppet, but its
> fleshless grin fell open in what might have been a soundless
> scream of triumph as it clasped its arms around Hermione's
> neck and pressed its face against hers. (I 147)

Hermione is found dead in the grave. Vicky then brings Rowan to
the cemetery and, as Rowan attempts to flee the horrible sight of
the dead Hermione, she hits her head on the tombstone and lies
unconscious.

Waking up some time later, Rowan is curiously disoriented.
She leaves the graveyard and trudges to the train station. She has
no money, but is certain that the conductor will let her go home
if he is informed of her situation; but no one makes any effort
to stop or question her. She is not even very certain how to get
home, so she disembarks at Chester, thinking to catch another
train. She can't find one, so she feels she has no option but to walk

all the way home, even though it will be many miles. Her sensations are becoming increasingly divorced from reality: "though
she was running, she didn't feel tired" (I 187). She also does not
seem to require any food or sleep, even though months must have
passed when she finally approaches her house: as she peeks in the
window, Christmas decorations have been set up. She then learns
a truth that has slowly been dawning on the reader: Rowan has
been reduced to pure spirit, while Queenie, having abandoned the
body of Vicky, has now occupied Rowan's body.

> So she was nothing. Even her feelings were suddenly more
> difficult to grasp, slippery and melting like the meaning-
> less shapes of sleet on the glass. Her experiences since the
> graveyard were catching up with her: not only had the world
> around her turned into a dream that was often a nightmare,
> she had been little more than a dream of herself. (I 207)

Rowan has no idea how to regain her body or even to notify
her parents of what has happened. Ever since "Rowan" (Queenie)
was rescued from the graveyard, she had been behaving oddly—
understandably enough, her parents think, given the traumatic
events she had witnessed and experienced. But some changes seem
highly anomalous: in school, for example, her spelling has suddenly improved, and no longer does she make the mistakes that
she used to do when writing in her private journal.

The spirit of Rowan goes to her parents' room while they sleep;
unnervingly, she fails to see herself at all in the mirror. Nevertheless, she attempts to call to her mother; and Alison—who had been
far more disturbed at "Rowan's" unusual behaviour than Derek
had been—seems to hear the ghost of a voice. She goes to the
bedroom where her daughter is supposedly sleeping: "The notion
that the child in the bed wasn't Rowan, whatever she looked like,
had seemed to illuminate the last few months with a clarity that
made Alison's mind feel seared" (I 216).

Gradually Alison becomes convinced that the spirit occupying the body of her daughter is not Rowan but Queenie; her intuition is dramatically confirmed when she finds the missing locket around "Rowan's" neck. A confrontation ensues, and Queenie lets down her disguise. But Alison's attempts at persuading Queenie to give up Rowan's body fail, so she begins throttling the little girl, knowing that Queenie would have no other body to enter if she were to die. Later Derek finds both of them unconscious but relatively unharmed; the spirit of Queenie has fled, and Rowan is allowed to re-enter her body.

The Influence uses a supernatural conception—psychic possession—that is not at all new, and Campbell has not done much to modify the basic idea. But this trope is merely an excuse for probing the pitiable helplessness of Rowan as she is exiled from her body and must wander about as a disembodied spirit. Her trip home from the graveyard is an evocative dream-fantasy reminiscent of the *Demons by Daylight* stories, and is the real core of the book.

As for Queenie, we may suspect that this is one more character based in part upon Campbell's mother, with her domineering ways and the terrifying effect she has on those close to her. The social snobbery evinced by Queenie seems to reflect some of his mother's traits as Campbell portrays them in the 1983 introduction to *The Face That Must Die*.

In spite of these features of interest, *The Influence* is on the whole a slight novel. Although it tells poignantly of a child's conflicting emotions as she encounters the world beyond the horizon of her own home and parents, its conventional supernaturalism and the somewhat flamboyant deaths of several characters place it among Campbell's lesser novels. It is, of course, a very satisfying read, but it does not seem to broach the broader personal and social issues found in many of Campbell's other works.

The Last Voice They Hear (1998) and *Silent Children* (1999), comprise, as Campbell has noted to me, "a pair . . . in terms of shared themes."[2] Both works derive much of their emotive power from their focus on the plight of children; but *Last Voice* deftly combines the child as victim and the child as villain—or, rather, shows how the one can lead inexorably to the other. At the start of this novel, however, we seem to be dealing with anything but childhood: this non-supernatural novel treats of a serial killer whose victims are at the opposite chronological pole from children—elderly couples. But it gradually becomes clear that the serial killer's motives reach back to his own childhood.

The Last Voice They Hear weaves several seemingly unrelated narrative strands together into a unified and gripping climax. The bulk of the novel focuses upon Geoff Davenport, the host of "Britain's most successful investigative television series" (LV 24), a news show devoted to exposing abuses by companies or individuals. We learn that Geoff had a half-brother, Ben, who disappeared when he was eighteen, although he has kept him a secret from almost everyone, including his wife Gail. Throughout the novel we are provided with glimpses of the shoddy, abusive treatment Ben received from his parents, who clearly preferred Geoff. Geoff had tried to be a loving brother to Ben and to mitigate the harshness of Ben's abuse, but to little avail. Eventually Ben is forced to stay with his mother's parents for years; some years later they die, and he finally returns to his family, although he is full of rage and resentment not only toward his parents but toward Geoff himself.

Ben begins to make enigmatic phone calls to Geoff and also to leave him a succession of envelopes at various locations, usually containing photographs of sites associated with their childhood. Things take a sudden turn for the worse when Ben causes Gail's parents' car to crash in Scotland. He then performs the sadistic ploy that he has used on the eight elderly couples he has previously killed: he uses glue to bind their arms around each other

2. Ramsey Campbell, letter to S. T. Joshi (28 April 1998).

and to seal their lips in an everlasting kiss—a grotesque parody of the affection he himself failed to receive from his own parents and grandparents. Gail's mother dies as a result, but her father survives and manages to escape, in spite of his serious injuries.

But Ben then contrives a still more heinous act: pretending to be Gail's father, he kidnaps Geoff's three-year-old son, Paul, from the television station's day care centre in London and takes him back to his hometown, Liverpool. Geoff is quickly on Ben's trail, but finds that Ben is not at their old home (now a hotel). He learns, however, that the landlady had recommended several other places to stay, and by a systematic search (which also includes a car chase in which he pursues to the airport a man who proves not to be Ben at all), he tracks Ben and Paul to an amusement park in Blackpool. Ben ascends a lofty tower, taking Paul with him; Geoff follows. After several tense moments, Geoff manages to save Paul, but Ben jumps off to his death.

The Last Voice They Hear manages, without overstating the matter, to convey a variety of social messages at once, but its central point is clear: the abuse of children can have lasting and catastrophic effects, and can actually engender psychopathic behaviour years later. Some readers might perhaps wish a more exhaustive dwelling on Ben's ill-treatment during his youth, but in a few deft strokes Campbell portrays the humiliation a boy must feel when his own parents or grandparents—figures whose authority he has been brought up not to question—display contempt or loathing for him. We are not surprised to learn, late in the novel, that Ben himself caused his own grandparents' death (LV 340).

To emphasise the point still further, Ben himself, during the time he kidnaps Paul, treats his nephew with just the kind of scorn he himself received—and, when he does so in public, is praised for it by passersby, who smugly imagine that Ben is merely being a stern and forceful parent. A scene in a travel agency, when Ben (who has sardonically adopted the name Mr Reaper) seeks to

THE CHILD AS VICTIM AND VILLAIN

purchase tickets for himself and Paul to go to Turkey, perfectly encapsulates the message:

> The child bowed forward—would have fallen off the counter if Reaper hadn't dug the corner of the brochure into the heaving chest. "Don't start," he said as he'd heard quite a few parents say in the open. "Nobody wants to hear you yell."
> He thought the warning had found a home until . . . the toddler unleashed the howl he'd been storing up. "Keep that up and you'll get another," Reaper responded as he'd observed parents did. That had no effect on the volume, and though the boy kept hiccuping that only punctuated the howl. Reaper did his best to ignore it as everyone else in the shop was doing . . . (LV 280)

Those who believe that parental "permissiveness" and reluctance to use corporal punishment on their children have produced today's unruly children and teenagers might want to think twice about the sadistic "tough love" that Ben—with the full approval of spectators—appears to be bestowing upon the helpless boy whose father he claims to be.

The Last Voice They Hear, although written with a lyrical grace that manages to augment the tensity of the scenario, is perhaps only in the middle range of Campbell's novelistic work; but to say that is simply to say that it still ranks high among suspense novels of its kind. One scene—when Paul wanders away from Ben's clutches by slipping out of a cinema, only to be caught by Ben some hours later—is somewhat too similar to an analogous scene in *The One Safe Place*, when Marshall Travis momentarily manages to escape from his captors, the Fancys. Many readers will regret the absence of the supernatural that made some of Campbell's more recent novels (notably *The House on Nazareth Hill*) so striking. But the vivid characterisation of all the central figures—notably Geoff, Ben, and the hardly articulate Paul—go far in redeeming this work.

Silent Children is a still finer work than its predecessor and ranks close to the summit of Campbell's non-supernatural work. While many of the incidents are those we would expect to find in a mainstream novel of family life, Campbell's treatment of them is such as to make generic distinctions meaningless, and the persistent undercurrent of unease that the reader feels while reading this work is perhaps singular in his output.

In the arresting first chapter we see a man, Hector Woollie, fall off a boat and apparently drown. We quickly learn that Woollie—who, with his wife Adele, had run a home for slightly retarded adults—had murdered several children; one of them Woollie had buried under the floor of a house that he was renovating in the suburb of Wembley. The house was owned by Roger and Leslie Ames, a married couple who subsequently divorced. After months of trying to sell the house, Leslie and her thirteen-year-old son Ian decide to move back into it, despite the unsavoury reputation it has now gained throughout the placid middle-class neighbourhood.

Leslie decides to hire out a room of her house to a tenant. The room is taken with surprising rapidity by Jack Lamb, an American writer of horror stories who is looking for a quiet place to work on his next novel. At this point we are led to expect a hackneyed romance between Jack and Leslie, and sure enough they become attracted to each other and have sex not long after Jack moves in. Leslie envisages marrying Jack, who might also provide an adult male authority figure for her wayward son.

But Campbell has lulled us into a false sense of security. Jack, it turns out, is none other than the son of Hector Woollie. Although by no means afflicted by Hector's psychosis, he is haunted by the possibility that, as a teenager, he may on occasion have unwittingly helped Woollie dispose of children while assisting in his father's renovation work. He deliberately sought out Leslie's house in order to write a book about the killings, but is jarred by unnerving phone calls he receives at the house—calls that must be from Woollie himself. Woollie had not in fact died, but had staged his own death so as to escape the police. Now he wanders the streets as a derelict, grotesque in his shabbiness and absence of teeth but still a menace. And at one point, as he speaks to his son on the phone, he voices Jack's most deep-seated fear: "I wonder how much like your dad you really are deep down" (SC 149).

Meanwhile, Leslie is harried by her son's misbehaviour. Inspired by Jack's example, Ian has written a horror story for a school class. A fellow student, Rupe Duke, brother of the girl who was killed at Leslie's house, reads the story and thinks it is about his sister. He tears it up, and Ian responds by striking at Rupe, inadvertently causing an injury to Rupe's eye. Ian is suspended for the rest of the term. Shortly thereafter, Leslie learns Jack's true identity and demands that he leave her house.

The novel's sense of foreboding bursts into full-fledged terror when Woollie comes on the scene. He kidnaps seven-year-old Charlotte, daughter of the woman Roger Ames has now married. Not long afterwards Ian enters the house next door to his—a house that he and Leslie are looking after while the occupants are on holiday. He discovers Woollie and Charlotte there, and Woollie quickly captures Ian as well. He forces Ian to write a note saying that he has gone away because his mother had suspected him of doing harm to Charlotte.

Woollie now plans his escape. Not wishing to give away his own whereabouts, he calls Jack and demands that he bring a car to Leslie's house. Jack arrives but does not find his father; he and Leslie eventually deduce that Woollie might indeed be next door. They burst in on him. Woollie, who has already smothered Ian with a pillow, possibly to death, now threatens to kill Charlotte unless Jack takes him away. But Jack wrestles the knife out of Woollie's hands. Leslie takes Ian—who, though injured, is still alive—and Charlotte out of the house as Jack confronts his father.

264 RAMSEY CAMPBELL: MASTER OF WEIRD FICTION

In a dramatic conclusion Woollie impales himself in the throat on the knife that Jack is holding.

Campbell does not opt for the expected happy ending, however. Jack and Leslie do not end up together, although Ian and Jack continue to meet occasionally. In the Epilogue Ian ponders, "He'd been looking for endings where there weren't any. Life wasn't a story unless you made it into one" (SC 359).

The one overriding feature of *Silent Children*—above its smooth-flowing prose, its tense moments of suspense, and its revelations of a diseased mind—is the vividness of its character portrayal. Even minor characters—Roger's wife, Hilene; Jack's overbearing mother, Adele; a pestiferous reporter whose sensationalistic stories about Leslie's house augment her difficulties in returning to it and leading a normal life—are rendered so crisply and vividly that they immediately come to life. Major figures such as Leslie and Jack are fully formed, complex personalities who are etched with increasing subtlety with each passing chapter. Campbell has depicted the teenager Ian Ames with especial felicity, capturing in all its paradoxical confusion the burgeoning character of a boy on the verge of young manhood. A distinctly satirical edge enlivens many descriptions of character and incident: Campbell is relentless in exposing the pettiness, hypocrisy, and selfishness that can typify middle-class suburban life. Few characters in the novel emerge as wholly admirable. Although the reader's sympathy resides chiefly with Leslie, and secondarily with Jack and Ian, even they are flawed individuals struggling as best they can to live up to their own ideals.

Oddly, Hector Woollie seems somewhat cloudy, specifically with regard to the psychological aberrations that led him to his multiple murders of children. There is, by design, no such intense and relentless focus on his psychotic mentality as there is on Horridge in *The Face That Must Die* or even on Jack Orchard in *The Count of Eleven*: Woollie is merely one of a network of characters whose accidental intermingling has produced the chilling scenario.

His past murders are only alluded to in passing, although in one harrowing passage he actually shows photographs of his victims to his captives, Ian and Charlotte, pretending that they are pictures of children who are merely "sleeping." We are led to believe that Woollie is so pained at the thought of children suffering—having watched his own brother die slowly and agonisingly as a child—that he has to "help" them by killing them. Throughout the novel Woollie sings to himself a nursery rhyme—

> Now I lay you down to sleep,
> Close your eyes goodnight.
> Angels come your soul to keep,
> Close your eyes goodnight.

Woollie has, of course, interpreted this song quite literally, and toward the end he reflects: "he was one of the angels himself—the angel that brought peace into the lives of children who were crying out for it" (SC 339). But this is about all we are given in regard to Woollie's motivations.

The question that will no doubt be asked of *Silent Children* is: is it a horror novel? I have already suggested that the strain of unease that underlies the entire work may make such a question moot. That unease takes many forms. Of course, the chief focus of terror is the fate of Ian and Charlotte at the hands of Woollie, especially in those scenes in which they come tantalisingly close to escaping, only to fall back into his clutches. But other questions haunt us. Will Leslie ever achieve peace in her own home, or will her neighbours, horrified at her mere occupation of what the newspapers call a "horror house," somehow rise up and drive her away? Will Jack turn out like his father, or instead have a reckoning with him? Will Ian let himself be influenced by his unruly friends and lapse into irresponsibility or even a life of crime?

Both *The Last Voice They Hear* and *Silent Children* are manifestly novels of society—a middle-class society that strives desperately to cover over, just as Hector Woollie has done, the crimes that have taken place in its midst; a society in which divorce has left lingering tensions and animosities that devolve upon children; a society that is unsure of the exact balance between permissiveness and discipline required to raise children responsibly. Social concerns have come to the forefront of Campbell's recent work, and society's treatment of children in particular has been a significant focus of his attention. That Campbell can probe the matter both supernaturally and non-supernaturally is only a credit to the versatility of his imagination.

In Campbell's next novel, *Pact of the Fathers* (2001), even the crime/suspense element is reduced to a minimum. Like classical Greek tragedy, all the "horrors" take place offstage and come to us only at second hand. This need not imply a diminution of the power of these episodes; it is only that those who want a more obvious jolt as part of their literary nourishment had best go elsewhere.

Pact of the Fathers reveals, with exquisite pacing and tempo, a scenario whose implications are appalling and grotesque. A young woman, Daniella Logan, grieves over the sudden death of her father in a car accident; but adding to her trauma is a scene she witnesses a few days later, in which a group of men appear to act out some mysterious ritual with knives over her father's new grave. Compelled to investigate the matter, she learns that her father had been one of a number of fathers who, to insure their success in business, had formed a pact to kill their first-born children. Described in this way, it can be readily seen that the novel bears some parallels to *The Long Lost*, in which we similarly see the working out of an age-old ritual in a modern world that seemingly has no place for such things. But the differences are also striking. There is never any suggestion in *Pact of the Fathers* that those who fulfil this pact receive supernatural aid; rather, it would appear that the others involved in the covert group provide assistance to those who carry through their dreadful mission and, conversely, destroy (as Daniella's father had been destroyed) those who lose courage and spare their first-born.

What distinguishes *Pact of the Fathers* is the suppleness, fluidity, and richly textured elegance of its prose. Campbell's writing has never been better; his etching of character has never been more telling and shrewd; his modulation of the narrative has never been surer. Consider this passage, describing a scene in Greece (where Daniella has fled to escape vengeance on the part of the other fathers):

> A line of squat white houses not much less rough than rocks straggled down the lumpy road to the harbour. Old women sat unmoving outside two adjacent houses, their faces wizened as dried fruit, their eyes black as their headscarves and the dresses that hid them from the neck down, their expressions no more welcoming than the priest's had been. A moped leaned in a doorway beyond which she heard the thumps and grunts of a martial arts game a solitary silhouette was playing on a television almost blank with sunlight. (PF 140)

Passages like this should make every other writer despair of ever hoping to equal the smooth rhythms, sharp observation, and painterly elegance that Campbell has developed over a lifetime of unremitting work as a prose stylist.

But is it horror? Is it even suspense? We are, at the outset, puzzled as to why Daniella has fled to Greece, away from all her friends and family, but the astute reader will have resolved this point some time before Campbell himself reveals it; and the only obviously horrific scene might be one that describes the hideous fate of another father who failed to offer up his first-born. As I say, those who want a book to make them jump out of their skins on every other page will surely be disappointed; but other readers—may they not be few!—who look to a novel for some insight into how people actually act and think will find *Pact of the*

Fathers one of the quiet triumphs in Ramsey Campbell's novelistic output.

Campbell has, of course, written much about children in a number of other works. Several of his novels feature a girl and a boy roughly parallel in age with Campbell's own children at the time of the novels' writing, although it would be simplistic to assume that these characters are mere portraits of his children. One piquant work is "The Maze" [1994], explicitly co-written with his children, Tammy and Matt. More than a literary curiosity, this tale is an effectively shuddersome account of two children who wander into a strange hedge-maze and are ultimately replaced by the supernatural occupants within. Since his children were well into their teenage years at the time of the story's writing, Campbell's remark that "Much that is best in this story belongs to Tammy and Matt"[3] need not be regarded as flattering exaggeration.

In the introduction to *Waking Nightmares* (1991), which contains many of his stories of children, Campbell addresses the whole issue directly:

> Jim Herbert told me recently that since he became a father he has tried to steer clear of the theme of children as victims. For my part, parenthood seems to keep sending me back to the theme of the vulnerability of children . . . Ideally—though in fact, I fear, too seldom—having children reminds one of what it was like to be one. (WN 2)

In many of Campbell's works children are, to be sure, victims; but on occasion (*The Nameless*) they can be villains also, and

3. Author's note to "The Maze," in *Great Writers and Kids Write Spooky Stories,* ed. Martin H. Greenberg, Jill M. Morgan, and Robert Weinberg (New York: Random House, 1995), 96.

even ("Apples") heroes of a sort. And perhaps their games, make-
believe, and lack of the onerous responsibilities of adulthood make
them unusually susceptible to supernatural adventure. But it is a
sad fact, too, that their victimisation frequently occurs not at the
hands of a ghost or goblin but of those adults who ought most to
cherish them.

"Dragged Down" (JB) is a splendid depiction of the wrenching
class conflict inherent in a lower-class teenage boy's longing for
an upper-class girl at school; but we are not given sufficient clues
as to what kind of creature could have caused their drowning in a
tunnel separating the districts where they live. In "Fear the Dead"
(JB), a small boy's fears that speaking ill of the dead will have
dreadful consequences proves all too true.

In *The Kind Folk* (2012) the narrative focuses entirely—and
obsessively—on a single character, the young Luke Arnold, who
is astounded to discover (on a nationally broadcast television
show) that he is not the biological son of his parents, Maurice and
Freda Arnold. The existential unease that this revelation creates
is only augmented by subsequent developments. What of the fact
that his beloved uncle, Terence, dies of a heart attack before he
is able to tell Luke something important about his origins? What
are we to make of a rambling and seemingly incomprehensible
diary that Terence left behind—one that suggests that he may
have developed an interest in the occult (both John Strong—a
baleful figure from Campbell's first novel, *The Doll Who Ate His
Mother* [1975]—and Roland Franklyn, from "The Franklyn Paragraphs," are cited in it)? Why does a nurse whom Luke tracks
down first say that she knows what happened during Luke's birth,
then frantically deny it?

The title of course refers to fairies—the euphemism "kind folk"
being exactly analogous with the ancient Greek term Eumen-
ides ("the well-intentioned") in reference to the Furies. These
fairies are, accordingly, very different from the airy sprites of Walt
Disney; and their sinister presence lurks in the background of

the entire novel. In one harrowing chapter, Luke actually pursues what he takes to be one of the kind folk, only to lose track of him (or her or it). Later he strikes one with his car:

He's nearly at the junction when the shape lurches in front of the car, flinging its arms wide and thrusting its mouthless head forward so violently that the eyes almost sink out of sight. He doesn't brake; he floors the accelerator, and the car runs the scrawny figure down, having struck it in the region where its genitals should be, a withered tangle more like bone than any species of flesh. Luke doesn't feel an impact, but the car shudders as though it has been seized by a wind across the moors. As he races past the Crakemoor road he sees a dim glimmering shape stagger to its feet in the mirror and stretch out its claws to the car. The arms are lengthening; they're yards long now—they're even longer. Then they appear to merge with the night, and eventually Luke lets the car lose speed on the ascent to the highest moor. (KF 171)

It is bad enough that Luke at times suspects that he himself is a child of the fairies; but he finds it much worse to contemplate the fate of his own child, being carried by his partner, Sophie. Initially the child seems normal, but it soon makes a bizarre hand gesture that ought to be physiologically impossible for human hands (this is the focus of the rather amateurish jacket art by Erika Steiskal). In a conclusion that vaguely echoes Lovecraft's "The Shadow over Innsmouth"—where the protagonist first flees the hybrid horrors of Innsmouth, only to embrace them later once he realises he is biologically related to them—Luke concludes the novel by feeling "wistfully relieved that there's still magic in the world" (KF 216).

The Kind Folk is written with a fluidity of prose rhythm that Campbell has mastered, along with an ever-growing sense of existential terror that is perhaps unlike anything in his previous works. It seems on the surface deficient in explicit physical horror, but it achieves its effects in a far more profound and psychologically resonant manner, as the horror interweaves itself into the very fabric of a family's most intimate relationships.

IX. MISCELLANEOUS WRITINGS

The work of a writer so prolific and multifaceted as Campbell is difficult to encompass even in a broadly thematic or generic study. Inevitably, some works will fail to fit within the given rubrics, even though they may be significant in themselves; other works may simply be false starts or the product of external impetus rather than inner compulsion. Although the bulk of Campbell's work falls very clearly within the range of either supernatural horror or psychological suspense, he has experimented in nearly all phases of imaginative fiction, with the possible exception of pure fantasy (unless *Needing Ghosts* is to be so categorised). It may be of interest, then, to discuss briefly some of his works that are perhaps not central to his output but are of interest nonetheless, if only from a biographical perspective.

In 1976, when Campbell was making relatively little money from his fiction-writing, he accepted an offer to write novelisations of Universal horror films under a house name, Carl Dreadstone. Campbell produced three books, all written in 1976 and published the following year: *The Bride of Frankenstein*, *The Wolfman*, and *Dracula's Daughter*. (Three other novelisations—*The Mummy*, *The Werewolf of London*, and *Creature from the Black Lagoon*—were written by other hands.) The attribution of these three books to Campbell had long been suspected, but only recently has he acknowledged them as his.

Campbell performed his task with relish, not only because he genuinely enjoyed the three films he was to novelise but perhaps because he felt he might gain useful practice in writing a novel-length work: he had written only one full-length novel (*The Doll Who Ate His Mother*) at this time. No one should regard these items as masterworks, but they prove far more entertaining and substantial than the usual dreary hackwork of this kind.

It is scarcely worth examining these works in detail, for of course they follow the basic scenarios of the films on which they are based, with provocative alterations. In each instance Campbell based his novels on the screenplays, although he clearly derived many touches from the films themselves. Introductions to each of the volumes, written under his own name, provide clues as to how he went about his task.

Campbell's overall challenge is to flesh out the characters beyond merely what they say on screen and the settings beyond merely what is seen by the viewer. To this end, he devotes much space in all three works to the psychological motivations of the characters and to their pasts, so that they become fully rounded figures instead of merely voices mechanically uttering words put in their mouths by the screenwriter.

The Bride of Frankenstein is the most "faithful" of the novelisations, following the film (and the screenplay by William Hurlbut) closely. Of course, the original *Frankenstein* film (1931) had adapted only about half of Mary Shelley's novel, and *The Bride of Frankenstein* (1935) picks up the story, especially its critical element whereby the monster demands that Frankenstein create a mate for him. Because the monster makes almost no utterances in the film, Campbell must expend still more effort in portraying his fluctuating emotions as the film progresses. In his introduction Campbell rightly sees the monster as the central component of the film:

... the monster kills less from malice than out of suffering, incomprehension, and loneliness. The true horror is not what he does but what is done to him. He is one of the cinema's archetypes—an outcast who is either exploited or more often rejected as intolerably monstrous, even by himself.[1]

To this end, Campbell has eliminated much of the comic relief and buffoonery that frequently threatens to destroy the atmosphere of horrific pathos in the film, especially the now corny opening in which characters representing Mary Shelley, Percy Bysshe Shelley, and Byron discuss the writing of horror stories. (The segment is of interest in the film only because Elsa Lanchester, who plays Mary Shelley, returns at the end as the Bride.) Campbell's entire novelisation focuses unremittingly on the complex emotions of the monster as he moves in a world he scarcely understands.

The Wolfman differs in significant particulars from the film, *The Wolf Man* (1941), especially in its dialogue: Campbell announces in the introduction that the novelisation restores some of the alterations made in Curt Siodmak's screenplay during the shooting of the film. One scene in particular—in which Larry Talbot, later to become the Wolfman, wrestles with a bear at a carnival—is omitted from the film altogether, although Campbell declares that stills for the scene exist. Talbot's first transformation into a wolf—really more a psychological change than a physical one—is described in a typically Campbellian stream-of-consciousness manner:

A movement made him glance up snarling, toward a rectangle of glass. Beyond it was a room exactly like this one. On the floor of that room crouched a dark shape. Its teeth gleamed; threads of liquid dangled from its mouth. It made ready to spring as he did.

1. Introduction to *The Bride of Frankenstein* by Carl Dreadstone (New York: Berkley, 1977), xi.

Perhaps this was its den. He backed off, and was relieved when it did the same. He turned, enthralled by the sudden ease of his body, the directness and simplicity of his thoughts. He felt almost free. Only the room oppressed him.

The window swayed above him. The great vague light drew him on. He must leap. Out there was freedom, the joy of the run, of the hunt. He felt his teeth levering his lips wide. The promise of the wide night made him ravenous. The power that throbbed impatiently through his body excited him, made him yearn to hunt something soft and warm. He leaped. With a shock like the breaking of ice, the cold shining night rushed up to embrace him.[2]

Dracula's Daughter (1936) is perhaps the least-known of the films Campbell novelised and is not highly regarded, although Campbell in his introduction speaks of it with enthusiasm as "a quietly serious piece of filmmaking, one of the most delicate and understated of all vampire films."[3] The large number of characters in this film allows Campbell to inaugurate a technique he would perfect in his own later novels: the rapid shifting of point of view from one character to the next, not only to introduce them to the reader but to trace the complex chain of events that leads them to come into contact with one another. Here again Campbell has condensed some of the film's dialogue and also cut out much of the comic relief. The narrative voice is unusually tart and satiric.

It would perhaps be making too much of these novelisations to say that they were somehow instrumental in Campbell's later novelistic output. Certainly, his next novel—*The Face That Must Die* [1976]—reveals all the tightness and compactness of construction that one would expect from a veteran novelist, but it does

2. *The Wolfman* by Carl Dreadstone (New York: Berkley, 1977), 126–27.
3. Introduction to *Dracula's Daughter* by Carl Dreadstone (New York: Berkley, 1977), ix.

not seem to owe much to the novelisations in point of technique. Suffice it to say that these three works brought in much-needed income for Campbell; and his lifelong love of horror films allowed him to undertake the task with a vigour and enthusiasm all too rarely found in such works. They are hardly essential works in Campbell's output, but the wholesome entertainment they pro-vide is sufficient justification for their writing.

The origin of the subgenre of imaginative fiction known as "sword-and-sorcery" is much debated by scholars and historians. Some trace it to the prose epics of William Morris (chiefly *The Well at the World's End* [1896] and *The Wood Beyond the World* [1894]), which, although set in fantasy realms, evoked the imagery of mediaeval battle; others find it in the early work of Lord Dun-sany, especially the striking tale of fantastic combat, "The Sword of Welleran" (1908). Still other sources have been put forward.

All agree, however, that the subgenre as we know it was first coherently systematised in the prodigally bountiful, if sadly uneven, work of the American writer Robert E. Howard (1906–1936), who in a career spanning barely a decade produced a mountainous array of fiction for the pulp magazines of the 1920s and 1930s; much of it, indeed, was rejected by those magazines and was pub-lished posthumously. Howard's work—almost exclusively short stories and novelettes—divides broadly into a number of separate cycles, each with its distinctive locale, historical setting, and hero: the tales of Bran Mak Morn, a British chieftain during the days of the Roman occupation of Britain; stories about Solomon Kane, a seventeenth-century Puritan who roams the globe in the name of justice and religion; and, most famously, the tales of Conan, a barbarian living in the prehistoric realm of Cimmeria, of which he eventually becomes the king.

Howard's prodigious imagination in conceiving the life and actions of primitive peoples is certainly remarkable. It was

probably derived from his own fascination with what he perceived to be the freedoms of barbarian life and his implacable
hostility to civilisation—attitudes fostered by his being the
descendant of one of the original settlers of Texas and his lifelong residence in the remote village of Cross Plains. These
provocative conceptions are, however, frequently offset by
a lamentable crudity of expression and a yielding to the most
hackneyed conventions of pulp fiction: characters who are broad
caricatures rather than living beings; lurid bloodletting and
melodrama; implausibility of action, especially with regard to
supernatural phenomena; and a general slovenliness in diction
and plot development. Howard and his work have attracted a
small but vocal band of cheerleaders who are determined to give
him high rank as a writer and thinker, but it is unlikely that he
will ever have as high a standing as, say, his friend H. P. Lovecraft in general literature.

Fritz Leiber (1910–1992), only a few years after Howard's death,
began the literary rehabilitation of this subgenre, taking the best
elements of Howard's work—its evocation of primitivism and its
sense of high adventure and conflict—and engrafting upon them
a psychological sophistication that makes his work a genuine contribution to literature. Leiber, also a leading science fiction author,
wrote dozens of stories around two piquant characters, Fafhrd and
the Gray Mouser, a pair of comically ill-matched individuals who
roam the ancient world in search of adventure. The self-depre-
cating wit of these stories is not the least of their virtues.

I am not clear how much of Leiber's work Campbell has read;
but he has certainly read Howard's, for in 1976 he was actually
asked to "complete" some Solomon Kane stories that Howard
had left unfinished at his death. It would be difficult to imagine
two writers more different than Campbell and Howard, and yet
Campbell's tales are so successful that few have been able to detect
the exact point in the three tales—"Hawk of Basti," "The Castle of
the Devil," and "The Children of Asshur"—where Howard ends

and Campbell begins. In the first, Campbell has written about the last three-fifths of the story; in the second, the latter four-fifths; and in the third, the latter third.

Campbell was presumably asked to write these completions because he had by this time written "sword-and-sorcery" tales of his own, mostly for anthologies compiled by andrew j. offutt. Again, these four stories—which grew out of his early fantasy tales set on the mythical planet Tond—are thoroughly entertaining in their own right, although they offer few insights into Campbell's literary personality. The stories focus around a Conan-like nomad named Ryre, who roams the world—presumably in primitive times—as a mercenary, but who has a keen eye for injustice and a yearning to overwhelm it. Now and again some striking horrific imagery enters into the tales, as in "The Sustenance of Hoak" [1974], when Ryre unearths a coffin containing the remains of a fellow warrior, Glode:

> At first, in the twilight, he couldn't distinguish what was in the box. A mixture of earth and pale objects: the pale things were entangled—there were large glistening pale surfaces and paler forms coiled about them. The pale thick tendrils were dragging the larger object, or objects, through the bottom of the coffin. One extremity of the large object slipped an inch lower in the hole, amid a strained creaking and rattling of earth. Although the large object was losing its form, as if melting, it had Glode's face. (FAN 15)

But, on the whole, these tales are *jeux d'esprit* in which Campbell seeks to apply his talents in a mode and idiom as far removed from his grim, contemporary, psychological horror tales as possible.

A fifth tale appears to qualify as sword-and-sorcery, although its genesis is peculiar. "The Ways of Chaos" [1978] constitutes chapter fourteen of a round-robin novel entitled *Genseric's Fifth-Born Son*, which was to have appeared in the small-press magazine

Fantasy Crossroads. Given its origin, the work can scarcely stand
on its own; but it is nonetheless an interesting piece, combining
rousing battle-scenes with a suggestion of Lovecraftian horror:
the protagonist is able, by uttering the "words of change," to
become an animal who leads the Hounds of Tindalos (creatures
invented in Frank Belknap Long's early "Cthulhu Mythos" tale,
"The Hounds of Tindalos" [1929]) on a murderous rampage
against his enemies.

Three decades later, Campbell was commissioned to write
Solomon Kane (2010), a novelisation of the film of the same title
(2009) written and directed by Michael J. Bassett. No doubt
Campbell was chosen for this work because of his prior involvement with the Robert E. Howard character. Both the film and
the novel are chock full of stirring incidents, although they begin
with the startling tableau of Kane being pummelled by thieves as
Kane declares, "I have renounced violence." The pledge does not
last long, as Kane is compelled to rescue the daughter of a family,
the Crowthorns, who have nursed him back to health after his
beating. The novelisation is written with tremendous energy and
verve, matching the film's relentless pace.

In the early 1970s Campbell attempted several tales that are clearly
within the domain of science fiction. Few of these are entirely successful, and several remain unpublished. The problem, in almost
every instance, is excessive obscurity, rendering the events and
their significance opaque to the point of unintelligibility. Consider "Murders" [1973]: the tale apparently deals (prophetically)
with a kind of "virtual reality" and the legal and moral difficulties
involved in the characters' inability to distinguish between media-
created fantasy and the real world; but the narrative is so indirect
that only confusion results.

Medusa [1973] has the distinction of being perhaps Campbell's earliest excursion into the novella form, a form he utilised

so powerfully in *Needing Ghosts;* it was published separately in 1987. But this long, rambling tale of a telepath, An, who comes to a planet named Fecundity and, in the company of a gay couple there, explores a nearby planet of living crystal, is too unfocused and overly intellectualised to deliver much of an emotional impact, for all its exploration of such issues as racism and the business mentality. Campbell himself later delivered a just verdict on this and his other science fiction tales: "Whereas I wrote a handful of sword and sorcery tales ... in order to develop images that seemed too extravagant to be accommodated in my usual stuff, my science fiction stories tried to deal with Themes, too consciously, I feel."[4]

Perhaps the only meritorious tale of this kind is "Slow" [1975], also published separately, in 1986. Here a man is supposedly "saved" from his ruined spaceship by nameless outer forces and placed in a cottage on a remote planet. An egglike object enters the cottage, moving anomalously slowly, but seeming also to cause the protagonist to move with corresponding slowness. This fascinating premise allows Campbell to delve into the disturbed psyche of his character in very much the same way he does in his tales of pure horror:

He began to writhe frantically within himself, within his stopped body. All he managed was a scream, and even that seemed weak; he tried to make it louder, more raw, but it sank into the silence. Darkness was seeping into the dim glow now. He heard the oppressive silence of the cottage, of the dead clock. He heard his slow harsh breathing, each breath slower than the last. The thing waited near him in the dark, mouth ready.[5]

---

4. Introduction to *Strange Things and Stranger Places* (New York: Tor, 1993), 14–15.
5. *Slow* (Round Top, NY: Footsteps Press, 1986), n.p.

Other, unpublished stories certainly sound provocative, at least in Campbell's own descriptions, such as "Point of View" [1973] ("A teacher's perceptions become uncontrollable as alien beings use him as a device to spy on our world") and "Hain's Island" [1974] ("Colonists on a distant planet encounter an entity which feeds on emotional power and domination");[6] but in all likelihood their themes have been touched upon more effectively in his supernatural and psychological suspense work.

To probe the history of the horror anthology would be a fascinating exercise. Perhaps one of the first of them is "Monk" Lewis's *Tales of Wonder* (1801), a volume of weird balladry so extravagant that it immediately spawned a parody, *Tales of Terror* (1801). In 1891 George Saintsbury compiled a volume entitled *Tales of Mystery*, consisting of excerpts from the novels of Ann Radcliffe, "Monk" Lewis, and Charles Robert Maturin—excerpts that are, by and large, far more readable than the bulky novels themselves. Julian Hawthorne produced a mammoth ten-volume *Lock and Key Library* (1909) that contained a wealth of superb material, much of it from continental Europe; while Joseph Lewis French produced some able anthologies in the 1920s.

But it was the mystery writer Dorothy L. Sayers who, in 1928, compiled the first of three monumental anthologies of mystery and horror tales whose intelligent selection and learned introductions set a standard perhaps never excelled before or since. Slowly a canon of horror fiction was being assembled, and Herbert A. Wise and Phyllis Fraser's *Great Tales of Terror and the Supernatural* (1944) came close to giving this much-neglected genre a fleeting recognition in the literary mainstream.

6. See Ramsey Campbell, Stefan Dziemianowicz, and S. T. Joshi, *The Core of Ramsey Campbell: A Bibliography and Reader's Guide* (West Warwick, RI: Necronomicon Press, 1995), 37, 41.

As the decades passed, such prolific anthologists as Alfred Hitchcock (who, in fact, compiled few of the volumes himself but only
lent his name to them), Peter Haining, Hugh Lamb, and others
did much to rescue forgotten horror writing of the nineteenth and
early twentieth centuries. August Derleth also assembled many
anthologies in both the horror and science fiction fields.

A new tendency (although evident as early as 1927 with Lady
Cynthia Asquith's *The Ghost Book*), emerging as a result of the
"horror boom" of the late 1970s, was the "original anthology,"
in which previously unpublished material by leading contemporary writers was gathered. Kirby McCauley's excellent *Dark Forces*
(1980) was the pioneer, and it has had many successors, to such a
degree that the reprint anthology was for a time nearly relegated
to extinction. Many of these original anthologies, however, leave
much to be desired, as their editors do not always seem to practise
good critical judgment and feel the need to include even mediocre
work by a celebrated name for marketing purposes. Probably the
overall quality of many original anthologies is no lower than that
of an average issue of a pulp magazine of the 1930s; but it is, in
most cases, certainly no higher.

Ramsey Campbell has made forays in both the reprint and the
original anthology, and has achieved a markedly higher level of
success than many of his predecessors or contemporaries. It should
be clear by now that he himself is widely read in the field and
gifted with acute critical judgment; so that the general excellence
of his anthologies comes as no surprise. His original anthologies
are *Superhorror* (1976; later titled *The Far Reaches of Fear*), *New
Tales of the Cthulhu Mythos* (1980), and two volumes of *New Terrors*
(1980). His reprint anthologies are *The Gruesome Book* (1983), *Fine
Frights: Stories That Scared Me* (1988), five volumes of *Best New
Horror* (1990–94) edited with Stephen Jones, and *Uncanny Banquet*
(1992).

Of the original anthologies, *Superhorror* and the *New Terrors*
volumes are very mixed bags, their most distinguishing feature

perhaps being the inclusion of two tales by Robert Aickman ("Wood" in *Superhorror* and "The Stains" in *New Terrors 1*). It is clear that Campbell wished to promote some writers with whom he had come into personal contact or whose work he admired, notably R. A. Lafferty, Daphne Castell, David Drake, Steve Rasnic Tern, and Karl Edward Wagner.

New Tales of the Cthulhu Mythos was commissioned by Arkham House, and Campbell was clearly given a free hand in its compilation. By the late 1970s it had become evident that the "Cthulhu Mythos" was being increasingly played out by mechanical or unoriginal treatments; and Campbell, in his introduction, expressed his wish to return to "the first principles of the Mythos—to give glimpses of something larger than they show."[7] On the whole he has fulfilled his wish. Although the volume contains mediocre tales by Stephen King and Brian Lumley, and although Campbell commits the gaffe of allowing one Martin S. Warnes to "complete" a fragmentary story by Lovecraft, the volume contains scintillating works by T. E. D. Klein ("Black Man with a Horn"), David Drake ("Than Curse the Darkness"), and Campbell himself ("The Faces at Pine Dunes"). But the jewel of the volume—the one to which Campbell alludes in his introduction when he notes that "one of our tales hints at the ultimate event of the Mythos without ever referring to the traditional names"[8]—is Basil Copper's "Shaft Number 247," a magnificently brooding science fiction/horror hybrid whose poignancy is matched by its horrific suggestiveness.

Gathering the Bones (2003), an enormous original anthology coedited by Campbell, Jack Dann, and Dennis Etchison, contains thirty-four stories from some of the leading figures in contemporary weird fiction (Kim Newman, Lisa Tuttle, Steve Rasnic Tem, Graham Joyce), along with several contributions by authors who could be considered disciples or even protégés of Campbell (Joel

---

7. *New Tales of the Cthulhu Mythos*, ed. Ramsey Campbell, xi.
8. Ibid.

Lane, Adam Nevill). It is an impressive compilation that boasts a previously unpublished story by Ray Bradbury.

One other original anthology must be cited if only to be dismissed. *Horror Writers of America Present: Deathport* (1993) bears Campbell's name as co-editor (with the ubiquitous Martin H. Greenberg), but Campbell mercifully had little input into this thoroughly mediocre volume, one of the annual "shared world" anthologies issued by the Horror Writers of America.

Of the reprint anthologies, *The Gruesome Book* is a compact little volume containing fine tales by several veteran writers (August Derleth, Robert Bloch, Donald A. Wollheim, Richard Matheson, Henry Kuttner). *Fine Frights* is interesting in that it features those tales—many of them by quite obscure or new writers—that frightened Campbell himself. In particular, Campbell wished to show the many readers who had been attracted to horror fiction in the 1980s that weird fiction had a long ancestry, and to this end he reprinted two classic British ghost stories from the early twentieth century, "The Necromancer" by Arthur Gray and "Thurnley Abbey" by Perceval Landon.

But *Uncanny Banquet* is clearly Campbell's most distinctive reprint anthology, as well as his finest anthology altogether. It is therefore regrettable that it has been published only in England. While containing fine tales by Russell Kirk, Fritz Leiber, Robert Aickman, Donald Wandrei, and others, its chief feature is a nearly forgotten short novel, *The Hole of the Pit* (1914) by Adrian Ross. Campbell notes that Ross was a friend of M. R. James and dedicated his book to James, but that the novel "owes at least as much to William Hope Hodgson."[9] What Campbell means is that the novel is not merely written in the seventeenth-century idiom that Hodgson attempted but lamentably botched in *The Night Land* (1912), but that its evocation of horrors from the sea certainly

9. *Uncanny Banquet*, ed. Ramsey Campbell (London: Lttle, Brown, 1992), 173.

brings Hodgson's novels and tales to mind. *The Hole of the Pit* tells of a strange slimy creature that dwells in a marsh near a castle, victimising a small band of Royalists who are defending themselves against a siege by an army of Roundheads during the English Civil War. The archaic diction is flawless, the characters fully realised, and the horror kept in the distance until the very end. The work is rarely even cited in many reference works on horror fiction, and Campbell's rediscovery of it is a notable achievement.

The five *Best New Horror* volumes are difficult to treat in detail. They represent perhaps the finest of the three competing "best of the year" anthologies in the field, the others being Ellen Datlow and Terri Windling's *The Year's Best Fantasy and Horror* (rather too given over to archly sophisticated mainstream contributions) and Karl Edward Wagner's *The Year's Best Horror Stories* (a series notable for its diligent combing of small-press journals, and now defunct as a result of Wagner's untimely death). Here again many of those writers whom Campbell favours—Steve Rasnic Tern, Thomas Ligotti, Wagner, K. W. Jeter, Nicholas Royle, Kim Antieau, D. F. Lewis, Dennis Etchison, Joel Lane, M. John Harrison, Michael Marshall Smith—appear repeatedly; although, of course, Campbell and his co-editor Stephen Jones had to agree on all the selections. Campbell left the project after the fifth volume, and Jones is carrying it on alone; and recently Campbell has bluntly explained the reasons for his departure:

> The pure truth is that I became dispirited by the amount of rubbish we had to read in order to reject it—material already published elsewhere which persuaded me that the mass of contemporary work in our field is becoming as contemptible as detractors of the genre suggest.[10]

Campbell's assessment—which no doubt will elicit howls of

---

10. "Ramsey Campbell, Probably," *Necrofile* No. 20 (Spring 1996): 17.

protest from those many valiant hacks who are striving to make a name for themselves in this field—will be judged by acute commentators as sadly accurate.

Hardly to be classified as an anthology assembled by Campbell, but not to be entirely ignored, is *Made in Goatswood* (1995), edited by Scott David Aniolowski. This volume gathers together original stories written by a variety of authors in imitation of Campbell's early "Cthulhu Mythos" stories, and utilising his fictional English topography. Most of the contents are mediocre, but one tale—"The Undercliffe Sentences" by Peter Cannon—must be singled out as an exquisite homage to (and an affectionate parody of) Campbell's style and personal mannerisms. Many of the details in the story are derived from Campbell's columns in *Necrofile*.

Meddling with Ghosts (2000), published by the British Library, is an anthology of stories "in the tradition of M. R. James," an author whose subtlety and deceptively bland manner of introducing ghostly phenomena into the fabric of daily life are much admired by Campbell. The title is somewhat deceptive: rather than including contemporary stories using James's manner or conceptions as inspiration, the volume features some stories that preceded James's own work—J. Sheridan Le Fanu's "The Familiar" (1872), F. Marion Crawford's "The Upper Berth" (1885)—that only by an imaginative stretch could be called "Jamesian." But as the volume progresses through the twentieth century, it displays tales that do in fact reflect a Jamesian sensibility, even if obliquely—from Fritz Leiber's "Smoke Ghost" (a prototypical example of Leiber's relocation of weirdness into the contemporary urban world) to T. E. D. Klein's "Petey" (1979) to Campbell's own "The Guide."

It could well be said that Campbell's anthological work is a concrete embodiment of the preferences he has shown as a critic in the field. His body of nonfictional writing is not extensive, but is indicative of both his defence of the long traditions of horror writing and his championing of selected new writers whom he sees to be extending that tradition.

In 1983 Campbell wrote an introduction to the six volumes of the *Books of Blood* (1984–85) by fellow Liverpudlian Clive Barker, remarking that Barker "is the most original writer of horror fiction to have appeared in years, and in the best sense, the most deeply shocking writer now working in the field."[11] Barker has, regrettably, lost some of his boldness and distinctiveness, writing drearily ponderous novels that attempt to fuse fantasy and horror.

Even more foresightedly, Campbell wrote an introduction to a meagrely produced small-press volume, *Songs of a Dead Dreamer* (1986), by a little-known American writer, Thomas Ligotti. At the time few would have credited Campbell's assertion that the volume "has to be one of the most important horror books of the decade";[12] but Campbell has been proven correct, and Ligotti has taken a place with Campbell himself, T. E .D. Klein, and a few other recent writers who both draw upon the heritage of horror fiction and carry it into radically new directions. Unlike Barker, Ligotti is by no means a best-selling author, and his contorted style and idiosyncratic horrific conceptions make him an acquired taste; but Campbell's imprimatur helped Ligotti to gain an audience, and his subsequent work confirms Campbell's confidence in him.

Campbell has also written introductions to books by Donald R. Burleson, Dennis Etchison, Terry Lamsley, Tim Powers, Peter Straub, and several others. In all cases these introductions were the joint products of Campbell's friendship with these writers and his genuine conviction as to the merits of their work.

Otherwise, Campbell's nonfiction writing is largely restricted to his occasional columns in *Fantasy Review* (1984–86), which run the gamut of topics, from defences of the dignity of horror fiction

11. Introduction to Volume 1 of Clive Barker's *The Books of Blood* (1984; New York: Berkley, 1986), xi.
12. Introduction to *Songs of a Dead Dreamer* by Thomas Ligotti (1986; London: Robinson, 1989), ix.

to discussions of undeservedly forgotten horror films to studies of the horror element in detective or suspense fiction, and his quarterly columns in *Necrofile* (1991–99), which range even more widely from pensive discussions of Campbell's occasional depression to outrageous lambastings of the British schlockmeister Shaun Hutson to complaints about the shoddy translation of his own work. His sensitive essay on James Herbert (1986) is one of the few assessments that popular British writer had received up to that time. Campbell has published a substantial volume of his essays, columns, and introductions under the piquant title *Ramsey Campbell, Probably* (2002), and a second volume of further nonfiction pieces is in progress.

It is not surprising that a writer of such prodigal imagination and boundless energy as Ramsey Campbell has ventured, with more than occasional success, into such varied realms as heroic fantasy, science fiction, and the critical essay; and, like any writer who has read widely in his field, he has frequently felt the need to preserve his personal favourites in anthologies. But it is for his own horror work that Campbell will predominantly be remembered, and his peripheral writing will only add nuance to and shed light on that work. His output, both in volume and in substance, is difficult to grasp, but I hope to offer a few general comments in the concluding chapter.

CONCLUSION

Ramsey Campbell's distinctiveness derives from the union
of a seemingly inexhaustible imagination with a prolificity
virtually unrivalled in the field. Not even Algernon Blackwood,
his only conceivable rival, can match either the quantity or the
consistently high quality of Campbell's work. Beyond his first few
novels, Campbell has rarely allowed himself to be led by market
considerations to give readers what he thinks they want; instead,
he has preserved his artistic integrity by producing an array of
novels and tales whose only goal is the working out of their own
inner logic. While it is difficult to specify the means by which
Campbell achieves his effects, some general remarks may help to
clarify both the intentions and the methodology of his work.

How does Ramsey Campbell produce that *frisson* of horror we
find so bountifully in his novels and tales? Indirectness, allusiveness, ambiguity: these terms all suggest that it is a deliberate
vagueness as to the nature of the weird phenomena that allows
the reader momentarily to experience the sensation of the strange
reality of the unreal. The technique certainly has its pitfalls: just

as overexplicitness can lapse into absurdity and unintentional humour, so can excessive vagueness lapse into obscurity and confusion. On the whole, however, Campbell manages to walk the tightrope with notable success.

Certain choices of language are immediately recognisable as harbingers of the weird in Campbell's work. Since so many of his tales focus on an individual—whether mentally disturbed or not—perceiving, or seeming to perceive, some anomalous entity or event, the supernatural is most often a result of a fleeting glimpse out of the corner of one's eye. "He was drifting, or being dragged, towards the centre of the pool by a half-submerged heap of litter" (AH 294): this is the narrator's first perception of the supernaturally animated derelict in "Mackintosh Willy"; the analogy is chosen not merely as a sociological commentary, but as the narrator's distracted attempt to encompass the entity within the bounds of the natural world. Another frequently used turn of phrase—"It must be . . . "—has the same effect. "It must be some lunatic, someone unable to cope with life over there" (AH 453), concludes the protagonist of "The Other Side" when seeing the weird phenomenon: he cannot bring himself to acknowledge the supernatural, and so he must adopt some makeshift excuse to bring the vision within the domain of the real.

Campbell is gifted with many other literary strengths aside from the mere ability to frighten. He is, for example, sensitive to the subtle overtones of emotion found in human beings' interactions with one another, especially in speech. Dialogue in Campbell's work is constantly qualified with remarks on the precise intonation of the utterance and its psychological effect upon its recipient. It is here that we can trace most clearly the influence of the several mainstream writers—notably Vladimir Nabokov—whom Campbell read immediately after writing his early Lovecraft pastiches.[1]

1. See Dziemianowicz, "An Interview with Ramsey Campbell," for Nabokov's influence on Campbell. See also Jones, "*Weird Tales* Talks with

The novels can, clearly, exhibit this feature better than the short stories; consider this passage from so early a novel as *The Face That Must Die*, when Peter and Cathy Gardner visit some friends:

> Unbuttoning his waistcoat, [Frank] sank into his chair, which humphed. "I hear you're thinking of buying a house," he said to Peter.
>
> "You hear wrong."
>
> "That isn't what I said, Frank. He knows what computers are talking about but doesn't understand me," Angie complained.
>
> "Sorry, sorry. Still, it's worth thinking about," Frank said. "Apart from all the other advantages, property is an investment."
>
> "Don't give me that stuff, brother. I've had one capitalist at me today already."
>
> Peter looked bored, excluded. "When are you finishing work?" Angie asked him.
>
> "Tomorrow."
>
> "Eighteen more months as a student, isn't it? Will you be glad when it's over?"
>
> "I don't know. It isn't a bad life."
>
> "Living off us poor overtaxed workers, you mean?"
>
> She smiled to show that was a joke, but his voice was low as a dog's warning as he said, "I thought all the workers were on the factory floor. That's who I'd call workers."
>
> "That doesn't say much for your library work then, does it?"
>
> "Right." (FD 130–31)

Every utterance not only increases the social tension of the entire

Ramsey Campbell," 47, where Iris Murdoch, Graham Greene, Lawrence Durrell, Malcolm Lowry, and Samuel Beckett are cited.

scene but adds to the distinctive etching of each character. In this sense, many of Campbell's novels are as tightly written and constructed as his short stories.

A somewhat peculiar feature of Campbell's work is the relative absence of first-person narration. Given the degree to which Poe, Lovecraft, and other weird writers utilised the first person to compel the reader to witness events through the protagonist's eyes, and given how frequently Campbell himself is concerned with the shifting perceptions of his protagonists, the lack of first-person narration is puzzling Many of his third-person narratives are, of course, virtually equivalent to first-person; but perhaps Campbell's rationale for the ubiquity of third-person narration is the freedom it gives him to present all facets of a scene or tableau without the limitations that a single viewpoint might cause. Certainly, the shifting of perspective from one character to another—a distinguishing feature of such novels as *Obsession, Incarnate, The Long Lost*, and many others—would be impossible in a first-person narrative.

It is interesting to note that Campbell uses the first person frequently in his tales of childhood; in this way he can not only tell the story in the language of children, but also adopt the perspective of a child in looking upon events that an adult would comprehend very differently. In the resulting dramatic irony, the reader is chillingly aware of the potential dangers or anomalies in a given situation to which the child remains oblivious.

One rather peculiar criticism that has been levelled at Campbell is that his work is too uniformly gloomy. Certainly, his tales throughout the 1970s were quite grim, and few works are as dispiriting as *The Face That Must Die*; but to fancy that the horror story should somehow be cheerful and comforting is more than a little strange. Even so astute a commentator and writer as T. E. D. Klein has fallen into this blunder:

It's absurd, of course, to take a horror writer to task for writing horror, especially when he does it with such originality and grace; indeed, I think Campbell reigns supreme in the field today. Yet horror *per se* can be, in the end, somewhat limiting; and now that he has mastered it, one might hope for an occasional ray of light to alleviate the gloom.[2]

What this ignores (and to be fair to Klein it should be remembered that his essay only covers the *Demons by Daylight* stories) is, firstly, that the powerful atmosphere of dreariness in many of Campbell's tales is a positive asset and a tribute to his skill in mood-painting, and, secondly, that the wealth of tonal and thematic variation in the whole of his work emphatically refutes the facile notion that he is a mere "Johnny one-note." Perhaps, in the 1970s, he wrote too many stories that, although each was effective in its own right, became somewhat formulaic in their depiction of a harried protagonist who dimly spies the presence of the supernatural until at the end it finally overwhelms him or her; but certainly no one, taking the entirety of Campbell's novels and tales into consideration, can find any significant degree of repetition.

Indeed, of late Campbell has developed into one of the finest comic writers of his time, even if—as in *Needing Ghosts* and *The Count of Eleven*—the element of humour is constantly accompanied by unease. Puns, wordplay, and wildly ludicrous situations of buffoonery lace his later tales and novels, to such a degree that one wonders how they can be translated at all effectively.

Campbell's fictional techniques may be impressive, but to what end are they utilised? What, in essence, is Campbell trying to say? It should be abundantly evident that he is doing more than merely sending a shudder up the reader's spine; that his work, in fact, is

2. T. E. D. Klein, "Ramsey Campbell: An Appreciation," in *Discovering Modern Horror Fiction II*, ed. Darrell Schweitzer (Mercer Island, WA: Starmont House, 1988), 99.

laced with philosophical, moral, social, and political reflections. Perhaps it is not possible to sum up the thrust of his work in a single sentence, as it may be for Lovecraft (who seeks to depict the appalling vastness of the cosmos and the insignificance of humanity within it), Dunsany (who stresses the need for human reunification with the natural world), Blackwood (who strives to convey a kind of mystic pantheism whereby all entity is equally vital), or Machen (whose religious sensibility was offended by modern humanity's secularism and lack of imagination). But certainly, some themes are clearly evident.

Perhaps we might call Campbell a *humanist* in the best and broadest sense of that much-abused term. He shows how difficult it is to be a fully moral human being, and what courage it takes to be so. Obstacles encompass us on all sides: the emotional crippling of early abuse and poverty (*The Face That Must Die*), the scourge of drugs, the culture of violence (*The One Safe Place*). Analogously, easy solutions to personal and social trauma are ready to hand: mindless fundamentalism (*The Hungry Moon*), the descent into neurosis and paranoia (*The Face That Must Die, The Count of Eleven, The Long Lost, Secret Stories*), blanket censorship (*Ancient Images, The One Safe Place*), the shield of snobbery (Queenie in *The Influence*). One character after the next is put to the test, either by external forces or internal demons; and that test is whether one can maintain the decency, honour, and sense of personal and social responsibility that society requires of each of us if it is not to turn into a nightmare of mutually resentful classes and explode in a cataclysm of violence. If so many of Campbell's characters fail that test, or gain a fleeting triumph only after losing everything they cherished (Oswald Priestley in *The House on Nazareth Hill*), then perhaps we should not blame Campbell for some sort of habitual pessimism but rather society itself for the deficiencies of its members.

It is of interest that social and political concerns seem to have come to the fore in Campbell's more recent works. They were not wholly absent in his earlier writing—class consciousness is broached in so early a tale as "The Scar," and the social dangers of the psychotic are manifestly the subject of *The Face That Must Die*—but such novels as *The Hungry Moon*, *The Long Lost*, and especially *The One Safe Place* broach these issues more bluntly than their predecessors. By no means should it thereby be assumed that Campbell is moving toward becoming a "mainstream" writer: firstly, it is unjustly condescending to the horror tale to assume that social and political issues cannot come within its compass, and Campbell himself clearly envisages his works to be in the realm of horror; and secondly, such a work as *The House on Nazareth Hill* is avowedly supernatural while at the same time keenly etching domestic conflict at its worst. But certainly it could be said that Campbell's earlier treatments of paranoia and neurosis seem generally focused on the disturbed individual rather than on that individual's interaction with society. *The One Safe Place* will perhaps always remain an anomaly in Campbell's output for its raw display of societal problems with only the faintest admixture of psychological suspense.

A question that will inevitably be asked as part of the assessment of Campbell's work is the relative quality of his novels as compared with his short stories. Readers unfamiliar with horror writing prior to the "boom" of the 1970s will be surprised at how few genuine "horror novels" there have been, and how few of even these have been truly successful. Of J. S. Le Fanu's many novels, perhaps only *Uncle Silas* (1864) is meritorious, just as few of Bram Stoker's several novels aside from *Dracula* (1897) are worth the bother of reading. William Hope Hodgson's four novels, certainly, each have their virtues, but after this time the horror novel virtually disappeared for more than a half-century. The novels of Arthur Machen and Algernon Blackwood are more fantastic than horrific, while even the longest of H. P. Lovecraft's three very short novels, *The Case of Charles Dexter Ward* (1927), has all the "unity of effect" he sought in his short stories. Conversely, the tales of Poe, Le Fanu, Bierce, Lovecraft, and so many of their congeners testify overwhelmingly to the notion that horror works best in short compass.

But in the 1970s, when so many writers attempted to make a career out of horror, the outpouring of novels began, reaching a peak in the late 1980s. How many of these are of the highest quality? Not many, by even the most charitable standard. Campbell has without question produced the greatest proportion of novelistic successes of any writer in his field.

In a sense, however, novel writing was imposed on Campbell by external necessity. No writer can expect to make a living on short stories alone, and by the mid-1970s Campbell realised that novels would help to support him while he continued to bestow his short stories upon poorly paying small-press markets. Statistically, the shift is easy to detect. If we commence the beginning of Campbell's career as a writer at 1960, the breakdown of novels (including his three novelisations of films) and short stories would be as shown in Table 1. In several of the years between 1975 and 1995, he wrote no short stories at all.

TABLE 1. CAMPBELL'S SHORT STORIES AND NOVELS, 1960-1995

PERIOD	SHORT STORIES	NOVELS
1960–1974	120	0
1975–1984	58	10
1985–1995	35	8

This tendency has only continued in the past two decades.

Of course, a strict comparison of quality between novels and stories is meaningless, since they require such radically different methods of composition and aim for such different goals. The gripping intensity that Campbell can achieve in his short stories would become oppressive in his novels, while the obliqueness of many of the supernatural phenomena found in the tales would only produce frustration if incorporated into a novel.

But the chief difference between the two forms lies, of course, in the treatment of character. In the compass of a short story Campbell is not obliged to present sympathetic characters; indeed, *The Face That Must Die* is a tour de force largely because it focuses so insistently on a character whom every reader will loathe. Conversely, character development requires the space of a novel for full realisation, and one of the chief strengths of Campbell's novels is the insidious way in which, over the course of a work, a character can slowly change from seeming normality to monstrousness. Liz Knight in *The Claw*; Jack Orchard in *The Count of Eleven*; Oswald Priestley in *The House on Nazareth Hill*; Dudley Smith in *Secret Stories:* these are only three of the many characters who undergo such profound psychological change that they become scarcely recognisable to those close to them.

Even in novels, however, Campbell can etch a character in a few sharp strokes as he frequently does in short stories, as in this example from *The Parasite:*

Ahead along the promenade, an elderly couple emerged from Seabank Road. They were almost a memory, but their faces were disappointing: the woman's deadened by powder, the man's moustache stiff as a silver comb—they looked like stylized posters for British intolerance of nonsense. He carried the *Daily Telegraph* like a club, ready for use. They stalked by, their voices creaking. (P 139)

Nevertheless, in a very real sense the characters in Campbell's novels seem, on the whole, more "normal" and "reader-friendly" than do those in his short stories, as if Campbell realises that the novels will reach a wider audience of readers who will not tolerate excessive peculiarity in characters with whom they expect to identify.

As a result, readers well-versed in the horrific tradition might be excused for preferring the wondrously twisted vision found in so many of Campbell's short stories to the somewhat more "normal" perspective of the novels. Whether Campbell is in fact consciously tailoring his novels to a wider (and, perhaps, less critical) audience is a question only he can answer; he has at least not yielded to the "happy ending" contrivance on too many occasions, or, if he has done so, has managed it in such a way that it seems a natural outgrowth of the events.

Ramsey Campbell has already produced an array of work that would do any writer credit for a lifetime's achievement; and the continued vitality of his recent output shows that he has by no means finished saying all that he has to say. Certainly, one would wish for Campbell a greater degree of popular acclaim (and, in this regard, one can wonder why so few of his works has been adapted into film, even though many of them would naturally lend themselves to this medium), so long as that acclaim does not compromise his aesthetic standards, as it is not likely to do. Each new work is a revelation both to his readers and to himself, and he continues to explore the anomalies of human life as we uneasily enter a new millennium. If the horror "boom" of the past 1970s and 1980s is truly over, then it may allow sincere authors such as Campbell to write as the spirit moves them without undue consideration for market demands. Campbell has benefited from those many horror writers who worked in relative obscurity in the generations preceding his; and he has in turn left a legacy of sound work that will carry on the tradition of horror literature well into the twenty-first century.

BIBLIOGRAPHY

Note: The editions of Ramsey Campbell's works cited in the text are indicated by an asterisk.

A. PRIMARY

i. Novels

Ancient Images. London: Legend/Century, February 1989. *New York: Charles Scribner's Sons, June 1989. New York: Tor, 1990. [AI]

Born to the Dark. Hornsea: PS Publishing, 2017. [BD]

The Claw. *London: Futura, 1983 (as *Claw*). New York: St Martin's Press, 1983 (as *Night of the Claw*). London: Little, Brown, 1992. London: Warner, 1992. As by "Jay Ramsay." [C]

The Count of Eleven. London: Macdonald, 1991. *New York: Tor, 1992. [CE]

Creatures of the Pool. Hornsea: PS Publishing, 2009.

The Darkest Part of the Woods. *Harrogate: PS Publishing, 2002. New York: Tor, 2003. [DP]

The Doll Who Ate His Mother. New York & Indianapolis: Bobbs-Merrill, 1976. *New York: Jove/HBJ, 1978. Rev. ed. New York: Tor, August 1985. London: Arrow, 1987. London: Headline, 1993. North Webster, IN: Delirium, 2004. [DM]

The Face That Must Die. London: Star, 1979. *Restored text Santa Cruz, CA: Scream/Press, 1983. New York: Tor, 1985. London: Futura, 1990. London: Macdonald, 1991. [FD]

Ghosts Know. Hornsea: PS Publishing, 2011.

The Grin of the Dark. *Harrogate: PS Publishing, 2007. London: Virgin, 2008. New York: Tor, 2008.

The House on Nazareth Hill. London: Headline, 1996. *New York: Tor, 1997 (as *Nazareth Hill*). [HNH]

The Hungry Moon. *New York: Macmillan, 1986. New York: Tor, 1987. London: Headline Feature, 1995. [HM]

Incarnate. New York: Macmillan, 1983. *New York: Tor, 1984. Complete ed. London: Futura, 1990. [I]

The Influence. *New York: Macmillan, 1988. Need York: Tor, 1989. London: Headline Feature, 1996. [In]

The Kind Folk. Hornsea: PS Publishing, 2012. [KF]

The Last Voice They Hear. New York: Tor/Forge, 1998. [LV]

The Long Lost. *London: Headline, 1993. New York: Tor, 1994. [LL]

Midnight Sun. London: Macdonald, 1990. *New York: Tor, 1991. London: Warner, 1993. [MS]

The Nameless. Glasgow: Fontana, 1981. New York: Macmillan, 1981. *Rev. ed. New York: Tor, 1985. London: Warner, 1992. [N]

Obsession. *New York: Macmillan, 1985. New York: Tor, 1986. London: Futura, 1990.

The One Safe Place. *London: Headline, 1995. New York: Tor, 1996. [OSP]

The Overnight. *Harrogate: PS Publishing, 2004. New York: Tor, 2005.

Pact of the Fathers. New York: Tor/Forge, 2001. [PF]

The Parasite. London: Millington, 1980 (as *To Wake the Dead*). *Rev. ed. New York: Macmillan, 1980. New York: Tor, 1989. North Webster, IN: Delirium, 2004 (includes two deleted chapters). [P]

The Searching Dead. Hornsea: PS Publishing, 2016. [SD]

Secret Stories. *Harrogate: PS Publishing, 2005. New York: Tor, 2006 (abridged; as *Secret Story*).

The Seven Days of Cain. Hornsea: PS Publishing, 2010.

Silent Children. New York: Tor/Forge, 1999. [SC]

Solomon Kane. London: Titan, 2010.

Somebody's Voice. London & New York: Flame Tree Press, 2021.

Thieving Fear. Hornsea: PS Publishing, 2008. *London: Virgin, 2009. [TF]

Think Yourself Lucky. Hornsea: PS Publishing, 2014. [TYL]

Thirteen Days by Sunset Beach. Hornsea: PS Publishing, 2015. [SB]

The Way of the Worm. Hornsea: PS Publishing, 2018. [WW]

The Wise Friend. London & New York: Flame Tree Press, 2020.

ii. Short Story Collections and Separately Published Novellas

Alone with the Horrors: The Great Short Fiction of Ramsey Campbell 1961–1991. *Sauk City, WI: Arkham House, 1993. London: Headline, 1994. [AH]

Contents: "The Room in the Castle"; "Cold Print"; "The Scar"; "The Interloper"; "The Guy"; "The End of a Summer's Day"; "The Man in the Underpass"; "The Companion"; "Call First"; "Heading Home"; "In the Bag"; "Baby"; "The Chimney"; "Stages"; "The Brood"; "Loveman's Comeback"; "The Gap"; "The Voice of the Beach"; "Out of Copyright"; "Above the World"; "Mackintosh Willy"; "The Show Goes On"; "The Ferries"; "Midnight Hobo"; "The Depths"; "Down There"; "The Fit"; "Hearing Is Believing"; "The Hands"; "Again"; "Just Waiting"; "Seeing the World"; "Old

Clothes"; "Apples"; "The Other Side"; "Where the Heart
Is"; "Boiled Alive"; "Another World"; "End of the Line."
Black Wine (with Charles L. Grant). Edited by Douglas E. Winter.
Niles, IL: Dark Harvest, 1986. [BW]
Contents (Campbell material only): "After the Queen";
"Broadcast"; "The Previous Tenant"; "Accident Zone"; "The
Sunshine Club"; "The Other House."
The Booking. Portland, OR: Dark Regions Press, 2016.
By the Light of My Skull. Hornsea: PS Publishing, 2018.
Contents: "Find My Name"; "The Moons"; "At Lorn Hall";
"On the Tour"; "The Callers"; "Fetched"; "The Impression";
"The Page"; "Reading the Signs"; "Know Your Code"; "The
Watched"; "The Wrong Game"; "Her Face"; "The Words
Between"; "The Fun on the Fair."
Cold Print. Santa Cruz, CA: Scream/Press, 1985. New York: Tor,
1987.
Contents: "Chasing the Unknown" (introduction); "The
Church in High Street"; "The Room in the Castle";
"The Horror from the Bridge"; "The Insects from Shaggai";
"The Render of the Veils"; "The Inhabitant of the Lake";
"The Will of Stanley Brooke"; "The Moon-Lens"; "Before
the Storm"; "Cold Print"; "Among the pictures are these:";
"The Tugging"; "The Faces at Pine Dunes"; "Blacked Out";
"The Voice of the Beach."
Cold Print. London: Headline, 1993. [CP]
Contents: "Chasing the Unknown" (introduction); "The
Church in High Street"; "The Room in the Castle";
"The Horror from the Bridge"; "The Insects from Shag-
gai"; "The Render of the Veils"; "The Inhabitant of the
Lake"; "The Plain of Sound"; "The Return of the Witch";
"The Mine on Yuggoth"; "The Will of Stanley Brooke";
"The Moon-Lens"; "The Stone on the Island"; "Before the
Storm"; "Cold Print"; "The Franklyn Paragraphs"; "A Mad-
ness from the Vaults"; "Among the pictures are these:"; "The

Tugging"; "The Faces at Pine Dunes"; "Blacked Out"; "The Voice of the Beach."

Dark Companions. *New York: Macmillan, 1982, New York: Tor, 1985. Cincinnati, OH: Samhain Publishing, 2012. [DC]
Contents: "Mackintosh Willy"; "Napier Court"; "Down There"; "Heading Home"; "The Proxy"; "The Depths"; "Out of Copyright"; "The Invocation"; "The Little Voice"; "Drawing In"; "The Pattern"; "The Show Goes On"; "The Puppets"; "Calling Card"; "Above the World"; "Baby"; "In the Bag"; "Conversion"; "The Chimney"; "Call First"; "The Companion."

Dark Feasts: The World of Ramsey Campbell. London: Robinson Publishing, 1987.
Contents: "The Room in the Castle"; "Cold Print"; "The Scar"; "The Interloper"; "The Guy"; "The End of a Summer's Day"; "The Whining"; "The Words That Count"; "The Man in the Underpass"; "Horror House of Blood"; "The Companion"; "Call First"; "In the Bag"; "The Chimney"; "The Brood"; "The Voice of the Beach"; "Out of Copyright"; "Above the World"; "Mackintosh Willy"; "The Ferries"; "Midnight Hobo"; "The Depths"; "The Fit"; "Hearing Is Believing"; "The Hands"; "Again"; "Just Waiting"; "Seeing the World"; "Apples"; "Boiled Alive."

Demons by Daylight. *Sauk City, WI: Arkham House, 1973. New York: Carroll & Graf, 1990. [DD]
Contents: "Potential"; "The End of a Summer's Day"; "At First Sight"; "The Franklyn Paragraphs"; "The Interloper" (as by Errol Undercliffe); "The Sentinels"; "The Guy"; "The Old Horns"; "The Lost"; "The Stocking"; "The Second Staircase"; "Concussion"; "The Enchanted Fruit"; "Made in Goatswood."

Far Away & Never. West Warwick, RI: Necronomicon Press, 1996. [FAN]

306 RAMSEY CAMPBELL: MASTER OF WEIRD FICTION

Contents: "Introduction"; "The Sustenance of Hoak"; "The Changer of Names";"The Pit of Wings"; "The Mouths of Light"; "The Stages of the God"; "The Song at the Hub of the Garden"; "The Ways of Chaos."

Ghostly Tales. Mount Olive, NC: Cryptic Publications, 1987. Special issue of *Crypt of Cthulhu* No. 50 (Michaelmas 1987). [GT]
Contents: "The Haunted Manor"; "The Oak Chest"; "The Hollow in the Woods"; "Things from the Sea"; "The Grave in the Desert"; "Accident"; "The Friend"; "The Devil's Cart"; "Tern Basish"; "The Whirlpool"; "The Whispering Horror"; "Bradmoor"; "Hybrid"; "The Tower"; "Conversation in a Railway Carriage"; "The Mask"; "Premonition."

Ghosts and Grisly Things. *Nottingham: Pumpkin, 1998. New York: Tor, 2000. [GGT]
Contents: "Introduction"; "The Same in Any Language"; "Going Under"; "The Alternative"; "Out of the Woods"; "A Street Was Chosen"; "McGonagall in the Head"; "Through the Walls"; "This Time"; "The Sneering"; "Between the Floors"; "Where They Lived"; "Root Cause"; "Looking Out"; "The Dead Must Die"; "A Side of the Sea"; "Missed Connection"; "The Change"; "Welcomeland"; "See How They Run"; "Ra*e."

The Height of the Scream. Sauk City, WI: Arkham House, 1976. London: Millington, 1978. London: Star, 1981. Northridge: Babbage Press, 2004. [HS]
Contents: "The Scar"; "The Whining"; "The Dark Show"; "Missing"; "Reply Guaranteed"; "Jack's Little Friend"; "Beside the Seaside"; "The Cellars"; "The Height of the Scream"; "Litter"; "Cyril"; "Smoke Kiss"; "The Words That Count"; "Ash"; "The Telephones"; "In the Shadows"; "Second Chance"; "Horror House of Blood."

Holes for Faces. Ashland, OR: Dark Regions Press, 2013. [HF]
Contents: "Passing through Peacehaven"; "Peep"; "Getting

It Wrong"; "The Room Beyond"; "Holes for Faces"; "The Rounds"; "The Decorations"; "The Address"; "Recently Used"; "Chucky Comes to Liverpool"; "With the Angels"; "Behind the Doors"; "Holding the Light"; "The Long Way."
Inconsequential Tales. Edited by S. T. Joshi. New York: Hippocampus Press, 2008.
Contents: "Truth or Consequences" (introduction); "The Childish Fear"; "The Offering to the Dead"; "The Reshaping of Rossiter"; "The Void"; "The Other House"; "Broadcast"; "The Urge"; "The Sunshine Club"; "Writer's Curse"; "Property of the Ring"; "The Shadows in the Barn"; "Night Beat"; "The Precognitive Trip"; "Murders"; "Point of View"; "The Grip of Peace"; "Only the Wind"; "Morning Call"; "Pet"; "Hain's Island"; "Bait"; "Snakes and Ladders"; "The Burning"; "A Play for the Jaded."
The Inhabitant of the Lake and Less Welcome Tenants. Sauk City, WI: Arkham House, 1964.
Contents: "The Room in the Castle"; "The Horror from the Bridge"; "The Insects from Shaggai"; "The Render of the Veils"; "The Inhabitant of the Lake"; "The Plain of Sound"; "The Return of the Witch"; "The Mine on Yuggoth"; "The Will of Stanley Brooke"; "The Moon-Lens." Complete contents now reprinted in *Cold Print* (1993 ed.).
The Inhabitant of the Lake and Other Unwelcome Tenants. Hornsea: PS Publishing, 2011. [IL]
Contents: "A Word from the Author"; "The Room in the Castle"; "The Horror from the Bridge"; "The Insects from Shaggai"; "the Render of the Veils"; "The Inhabitant of the Lake"; "The Plain of Sound"; "The Return of the Witch"; "The Mine on Yuggoth"; "The Will of Stanley Brooke"; "The Moon-Lens"; "The Box in the Priory"; "The Tomb-Herd"; "The Face in the Desert"; "The Horror from the Bridge"; "The Tower from Yuggoth"; "The Insects from

Shaggai"; "The Church in High Street"; "Afterword"; "Correspondence."

Just Behind You. Hornsea: PS Publishing, 2009. [JB]
Contents: "Fear the Dead"; "Digging Deep"; "Double Room"; "The Place of Revelation"; "The Winner"; "One Copy Only"; "Laid Down"; "Unblinking"; "Breaking Up"; "Respects"; "Feeling Remains"; "Direct Line"; "Skeleton Woods"; "The Unbeheld"; "The Announcement"; "Dragged Down"; "Raised by the Moon"; "Just Behind You"; "Afterword."

The Last Revelation of Gla'aki. Hornsea: PS Publishing, 2013. [LR]

Medusa. Round Top, NY: Footsteps Press, 1987.

Needing Ghosts. London: Legend/Century, 1990. [NG]

Night Visions 3 (with Lisa Tuttle and Clive Barker). Edited by George R. R. Martin. Niles, IL: Dark Harvest, 1986. New York: Berkley, 1988 (as *Night Visions: The Hellbound Heart*). Contents (Campbell material only): "In the Trees"; "This Time"; "Missed Connection"; "Root Cause"; "Looking Out"; "Bedtime Story"; "Beyond Words."

The Pretence. Hornsea: PS Publishing, 2013. [Pr]

Scared Stiff: Tales of Sex and Death. *Los Angeles: Scream/Press, 1986. New York: Warner, 1988. London: Futura, 1991. New York: Tor, 2002. [SS]
Contents: "Dolls"; "The Other Woman"; "Lilith's"; "The Seductress"; "Stages"; "Loveman's Comeback"; "Merry May." [Tor edition adds "The Limits of Fantasy," "The Body in the Window," and "Kill Me Hideously."]

Slow. Round Top, NY: Footsteps Press, 1986.

Strange Things and Stranger Places. New York: Tor, 1993. [STSP]
Contents: "Introduction"; "Cat and Mouse"; "Medusa"; "Rising Generation"; "Run Through"; "Wrapped Up"; "Passing Phase"; "A New Life"; "The Next Sideshow"; "Little Man"; *Needing Ghosts.*

Told by the Dead. Harrogate: PS Publishing, 2003. [TD]

Contents: "Return Journey"; "Twice by Fire"; "Agatha's Ghost"; "Little Ones"; "The Last Hand"; "Facing It"; "Never to Be Heard"; "The Previous Tenant"; "Becoming Visible"; "No End of Fun"; "After the Queen"; "Tatters"; "Accident Zone"; "The Entertainment"; "Dead Letters"; "All for Sale"; "No Strings"; "The Worst Fog of the Year"; "The Retrospective"; "Slow"; "Worse Than Bones"; "No Story in It"; "The Word"; "Afterword."

The Tomb-Herd and Others. Mount Olive, NC: Cryptic Publications, 1986. Special issue of *Crypt of Cthulhu* No. 43 (Hallowmass 1986). [TH]
Contents: "The Tomb-Herd"; "The Face in the Desert"; "A Madness from the Vaults"; "The Tower from Yuggoth"; "The Plain of Sound"; "The Return of the Witch"; "The Mine on Yuggoth"; "The Stone on the Island"; "A Madness from the Vaults" (final version).

Twilight Tales from Merseyside. [Audiotape.] Read by Ramsey Campbell. West Warwick, RI: Necronomicon Press, 1995.
Contents: "Calling Card"; "The Guide"; "The Companion"; "Out of the Woods."

Two Obscure Tales. West Warwick, RI: Necronomicon Press, 1993.
Contents: "The Void"; "The Urge."

Visions from Brichester. Hornsea: PS Publishing, 2015. [VB]
Contents: "The Stone on the Island"; "Before the Storm"; "Cold Print"; "The Franklyn Paragraphs"; "A Madness from the Vaults"; "Among the pictures are these:"; "The Tugging"; "The Faces at Pine Dunes"; "Blacked Out"; "The Voice of the Beach"; "The Horror under Warrendown"; "The Other Names"; "The Correspondence of Cameron Thaddeus Nash"; "The Last Revelation of Gla'aki"; "The Successor"; "The Franklyn Paragraphs" (first draft); "Mushrooms from Merseyside"; "Two Poems by Edward Pickman Derby"; "The Horror in the Crystal" (fragment); "Rusty Links"; "Lovecraft in Retrospect"; "On Four Lovecraft Tales"; "Afterword."

Waking Nightmares. *New York: Tor, 1991. London: Little, Brown, 1992. [WN]
Contents: "The Guide"; "Next Time You'll Know Me"; Second Sight"; "The Trick"; "In the Trees"; "Another World"; "Playing the Game"; "Bedtime Story"; "Watch the Birdie"; "Old Clothes"; "Beyond Words"; "Jack in the Box"; "Eye of Childhood"; "The Other Side"; "Where the Heart Is"; "Being an Angel"; "It Helps If You Sing"; "The Old School"; "Meeting the Author."

iii. Novelisations

The Bride of Frankenstein. *New York: Berkley Medallion, 1977. Restored text London: Universal Books, 1978.
Dracula's Daughter. New York: Berkley Medallion, 1977. London: Star, 1980 (as by "E. K. Leyton).
Solomon Kane. London: Titan, 2010.
The Wolfman. New York: Berkley Medallion, 1977. London: Star, 1980 (as by "E. K. Leyton").
All three as by Carl Dreadstone.

iv. Nonfiction and Poetry

The Core of Ramsey Campbell: A Bibliography and Reader's Guide (with Stefan Dziemianowicz and S.T. Joshi). West Warwick, RI: Necronomicon Press, 1995.
Letters to Arkham: The Letters of Ramsey Campbell and August Derleth, 1961–1971. Edited by S. T. Joshi. Hornsea: PS Publishing, 2014. [LA]
Ramsey Campbell, Probably: On Horror and Sundry Fantasies. Edited by S. T. Joshi. Harrogate: PS Publishing, 2002 (*rev. ed. 2015). [RCP]

Ramsey Campbell's Limericks of the Alarming and Phantasmal. Hornsea: PS Publishing, 2016.

V. ANTHOLOGIES

Best New Horror (with Stephen Jones). London: Robinson, 1990.
Best New Horror 2 (with Stephen Jones). London: Robinson, 1991.
Best New Horror 3 (with Stephen Jones). London: Robinson, 1992.
Best New Horror 4 (with Stephen Jones). London: Robinson, 1993.
Best New Horror 5 (with Stephen Jones). London: Robinson, 1994.
Fine Frights: Stories That Scared Me. New York: Tor, 1988.
Gathering the Bones (with Jack Dann and Dennis Etchison). London: Voyager/HarperCollins, 2003. New York: Tor, 2003.
The Giant Book of Best New Horror (with Stephen Jones). London: Magpie/Robinson,
1993. (Selection from the first three volumes of *Best New Horror.*)
The Giant Book of Terror (with Stephen Jones). London: Magpie, 1994.
The Gruesome Book. London: Piccolo, 1983.
Horror Writers of America Present: Deathport (with Martin H. Greenberg). New York: Pocket, 1993.
Meddling with Ghosts: Stories in the Tradition of M. R. James. London: British Library, 2000.
New Tales of the Cthulhu Mythos. Sauk City, WI: Arkham House, 1980.
New Terrors 1. London: Pan, 1980.
New Terrors 2. London: Pan, 1980.
Omnibus of New Terrors. London: Pan, 1985.
Superhorror. London: W. H. Allen, 1976. New York: St Martin's Press, 1977. London: Star Books, 1980 (as *The Far Reaches of Fear*).
Uncanny Banquet. London: Little, Brown, 1992.

vi. Uncollected Short Stories

"The Address." In *Cut Corners, Volume 1* (with Bentley Little and Ray Garton). Austin, TX: Sinister Grin Press, 2012.
"The Castle of the Devil" (with Robert E. Howard). In *Solomon Kane 1: Skulls in the Stars* by Robert E. Howard. New York: Bantam, 1978. 64–78.
"The Children of Asshur" (with Robert E. Howard). In *Solomon Kane 2: The Hills of*
the Dead by Robert E. Howard. New York: Bantam, 1979. 129–38.
"The Christmas Present." In *Nameless Places*, ed. Gerald W. Page. Sauk City, WI:
Arkham House, 1975. 255–61.
"The Face." *Footsteps* No. 7 (November 1986): 6–10. Tampa, FL: Camelot Books and Books, Inc., 2003.
"Hawk of Basti" (with Robert E. Howard). In *Solomon Kane 2: The Hills of the Dead* by Robert E. Howard. New York: Bantam, 1979. 33–47.
"The Maze" (with Tammy and Matt Campbell). In *Great Writers and Kids Write Spooky Stories*, ed. Martin H. Greenberg, Jill M. Morgan, and Robert Weinberg. New York: Random House, 1995. 97–108.
"Midnight Appointment." *St Edward's College Magazine* 1, No. 4 (1958): 201–2.

B. SECONDARY

i. Interviews

(Ramsey Campbell has given a great many interviews. The following is only a representative selection.)

Barnard, Simon. "A Demon by Daylight." *Cold Print* No. 1

(Spring 1996): 17–20. B[romley], R[obin]. "Breaking In: Ramsey Campbell." *Twilight Zone* 6, No. 1 (April 1986): 28–29.

Cerasini, Marc A. "A Talk with Ramsey Campbell." In *How to Write Horror and Get It Published.* Brooklyn Heights, NY: Romantic Times, 1989. 110–17.

Crowther, Peter. "Ramsey Campbell: An Interview." *Midnight Graffiti* No. 5 (Spring 1990): 55–62.

Dziemianowicz, Stefan. "A Conversation with Ramsey Campbell." *Cemetery Dance* 9, No. 1 (1998): 13–22.

———. "An Interview with Ramsey Campbell." In *The Count of Thirty: A Tribute to Ramsey Campbell,* ed. S. T. Joshi. West Warwick, RI: Necronomicon Press, 1993. 7–26.

Elliot, Jeffrey M. "Ramsey Campbell: Journeys into the Unknown." *Whispers* 4, Nos. 3/4 (1982): 15–24.

Ford, Carl T. "Ramsey Campbell, Transcendent of Terror." *Dagon* No. 15 (November–December 1986): 9–15.

Griffin, Marni Scofidio. "Profile of Ramsey Campbell—'The Grand Old Man of Horror.'" *Deathrealm* No. 24 (Summer 1995): 24–28.

Jamneck, Lynne. "Ramsey Campbell." *City Slab* No. 3 (2003): 43–46.

Jones, Stephen. "*Weird Tales* Talks with Ramsey Campbell." *Weird Tales* No. 301 (Summer 1991): 44–51.

McDonald, T. Liam. "The Dangerous Edge of Things: Ramsey Campbell." *Cemetery Dance* 3, No. 4 (Fall 1991): 20–27.

Nicholls, Stan. "Finds Dreaming on the Page Bloody Hard Work." In Stan Nicholls, *Wordsmiths of Wonder.* London: Orbit, 1993. 397–403.

Proposch, Steve. "Ramsey Rambles." *Bloodsongs* No. 1 (January 1994): 16–21.

Proulx, Kevin. "Ramsey Campbell." In Kevin Proulx, *Fear to the World: Eleven Voices in a Chorus of Horror.* Mercer Island, WA: Starmont House, 1992. 11–23.

314 RAMSEY CAMPBELL: MASTER OF WEIRD FICTION

Schweitzer, Darrell. "Interview: Ramsey Campbell." *Fantasy Newsletter* 3, No. 4 (1980):

15–20. In Darrell Schweitzer, *Speaking of Horror: Interviews with Writers of the*

Supernatural. San Bernardino, CA: Borgo Press, 1994. 23–36.

———. "A Talk with Ramsey Campbell." *H. P. Lovecraft's Magazine of Horror* No. 1 (Spring 2004): 35–39.

Simmons, William P. "A Conversation with Ramsey Campbell." *Cemetery Dance* No. 43 (2003): 4–10.

Tibbetts, John C. "From Providence to Liverpool: Ramsey Campbell." In John C. Tibbetts, *The Gothic Imagination: Conversations on Fantasy, Horror, and Science Fiction in the Media.* New York: Palgrave Macmillan, 2011. 35–50.

Vine, Phillip. "Ramsey Campbell." *Interzone* No. 28 (March–April 1989): 11–16.

Wiater, Stanley. "Ramsey Campbell." In Stanley Wiater, *Dark Dreamers: Conversations with the Masters of Horror.* New York: Avon, 1990. 35–42.

Williams, Conrad. "Ramsey Campbell Speaks Out." *Dementia* 13, No. 10 (1993): 21–26.

Winter, Douglas E. "Ramsey Campbell." In Douglas E. Winter, *Faces of Fear: Encounters with the Creators of Modern Horror.* New York: Berkley, 1985. 65–78.

ii. Books and Articles

Aniolowski, Scott David, ed. *Made in Goatswood: A Celebration of Ramsey Campbell.* Oakland, CA: Chaosium, 1995.

Ashley, Mike, ed. *Fantasy Reader's Guide #2: Ramsey Campbell.* Wallsend, UK:

Cosmos, 1980. Rpt. San Bernardino, CA: Borgo Press, 1984. (Contains essays by T. E. D. Klein and Jack Sullivan along with rare material by Campbell.)

Campbell, Ramsey; Dziemianowicz, Stefan; and Joshi, S. T. *The Core of Ramsey Campbell: A Bibliography and Reader's Guide*. West Warwick, RI: Necronomtcon Press, 1995.

Carroll, Noël. *The Philosophy of Horror*. London: Routledge, 1990.

Crawford, Gary William. *Ramsey Campbell*. Mercer Island, WA: Starmont House, 1988.

————. "Urban Gothic: The Fiction of Ramsey Campbell." In *Discovering Modern Horror Fiction I*, ed. Darrell Schweitzer. Mercer Island, WA: Starmont House, 1985. 13–20.

Crawford, Gary William, ed. *Ramsey Campbell: Critical Essays on the Modern Master of Horror*. Lanham, MD: Scarecrow Press, 2014.

Hadji, R. S. "Campbell, [John] Ramsey." In *The Penguin Encyclopedia of Horror and the Supernatural*, ed. Jack Sullivan. New York: Viking, 1986. 67–69.

Jackson, Rosemary. *Fantasy: The Literature of Subversion*. London: Methuen, 1981.

Joshi, S. T. "Ramsey Campbell: The Fiction of Paranoia." *Studies in Weird Fiction* No. 17 (Summer 1995): 22–33 (abridged). In S. T. Joshi, *The Modern Weird Tale*. Jefferson, NC: McFarland, 2001. 133–74.

————. "Ramsey Campbell: Horrors of the city." In *Unutterable Horror: A History of Supernatural Fiction*. Hornsea: PS Publishing, 2012. 2.662–70.

————. *The Weird Tale*. Austin: University of Texas Press, 1990.

Joshi, S. T., ed. *The Count of Thirty: A Tribute to Ramsey Campbell*. West Warwick, RI: Necronomicon Press, 1993. (Aside from the Dziemianowicz interview [see above], this booklet contains a study by Joshi on Campbell's Lovecraftian fiction, an essay by Simon MacCulloch on Campbell's "concept of evil," and two essays by Joel Lane on the progression of Campbell's novels.)

Jurkiewicz, Kenneth. "Ramsey Campbell." In *Supernatural*

Fiction Writers, ed. E. F. Bleiler. New York: Scribner's, 1985. 993–99.

Klein, T. E. D. "Ramsey Campbell: An Appreciation." *Nyctalops* No. 13 (May 1977): 19–25. Rpt. in *Discovering Modern Horror Fiction II*, ed. Darrell Schweitzer. Mercer Island, WA: Starmont House, 1988. 88–102.

Lane, Joel. Review of *Waking Nightmares* and *The Count of Eleven*. *Studies in Weird Fiction* No. 11 (Spring 1993): 31–33.

———. "Shattered Visions" (review of *The Long Lost*). *Necrofile* No. 12 (Spring 1994): 8–10.

———. "Writers in the James Traidtion: Ramsey Campbell." In Joel Lane, *This Spectacular Darkness: Critical Essays*. Ed. Mark Valentine and John Howard. Leyburn: Tartarus Press, 2016. 225–32.

Leiber, Fritz. "A Literary Copernicus" (1949). In *H. P. Lovecraft: Four Decades of Criticism*, ed. S. T. Joshi. Athens: Ohio University Press, 1980. 50–62.

Lovecraft, H. P. *Selected Letters*. Ed. August Derleth, Donald Wandrei, and James Turner. Sauk City, WI: Arkham House, 1965–76. 5 vols.

———. "Supernatural Horror in Literature." In *The Annotated Supernatural Horror in Literature*. Ed. S. T. Joshi. Rev. ed. New York: Hippocampus Press, 2012.

Mariconda, Steven J. "The Campbell Renaissance" (review of *Strange Things and Stranger Places*). *Necrofile* No. 10 (Fall 1993): 6–8.

———. Review of *Needing Ghosts* and *Midnight Sun*. *Studies in Weird Fiction* No. 9 (Spring 1991): 32–34.

Morrison, Michael A. "The Forms of Things Unknown: Metaphysical and Domestic Horror in Ramsey Campbell's *Incarnate* and *Night of the Claw*." *Studies in Weird Fiction* No. 6 (Fall 1989): 3–9.

———. "Patterns, Demanding to Be Read . . ." (review of

Midnight Sun, Waking Nightmares, Needing Ghosts, and *The Count of Eleven). Necrofile* No. 2 (Fall 1991): 4–6.

Nevill, Adam L. G. "Wonder and Awe: Mysticism, Poetry, and Perception in Ramsey Campbell's *The Darkest Part of the Woods.*" In *21st-Century Gothic: Great Gothic Novels Since 2000,* ed. Danel Oilson. Lanham, MD: Scarecrow Press, 2011. 149–57.

Punter, David. *The Literature of Terror: A History of Gothic Fiction from 1765 to the Present Day.* London: Longman, 1980 (rev. ed. 1996).

Sullivan, Jack. "Ramsey Campbell: No Light Ahead." In *Shadowings: The Reader's Guide to Horror Fiction 1981–1982,* ed. Douglas Winter. Mercer Island, WA: Starmont House, 1983. 79–86.

Underwood, Tim, and Chuck Miller, ed. *Bare Bones: Conversations on Terror with Stephen King.* New York: Warner, 1989.

INDEX